Finding My Invisible Sun

L. M. King

Publisher: Inspiring Publishers,
P.O. Box 159, Calwell, ACT Australia 2905
Email: publishaspg@gmail.com
http://www.inspiringpublishers.com

A catalogue record for this book is available from the National Library of Australia

National Library of Australia The Prepublication Data Service

Author: L. M. King
Title: Finding My Invisible Sun
Genre: Non-fiction

Print ISBN: 978-1-922920-21-8
eBook ISBN: 978-1-922920-22-5

Praise for Lisa M. King

An incredibly brave, honest, and eloquent personal story that takes you on a journey through early trauma, its impact on adult life and ultimately into hope. Lisa delves into her lived experience and provides an insightful account of how one assimilates early raw traumatic experiences while growing up in an indifferent world, its negative impact, and how she found herself through therapy. This is a brilliant read, enriched with powerful paintings and poetry.

Dr. Kris Rao, MScMed (Psychotherapy), Psy.D.

Finding My Invisible Sun is beautifully written and eloquent, with moments of playfulness, intensive reflective insight, heart-wrenching sadness and clarity. A true artist: the internal workings of Lisa's mind are vividly illustrated and amplified with references to song lyrics, sounds, quotes, and books that have been instrumental at different ages and stages in her life. I hope you read it as I did, with a smile, in awe of such masterfully crafted writing. I have no doubt that *Finding My Invisible Sun* will resonate with, and help many people who read it.

Amanda Bendt,
Accredited Mental Health Social Worker/Trauma therapist

An extraordinary and very unusual book. Partly a courageous and searingly honest account of personal trauma and recovery. Partly a textbook on trauma and trauma therapy – with plenty of academic references to follow up. Partly and ultimately a message of hope for both those who need help and those who do their best to provide it. For the client, read it with the support of a skilled helper. For the trauma therapist, read it a chapter at a time – and take time to process the contents. You will learn more from this book than just about any book on trauma that I know.

Graham Taylor, Clinical Psychologist, Accredited EMDR Trainer,
Accredited Schema Therapy Trainer, Accredited ACT Trainer

Creative and resilient, quick witted and deeply intellectual: this is a handbook for humans – whether you're a citizen of the world, a therapist, a health professional or a carer. Lisa prompts you to pay attention with curiosity and without judgement. Her vulnerability and honesty in telling her story, make you want to embrace her and celebrate her victories as an adult; and go back and protect her as a child. A story of recovery and transformation but one that goes that extra step – to bestow her learnings, knowledge, lived experience and passion to invest in others what she has learnt all by herself, through blood, sweat and tears. Lisa's selfless regard for others and passion for questioning the status quo, have led to recovery in herself and many others. This book will be a lighthouse for anyone who has ever experienced mental illness, the systems that work against them and the powerless and vulnerable position they find themselves in when asking for help. Essential reading for health professionals – when you know better, you do better.

Eliza Pike, Accredited Mental Health Social Worker,
Director Blackbird Counselling, Program Manager Gidget Foundation

*Thankyou Spencer, for gently blowing
on my smouldering embers.*

*Thankyou Noelene and Geraldine
for always believing in me.*

Thankyou Fiona, for setting me free.

*Thankyou trauma responses for protecting
my youngest part until I could protect her and love her.*

Contents

Illustrations

Recommended Music Playlist

1. The Beatles *Within you, without you.*
2. Carl Orff *O Fortuna*
3. Al Stewart *Year of the cat*
4. The Beatles *Because*
5. Al Stewart *If it doesn't come naturally, leave it*
6. Sting *When we dance*
7. Bruce Springsteen *Cover me*
8. The Carpenters *Top of the world*
9. U2 *With or without you*
10. The Cure *Catch*
11. Sting *Let your soul be your pilot*
12. Rolling Stones *Gimme shelter*
13. Rolling Stones *Paint it black*
14. The Kinks *I'm not like everybody else*
15. XTC *Senses working overtime*
16. Tim Minchin *It's not perfect*
17. George Harrison *All things must pass*
18. Rolling Stones *Sympathy for the Devil*
19. Dire straits *Les boys*
20. The Beatles *Fixing a hole*
21. David Bowie *Heroes*
22. Police *Invisible sun*
23. The Beatles *Here comes the sun*

Prologue

We were talking about the love that's gone so cold and the
people,
Who gain the world and lose their soul
They don't know, they can't see
Are you one of them?
When you've seen beyond yourself then you may find
Peace of mind is waiting there
And the time will come when you see
We're all one, and life flows on within you and without you.

George Harrison[1], Within you, without you,
Sgt. Pepper's Lonely Hearts Club Band.

Have you ever listened to music? Truly listened? Listened, not just
with your ears, but with every fibre of your being? Close your eyes,
shut out the rest of the world, let the music become your world and
allow yourself to become the music. Feel the waves of music as they
embrace you, envelope you, accept you. You don't need to think now
– just be.

My internal music, my being, my truth: the parts that make me
whole define me, and are to the most part largely invisible to the
human eye. Ah … if only you could hear my music. It is beautiful:
unbearably exquisite, poignant, and terrible. It is complex, layered,
impossible to keep pace with, fiercely defended; yet, surprisingly
simple, comprehensible, penetrable and vulnerable. Perhaps you

cannot hear my music. Perhaps my music is not to your taste, and is at times unenviable. Nevertheless, it is valuable and loveable.

Music is sacred. Music *is* life and reminds us *of* life. It is both within us and around us. Music is the medium individually and collectively used to create, communicate, celebrate, inspire and unite. It allows us to share our thoughts, ideas, and emotions. If you listen carefully, listen openly, you may hear and feel that which you have never heard, never felt, never experienced before. You may discover new truths, unbearable truths, liberating truths. You may catch a glimpse of someone else's truth – a new rhythm, a new melody. Perhaps those new notes will touch your notes – merge, harmonise, and become more beautiful.

What do you do when someone else's music initially sounds discordant, perhaps even painful? Do you ask yourself why it disturbs you? Is the music in some way threatening: disturbingly affective, distantly familiar? Perhaps the music feels like dark energy: a negative pressure that counterbalances your own gravity and threatens to expand your understanding of self and truth too quickly – if you were to allow it. Do you turn his or her volume down? Do you increase your own volume and drown out his or her music; thereby rendering it non-existent, worthless, separate from the universal symphony, and somehow not quintessentially human? Perhaps you close your eyes, open your senses, listen to the music more closely, and discover the beauty of the music's nuances.

I describe my internal music, and therefore the essence of who I am, as 'beautiful: unbearably exquisite, poignant, and terrible'. Perhaps my choice of words may give the impression of self-indulgent introspection or an overt, attention-seeking ploy. The previous two sentences reveal personal insights, an enduring private struggle to establish and maintain self-worth, and hypervigilance regarding believability: all of which compel me to share my experience with you. Why am I exposing myself to the potential reinforcement of a feeling of isolation and difference, and to my very real fears of being misinterpreted, rejected, and worst of all, not believed?

I am compelled by a deep-seated sense of social justice and an enduring belief that words have the power to enlighten, modify, and improve human behaviour and social well-being. Despite the many physical, psychological, social, and financial obstacles I have encountered and continue to be restricted by, my automatic survival switch continues to be triggered and provides me with one simple message: DON'T GIVE UP. I must draw on all my courage, and employ all the skills I possess to fulfil my own potential. I have realised that my volume needs to be amplified so that others might listen, understand, accept and share my music. I am hoping that my music will resonate with you and then be passed on to others so that it is sufficiently amplified to reach the minds and hearts of those with the power to help people like me.

I have deliberately provided you with an apparition of my character: a barely visible, intangible, possibly not real impression of who I am. I will provide you with a narrative that is not unlike a mystery to be solved. You will gather my memories, my experiences, my feelings, my values, my flaws, and my strengths. You will enter my world, stare into my abyss, be blinded by darkness and robbed of all hope. You will know of my pain but you will not feel my pain. I offer you an evanescent self-portrait because that is how I have been perceived for most of my life. I have pieced together my mystery in an effort to cling onto the treacherously slippery, rocky sides of the abyss. I employ powerful imagery, whether in words or paint, to describe what is impossible to see: and for many people, what is beyond their capacity to imagine – or what they want to imagine. If nothing else, I want you to learn that the worst pain I have endured has been served up as a lethal cocktail of ignorance, prejudice, patronisation, indifference, disbelief and dismissal from too many health professionals who represent my very leaky lifeboat.

Chapter 1

Sentient

"What a piece of work is a man!
How noble in reason! How infinite in faculties!
In form and moving, how express and admirable!
In action how like an angel!
In apprehension how like a god!
The beauty of the world!
The paragon of animals!
And yet, to me, what is this quintessence of dust?"

William Shakespeare[1], *Hamlet*

Everyone thinks writers must know more about the inside of the human head, but that is wrong. They know less, that's why they write.... Trying to find out what everyone else takes for granted.

Margaret Atwood[2], *Dancing Girls.*

A novel that does not uncover a hitherto unknown segment of existence is immoral. Knowledge is the novel's only morality.

Milan Kundera[3], *Immortality.*

Sometimes I cannot bear to listen to music: I want to extinguish it. Not because it is too loud. Not because it is not my kind of music. It is because it is too beautiful. Purity of voices and the masterful manipulation of rhythm, and melody that manifests the best of human creative potential overwhelm my senses and leave me destitute of hope. How can people, as a species, be capable of working so well together to create something so novel, and universal in its apparent inspiring truth, yet simultaneously reek callous destruction in their attempt to transcend the reality of being human: of being connected with others?

This question is always associated with a memory I have of listening to Orff's 'O Fortuna'[4] for the first time, when I was 21. I had heard and enjoyed excerpts from *Carmina Burana* previously but I had never really listened to it at the exclusion of all other sounds. Probably motivated by the whim of a positive mood I requested to listen to *Carmina Burana* in a popular music shop in Brisbane's Queen Street. It was a relatively new trend for music shops to offer potential customers the opportunity to sample music whilst wearing headphones. I was not prepared for the consequent assault on my sensibilities. The chorus was urgent in its intent, powerful and exquisitely positive. It devastated me. I was almost unaware of the fact that I was crying in a very public place but it did not seem to me to be inappropriate. I was the music and the music was me. This experience has punctuated my life's narrative. It was at that moment that I realised what it meant to be human. The music had captured core themes running through Nietzsche's and D. H. Lawrence's writings: the destruction and creation of human reality and potentiality. Whilst, sometimes I cannot bear to listen to the pain of that realisation I am still compelled to embrace the message of that reality: we are what we make of it.

Perhaps other customers saw me crying and thought my behaviour strange because they could not hear my music. What if I had shared my music with them? Would they have understood it and shared my awareness? Would Carl Orff have been able to compete with The Police and Cold Chisel? Probably not. I also love The Police and Cold Chisel – their songs are fabulously fun to dance to, but the reality is that I would have had MAD stamped on my forehead if I had attempted to share my thoughts and feelings with the other humans in that shop.

I began to protect my difference during early childhood. Sometimes it involved being described by others as *independent*, a *dark horse*, or *fey*. More often it meant pretending to be confident, fun, and happy, whilst inwardly withdrawing, reserving my thoughts and feeling a terrifying, disturbing sense of difference. Sharing my story is similar to navigating a labyrinth with me because it has taken me so many years of rummaging around inside my mind and body; having to live with huge, dark, insidious and enduring secrets, occasionally glimpsing hope for medical help that has all too often been the Minotaur. Years of intentional reading and researching have been necessary for me to understand myself, others, and to help myself when help has been limited, and at worst extremely damaging. In fact, climbing out of my labyrinth to share my story is proving simultaneously extremely challenging and motivating. My negotiation of life's labyrinth is a huge puzzle – a problem to be solved and I love problem-solving. It is just my luck that I have to be my own lab rat.

I did not enjoy primary school. For the most part, I was bored. I loved reading because it inspired my imagination, taught me new things, entertained me, and most of all it represented my portal of escape. My parents taught me to read by the age of three and a half. Having to 'learn to read' at school was just a waste of time and switched off my engagement in class. One of my other favourite things to engage in was conversation. I especially loved talking with my maternal grandfather (or more likely listening) and my adopted grandfather. They were similar in that they were articulate, highly intelligent, knowledgeable, asked me questions, expected me to understand them, and I developed the *sense* that I was an intellectual equal. I emphasise the fact that it was a sense of intellectual equality because obviously one cannot possibly be conscious of such a concept at that age. However, my relationships with these two men whom I dearly loved and aspired to be like certainly influenced my development of core beliefs founded on a biological potentialist view of Humanism, that is; people are agents of their own self-development[5].

I had a master plan: a) to grow up to be just like my mother who I considered to be beautiful and a real grown-up, and b) to marry my father. Sentiments horribly representative of Freud's Oedipus[6] phase but I assure the reader that I certainly did not envy my father's penis! I remember asking my mother if I could start calling her Margaret. My simple solution to the complex relationship obstacle, namely that of changing my mother's identity from Mummy to Margaret, was immediately and resoundingly quashed. My parents consistently modelled important living skills and provided me with many rich, educational opportunities which I increasingly appreciate with age. The four most valued gifts they have empowered me with are love, the ability to read, the ability to think for myself, and self-mastery beliefs[7]. My father was particularly instrumental in my development of independent thinking and my expectations for self-mastery. When I asked him questions, he would often ask me, 'What do you think first?' When I doubted my ability to do something he would say, 'But you can try'. These gifts have been, and continue to be my life raft – especially when I have struggled to maintain a hold on reality.

At five years of age, I found it impossible to 'play horses' with other little girls because quite evidently, we were not horses. It confounds me that someone with quite a vivid imagination could not make the abstract leap but it certainly made making friends at that age difficult. I recall regularly doing 'playground duty' at lunch with a very tall, impressive principal because I found it easier to chat with him than my classmates – poor man. Playground duty was almost as pleasurable as taking myself to the school's library and reading books to myself. My favourite memory of my years at state primary school was reading Eric Carlyle's *The very hungry caterpillar*[8] to myself during lunch one day when I was in year one. The magic of the colours, the holes in the pages, the repetition that built up the excitement, and the wondrous transformation of the caterpillar into the beautiful butterfly were damned hard to beat. The story is also a wonderful message about self-renewal which I have been personally attempting to emulate since Carlyle's chrysalis of hope opened in my consciousness.

Chapter **2**

White Bears and Lost Innocence

'We can never hold an image of totality because our consciousness is too narrow; we can only see flashes of existence. It is always as if we were observing through a slit so that we only see a particular moment; all the rest is dark and we are not aware of it at that moment.'

Jung[1], *Analytical Psychology: It's theory & practice.*

Memory is a way of telling you what's important to you.

Salman Rushdie[2]

I don't remember my year two classroom. I have no recollection of its layout, where I sat, my teacher, or my classmates. When I try to remember, my mind can only conjure an inky black. It is the only year of school that I cannot recall. In fact, the only memories of 1975 that I have tried so hard to obliterate are rooted deeply in my subconscious and conscious, and have spread like a noxious weed through my mind, my heart, my very existence. Those moments and the memories of those moments have caused irrevocable psychological damage that has directly affected my development, my cognitive functioning, my relationships, my career, my earning capacity, and my quality of life. Attempting to share some of my memories of those cataclysmic turning points in my life is so distressing that I am experiencing tightening of my chest, intense muscular tension, difficulty in breathing, and an almost overwhelming dread of conveying those mental images and their emotional impact with the power of words. This process seems to increase the proximity of my experiencing, and immediately evokes a flight or fight response. I am only six or seven years old now and I am completely and utterly vulnerable.

I am suffused with disgust, shame, guilt, fear. Who do I loathe more now: her or me? My hatred died a long time ago. My anger sometimes resurfaces when I allow myself to feel angry that she and her mother stole my potential; robbed me of years of possible closeness and warmth from my mother and brother; and prevented people I valued from understanding me and trusting me. Ah – I am crying now. Mostly inside me. Don't look because I hate making people sad.

I am safe now; she can't hurt me anymore.

But she is.

I have power now and ways to look after myself. I can give myself time and emotional space to gather the courage to continue telling my story because there is purpose in the pain.

You see? The internal chatter has become useful again. It was amplified in 1975. It was a defence mechanism then: somehow restoring order in my head. It was different then; it always began with *We*. Somehow, I felt safer when I had a type of invisible special force team. Accumulative years of anxiety founded on a lack of understanding of what had happened to me and its enduring effects simply amplified the internal chatter to a distracting volume and became more disturbing when I observed that other people did not appear to experience the same phenomenon. They could concentrate when they did not understand something at school. They were not overwhelmed by the fear of being seen as bad or stupid because they were not quick at learning something like they used to be.

I had to hide this difference: I knew that much. The puzzle pieces were there but they were much, much bigger than me. I was actually buried alive in them and it has taken 40 years to sort those pieces into the corner pieces, the boundaries, and the internal pieces that would eventually come together to make sense of who I was, who

I am, and to believe in who I may be. Is this story one of anger and blame: a great cathartic purge on my readership? No. It is intended to increase awareness about the ways in which all levels of society can work together to encourage, support, and help provide the resources necessary for young people to develop resilience. It is an amplified request of society, and in particular, politicians, government departments, and health professionals to look beyond numbers, statistics, and medical journals funded by giant pharmaceutical companies, to *listen* to their patient's or client's language and treat them individually as opposed to a predictive script. Enable their client to be proactive in their health management. There are many *if onlys* in my life that I refuse to give in to. However, there is a way of protecting children through education and there are ways to help individuals who live with mental illness because *we* often have, often do, and can make great contributions to society given a real opportunity. This message is so important that I have to force myself to tell you more of my story.

I do not want to remember their house but I do. I had to live next to it for 14 more years. I could not block it from my view and whenever I visited my parents' house, I could see it. I hated that house. I still hate that house. It was such a relief when neighbours built a two-storey house on the paddock in between and blocked the view of that constant traumatic trigger. I recall much of the layout of their house and I remember their faces. Those were the kind faces that I had trusted. They were *good people*. My father loves those neighbours. Although he was wary of any attempt they might have made to convert me from Anglicanism to Christadelphianism, he approved of their uncommonly good knowledge of the Bible and their dedication to carpentry and the simple life, because my father is an Anglican priest. I used to love patting their cow and watching their chickens. Their big brother, Jaimie, helped me ride on their cow: a happy memory. But that happiness was decimated by what I experienced in their dark house.

I admired her because she was a *big girl*, possibly seven or eight years older than me: old enough to know precisely what she was doing. She knew how to use nail polish and eye shadow: *just like*

Mummy. She promised that if I would 'not tell anyone', she would paint my nails: *I would be just like Mummy.* I did not know what I would have to do to have my nails painted and I did not understand why we had to go to her bedroom or turn out the light. I did not know why she was whispering and I did not expect her to remove some of my clothes. But she was a big girl and I was scared. I was scared of being in trouble and somehow, I knew we were doing something bad but I did not know or understand what it was. Whilst she was enjoying touching and petting my *wee wee*, she was telling me how I should never do this with boys, only girls do this. She told me her sister showed her how to do it. Whilst she was making me *ride her,* she was telling me that my mother did not love me as much as my little brother because the youngest child is always loved the most. It did not hurt me physically and it was apparent to me that she was excited and gaining some immense pleasure that I could not comprehend. She finished abruptly, made me dress and turned on the light. Then she smeared some white nail polish on my nails and sent me home.

I feel sick now and am resisting the urge to vomit. I am feeling acute sadness. I am crying. I have put headphones on and am listening to the choir of monks of the *Abbey of Santo Domingo de Silos*[3] singing Gregorian chants. It soothes me. My defence mechanisms have kicked in to protect me from feeling too much pain so that I can continue telling you my story.

Why did I allow her to do this again? I was terrified when she led me down the dark hallway to her older brother's room. She proudly showed me the magazine pictures of girls she had stuck up on Mark's bedroom walls. I did not understand why she would do this. She did not mess around with what I have come to understand as foreplay this time. As I see it now, I just had to be the man and ensure that she reached satisfaction. She did and then she put eye shadow on me. I remember her making me dress up in a bra filled with tissues and parading me in front of her mother. Her mother did not appear to think this strange.

I now understand the automatic horror I experienced when my mother told me that I had to be fitted for a bra when I was 12, and my enduring avoidance of assistance in lingerie fitting rooms. It has only recently occurred to me that Esther's mother must have been aware of Esther's behaviour, and must have been aware of her daughters' behaviours. What good Christadelphian mother would allow her daughter to decorate her older brother's walls with magazine images of scantily clothed women? Why didn't she raise an eyebrow at her teenage daughter parading the little girl from next door, dressed in a stuffed bra in the kitchen where she was preparing food, just outside her daughter's open bedroom door that, moments before, had been closed with the lights off?

I learnt to make a bed in her grandmother's bedroom but I cannot recall what else happened there. It was hard to avoid her. My mother assured me that "you weren't friends for long" but I was not friends with her: I just had to appear to be friendly with her for my parents. I had to share the backseat of my father's car with her whilst he dropped me off at primary school and took her to high school where he taught. In the backseat, she would explain to me that my blue eyes and blonde hair were not as beautiful as her brown eyes and blonde hair because hers were more unusual. The sexual abuse did not continue but the effects of that abuse, and the emotional and psychological abuse that accompanied those incidents and other encounters, impacted my life with such force that it brings to my mind the image of the sickening wreckage left by a train collision with an oncoming train. My mind, my worldview, and my childhood were picked up, twisted, wrenched apart and left in a heap for me to mend without anyone knowing.

I have never been able to communicate these memories to anyone with such detail before. I have never made myself relive those moments so intensely that I could communicate what I was thinking as a child. It is not that I could not remember: it is because it is so painful. In order to continue telling my story I have had to stop, make myself a cup of green tea, and cry in my bathroom. More accurately, my insides felt like someone had taken a grater to my heart, left me bleeding internally, and my mouth was emitting sounds that could only be described as sobs of grief. Since I was six or seven years old, I have felt disturbed by dark rooms during the day. They make me feel trapped and sad. I find it hard to trust people with brown eyes. This makes me sad because my husband and sons have brown eyes.

How does a young child cope with experiences and information that are not developmentally appropriate? How does that information and those experiences affect her? Current research[4,5,6,7] postulates that severe stress or traumatic events, such as sexual abuse, alters the structure and operation of brain regions necessary for emotional and cognitive functions. Adverse alteration of areas like the hippocampus and amygdala during childhood development, when the central nervous system is more plastic or malleable, is conjectured to have greater, enduring, deleterious effects on the physical and mental health consequences for individuals with severe mental illness[7]. Larsson, et al. report that sexual abuse before 12 years of age, is correlated with diminished grey matter located in the visual cortex[5]. For the non-specialist reader, that information may sound very sciencey, and somewhat scary. Having a psychology degree, and an interest in how the human brain works, it came as no surprise. For someone who experienced this type of trauma during the most vulnerable stage of human development, with the added awareness that I appear to be personally confirming some rather horrid scientific and medical research theories and findings, the news isn't good.

So, how did I cope with the trauma? I knew that what had happened was wrong: it felt wrong. Therefore, there was a great possibility that I would be in serious trouble if my parents found out. Even though I believed that I had not been the bad person, that is, committed a sin like they talked about in church, I felt bad. I felt intense shame, guilt, and a sense of dirtiness. I have not really been able to rid myself of those feelings when I feel down.

I recall trying to show my little brother what had happened to me. I suppose I was just trying to work it out for myself because she had said that you don't do this with boys. I wish with all my heart that I had not tried to show him. He would have been only four or five years old. We did not have a clue what we were doing and it certainly did not add up to any sexual experience but I still feel bad. Does he remember it? Is that why he stopped talking to me for two years when we were adolescents? I do not know and that is something people just do not talk about. However, that night during dinner he told my parents that, "Esther touched Lisa's wee wee". Of course, I denied it when they asked me if it was true. Perhaps if one of them had approached me again quietly, in privacy and had made me believe that I would not be in trouble, I might have felt safe to tell them and I might have received help. I do not blame them. Public awareness campaigns have made society more aware of the dangers of child sexual abuse and now everyone should be responsible for listening carefully to what children say, how they say it, and observe changes in children's behaviour. If they are exhibiting unusual behaviour, *observe very closely*, and if your internal alarm bells are ringing, *investigate*.

There seemed to me to be one very big problem. I was a girl. If only girls did those things, I most certainly did not want to be a girl. Back to the simple solution: I changed my name at school. My friends who were girls accepted my new name and called me Charlie for the next five years. I recall being about 11 when I sat down on my bedroom floor and whited out my name on my ballet certificate (signed by Margot Fonteyn), and wrote *Charlie*. Charlie gave me courage and helped me to confront moments of fear when every fibre of my being was telling me to run away. My father interpreted this new behaviour as amusing so Charlie was only ever in my head at home.

My levels of anxiety sky-rocketed. Every day I have ever attended school (as a student, as a teacher, and as a counsellor/community educator) I have felt nauseated simply approaching the entrance gate. I just wanted to run in the opposite direction. I learnt to internally "whistle a happy tune" so that no one knew I was afraid. Whilst I am a very sociable person who loves to learn and teach, I am also largely introverted and do not like large groups, public performances, uniforms, regimental-like rigidity in behaviour and thinking, bells that tend to have a Pavlovian effect on people's behaviour, conformity, mediocrity, and I am allergic to chalk. So, I acted my way out of fear every time I needed to and excelled in oratory presentations. I appeared at ease and confident. Thanks to Charlie and his metamorphosis into someone more like Clint Eastwood as I grew older, I challenged life's obstacles and continued to believe that I could overcome fear and solve my problem.

Charlie helped me when I felt out of control, especially when I showered. I hated my body and I lived in fear of being exposed. Self-talk is a handy thing when you know how to use it. Unfortunately, at seven years of age I did not know about positive self-talk so I had to invent my own form. This typically involved Charlie talking me through my showering routine, saying assuredly, "We're going to wash our hair now because …". It was like meditation and I felt in control again: very much like listening to Gregorian chants, just crazier.

My biggest problem was that I did not know that my problem was bigger than me. That the more I kept my problem to myself, the bigger it became. Her pernicious words had buried themselves deep in my subconscious and attracted confirmatory bias. I now believed that my mother did not love me but she did love my brother. When I was feeling insecure about my appearance, I asked her for her opinion. She replied, "Every mother warthog loves her baby warthog". A strange reply but apparently, she had said the same thing to my brother and it had not affected him one iota. She did not know that I already believed that I was ugly: the seed had already been planted and had now been fertilised by a typically dry English wit. It was a fact – I looked like a warthog. It only took 31 years to question my mother about the meaning of her statement and for me to privately question why it had affected me so much. She does not know how it was so strongly linked to a traumatic experience. My confirmation bias would have blocked any positive thing she might have said to me in a hypervigilant effort to gather evidence that my mother believed I was unlovable and ugly. Cognitive-behavioural therapists would describe that type of erroneous thinking *selective abstraction*[8] and would, no doubt, challenge my thinking by asking questions that would penetrate the filter but I did not have a therapist at my disposal.

Unlovable and ugly are themes in my life. I battle with those internal enemies fairly constantly, even though I am surrounded by family members and friends who love me dearly and I certainly do not look like a warthog. Children watch their parents closely and learn from their behaviour. Much of that learning is unconscious, and children learn both desirable and undesirable skills and behaviours. By observation of facial expressions, eye contact, and vocal tones they also learn to evaluate people's emotions and levels of parental approval. Believe me, we all instinctively long for parental approval and many of us consciously and unconsciously strive to obtain it. Perhaps individuals who do not feel the need to obtain parental approval may have; (a) assumed philosophical acceptance, (b) given up in despair and possibly self-loathing, or (c) are simply psychopathic. Even then, Freud would blame it on their mothers!

I do not think I ever really felt as though I had to strive for my father's approval. There were times when I knew I had disappointed him but he always seemed to emit a sense of hope that I would "see the light": that I had not strayed beyond the realms of his approval. I *knew* that he loved me. I believed that I had to win my mother's approval and I was highly sensitive to any perceived signs of disapproval; lack of warmth; criticism; or rejection. Unlike my father, she was not a naturally huggy type of person and I am sure it would have been hard to compete with Dad to hug me when I was little because I was a *Daddy's girl*. It was not her fault that we did not share the same type of relationship. We now share a different, special relationship that involves love, approval and friendship. Best of all, we share some beautiful hugs. However, you will have to read the rest of my story to learn how we achieved that.

From all historical accounts the evidence points to my having been born a neat freak. It is true that my father nick-named me "Fusspot baby". I am an aesthete and highly sensual. I feel more comfortable being surrounded by beautiful colours, textures, sounds, and smells. When I am at home, I will arrange my environment until it feels and smells beautiful (which usually means arranging everything so it appears like a paradoxically dynamic still life (including the pantry and the laundry). Crazy, I know but that is who I am. I have a painful appreciation of beauty. After my trauma I needed to control my environment. I needed to feel safe. There was no space in my head because it was crowded with anxious, internal dialogue (not to be confused with psychosis) involving what I call *metacognition-gone-wrong.*

Metacognition[9] is a thinking process that involves thinking about thinking, and ultimately demands regulation of thought: in short, mental control. Have you ever consciously tried not to think: to clear your mind for a set period of time? It never ceases to amaze me when I sometimes ask my husband what he is thinking about and he declares that he is thinking about nothing. Having viewed a comic routine on YouTube (presented by a comedian) regarding the structural differences of male and female brains, I now understand that male brains are organised into thought boxes, and that one is permanently labelled, *Empty.* This is in sharp contrast with the female brain which is a complex network of extremely active neural pathways responsible for organisation and decision-making. Whilst I am aware that not everything you see on the Net is to be believed, I would love to have a brain region designed to be an empty box. Learning to meditate, to clear one's mind of all thoughts, involves great mental control and illustrates the paradox of metacognition. Metacognition requires conscious thought because we are aware that we are thinking about thinking. However, much of what we think involves automatic thoughts, thoughts that are linked by association and exist outside of our consciousness, or subconsciously[9]. Focusing one's attention on clearing one's mind of thought requires the thought, "I must not think any thoughts," which inevitably triggers a thought about not thinking, which elicits the thought, "Damn, I just had a thought. I have to stop thinking. How do I stop thinking?" Then one might try to imagine a peaceful scene, automatically remember a pleasant experience in a similar setting and struggle with all the thoughts that come to mind whilst one valiantly reminds oneself not to think. I know – it sounds hopeless but one can learn to regulate thought (and mood) with practice.

However, when you are trying to block a traumatic event from your mind while trying hard not to think about a future event that you know will trigger undesirable feelings, *metacognition-gone-wrong* is akin to open warfare. Wegner's[9,10] famous white bear study elegantly illustrated the irony of employing meta-cognitive processes to suppress unwanted thoughts. His thought suppression experiments required participants to think audibly whilst attempting to not think of a white bear[11]. The participants reported their conscious efforts to suppress thought using distraction, and occasionally succeeded[11]. However, participants rarely completely blocked the white bear from their minds (Wegner, et al., 1987). Every time the bear reappeared, participants had to re-initiate their thought distraction process, often resulting in a repetitive cycle. Participants also reported their development of a preoccupation with the undesired thought of the white bear[11]. Wegner postulates that our capacity for thought suppression is affected by four factors[10]. Firstly, our purpose to suppress thought, that is, our reason and level of desire to stop the thought. Secondly, our capacity to control our states of mind and mood. Thirdly, our ability to manifest and maintain the effort required to consciously work on thought suppression and to continuously consciously and unconsciously monitor the thought suppression process. Finally, the range of the associated wanted thoughts and unwanted thoughts that the monitoring process has to work through to enable thought suppression[10]. Hence, if an individual is time-constrained, attempting to perform many simultaneous tasks, mentally fatigued, feeling stressed, or feeling a particularly strong emotion, it is probable that he or she will fail to suppress unwanted thoughts, and will in fact increase the frequency of the unwanted thoughts: *metacognition-gone-wrong*[11,9].

Perhaps I cannot remember details about my second year of school that one would normally recall because the light in *my* world had been extinguished. My world had been painted black. My mind was consumed by my traumatic experiences to the extent that when I mentally try to walk into the classroom, I walk into a room without light. I cannot see it. I lost my world when I was six or seven. I no longer felt safe, and I had lost my sense of factual information: what to believe and what was necessary in order to hold myself together. To be me.

How does a child assimilate aberrant experiences, coupled with psychologically-shattering information into his or her worldview? Furthermore, how much does that child have to change to cope with that new information? I can only tell you about how I learnt to exist. I use the word *exist* deliberately. I could continue being but I had lost the ability to live. I could continue loving but I believed I had lost my lovability. I had one secret weapon: the belief that I had to find out how to be me again, how to be loved again, and how to live. I began to tread water and I did what any good daughter of a librarian and teacher librarian would do to solve a problem: I read.

Fiction provided me with escape routes into other worlds that were comparable with my own. I had the freedom to learn about how other people solved their problems, with and without help. Enid Blyton provided me with the idea that children of my own age were smart enough to solve adults' problems and that ginger beer is an essential aid to think, rest and celebrate. A belief I still like to endorse. A. A. Milne's characters offered a rich array of personalities and thinking styles that are still easily identifiable in so many people I live with, including myself. I know to walk the Eeyore within me to a different corner to find a better perspective and find my Tigger. Best of all, I can usually walk the middle path that Winnie-the-Pooh knows is most comfortable and generally provides inner peace. Pooh knows to ask for help[12]. I love A.A. Milne's writing. I read his book as a child but his lessons grew in power and richness as I grew, and my capacity to learn from them developed.

I favoured reading stories about characters who were courageous, generally self-sacrificing and true to themselves. Stories like *The wooden horse*[13], *Carve her name with pride*[14], *The spy who came in from the cold*[15], *The great escape*[16], are some of the books that helped form a belief that I had to be brave to face fear. Orwell's *Animal Farm: A fairy story* reinforced the importance of thinking for oneself, and being true to oneself[17]. Those beliefs helped me to face the fears associated with being sent to a girls' school when I began grade seven.

I read my favourite book, the most influential book I have ever read and will probably ever read in my life when I was 12 years old. I have re-read that book almost every year since then because I identify with the heroine: *Jane Eyre*[18]. She was different, she was vulnerable, she suffered cruelty, she was sad, she was honest, she was intelligent, she was resourceful and competent, she loved to read and learn, she loved to draw, she had warmth and support from friends and mentors, she had a great capacity to love, she was true to herself, she refused to compromise her values, she was forgiving, and she loved Mr Rochester with all her heart. Because of these things and because she was Jane, he loved her. Because of these things she found happiness. Jane did not give up and Jane was a survivor. I believe that Bronte's nineteenth century novel is a masterful study of the vital factors necessary for the development of resilience: a concept that surfaced as an important field of psychological study more than 100 years after *Jane Eyre* was written. It took 32 years for me to realise that I was like the character I most admired and loved: I am resilient.

Chapter **3**

Shattered

"Life's but a walking shadow, a poor player, that struts and frets his hour upon the stage, and then is heard no more; it is a tale told by an idiot, full of sound and fury, signifying nothing."

William Shakespeare[1], *Macbeth*

"*I think, therefore I am,* is the statement of an intellectual who underrates toothaches."

Milan Kundera[2], *Immortality*

"Reality is merely an illusion, albeit a very persistent one."

Albert Einstein[3]

"Who in the world am I? Ah, that's the great puzzle."

Lewis Carroll[4], *Alice's adventures in Wonderland*

Have you ever attempted to desperately fumble around in the dark, in search of an object that you know you need? It is inevitable that you will take hold of objects that you immediately reject because you know they are not what you need. Sometimes you will pick up objects that hurt you before you instinctively drop them. It is a great relief when you find what you know you have been looking for. My very short period of childhood and adolescence resembled a prolonged and torturous fumble in a bedside table for an object that would help me breathe. The only problem was, I did not know where the hell it was or what it felt like. Ironically, my allegorical search for reality, self, and life transmogrified from my internal world to my physical world.

My secret world, my secret grief and anxiety, my intimate music, began to slowly leak out of cracks in my internal fortification. I was unaware of the leaks but they were apparent, they were significant, and in hindsight, they quite elegantly symbolized my security system alarm bells. In an effort to hide my inner world, my outer world muffled my music; distorted it so that when it leaked, its acid seeped back into my pores. My rogue defence system attacked my immune system, my lungs, my eyes, my skin, my physical and sexual development, and my academic progress. All of these physical realities were markers of stress, and if laid out, in order on a table, spelt HELP!

I developed chronic life-threatening asthma that was exacerbated by allergies to household dust, dust-mites, and cats. I suffered from excruciatingly painful eye ulcers that affected both eyes, sometimes simultaneously. I suffered from eczema as a baby, and it is commonly associated with people who have asthma and allergies. However, my eczema was quite debilitating for extended periods of time when I was most stressed. In fact, during my final year of school I suffered from chronic asthma, I suffered pneumonia, had the inside of my thighs scraped to treat chronic eczema, was hospitalized for irritable bowel syndrome, and hospitalized to have ulcers wiped from the corneas of both eyes. If doctors thought I was a mess on the outside they should have seen the mess on my inside.

Not one teacher during my entire school life asked me how I was going. Not one teacher offered me extended time to work on an assignment, or asked for some type of concession for my overall final tertiary entrance score. Not one teacher took the time to think, "That child is capable of so much more than they are giving. Why isn't she achieving her potential in my class? I should help her". I was a well-behaved, polite student whose report cards revealed that I could achieve top grades in all subjects but not consistently. Why? Naturally, it was decided that it was explained by my attitude and my effort. I have a much better, informed and accurate explanation.

I am fairly certain that if I had been asked the right questions by a therapist who could listen to the language of his or her client, that I would have been able to tell them when I was 10.

I recall a strange school-yard conversation I was audience to when I was nine years old. A popular classmate was talking about how she was going "to do it with Darren down on the oval". The other kids seemed excited and from what I gathered, they were talking about doing things with their private parts. I was extremely shocked by this because my previous experience had taught me the reverse, "You never do this with boys". My worldview was being penetrated by new, challenging information which I was privately rejecting. I was safe with boys because boys could be trusted. Those girls did not have their facts right. I had to continue fighting the repulsive, unnatural urge to self-stimulate that I had needed to do since the switch had been flicked by my abuser when I was too young to handle the effects. I had to retreat further into my hole.

I could not escape the horrible truth that I was destined to endure more repulsive changes to my physicality: radical changes to my understanding of the external world, and the knowledge that I could never tell anyone what had happened to me and what I had done. Not long after I had listened to the bizarre conversation, my mother gave me a couple of picture books to read. I remember she was grouting tiles in the shower when she told me to read them, and gave me instructions about the order in which I was to read them and the sections I was allowed to read. I was not prepared for the content and how that would impact my world. I read *Where did I come from?*[5] largely in a state of shock. The content of the book was believable despite previous experience. The implications of the new knowledge were extremely stressful. I had been lied to about sex. Older girls, hence all women were not to be trusted, no matter how much I loved them or wanted to trust them. I could no longer grow up to be a boy no matter how much I wanted to feel safe (I had always known I was kidding myself). I needed to avoid ever feeling or being vulnerable, manipulated, or violated again.

I read two sections in *What is happening to me?*[6]: one describing the growth and purpose of breasts and one explaining menstruation.

I never read any other sections because I was so appalled. To this day, I have never been able to utter the medical terms used for my private body parts. I have to close my eyes when I attempt to discuss any medical concerns with my doctors. I abhor discussing bodily functions and certain environments or social situations can trigger immediate feelings of panic, or distress, and worst of all: they have often detrimentally impacted my mood and self-esteem.

There was no way out of this. I could not avoid more change and I had to somehow assimilate this new information into my understanding of how the world operates. After I returned the undesirable books to my mother she asked if I had any questions. Quite frankly, I did not want to know any more. My mind had been blown. I asked one question: what does it feel like? I did not receive a direct answer and certainly no eye contact because Mum continued grouting. She was just as uncomfortable as I was.

Those books were introduced to me with remarkable timing because it was not long after that I began menstruating, aged 10. I was horrified. I was teased by the boys at school for having breasts, and one of the boys nick-named me "pregnant lady" and mimicked me. I died internally. I could not understand or learn mathematical concepts. I suffered a lack of confidence when examined and would forget everything I knew just prior to examination.

Years five and six were composite classes: the class size was overwhelming making it difficult for me to concentrate. Worst of all, I had a female teacher whom I was terrified of. She had absolutely no understanding of how to instil confidence or trust in a child who obviously needed warmth and encouragement. Had she been skilled, she could have used my outstanding language skills, and comprehension skills to my advantage. Instead, she resorted to shouting at me to hammer the mathematical facts into my stupid head. Digging her nail into the nape of my neck whilst she shouted at me was presumably supposed to eek the hidden knowledge out of my lazy brain but it had the opposite effect and only taught me not to ask questions. I was a failure because I failed maths. I was stupid because I failed maths. I was bad and unlovable because I failed maths and because the latter fact had been a fact since I was seven.

Humiliation, vulnerability, violation, entrapment: all of these factors, coupled with rapid hormonal changes led to deep depression. I did not know that I was depressed. I believe that during the late 1970s there was not much public awareness of depression or stress. I was more aware of the versatility of pasta (that is, you can eat it, use it for art, or wear it as jewellery) but I was not aware that there was a name for how I felt. Nor did I know that I should ask for help. I know that I used to think of it as feeling homesick although I was at home. I remember writing a poem about walking off the end of a jetty when I was 10 or 11 years old. That is my first recollection of expressing my wish to die.

My parents were concerned about my fear of maths and exams. They tried to help in every way they could think of. I had coloured blocks to help me with addition and subtraction. My parents gave me orange coloured "confidence tablets" before exam days (for school, ballet, and piano) but I still felt like passing out or vomiting. My performance anxiety was debilitating, and I still broke out in hives before my dance exam. The placebo did not work, especially when I glimpsed the vitamin c label. They accompanied me to the school office and explained that I was nervous before exams. They trusted that someone, presumably my teacher, would take special care of me. She did address the issue. All I can remember of that exam day was standing up in the middle of the class when she gave the direction to, "Stand up the little girl who is scared of tests".

I did have a number of friends who seemed to truly regard me as fun to be with. I appreciate them more in retrospect than I did at the time. It took all my energy to find and summon up a fun, funny, brave, entertaining and confident person for them. I cared about them but I am sure that they felt a greater sense of friendship with me than I did with them. I did have a best friend who I admired very much. I believe we developed our friendship when we were in grade four. She was everything I wanted to be. She oozed natural confidence, grace, intelligence, and she was beautiful. She liked to draw and taught me how to sketch rather than to draw in one contained outline like I had taught myself from trying to study Beatrix Potter's illustrations. She could cut along a straight line and draw straight lines with her ruler, and was never reprimanded by the class teacher for finding this task almost impossible to do. If only I had known that my eyesight was flawed rather than my brain. Her very presence inspired a sense of safeness – that someone that I admired might seek my company. The sun shone out of her the day she taught me what others had seemingly failed to: she taught me to tie up my shoe laces.

I was often paired with children who experienced difficulty in learning to read. I was patient with them and concentrated on teaching them to read phonetically, teaching them to read with feeling, and encouraging them. This is how my parents taught me. I was compassionate with my "students" because I intrinsically understood what it was like to be different, and to experience difficulty with learning. This pattern of pairing me with someone who floundered with literacy, in order to boost his or her understanding and skills, repeated throughout my senior years at school. It quite frankly helped my teachers and cohorts but it seriously exploited and diminished my own potential which my teachers should have deliberately challenged and enriched. Apparently, I was useful sometimes, compliant and hence, easily invisible when not asking questions or choosing to make my own path. One can be a thinking person and maintain this type of existence for only so long before something has to give.

Despite the fact that I found many aspects of my school life demanded a constant supply of limited inner resources to maintain a normal appearance, the daily horrors were generally predictable. Therefore, I had managed to create a persona, that is, a public image, and a set of known ways to cope: to hold myself together. My home life also offered a sense of certainty. My parents understood the importance of routine, consistency in rules and consequences, regular meal times, bath times, bedtime stories, homework, and set bedtimes. My brother and I could be assured that we would attend piano lessons, ballet lessons, or sports training and events without fail and that those activities would involve practice.

Sunday was substantially sacrificed to church. We rose early, dressed in our best clothes, attended the morning service, spent our time learning the rituals, absorbing the general messages, appreciating the music, and learning about the different stages of life from a cultural perspective marked by rites of passage. We were growing up in a community of generally conservative people who largely shared my parents' values, expectations, beliefs, and faith.

Sometimes I enjoyed the social aspects of the community and the opportunity to wear clothes that were not school uniforms. I loved the beautiful music, listening to my mother's singing, and remember discovering with pride that I could read the music and when no one was listening, could sing the notes in tune. I learnt that I could take pleasure in singing hymns when I was capable of not critically thinking about the lyrics. I loved the beautiful architecture, the candles, the colours, the flowers, and my father's holistic teaching style when he delivered sermons. Church, as we referred to it, permeated every aspect of my life, and certainly did not afford me the tolerance and respect it demanded of me.

Before I lost my childhood, I accepted that what adults said was fact. I was eager to learn everything they taught me. I quite enjoyed learning how to say simple French phrases and impressing adults before I was four. I particularly loved listening to my mother's records of *The Man of La Mancha:* a musical rendition of Miguel de Cervantes' novel, *Don Quixote*[7]. I was enthralled by the passion of the story as it unfolded, despite the fact that I had no real understanding of the story when I first began to listen to it. I sang along with the characters: any words that I did not know I made up. I knew that Don Quixote (or Donn key Hoh! Tea as I sang it) loved Dulcinea with all of his heart. This significantly impressed me to the point that when my great uncle gifted me with a stuffed pink bear, I named her Dulcinea. I still recall the faces of adults when they asked me what my bear's name was (in the special way adults engage with small children). They never expected to hear my answer and I never expected to see their astonishment. Perhaps, had I been Spanish, it would have not been so unusual.

I believe that I had always been encouraged to think for myself, and this was something I took to like the proverbial duck to water. It was a skill that, when I was seven years old, simultaneously tortured and liberated me. I began to work over-time on my reassessment of my understanding of who to trust, what to believe, what was real, and how I fitted into the scheme of things. I began with nihilism. I favoured reasoning and logic (based on observation, experience, and a process of elimination) to help reconstruct my world, and to distance myself from the unbearable proximity of the experiences and their enduring effects. I stopped reciting prayers and mentally scrutinised their validity when applied to my personal relationship with God. I then attempted to honestly assess whether I could love and worship my parents' and my inherited religion's version of God. Finally, I asked myself if I even needed or could possibly believe in a God according to any description or definition.

I found myself silently rejecting the notion of asking forgiveness for my sins when I knew I had not committed any. That prayer simply made me angry. I inwardly asserted my worthiness to share the same table as this god and declared that I deserved to eat much more than the crumbs left under his table. I found his understanding of his main message and his self-assumed super-power lacking. His love was conditional. I deserved and needed more than that. My shepherd definitely needed sacking.

Ironically, I initially employed a mathematical tool to assess my ability to accept God. I recall one important night when I was seven years old. Using the time I usually devoted to reciting my night time prayer, I lay in bed with my eyes shut and imagined a pie graph. I then asked myself, "Can I love God with *my whole heart*?" I mentally divided that pie, and labelled each portion with the names of the people I loved most, including my father, my mother, my brother, each of my maternal grandparents, and my cat. There simply was no room for God. I did not, and could not love God; nor did I need to. It was my Nietzschean[8] moment: God was dead. My mind has never changed, and I have never found any evidence to the contrary. I just had to protect myself from the damaging messages I received about myself that derived from dominant culture and social mores.

My rejection of the notion of God, in any form, was not a knee-jerk reaction to my experience. It was not because this great invisible being had failed to protect me. This would be a misunderstanding of my thought processes. I discovered that I am an atheist because religion fell short of an adequate, reasoned explanation for the existence of our universe, the evolution of life, and the complexities of human behaviour. From my perspective, those who had faith were absolving themselves from thinking for themselves, and were prevented from fully appreciating the true, unlimited wonders of our universe. Their self-created God had shackled them in an effort to find safety and social regulation.

I did not need fear to keep me on the straight and narrow: I knew what was right and wrong, and I knew that there were grey areas. Furthermore, I was capable of respecting and tolerating other people's beliefs and of preventing myself from shattering their belief systems by overtly conforming when necessary, and unwaveringly maintaining personal integrity. I have developed an excellent intimate knowledge and understanding of heaven and hell, and I assure you that I have not needed to die to experience either. There have been times in my life when I would have preferred the cessation of my existence (with full awareness that my death did not involve an extended life warranty) to my living hell. However, my will to survive, my will to live, and my will to love and be loved, have out-lived and surmounted those times.

At 11 years of age my life resembled a murky existence just below the surface of a mangrove colony. I can imagine this because I spent many hours of my childhood exploring these environments close to where I grew up. Such existence might be desirable for a crustacean evolved to thrive in generally submerged, turbid environments, but I was not ready for constant, and for the most part, radical change. I needed the ability to see what was coming around the corner: to be prepared. Analysing in order to minimise pain, self-distraction, and creating an alter ego to deal with anxiety and fear are restricted and restrictive in their effectiveness. My worldview had changed, my body was changing, and my sense of self had changed. I was experiencing heightened emotionality, was hypervigilant to danger and had very low self-esteem. I seemed to be unaware of my impending transition from primary school to secondary school: I was just relieved to be picked up from school at the end of each day.

Discovering at the end of year six that I was to attend an Anglican private school for girls in my final year of primary school impacted me like a meteor crashing into a stone-age village. Totally unexpected, incomprehensible, earth-shattering, and I had even fewer resources to work with. Furthermore, I was unaware of the catalytic effect it would have on my identity development. Infiltrating my new school world involved either embracing or contending with the unanticipated advantages and disadvantages concealed within the alien environment. I was parachuted into a foreign land, minus a guidebook, and had found myself surrounded by a population I most feared: females. I had no camouflage. In fact, I discovered I was wearing a bright orange visibility vest labelled, CHAPLAIN'S DAUGHTER. It could easily have been the straw that broke the camel's back, but fortunately this camel was made of sterner stuff and had its eyes set on a distant horizon. That horizon's clouds had silver linings that indicated to me the opportunity to create a new social identity which involved redefining who people would think I am.

No doubt my father's new job was a challenge for him. He had moved from teaching in a state system to working in the private system. He had adopted the official role of the shepherd of an enormous population comprising, nuns, female teachers, secondary school girls, and primary school girls. He was doing the same kind of work Jesus had done: teaching, guiding, inspiring by example, loving his flock, working for his Father. He was in his element.

His job, including its very location, certainly re-arranged and dominated family life. Sunday was now Chapel Day. This meant I now attended school six days a week. During Lent, I attended chapel services three times a week: Wednesday mornings before school, Wednesday evenings after school, and Sunday mornings. During Lent, I became an honorary boarder; breakfasting with the nuns and boarders on Sunday and Wednesday mornings, and dining with them on Wednesday nights. I do not recall how many times a week my conscious self floated off into the slipstream of imagination during Divinity. I had to go somewhere. Secular, state school had provided me with a type of buffer from god people and god world. Despite my absolute belief that one omniscient, omnipotent, creator does not exist, I could not avoid this man-made god. He was everywhere.

Travelling from home to school involved military-style routine and self-discipline: adherence to a timetable, uniforms, an unspoken code of conduct, and complete compliance. Estimated times of departure and estimated times of arrival were significant because, in 1979, travel time from our home to school involved at least approximately 90 minutes. Days began early, and often seemed to last a hell of a long time. Dad has often fondly recalled that I "always woke up with a smile" and marvelled at my good-natured behaviour during that time. Perhaps it takes a good deal of wisdom to know that there is no real point to attempting to alter what you know you have no power to alter.

Furthermore, Dad and I enjoyed each other's company in the car. He loved me and I loved him. Sometimes we would sing his childhood songs together. He would sing "Will ye stop your tickling Jock?" with a Scottish accent that made me laugh until tears ran down my cheeks. During my adolescent years he used to enjoy singing "I'm the happiest girl in the whole USA" just like Dolly Parton. He was and still is a natural entertainer and completely eccentric. How could I not love him? Other times, he would listen to the car radio whilst I read novels. At that age I had an ability to mentally block out distractions so that I could concentrate on reading. I do remember sobbing in the car when my favourite character in *Seven little Australians* [9] died. She had attempted to run away from boarding school where she was deeply unhappy. Hmmm.

Dad has always been impressed with the way I empathise with people, real and imaginary. He also liked the way I played the piano "with feeling". I cannot help it. Sometimes I would like to lessen the depth of my feeling but I seem to be permanently tuned that way. I would never choose to switch it off. I suppose that is why I protect my father. He is a very loving and lovable man who loves me but does not understand or love *all* of me. He just thinks he does. He does not know when, how or why my childhood ended. He does not know or understand why I have made some of the decisions I have made in my life, nor does he know that so many of them were made because I loved him and because I loved Mum.

For him to know these things, to ultimately know me, and perhaps to have the opportunity to love me unconditionally, I would have to risk shattering his worldview. I would have to rewrite the history of our shared lives. I would have to rob him of his trust in people he loves, soak decisions that he made for me in guilt and self-blame, force his redefinition of self, challenge his core beliefs, steal his innocence, and perhaps annihilate his god. I will not do it.

Chapter 4

The Year of the Cat

Acrylic on canvas 61 x 30 cm *Year of the Cat* (2022). Acrylic on canvas 40 x 60 cm

She comes out of the sun in a silk dress running
Like a watercolour in the rain
Don't bother asking for explanations
She'll just tell you that she came
In the year of the cat
       Al Stewart[1] Year of the cat, *Year of the Cat*

Because the world is round it turns me on
Because the world is round
Because the wind is high it blows my mind
Because the wind is high
Love is old, love is new
Love is all, love is you
Because the sky is blue, it makes me cry
Because the sky is blue

Lennon-McCartney[2], Because, *Abbey Road.*

St Alias was a culture shock. In retrospect, I view it with wry amusement. It brings to mind a vision of country mouse meets city mouse and wishes it had found la résistance Française instead. My primary school had consisted of roughly four permanent blocks, a couple of demountable schoolrooms, a toilet block, a tennis court, an oval with a cricket pitch, and an office. At the end of the very dry oval was bush which was eventually cleared to make room for the Opportunity School (i.e., special needs school). During summer, we travelled in a bus to our council's public swimming pool, for swimming lessons. Our class teachers were responsible for teaching us in every subject (whether they were competent in the subject or not). The school's student population was possibly about 350-400 children.

St Alias was simply *gobsmackingly* awesome (Note. Apply original meaning of awesome). Yes, it is necessary to invent an adverb for St Alias, because I sincerely doubt that anyone had ever felt as simultaneously impressed and terrified by an educational institution as I was in 1980, since Shakespeare ceased being available to invent such words. Its very location, vast estate, layout, and architecture (much of which was steeped in history) belied its purpose: to produce well-educated, accomplished, well-mannered, well-behaved, obedient, devout girls who would, ideally, continue to achieve in their goodness and endeavours beyond their school lives. St Alias took a bit of getting used to.

My former primary school's uniform consisted of a simple dress, ankle socks, black school shoes, a pair of Volleys for sporting activities, some togs (bathing costume), and bottle green ribbons for hairstyling. I always wore my correct uniform and polished shoes because my parents were sticklers for uniforms. I was quite envious of girls who were allowed to wear sandals or high heels to school. Some boys wore their hair long over their ears and had pierced ears.

When kids talked about musical bands and their posters, I had no idea what they were talking about. Dad discouraged us from listening to popular music, explaining that music died when Glen Miller was killed in an aircraft accident during World War II. If we ever watched bands on TV Dad would immediately say that the musicians looked "constipated" and were "long-haired gits". Hence, I continued to listen to predominantly classical music, jazz music, and songs predating the 1950s. My strangeness was enhanced by Dad's concentrated interest in and enthusiasm for flight, especially Bert Hinkler and aircraft from World War II. Having watched and listened to the film, *Battle of Britain* [3], countless times, I can probably provide a quote from its script that would be suitable for any occasion. I have made models of spitfires (and I know any pilot worth his salt wears a yellow scarf). I also listened to sound effects from WWII, and learnt to identify the different sounds made by spitfires and hurricanes taking off. On reflection, I was standing on the outside and looking in to my contemporary world.

St Alias was a relief in the sense that there was routine, order, smaller classes, and more strangely, I was not bullied by my peers (as long as I did not encounter the high-school girls). I remember the layout of my year seven classroom, and I remember the light that poured through the windows. It had wooden desks that we were encouraged to keep tidy, and the teacher's desk had a bell on it, which was tinkled to remind students to keep quiet. I remember all of my St Alias's teachers with fondness. They treated me with kindness and warmth, which eventually managed to make me feel safe enough to be myself, and to discover that I could enjoy school.

My class teacher had a natural command of the classroom that simply inspired hard work that gave me a sense of accomplishment. This may be partially attributed to the fact that the majority of my classmates had attended St Alias for many years and had learnt to demonstrate excellent classroom behaviour. I do not remember fearing or hating any subject that she taught me. Somehow, she taught in a language that I understood, and this allowed me to understand and believe that I could master new skills and combine them with the skills I already had. The positive effect of combined warmth, encouragement, security, and support was evidenced by my ability to grasp an understanding of mathematics. I had left my state primary school with a morbid fear of maths and a great, big D (fail) stamped next to the subject, both on my report card and on my brain. I left that year seven class with an astonishing A (top score) for maths, and a renewed belief that I was not stupid.

This transformation of my view of myself and my perspective of my new world was not immediate, nor was it painless. I was deeply unhappy for much of the first academic term for significant reasons. Firstly, I had left a familiar school environment in which I had developed individualised (and to some degree dodgy) coping skills that I was forced to re-evaluate and modify. Secondly, I had lost the support of my familiar circle of friends, in particular my best friend. Thirdly, I was surrounded by females: the very population I feared, mistrusted, and felt particularly vulnerable to, and threatened by.

Toilets, bathrooms, showers, swimming pools were the places that automatically triggered a type of noise distortion in my head, a fuzziness equivalent to when your radio channel suddenly loses reception. They turned my organs inside out, made me want to hide, run away, freeze, cry, scream, vomit, and avoid needing to use the toilet: I was seven again and utterly vulnerable. I knew I could not escape this environment so I chose to develop quick change acts in toilet cubicles, to urinate when I knew that other sounds would disguise the noise of my disgusting bodily functions. I wore my togs in the showers and avoided looking at uninhibited, naked girls who apparently did not hate their own bodies. I now have the bladder of a camel, and still avoid the use of public toilets.

I also had a completely new dilemma. I was used to being the daughter of a priest in one part of my life and having to conform to people's expectations but at least at my old state primary school I was afforded secular protection and relief. At St Alias, I was now The Chaplain's Daughter: my identity had been recreated in my father's image, without my consent.

Adolescence is a word that we tend to associate with transition, change, and turbulence. It often conjures up the image of a stroppy, spotty, rebellious teen who either forgets what personal hygiene means or is perilously close to drowning in his or her reflection. The teen will undoubtedly swing from high to low moods without warning, spend too much time with undesirables, and will definitely challenge Copernicus's theory that the Earth revolves around the sun by constantly demonstrating to his or her parents that the Earth revolves around their adolescent offspring.

No doubt some readers will be nodding their heads, perhaps smiling at memories of their own adolescence. I know that there were definitely periods of time when I drove my mother to distraction with my chatter, or my moodiness. Undoubtedly, I was high maintenance. Some of my "moodiness" could possibly be attributed to puberty, and as a parent of adolescent boys, and having chosen to teach for 14 years in secondary education, I empathise with all parents and admit that it is not easy to completely understand an adolescent. However, how many of us can say we completely understand any human behaviour? The stereotypical description of an adolescent may bare some truth but it would be a horrible mistake for parents to assume that they should approach their adolescent child through a one-size-fits-all, stereotyped filter.

It may be presumptive of me to share my view of adolescents with you but I will take the opportunity whilst I still have your attention, if not your acceptance. Adolescents are amplified human beings. We need to appreciate the nuances of what they are amplifying. We do not necessarily need to agree with or like everything they do, but we do need to acknowledge that we may also need to grow with them. Shakespeare's[4] sonnet 116 has, for in excess of 400 years, contained a vital lesson that I believe everyone should adopt.

> "... love is not love
> Which alters when it alteration finds,
> Or bends with the remover to remove.
> O no, it is an ever-fixéd mark
> That looks on tempests and is never shaken; ..."

Love is not true love when it is conditional: when it depends on a fixed perception of the person one loves. Love is constant regardless of changing conditions. True love is unconditional: it is not withdrawn in order to force compliance. Perhaps, one of the greatest acts of love we must demonstrate to our children is the type of love that says, "I love you even when I do not like, or do not agree with what you do, think, or feel. My love will not be diminished by your difference." This requires persistence, and quite possibly ridiculous levels of unnatural tolerance but I believe all individuals need unconditional love.

My fourth and largest source of unhappiness required a different personal management approach. I used the new resources and opportunities made available to me to reveal parts of myself in creative ways that were socially attractive; I developed a somewhat extroverted persona; and I asserted my independent thought incrementally, testing how close I could sail to the wind.

I loved my art teacher dearly. She provided me with opportunities to experiment, encouraged me, and demonstrated a personal interest in me. I enjoyed music and actually chose to play the piano, whilst I sang "*Smoke gets in your eyes*", to my classmates, who responded with their usual camaraderie. My most powerful tool was my sense of humour, often combined with wit without malice. Perhaps my humour made me more likeable because it revealed that I was safe and open to friendship. I do not know. My classmates loved to hear me laugh so much that sometimes they would pin me to the floor while they tickled me (absolute torture to the ticklee but apparently delightfully amusing to the ticklers). What I do know is, laughter and shared humour lifts people's moods, and in so doing, lifts mine. Humour and I have a great relationship. My irreverent humour sometimes shared but mostly hidden in my mind helped buffer me from perceived threats to my identity formation.

Humour also saved me from being bullied by the secondary school boarders who initially associated me with their natural enemies: the chaplain and nuns. My protests that *I am the Chaplain's daughter but I am not a chaplain* failed to convince them. However, inventing a dessert game during Lent convinced them that I was not an enemy. Dessert for the boarder community predictably involved custard and prunes. The head table usually seated the Chaplain, the Mother Superior, and the Sisters. They were sitting ducks. Load your weapons (prune stones on dessert spoons), aim your weapons (at the black and white ducks), and flick. Five points for each nun, ten points each for the Mother Superior and the Chaplain. Delightfully irreverent and harmless fun: I cannot recall anyone being successful but I had won them over.

I failed Divinity (religious education). I remember Sister's disappointment but I suppose it was a quiet demonstration of passive resistance. I do not remember deliberately failing it after that year, in fact I am fairly certain that I generally approached it with a decent effort when it was a study of comparative religions or great acts of humanity because that involved considering human behaviour and beliefs. I quite enjoyed French lessons because Dad had introduced the language to me when I was very young and Mum and Dad often spoke to each other in French during meal times. Their cunning parenting tactics were later undone by their own effective teaching when I was able to translate their secret code. For instance, the words *petites choux* did not make Brussel sprouts any less disgusting.

I adapted to my new school and developed a new set of coping skills that in hindsight certainly seem more "normal" or healthy than my earlier coping style. I suspect that this is largely because St Alias's primary school culture was nurturing, and my classmates were not status conscious, or cliquey. I grew to be as happy as I could be in a girls' school, I had even become quite popular because I had a sociable disposition. However, I could not shake my depression. The white bear was always there and he was growing in strength. My memory is not clear on the chronological order in which my life was yet again dramatically changed during 1980 but it altered in two ways. One way was to my detriment, and the other, phenomenally opened my mind forever.

My father resigned from St Alias's at the end of third term and returned to the state education system. Public transport from my home to St Alias's did not exist, consequently I was enrolled in a new private girls' school for the final academic term of 1980. This school was different: the girls were different, the teachers were different, and

I had no real time or opportunity to create a social position or the means to discover new ways to buffer myself from this new, highly anxiety-generating environment. Everything changed. I was the new girl again, but this time I hit a social clique wall that was more effectively reinforced than the one that separated West Germany from East Germany.

These girls were highly competitive in ways that I simply had not even considered. They knew how to assess your social standing by how you wore your hair and by how you wore your uniform ankle socks. They were aware of fashion, money, your academic standing, and how you might affect their successful attainment of a sexual mate. My outstanding learning experience at this school was heavily grounded in evolutionary psychology and I had no desire to be a student in this hostile, largely unsupportive, competitive, survival-of-the-fittest, visually-enhanced swamp.

My easy popularity and sense of belonging had evaporated into the ether and I was left feeling quite alienated and at a loss as to how to adapt to my new world. My new world involved an all-girls' school that had an established history, was considered the top academic girls' school in Queensland and perhaps should have offered some sense of cultural or social familiarity. However, this school seemed to encourage a conservative culture that focused on academic excellence that was maths-science based and targeted towards tertiary education.

One's social status and associated success was heavily influenced by one's parents' occupation (barristers, fashion designers and opera singers ranked fairly highly) and whether one's family members were members of the Old Girls' Association. This school lacked warmth. It had an inner-city self-awareness that despite its beautiful late nineteenth century architecture and promotion of language and music studies, seemed to me to dismally fail to nurture an authentic sense of community.

If one conformed, if one learnt to walk the walk and talk the talk that was synonymous with the school's idea of leading social behaviour (and that included favouring realism rather than expressionism in art), one was destined to be happy and successful. I have never learnt to walk the walk and talk the talk, nor have I ever desired to do so. Once I realised that this kind of mentality existed in the world (a horrible and disappointing realisation) I simply decided that this new mentality would not be adopted in my world view and I resolved to protect and express my individuality in the least destructive manner that I could, with the few resources that a 12-year-old has.

My classmates did not go out of their way to welcome me, nor did my teachers. My existence probably represented a paperwork nightmare for the school administration and classroom teacher, and to my classmates, I just bore no particular importance so late in their final primary school year. I had no time to establish relationships with my various specialty teachers, nor with my class teacher. I do remember feeling a sense of pride when I mastered perfect copybook handwriting (a skill that had not been rated sufficiently important during my state primary education).

I maintained a conscientious attitude to all my subjects that year but the subject that I truly found stimulating in that last term of primary school was Latin Roots. I wish the opportunity to study Latin had been offered during our secondary education. I believe that I maintained my conscientious attitude to school because my St Alias's teachers had helped me to develop my belief in my ability to master new skills with effort. Managing depression, anxiety and an ever-increasing sense of difference within a social environment that by its very design would exacerbate my psychological pain and magnify my sense of difference was entirely another matter.

Perhaps my efforts to mentally block the simple biological facts of human reproduction, sexuality and the inevitability of future sexual relationship experiences limited my age-appropriate development of female competitiveness related to attracting mates. I was quite relieved to wear a uniform to school because I did not know anything about fashion other than normal adolescents wore jeans and I only owned a pair of second-hand jeans (which I had purchased with my own pocket money during a family holiday to New Zealand) because my father outlawed the wearing of jeans. I gather his hatred of jeans was related in some way to lax American values associated with rock 'n roll, Elvis Presley, and sexual liberation.

My wearing of my prized jeans was limited to one school occasion in which we could wear "civvies" clothes when I discovered that my peers were politely appalled at my effort to look fashionable in my apparently out-dated jeans and home-knitted, much loved and comfortable jumper. After that fashion faux pas, I tended to choose to wear my uniform on civvies day. I am not suggesting that I was in some way limited because I was economically deprived: I had simply been unexposed to teen culture as a consequence of my immediate family's conservative outlook, and because of my self-imposed inner-world buffers.

I knew what real love involved. I knew what it would feel like and I knew that I would recognise it when I experienced it. Above all else, I knew that it would be unconditional. How did I know this? I had read *Jane Eyre* and I was already in love with Mr Rochester: I just needed to be me and wait for him. Why the hell would I need to even consider folding my ankle socks as far down as they could go and shave my legs because I would "never get a boyfriend" if I didn't? What type of boy would be looking so closely at my impossibly fine, blonde hairs on my legs and think "I can't love her because she doesn't shave her legs even though she's 12"? I simply was not interested in that type of boy but I certainly felt the social pressure to make small, cosmetic adjustments to avoid unconcealed peer rejection and a resurgence of bullying.

I maintained my irreverent sense of humour, safely guarded my private life and vulnerability, whilst I outwardly appeared to be confident and affable with most of my peers. I had a couple of "best friends" whilst I attended the school but neither of them knew about my terrible secrets, my depths of utter despair, or the very fact that I could never completely feel comfortable or safe in their presence because they were female. Sadly, they did not really know me: nobody did.

My daily life developed a familiar routine organised around school, family, piano lessons, and church. I did not have the hectic social life that many of my school friends shared with mutual friends because I lived too far away from them and, I suppose I was simply waiting to discover some kind of social life that felt more comfortable, more essentially "real" than the one I knew I would spend with them. Despite the fact that Mum seemed to share my father's conservative perspective of social organisation she occasionally, sometimes quietly rebelled (but she is a huge story unto herself, and her story should only be told by her). However, I am eternally grateful for her deliberate rebellious act that flung open the slightly ajar doors of my psyche.

One very special day, Mum gave me three cassette tapes that a music teacher had copied for her to give to me: *Abba Gold*[5], *Year of the Cat*[1], and *Abbey Road*[2]. I had been vaguely aware of Abba and I still enjoy listening to them, but Al Stewart's atmospheric and passionate music, combined with his poetic story-telling, and The Beatles' radically masterful musicianship, harmonies, and true liberalist philosophy provided me with my personal age of enlightenment. The music seemed to tap in to my subconscious, my senses, my conscious and I discovered that combining these new ideas and sensations with the insights and values I had embraced from the nineteenth century effortlessly merged. I acknowledged these new sources of personal information as the most accurate descriptions, reflections, and expressions of my inner self: the self that most people cannot see.

When I reflect on this stage of my identity metamorphosis the somewhat iconoclastic thought that flashes through my mind is that God may have created man in his own image but I have invited literature and music to help create me. The truth of the music and ideas, that is the universality of the beauty and humanistic values, became my beacon and my lifeline. I have very rarely strayed from those truths, and never without the belief (whether accurate or not) that I would be compromising my values in order to protect someone else.

The previous statement sounds nauseatingly magnanimous: believe me, I am not. I have desperately needed to hang on to those core values, beliefs and understandings of my universe when the rest of my world felt so threatening, fragmented and perilously fragile. I needed to believe in me, and to know who I am, and to stay true to that self no matter how strong the pull of the great abyss, the Great Loss, was and can still be.

Chapter **5**

Fugitive

Let us then suppose the mind to be, as we say, white paper, void of all characters, without any ideas; how comes it to be furnished ...? To this I answer, in one word, from experience: in that, all our knowledge is founded; and from that it ultimately derives itself.

John Locke[1], *An essay concerning human understanding: Volume1.*

The statements of science are hearsay, reports from a world outside the world we know. What the poet tells us has long been known to us all, and forgotten. His knowledge is of our world, the world we are both doomed and privileged to live in, and it is a knowledge of ourselves, of the human condition, the human predicament.

John Hall Wheelock[2], *What is poetry?*

Well there was never a doubt that she had to get out
She was just looking out for a way
In the pit of the night there was nowhere to hide any more
She was out on a limb, she was reaching for things
That she wanted, but just couldn't say
And she had to be sure that she wouldn't get caught
like before.

Al Stewart[3], If it doesn't come naturally, leave it, *Year of the Cat.*

The year I turned 13 is best described from the perspective of an ear of wheat passing through a threshing machine: unperceivable from across the field but violent, painful, disorienting, transmogrifying, and impelled. Much of the threshing was done by the girls who were apparently in charge of deciding who survived the social gauntlet (appearance, behaviour, academic ability, sporting prowess, and potential social usefulness or threat), being submerged in a social environment that I simply was not psychologically equipped to independently adapt to, and my well-intentioned parents.

Adolescence involves pervasive cognitive, biological, and psychosocial change coinciding with intensified levels of stress associated with developmental change, and chronic, acute or daily hassles[4,5]. My stress associated with learning to read timetables, negotiate public transport, develop an awareness of time (*so that was what my watch was for*), transition from classroom to classroom, manage interpersonal challenges, and attempt to conform to parental expectations was developmentally normal. Having to conscientiously study 11 academic subjects, endure physical education, and study music privately was a challenge, and stressful, but my stress was completely normal when compared with my adolescent cohort.

Having to be a silent atheist living in a devout Christian household and strong Christian community; and having to be someone I was not was emotionally exhausting but was probably normal for priests' children who have their parents' reputations, identities and emotions to protect. Seemingly creating some distance from my parents and moving more towards the company of my peers (e.g., spending far too much time talking to my friend on the telephone) was to be expected. Perhaps on the face of it, I appeared to be a "normal teenager".

My levels of chronic stress, anxiety and unremitting depression were not normal for any stage of development. Needing to outwardly establish my own sense of self, knowing what I most needed to do, but feeling constantly powerless and thwarted essentially involved a superhuman will to hold on to my essence amidst the reality of a battle between creative and destructive forces. The only problem was I was not superhuman. I was losing my will and somehow, I had to gather my parts, re-inflate my safety vest, commit my cognitive and emotional energy where I knew I needed to, fix my eye on a distant, safe horizon and tread water.

I needed to escape. Whilst I was a student at that girls' school, whilst I was biologically and psychologically ready to become a sexual being, every part of my being was telling me to run. Whilst I was living with religious dogma a large mute part of me was screaming fight. Whilst I was living next door to the person who robbed me of my childhood, my sense of safety, and my wellbeing, I wanted to run. This relentless flight or fight response without doubt inhibited my learning processes, especially when those subjects did not fit my essential needs: to know myself, to express myself, and to safely allow me to be me. These three fundamental needs had to be met if I had any chance of rediscovering me, breaking free from the invisible barriers of my angst, and experiencing real joy.

My popular self, my funny self, my brave *Clint self*, and to a large degree, my short-lived academically-efficacious self, re-arranged themselves according to which self was best resourced and most needed. *Popular self* stepped out of the spotlight and became more comfortable with being able to communicate with most social groups by being a good listener to individual members of those groups. I certainly found that my closest friends sought my company and I could never understand what they found so attractive in me. One friend was desperate to make me find God, to the point that she would kick me in the shins, and drag me to the school Christian fellowship sessions. One does not need to wonder why her unique style of missionary work failed.

One friend whom I grew to love and admire dearly pursued me until I could no longer avoid a commitment to the friendship which existed for 21 years. Unfortunately, I could never feel completely comfortable or safe in her presence: she loved me too much. My commitment to my husband seemed to cause tension between us, as though she viewed him as a threat. Eventually my loyalty had to be directed towards my husband. I did not view the decision as taking sides, I just did not have the emotional energy to deal with my own worsening mental illness, working full-time, being a wife, being the mother of two small children, and providing my friend with all the love, time, and psychological support that she needed. Instinctively, correctly or incorrectly, I always felt like she loved me in more ways than I loved her: in ways that I could not love her and that instinctive feeling made me feel vulnerable. This saddens me because she deserved more than I could give her. She deserved to be loved completely and I will never stop wondering if she has found that happiness.

I loved studying English, history, German, and art. The teachers of those subjects that year were approachable and they fuelled my interests and passion for the subjects. Two of the set novels I studied for English that year inspired me greatly. *October Child* [6] is an Australian novel that touched me on a number of levels. Firstly, it describes the pain that can be associated with individual difference, equally individuals who feel alienated from society because they do not seem to conform with, or do not have the opportunity to conform with normal social behaviour; and with those who experience what Pauline Boss[7] would refer to as ambiguous loss.

Ambiguous loss is a type of grief that has no definite resolution because either there is no physical evidence of the death of the loved one the individual grieves, or because one is grieving the psychological loss of a loved one[7]. Ambiguous loss can be particularly painful for people whose grief intensifies incrementally with the gradual loss of someone who is dying with Alzheimer's disease. In the case of *October Child*, the grief may be understood from the perspective of the family members who are attempting to cope with grief for the loss of a loved one who might have been. Carl might have been a loving son, he might have grown up to have a life filled with wonderful opportunities, and he might have been a wonderful brother.

Secondly, it described autism, something I had never heard of. Autism seemed especially poignant to me because it was so different from my world: a world that was dominated with emotion that I knew I could easily identify, share and express in so many ways. It interested me, and years later I chose to research this area of psychology, and made a special effort to teach students who demonstrated behaviour on varying levels of the spectrum. I felt joy when I was able to help them learn ways to relax, to interact with each other, to play, or to communicate their feelings. Perhaps I was helping them to develop coping skills that I was essentially attempting to master myself. I may have only read *October Child* once in 1981 but I have continued to reflect on it and learn from it for the past 33 years.

The second novel, *I am David* [8], is one of the most beautiful, heart-wrenching, and deeply inspirational novels I have ever read. I still have my original copy which I have read many times, having chosen to teach it to a number of year 8 classes. This novel resonated with me at a time I needed most. I was very familiar with stories (both fiction and non-fiction) that were set during the Second World War. The stories I had read certainly described the horrors of the war and the great courage that individuals demonstrated (whether alone or in communities) in their efforts to overcome fear, to uphold their personal beliefs, and often to protect national values. The stories had been written by adults about adults' experiences.

I was also very familiar with Jane Eyre's identity development but somehow it had an adult's perspective, or perhaps her unwavering certainty about who she believed she was and her love for Mr Rochester eclipsed, for me, Charlotte Bronte's exploration of Jane's essential identity development [9]. Anne Holm created a sensitive and insightful depiction of a child refugee's courageous, perilous journey to find his home, to learn to live rather than to exist, to discover and appreciate beauty, to confront all his fears because he was driven by one essential need: the need to know who he was. When he reached his journey's end, and was able to say with conviction, "I am David", he felt safe. I named my first son David.

I enjoyed year 8 history. My teacher was passionate about her subject, bringing to life the practice of archaeology with her recounting of archaeological digs that she had participated in. I was fascinated. I had seen a Roman excavation in England when I was nine years old and had enjoyed reading historical fiction: I still do. Despite Sting's lament that "history will teach us nothing", I believe it ought to [10]. I chose to study history for the next four years of my schooling (both modern and ancient). I lost interest in it during years nine and ten (my rather young teacher failed to tell stories and connect me emotionally to the history) but I still believed that history could teach me about the human condition: who we were, who we are now, and who we may be.

I was interested in modern history, particularly Russia and India, but I always felt threatened in the classroom. My teacher definitely chose the students she was willing to support and encourage. High achievers were easy to encourage. She never asked me why I failed every exam (bar one on Indian Independence for which I achieved 98%) but excelled at research assignments. She never offered me help. She was the headmistress of the school and never offered me a kind word, encouragement or help in the two years that she taught me senior history. I believe she did not like me and I certainly, but never overtly, disliked her. If I could choose an actress to play the part of my modern history teacher, I would unhesitatingly choose someone who could convincingly resemble a butch, hardened female prison warden.

I felt safe during my ancient history lessons because my teacher genuinely liked people and animals, and was definitely a historian. If I could choose anyone to act the part of my ancient history teacher, I would choose Emma Thompson. Despite the fact that I had almost completely disengaged from school by the second half of my final year of school because I was physically and mentally ill, I scraped in to a university course that I thought would interest me: a Bachelor of Arts majoring in Literature and Modern History.

I have an ear for languages but not a memory. My husband has a memory for language but he unfortunately lacks a convincing native note to his pronunciation. We strangely complement each other. Sadly, my French teacher bored me. With my limited energy capacity, I dropped from an A to a B in French. Japanese was not particularly interesting despite the fact that I seem to remember more of the vocabulary and its pronunciation (dating back 21 years) than my youngest son did by the time he had completed his one term of language experience. I do not think I achieved more than a B for Japanese.

I absolutely loved German: it sounded so certain, so uncompromisingly real. My German teacher encouraged me to continue studying her language. She was the only secondary school teacher to personally encourage me to study their subject area and I wanted to. It was my parents' decision that I study French. Well-intentioned they may have been, but it was not a wise decision nor was it helpful in the short-term or the long-term. My tertiary studies of comparative literature and history focused on German philosophy and I favoured German and English literature.

My ability to translate and pronounce French phrases was useful when the rare occasion necessitated (e.g., ordering meals in French restaurants and watching quirky French films) but I can honestly say that I did not enjoy the structured style of French literature. Had I studied German with a teacher who had shown an interest in me when I was motivated, I may have been more engaged in school and advantaged in my university studies. Even my initial formal study of psychology began with Freud's theory of psychoanalysis. I may have only been 13 years of age but I had already spent a great deal of time inside my head and self-reflecting. I knew what interested me and motivated me. Sometimes parents need to trust their children's choices because children are capable of making wise choices, and when they're not wise, they have the chance to learn.

Art was disappointing and frustrating but I remained devoted to it. Creativity and originality were not celebrated nor were they promoted. Techniques were not taught and I refused to listen to warnings from girls whose sisters had learnt from previous experience that the art teacher who taught years nine to 12 did not like the colour red. She did have her favourite students and they seemed to belong to the same families.

She understood realism because that is how she saw the world and how she chose to paint it. I could never understand how I could not achieve a VHA (very high achievement or mark of excellence) for art because I lived and breathed it and applied so much effort. In year 12 I was surprised to be awarded first prize for a lithograph and two second prizes for paintings (which my teacher had marked as high achievements or Bs). It took artists from outside the school to give me real acknowledgement.

Art and English, beauty and self-expression, the absorption of knowledge, awareness and creation: these are my motivators. I always strove to excel in English because I loved literature and if I could have had the opportunity, I would have chosen to read all day. Once, when I was 16 years of age (during my final year of school) my English teacher told me that I wrote like D. H Lawrence. I had not heard of him and did not realise what a great compliment that was to me. She told me that he had written *Kangaroo* [11]. I suppose you either love his style or dislike it. I discovered that I loved his style and themes when I studied him during the second year of my arts degree course. I independently sought my teacher's guidance for how to improve my English results (which always seemed to be a High Achievement, or VHA -) but she gave me no advice. Why?

I do not have a problem with not being a top student or not being excellent, I have a problem with being wilfully prevented from fulfilling my potential because of bias, and lack of competent teaching. Australian anti-intellectualism and a severe national lack of genuine value placed on education is constantly reflected in national surveys and research reports focusing on Australian education levels, which leads to more government lip service that too often relies on sporting metaphors and similes to explain the current economic problems to its population. No wonder Australia has opted for mediocrity and lack of initiative and creativity: they're easier to understand.

So how did I manage to keep my eye on that safe, distant horizon when I was 13 to 15 years of age? I opted for a back seat where I could observe others. I could observe their behaviour, assess their views and self-reflect. I discovered that I could reserve emotional energy and sometimes increase that energy by spending some of my time with good-natured, quirky, arty and dramatic, or physical, water-sporty people who appeared to exalt life and knew how to avoid the darkness. Through them I could escape, and through observing their behaviour (like the effect of a brilliant smile, or through the sharing of laughter and energy) I learnt that with effort I had the ability to regulate my mood when it was absolutely essential. I also discovered that I quite liked the self that could hang out with these beautiful, comfortable-within-their-own-skin people, and the fact that I could still be myself.

I was not able to convince my parents to let me shift to the local public school so I had to find other safe ways to meet and spend time with the people I am most comfortable with: boys. I sometimes had the opportunity to chat with boys on the bus but I found that led to other older girls bullying me until I was in year 12. I began going to school dances that were organised between a select number of protestant private girls' and boys' schools. Although I found the new experience a little terrifying at first, I had the protection of my confident, beautiful friends, and the ability to feel uninhibited when I danced to the music of our generation.

I also enrolled in ballroom dance classes organised between my school and a private boys' school. I thoroughly enjoyed those classes because my best friend also chose to enrol. We were devoted to the concept of art for art's sake, constantly experimenting with music (both listening to and composing music, and spontaneously singing lyrics during our lunch breaks), sharing creative thoughts about design, fabrics, architecture, and lifestyles. We were Bohemian defined. Dancing with boys was another opportunity for us to say "yes" to life. We were not boy crazy but we were open to experience.

We probably shared a romantic view of having a boyfriend and experiencing true love but I was not looking for a boyfriend, nor did I expect to attract one. I simply enjoyed the opportunity to wear my choice of clothes and to be me, without having to wear a uniform and be a student or the priest's daughter. I never felt nervous interacting with boys or men, in fact I felt comfortable. They were people, and quite easy to understand and to read. They were not girls who were complicated, and who were capable of laying minefields without leaving warning signs.

In retrospect, I could not win. I was socially expected by my peers and parents to dress well, develop social confidence, socialise with boys, and attract nice boys. The appropriation of those social skills and values are markers of healthy psychosocial development. I appeared to be a natural, much to my surprise and to my competitive female socialite peers who had up until then, failed to register me on their radar. Because I was comfortable with boys I was not concerned about, and therefore not looking for signs of approval, or particular interest. I was obliviously unaware of this dynamic for at least 16 years.

Much to the initial pride and amusement of my mother, and to the consternation of my peers I discovered that I had attracted a remarkable number of smitten boys from each social venue that I frequented. I was always surprised, even when I had to instruct my mother to let me know the name of the boy who was phoning me. I did not feel flattered or excited by this phenomenon. I had already refused to kiss boys at school dances because, as I explained to them, I did not love them. One boy, whom I had quite grown to like over a series of dance lessons, wrote me an angry note that accused me of being "frigid". When I discovered the meaning of the word I was devastated. We had only ever held hands briefly yet he had applied that powerful word to my sexuality when it should never have been in contention.

I found myself agreeing to be the girlfriend of every boy who asked me to be because I did not want to hurt their feelings. I would talk to them on the phone, or meet them at school dances when I was with a group of friends but I never went out on an exclusive date with them, and they would always eventually feel confused (and probably hurt) and finally let go. Girls at school could not understand why I refused to be the girlfriend of an apparently very desirable and popular footballer from a prestigious boys' school. He was a nice boy, well-mannered and respectful. He was also quite serious about me and I liked him as a person but he did not *speak my language.*

By accident I met a lady on my school bus who told me about a naval cadet base that had been established near my home. Whilst wearing uniforms and most things military did not really appeal to me, the desire for freedom and new experiences did. I lived near the sea, and I escaped to it every day (whether physically or mentally). My family house had views of the sea and I only had to walk to the end of our road to be next to it. It is my favourite visual image to conjure up in order to feel peace and to use metaphorically to identify and describe deep emotion. My joining naval cadets represented a new beginning for me that offered me an opportunity to establish my own identity, to expose myself to new and exciting experiences like rowing and sailing, and being a beautiful water person. It represented freedom. This was my motivation for joining cadets and this was how it was for me for a brief period in my life.

I was bored in history, science, French, religious education and I hated maths. I was failing advanced maths and I wanted to leave the school. Mum organised private tutoring for my maths. My tutor was able to explain algebra and geometry in a way that I understood and in a way that I mastered easily. I scored 98% for algebra and for geometry and then maths fell out of my brain again. I could not accommodate the extreme levels of anxiety, and depression, the desperate need for escape, the superhuman effort to appear sane, and learn something new and complex that did not rank highly on my necessary-for-survival list.

I had to solve this on-going maths, and now science problem. I knew that it was not compulsory to study maths or science in senior levels. I had no real idea of what I wanted to do for a career (other than read and philosophise). Quite honestly, I could not visualise a future life for me because for much of my time I just did not want to be there. There was one simple solution that only required further loss of parental approval and diminishment of self-esteem (how low could it go?).

I deliberately failed advanced maths and then ordinary maths. There was no way the school would force me to select maths or any form of science in years 11 and 12. Choosing an all arts course would be time intensive, require hours of research, writing, study, creativity, and critical thinking but it would score lower on the Overall Position scoring system for university placement and my OP score would be translated in competitive parents' heads and conversations as IQ scores and social ranking. From my perspective, it was my only option.

I treaded water at school, threw my energy into my social life, and escaped into my head at home.

Chapter **6**

Salvation and Sacrifice

The priest has said my soul's salvation
is in the balance of the angels
And underneath the wheels of passion
I keep the faith in my fashion
When we dance, angels will run
and hide their wings
Sting[1], When we dance, *Symphonicities.*

Promise me baby you won't
Let them find us
Hold me in your arms
Let's let our love blind us
Cover me
Shut the door and cover me
Well, I'm looking for a lover who will
come on in and cover me
Bruce Springsteen[2], Cover me, *Born in the USA.*

These days she says, I feel my life
Just like a river running through
The year of the cat
Al Stewart[3], Year of the Cat, *Year of the Cat.*

"Just as the wave cannot exist for itself, but is ever a part of the heaving surface of the ocean, so must I never live my life for itself, but always in the experience which is going on around me."

Albert Schweitzer[4] *The philosophy of civilization:*
Part 1, the decay and the restoration of civilization;
Part 2, civilization and ethics.

"Pouring forth its seas everywhere, then, the ocean envelops the earth and fills its deeper chasms".

Nicolaus Copernicus[5], *De Revolutionibus*

I feel your presence before I see you. How is this possible? You are so close that I reach out and touch your face. Why hasn't it changed – grown older? My heart pounds as my body and mind are dragged under, submerged and rolled over by a wave of confused and ambivalent emotions: awe, excitement, fear, joy, guilt, anticipation, trepidation. Deep sorrow. Your face is as I remember it: masculine, sculpted, aristocratic and exquisitely beautiful. My fingers trace your high cheek bones and I feel your fine, sparse, soft stubble; your perfectly-formed black eyebrows, down your long, straight nose to your firm and responsive lips. Your hair is still glossy black, your dark eyelashes short, framing large tiger eyes: green, with the power to see straight into my soul to read my feelings and needs. For a moment I feel complete – I am within reach of my horizon. I can breathe. You smile at something someone has said but I do not hear that person because my father has just explained to me that he has chosen someone for me to marry who is more suitable – much older than me. He insists that a 46-year-old woman cannot marry a 21-year-old man. But I am 18. You disappear and I am left abandoned, bereaved, grief-stricken and awake.

This is not the first time I have dreamt of him. He has visited my dreams for 28 years – not so regularly in recent years but when he does, I am always rocked to the core. The deep physical pain I experience lies hidden within my chest like a gaping, silent mouth. Its sorrow pours through my veins, drowning my sense of now, and drags me back to then. Spring's incandescent colours, sweet bird songs, and soft breezes emitting ambrosial jasmine perfume carry him into my subconscious mind: a siren's paean of wish fulfilment [6]. What do I wish for? Forgiveness, understanding, autonomy – peace. I want pain's gaping mouth to close: to stop feeding on my sense of self and self-worth. I wish that I could say to him, "Yes, you're right: I do love you. My eyes still say, 'I love you'. I wish I had had the ability to explain that there are some things that are bigger than love and that I was not large enough to manage them. I wish that I knew a better and kinder way to hurt someone that I loved with all my heart, and mind and soul. I had a soul then.

I joined naval cadets to explore life and to just be me: free of any social constraints associated with *private school girl* or *priest's daughter*. I was not boy-crazy, nor was I looking for a boyfriend. I was searching for my horizon and a means to stay afloat. I never expected my life-raft to resemble another human but I felt the full impact of his presence when I first saw him. He moved with a comfortable self-assuredness and big-cat grace. I had time to observe him because I was not quite 15 and a beginner, whilst he was 17 and an officer.

He was popular with the other cadets because of his quick wit, natural athleticism, competence, friendly disposition, and initiative. He was humorous, good company, highly intelligent, a patient instructor and a born leader. His smile was immediately dazzling and genuine. One of the most amazing things I discovered about him was that he had immense respect for women which he demonstrated easily because he was emotionally intelligent. He understood the importance of communication, especially the communication of emotions.

I discovered his rather rare qualities over a period of approximately 12 suspenseful months during which we developed a solid friendship founded on common interests, values and aspirations. We were both romanticists who desired freedom and adventure: a love-conquers-all type of perspective. The year was suspenseful in the sense that it was obvious to outsiders that we felt deeply for each other, the spark had ignited but we physically danced around each other very slowly, and in so many cerebral ways we danced together very intimately.

We sailed together, played together and shared our fears, darkest secrets and dreams. We were good friends for a year before we held hands, kissed and admitted to each other that we were utterly in love. I recall the day that we shared a picnic in the botanical gardens and kissed for the first time. It was my first kiss with someone I was totally in love with and he had told me that he was in love with me. Despite the fact that Bruce Springsteen and Lionel Ritchie were dominating the top 10 hits I found myself privately bursting into elated renditions of The Carpenters' [7] *Top of the world.* It seems so old-fashioned now, but we knew each other before we loved each other and we considered this love to be sacred.

It is absolutely impossible for me to find words that are powerful enough to describe the blissful purity and depth of the love I felt for him. Nor can I adequately express the immeasurable gratitude I have for the greatest gift he gave me: a period of time in my life when I felt truly beautiful, untainted, and free to be me. I associate ultimate freedom with him: like flying without wings on an endless Morning Glory cloud. Perhaps this is because the first day we spent together as friends we sailed a catamaran on Moreton Bay and he taught me how to parasail from the mast. I have never felt so alive, like every cell of my body was open and connected with the blue sky, the blue sea, the salt, the wind, the sun, the Earth and me. I felt completely safe with him.

I remember we spent another evening as friends at a local hall dance during which we enjoyed sharing stories and dreams of exploring the world on a sailing boat whilst we waltzed, quick-stepped and cha-cha-chaed our way around the worn, wooden floor. I was quite oblivious to the other dancers and felt so at ease in his company and movement. He later told me that he had passed his ballroom teaching qualification test and his godlike qualities simply intensified for me.

He had rhythm, he had music and for me, he became my private, internal song of joy. One morning whilst my father was driving me to school, I excitedly shared our dream with him. I told him how we would like to live together on a sailing boat and travel from port to port. My father began to cry. I was horrified: I had not meant to hurt him and had I foreseen the consequence, would never have shared this dream. He had cried because he was devastated that I wanted to leave home and now as a parent I understand that he felt deep pain – some sense of rejection.

I do not think that I gave the impression that we wanted to *live together* in the modern social sense of the phrase because the thought had not crossed our minds. We just wanted to escape. I have relived this painful moment in my mind so many times. I wish that I could have explained that I was not rejecting my family in any way. I wanted to escape my unendurable pain and increasing anxiety. I wanted to obliterate the sight of my next-door neighbours' house – raise it to the ground. I still feel sick driving down my parents' street and consciously avoid looking at that site of depravity that violated my childhood, and worked its darkness through my mind and body like a gluttonous grub gorges itself on the flesh and heart of sweet, young fruit.

My father has on numerous occasions unwittingly proffered this invisible grub throughout my adult life simply by animatedly sharing news about his neighbours' family members. He sometimes says her name. Conjuring their faces, smells, physical sensations, heart beats, breathlessness – terror. I listen politely but I never encourage further discussion. Externally, I appear unaffected: at night I dream. My husband has to wake me from my night terror because I am unable to wake myself.

I wake up sobbing and I know that I have been trying to escape from the most primeval fear. Why would a 45-year-old woman be running from a wolf? Why would her father describe the noise she made in her sleep as howling? She has never been truly safe from the wolf. Her darkest, earliest experience of fear has scoured her heart, permeated her subconscious, invades her dreams, and threatens to leak into her conscious.

I needed to escape my cloying, grasping, claustrophobic school life that was quite simply doing my head in. I was me when I was with him. I was not me when I was without him. I said that I was a beautiful person for a brief period in my life: this is true. I was allowed to be a beautiful person for a brief period. When I joined naval cadets, I felt rather proud of myself because I independently and purposefully chose to do something for myself, something that would help me to find me and be me again. I did not expect my father to join not long after me. BOOM! Friendly fire equates to regrettable sinking of vessel. I had been me – now I was the padre's daughter and every movement I made near a boy was observed.

Dad expected me to rise through the ranks because he believed I had "leadership qualities". Not only did I most definitely not want to lead, I could not see the point in working for a rank that I would have to earn when I had to salute my father because he was automatically an officer because he had God on his side. It was quite impossible to reinvent myself this time. My sense of self was confused: I had grown yet I was being diminished. I loved my father and it was nice that he thought he shared a common interest with his daughter but I was angry with him for blindly snuffing out my flicker of autonomy in his unquenchable passion for leading a flock, order and ceremony.

My first cadet camp should have been a thoroughly wonderful experience: the first camp that I had wanted to attend and freedom from home, church, and school. My father came too. I knew I was in love but I was determined not to let my father know who I was in love with. I deliberately allowed my father to see me fraternising with a number of boys – even holding hands with one. This desperate decoy was not intended to disturb Dad; I just needed space to feel my own feelings without surveillance. The irony in the horribly painful and torturous three years that were to ensue from being in love and being in a relationship was the fact that Dad had originally thought John was wonderful. He was impressed with his striking smile, his manners, his leadership and obvious outstanding competence.

I can only describe this part of my life as turbulent. When I was with John I did not have to pretend and I felt safe. I felt genuine happiness, freedom and peace. He was the only person in the world that I told my secret to. He listened to me, he believed me, and his unconditional love and respect allowed me to be beautiful and for perhaps six months, to banish self-loathing.

Whilst I was at home, I was often aware of the shadow that prevailed from next door. When I was at church, I had to pretend to be someone I was not, whilst masking a deep-seated anger towards the very premise of a god and what Nietzsche would describe as *slave morality* [8]. At school I was pretending to be a sociable person but I was conscious of the fact that I was not like the other girls and that I was experiencing such a constant high level of anxiety that was equivalent to a suppressed, endless, inaudible scream. I had to manifest ridiculous levels of energy simply to maintain a functioning appearance – to some I appeared to be an extrovert. The flipside of manifesting energy is one occasionally has no reserves of energy left and one crashes.

I believe I had my first full-blown mental breakdown when I was 15, almost 16 years of age. I was in year 11, particularly unhappy at school, under pressure to go to university, and my menstruation cycle that had been regular for five years suddenly became unbearably erratic. I was heavily bleeding for two out of four weeks and I was a nervous wreck. I was forced to frequent the school bathroom, hence I felt even more vulnerable at school and I was experiencing an irrational sense of associated shame: one that sometimes infiltrates my current life. I believe that my body was communicating what I needed to be able to voice, what I had attempted to voice but what no adult in my life seemed to be able to hear: I could not psychologically cope in my environment and I needed help.

My mother took me to my family doctor and he prescribed the pill. My GP was marvellous and he treated me with respect, empathy and always believed me. Perhaps I should have told him but it did not occur to me. Sexual abuse, depression, anxiety and mental illness were not really talked about in the 1980s and whilst I was aware that I did not feel safe around girls and that I hated living next door to my abuser I did not consciously connect all the dots. The pill certainly helped me to regain some control of my body and I later discovered that it helped me to avoid experiencing dysphoria associated with hormonal fluctuation.

I did not discuss my misery with John because when I was with him, I felt better – I was in a safe and accepting environment. His oldest sister was a doctor in the army. I had met her at cadets and I had admired her. She immediately accepted me as part of her family because she loved her brother. His younger sister was my age and loved me because she loved her brother. She was the only female friend I had whom I completely trusted. I did not completely trust another until I was 33. I had never known such a warm, loving, trusting sibling relationship before I entered John's family. It was extraordinary and it was a positive influence on my personal growth at that time because John's relationship with his sisters endowed him with a powerfully positive perspective of women. He was comfortable in women's company, he believed they could do anything and did not view the world through a gender specific prism.

At first, I was shocked by the way he and his younger sister seemed to hold no secrets from each other and that they would seek each other's advice about personal matters. John was also sensitive, knowledgeable and respectful regarding the female body because he had grown up with sisters. I was fairly ignorant of such matters and learnt about myself as a result of having such a trusting relationship with him and his younger sister. I am so grateful for the opportunity of being accepted and loved by her: she was the closest and best sister I could have ever had.

Spending time with his family also exposed me to my own generation's normal culture – life beyond the ABC, classical music and my father's choice of music. I discovered *Hey, Hey, It's Saturday,* and went to Bruce Springsteen's concert at the QEII stadium. We went grass skiing, wind surfing, and I accompanied John when he had a paragliding lesson. It seems that we spent most of our time together listening to music and heading for the beach. I felt alive and whole when I was with him and I felt a part of him. I wanted to be part of him.

It is true that we were physically and sexually attracted to each other but that was not what brought us together and had our relationship been founded on merely an adolescent sexual urge we would not have fought so hard, for so long to make it work despite such cruel, blinkered (yet I know best intentioned) opposition from my parents. They did not know they were inflicting more damage because they could not know all of me, they were rejecting a large part of me, and I was unable to convince them that he was an essential part of my life because what would a 16-year-old know about life? From their perspective they needed to save me from a future in which I was destined to be a check-out chick.

Had they really known me, allowed me to talk about him and share my feelings about him they would have known that I had been attracted to him because he stimulated my thoughts, he was interested in science, enjoyed learning and loved people. He expanded my view of the world and encouraged me to attempt new activities and grow in confidence. I had been attracted to him for the same reason I had loved my grandfather: he was interested in how the world worked and he was physical.

He also made me laugh which was something I rarely felt like doing. When we were in our world, he filled my life with light. Had Dad respected my personal choices as part of my individual development and need for autonomy he would have discovered that he had so much more to appreciate, admire and love about John. My parents' world views and understanding of parenting eclipsed and engulfed my needs and I began my descent back into hell.

To be able to recognise hell one has to be familiar with heaven. From my atheistic perspective heaven and hell are our very real experiences of the best and the worst that life offers us. Some of us may need theological representations of the unimaginable: from the age of seven I didn't need any one's version of hell but my own. When I was 16, John and I knew heaven and I never wanted to leave. It is the most exquisite symphony of light, safety, uninhibited love and self-expression, truth, compassion, selflessness, and shared joy. It is a knowing – a union of thoughts, senses, feelings and cells. It intensifies the Earth's beauty; creating one's own magic realist landscape. He loved me and he made me feel loved: I never questioned that. He was a beautiful lover and he healed me. I no longer felt shame, dirtiness, and confusion. I did not feel pain or fear. I was not terrifyingly vulnerable and I could breathe. I had been freed with the gift of love. I was no longer a trapped, cowering seven-year-old who was sickened by her own sexuality: I was a beautiful 16-year-old woman.

I wanted to share that with my mother. I wanted to be able to trust her and I wanted her to trust me. Despite the fact that I trusted no female other than John's little sister (who of course knew) I confided in my mother because I wanted her to know me. Naively I believed that it was better she knew than to allow her to perhaps wonder or worry. Honesty, integrity, and trustworthiness have always been important to me. I suppose I am driven by a need to be known because so much of me is experienced imperceptibly. I did not tell my father – I wasn't that mad. It was not because I was afraid of him or because of guilt. I believed then, as I do now, that the relationship I shared with John was sacred and completely normal.

I did not share my parents' medieval values and I was not impervious to the effects of the liberating 1960s or the musings of the romantic poets. I was me and they were them and I respected that. I did not want to tell my father because I did not want to hurt him. I knew he would not understand and I knew he would think that John had robbed me of my innocence. I could not tell him that I had no innocence to lose and that John had actually saved me. I could not completely rock my father's world and I doubt that I would have been able to adequately articulate my story: my parents did not discuss such things.

Telling my mother was a mistake. She did not show any sign of appreciation that I had so honestly, courageously or trustingly shared with her such a private and precious part of my life. She didn't shatter that gift immediately nor did she hug me and thank me for offering her that gift and inviting her to develop a closer relationship. She received my gift politely and stiffly like someone who had been given a rather offensive present that she couldn't possibly toss in the nearest rubbish bin but would most definitely have to dispose of it somehow. My core values were not so different from hers – they just weren't restricted by religious beliefs or Victorian culture. They had also been modified through personal experience. I have forgiven her and I have made every effort to intellectually understand her context and actions but the memories of these events still hurt me.

My mother did not tell my father but she certainly changed her manner towards John. He did not feel comfortable in my home – we lived in different cultures and mine was certainly more difficult to feel at ease in. It was not that my parents are inhospitable or unsociable: quite the opposite. There is a projected reserve created by middle class, somewhat Victorian manners and social expectations that can erode an individual's confidence if he or she is simply trying to connect on a level that doesn't involve intellectual conversation regarding politics or social welfare, or mirthful recounting of BBC comedies and dramas. I love that world and I am most comfortable in that world but John was not and my parents certainly did not attempt to help him feel comfortable.

Those wonderful summer holidays ended in darkness. John had enrolled in marine biology studies at James Cook University which was approximately 1500 kilometres away from me. My life raft was going to be out of reach for months on end and our hearts were breaking. We wrote to each other at least twice a week and would look forward to brief long-distance calls. I would count down the days until he would ring or we would see each other during the school holidays.

Knowing there was a reason to live kept me afloat but I struggled. My studies were time consuming; my anxiety had increased and my depression was constant. My mother attributed my sometimes-average academic results to being "besotted" with John and applied incredible pressure on me to improve my results or I "would end up working in a checkout" – apparently the worst thing one could do. I started suffering from severe bouts of eczema on the insides of my thighs which were exacerbated by wearing my school stockings. No cream seemed to be effective. I was then hospitalised for irritable bowel syndrome. At no time was I asked if I needed to talk about something. I was slipping into my abyss but hanging on to my one life support – John.

Had we known that my father would spy on us we may have found another private location to make love but our opportunities during school holidays were scarce and we were not afforded the privacy that many young couples now are. My father confronted me and demanded to know if I had "been fornicating" with John. I initially denied that I had for two reasons: (a) I did not want to hurt my father even though I had told my mother months before, and (b) what John and I shared together could never be described as *fornication* and all that word implied. My father was so enraged that he threatened to use his gun – a reason I have never told him about his neighbour. I had to protect my father. John was banned from my house and I was not allowed to use our home phone to call him. I was not able to talk about him at home and my once all-too-beautiful world, my inner sense of beauty died. My lifeline now resembled a fine thread that was sometimes difficult to locate in my darkness.

We could still write to each other and I saved my pocket money, converted it to 20 cent pieces and walked in the dark to the phone box at the end of our very long street to hear his voice for several precious minutes once a week. Every time I walked up and down that street I was terrified for my life because I had heard that a girl had been attacked not far from that phone box. Every time I walked up and down that street, I was petrified that someone was following me. Years later my mother told me that she had sent my brother to follow me to make sure that I was safe. My brother had chosen not to speak to me so I never knew that he was following me.

I did not think that my father had stopped loving me – just that he was waiting for me to come back to the fold when I would inevitably see the error of my ways. I was absolutely certain that my mother saw me as spoilt goods and a cross that she had to bear. I do not remember events chronologically but I feel an intense physical pain when I relive my mother calling me "a slut". I hate that word and every time I hear it used the impact is like a slap across the face. The ramifications of my parents' view of me and their attempts to *save* me caused immediate and enduring psychosocial damage which I have endeavoured to overcome.

That was when my invisible sun died. That was when I began to be aware that there were some things bigger than love that I did not know how to manage. My perceived loss of value combined with the deliberate, punitive suppression of my identity and purpose for living snuffed out my spark. Their language and labels defiled what I held sacred and stripped me of my beauty. The power of their words revoked the healing effects of my relationship with John and violently, albeit unwittingly, transmogrified their lovable, validated, beautiful 16-year-old daughter into her worthless, unlovable, shameful, dirty, ugly, vulnerable seven-year-old self. I have never regained that beauty and for too much of my life it has robbed me of completeness. From 17 years of age, I merely existed. In fact, I recall walking down a school stairwell beside one of my beautiful water friends and stating that "I don't live – I exist".

The Plague (1985/1991). Acrylic on board, 68 x 51 cm

I am on a white, timber veranda of a low-set colonial house. It is surrounded by deep-green ferns and agapanthus with heavy, dark jacaranda blue heads. I am surrounded by light, by a brilliantly cobalt sky and I am caressed by a gentle breeze. It is beautiful and safe. But I am not free. I am in a cage – a tiny bird, and I can hear my mother's voice. I am frightened of a black cat. I am the black cat, so full of murderous rage and hatred. I am a white cat filled with love. I am the black cat and the white cat cannot contain me. She has no power. I have no power. I can smell my mother's blood and see it glistening: so much blood, white bone, her spinal cord partially covered in gobs of bright red flesh. The black cat is shredding my mother's back and I have to wake up.

I will never forget this dream and my terror. I woke up hyperventilating and sought the safety of my parents' bed where my mother helped me to calm down. I needed her, I loved her and I never wanted to hurt her.

I was mortified when I was summoned to the deputy principal's office. I had never been in trouble at school having kept my thoughts firmly locked in my head, and could not possibly fathom why he would request a meeting. He informed me that my parents had contacted him because they were concerned about my school results and that they believed I was distracted because I had a boyfriend. Humiliated does not truly describe how I felt. I did not know this man and he did not know me. I had been ambushed: powerless to defend myself against a multitude of authority figures who clearly knew what was best for me and how I should be behaving. There was no point attempting to defend my academic efforts or my private life that was apparently not so private. I had no armour, no back-up army and no escape route. He offered me no help and frankly my dear, he didn't give a damn.

My boyfriend was 1500 kilometres away from me – out of reach. I had no influence on a flawed assessment system based on a bell curve. I gave my best effort to my assignment work, research, writing, and oral presentations and always achieved very high marks for this work. I studied and worked on my practical artworks every night – sometimes all night. Examinations crucified my results because I did not know how to quell my debilitating anxiety. I was passing all my subjects and way above average in English and art. I was doing the best that I could but it was not good enough. More evidence that I was worthless, deliberately bad, and more than likely stupid.

As a parent and a former secondary school teacher with an arts degree, a psychology degree and a masters in guidance and counselling, I cannot understand how teachers in a top academic school did not feel compelled to investigate why a student in their class was achieving such a pattern of results. The student did not misbehave in class, was engaged in activities, and submitted her work on time. This negligence as professionals and as fellow human beings is inexcusable and is too often masked by general social ignorance that manifests itself as stereotyping of adolescent behaviour. Professionals working with adolescents need to have a good knowledge and understanding of human development, and children need to be given support and taught skills that promote resilience. I was 37 years old when I taught myself to overcome exam anxiety by overlearning: so, it only took 20 years for me to *almost* prove to myself that I am not stupid.

Home, school, church: there was no safe haven. The image of a Sumerian afterlife of perpetually eating clay and drinking ashes could have been an accurate representation of my final year at school except for one detail: it does not involve pain. I was riddled with pain. The pain that emanated from my heart coursed through my veins like black ooze. It infiltrated every part of my nervous system, and my brain; sending out warning signals, distress signals and messages that became lost and confused. Eczema, asthma, irritable bowel syndrome, pneumonia; the pressure erupted in the best way it knew how. I woke up screaming with pain. Both my eyes were ulcerated and normal treatment was ineffective. I was hospitalised and two leading ophthalmologists were required to wipe my eyes.

The rest of that short academic year was blurred by eye ointment and many nights studying by candle light because of the famous Queensland power strikes of 1985. I had no one I could share my nightmares with and no one I could possibly ask help from because I was overwhelmed, trapped, isolated and effectively made helpless by my own psychological and physical pain. Like so many people who suffer from depression and other forms of mental illness, I thought I was the only person who felt that way. I had to disguise my ceaseless internal dialogue, my deeply internalised pain, my unbearable loneliness, and my intense desire to escape me.

I completely *got* Hamlet [9]. He and I seemed to share the same dilemma. We were individuals who were consumed by grief (albeit from different sources); struggling with our deepest values; protecting those we loved; truly in awe of nature and the beauty of human potential but devoid of the desire to live. At 17 years of age, I was not scared of death: it seemed like a viable option. In fact, dreamless oblivion seemed attractive. I did not *want* to die. I just wanted the pain to end. This thought-feeling became an imperceptible personal mantra that played on a background loop: sometimes unbearably loudly; often expressing itself in daytime doodles; expressive paintings; or death-themed creative writing.

Sometimes it expressed itself in uncharacteristic behaviours that appeared reckless or shocking. More often it consumed my dream-filled sleep so that I was never free from it. Its power was sometimes so great that it orchestrated a psychological breakdown in which I became a physical and emotional heap that simply could not function. I became overwrought with helplessness, hopelessness, worthlessness, hurt, grief, and despair that were expressed with inconsolable, wretched sobbing, shaking, and an inability to describe how I felt or what I truly needed. This mantra played on that background loop for 26 more years. It was very rarely drowned out by another song and has, on a number of terrifying occasions lured me into playing its final notes. In the past three years it has sometimes attempted to subdue my healthy, beautiful song but my invisible sun has the strength to defeat it. *NB: Written in 2014. Please be aware that whilst I originally documented this observation in 2016, I have not discovered sufficient evidence to alter my view in 2022.

What help did I receive? I remember one occasion when I completely melted down and it was obviously apparent that I could not attend school, my mother (who was a counsellor) talked me through a progressive deep-muscle relaxation exercise. This exercise is remarkably effective for people suffering from anxiety or sleep disorders, and may be practised in many environments when one has mastered the relaxation technique. It did help me at the time for two reasons: (a) it demonstrated to me that I could regulate my physical state and gain some control over my mood, and most importantly (b) I felt momentarily valued by my mother. I attended one appointment with a local female general practitioner who listened carefully to me and seemed to observe my body language and presentation in a way that I trusted. I do not remember her diagnosing depression but I do remember feeling her empathy and the fact that she suggested my taking anti-depressants. My mother had accompanied me to my appointment and did not consent to the prescribed treatment.

I have struggled to understand this life event for many years. I have turned the puzzle around and around in my mind: sorting through the missing pieces in an attempt to view my identity, or my persona, from others' perspectives so that I can apprehend the assumptions they formed and the decisions they made. This life event is a significant event because it signalled a potential path for psychological investigation and healing but it was the first of many refusals to believe my desperate need for psychological support and intervention. It was the defining moment that was to be repeated on too many occasions when I felt compelled to expose my inability to cope: to ask to be heard, believed, and cared for.

Over the years I found myself mentally holding on to my inner conviction that *I am not a hypochondriac, I am not stupid, I am not crazy, and I am not ignorant.* I had to tell myself this, sometimes out aloud, because these were the messages I too often received, both literally and inferred, from medical professionals who were limited by their own prejudices, limited life experiences, time, insensitivity, or ignorance regarding mental health. Most often they meant well and believed they were making the best decisions for my health and future; favouring either a *stop taking life so seriously,* or *this is how you must fit into this box* approach.

From my perspective my parents appeared to reward good behaviour (i.e., behaving in ways that I knew pleased them, fulfilling their parental expectations to my best ability, and attempting to appear "normal"), provide special support where they understood I needed it (e.g., tutoring, supervision, and medical treatment), and to punish bad behaviour (i.e., any behaviour that did not appear conducive to my future happiness and success from their perspective). They must have wondered why my academic results were not reflecting my obvious potential and why I was seemingly not trying hard enough and choosing to *throw it all away.* I know they were at their wits end and blaming my boyfriend. I know they felt betrayed, disappointed, angry, sad, confused, frustrated – helpless. I wish they had not felt at fault.

They were and are good parents and I know they love me. They were parenting in the dark. I believe that if they had known my secret, they would have been able to provide the support I needed and my life would have been very different. I believe that early psychological intervention would have alleviated, if not prevented, the development of my mental illness and the severe clinical presentation and progression of the illness. I also believe that social stigma surrounding mental illness, fuelled by social fear and relative ignorance regarding psychological health within the general public and the health professions, has an enduring negative influence on my ability to fulfil my potential: to truly be me.

Living on the inside has created an unenviable, inescapable, personal dual role of researcher and laboratory rat. I peer at myself through a microscope as I navigate my way through an endless maze. I am fascinated, compelled, challenged, repulsed and exhausted. I am exhausted by my own introspection that has developed from many years of unperceivable withdrawal from the *real world.* Necessary withdrawal. Necessary sacrifices.

Chapter **7**

Event Horizon

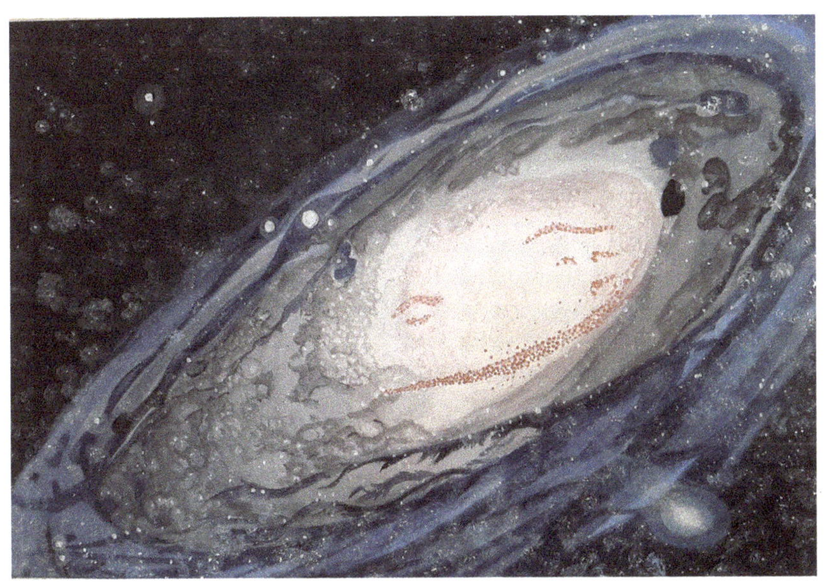

An event from which there is no turning back. (2016).
Acrylic on canvas. 61 x 91 cm

"Doubt thou the stars are fire;
Doubt that the sun doth move;
Doubt truth to be a liar;
But never doubt I love."

William Shakespeare[1], *Hamlet.*

I am in you and you in me, mutual in divine love.
William Blake[2], *Jerusalem the emanation of the giant Albion.*

One must learn to love, and go through a good deal of suffering to get to it ... and the journey is always towards the other soul.

D. H. Lawrence [3]

It is a fine thing to establish one's own religion in one's heart, not to be dependent on tradition and second-hand ideals. Life will seem to you, later, not a lesser, but a greater thing.

D. H. Lawrence [4]

Where choice begins, Paradise ends, innocence ends, for what is Paradise but the absence of any need to choose this action?

Arthur Miller[5], *After the fall.*

With or without you
I can't live
With or without you

U2[6], With or without you, *Joshua Tree*

1985 was riddled with pain and a multitude of decisions to be made regarding choices I did not want to consider: some of those choices did not bear thinking about. I had to choose a university course which had to relate to a career, preferably a career that would sound impressive if one had to refer to it. I had no real idea what I wanted to do other than to read novels and think. I seriously fancied being a philosopher but even I was aware that employment opportunities would be extremely limited. I absolutely loved Orwell's writing and believed that perhaps journalism would provide me with the opportunity to investigate, write and expose truths about corruption and my favourite platform: the dehumanisation of man. In 1986 I enrolled in a Bachelor of Arts (comparative literature and modern history) because all of the subjects sounded fascinating and I loved literature.

Other than note-taking during lectures and researching and writing 3000–4000-word essays I was completely unprepared for university life. I did not want to learn to drive a car because they seemed so dangerous: the very proposition of changing out of third gear into fourth gear (which suggested *high speed*) was preposterous! This was a problem because there were no forms of public transport available between my home and the university I was to attend. Furthermore, if I hoped to ever arrive on time for early-morning lectures without the aid of a TARDIS I would definitely have to summon up the courage to shift into fifth gear.

I earned my driver's license at the eleventh hour and learned to thoroughly enjoy driving. In fact, I thought my license was so special that having arrived late one morning in the university car park and discovering that there were no usual carparks I parked in a park reserved for *Special Permits*. Apparently, the word special did not mean *highly valued by the licensee* (as I had interpreted the sign) and I learnt this sad lesson via a parking ticket. I had thought that libraries were *sacred places of learning* only to be eclipsed by the truly holy intellectual realms of universities. Here I imagined students would spend hours debating philosophical arguments and writing important essays and plays. I imagined that my fellow students would think in the same way that I did: that they would speak the same language and that I would not feel like a foreigner.

I had been living the life of a legal alien my whole life: pretending to be a part of society but not being aware of how real life worked because I was trapped inside myself and holding on to idealist dreams woven by my favourite novelists to keep afloat. Even now as I recall my first year at university I shake my head at my own remarkable naiveté, absolute cluelessness, unshakeable faith in intellectualism, and I marvel at the fact that I managed to learn anything that year given my combined lack of savoir-faire and undiagnosed, untreated mental illness. It certainly explains how I could successfully complete my first academic year without realising that the reason why there was always a dissatisfying number of good reference books in the library was because I was unaware that there was a *Frozen Section* in the library for research work. Unbelievable.

John had accompanied me to my orientation week, providing me with the emotional support I had needed. Our time together during the summer holidays had been too short: he returned to Townsville and I was faced with another year of heartache, loneliness, anxiety, depression, and decisions that I had to make. When I was with John, I was me or at least the best that I could be. He gave me strength, support, and love. He believed in me in a way that I could not possibly comprehend. He had asked me to marry him and I had of course said yes.

We already felt married and had known that from the moment we fell in love. I was faced with the cruellest choices that would leave me incomplete and hurting no matter which one I chose. The consequence of either choice equated to self-neglect: a "vile sin" according to Shakespeare, and an opinion I have lately come to share. I knew that John was my soul mate and my best friend. I knew that I wanted to spend the rest of my life with him and his little sister. I knew that the only time I felt any happiness and sense of peace was with John. I knew that I loved my family beyond my own sense of happiness and self-worth. I knew I needed their acceptance. I could not choose both.

How does one continue to function when one's head is filled with a high-frequency buzzing – a constant dialogue and flashes of one's own death scenes which leak into doodles amongst pages of lecture notes? How does one continue to function when one's mind is consumed by an unsolvable puzzle when one considers oneself a problem solver? How does one continue to function when one's insides feel like they're haemorrhaging?

One foot in front of the other. Look like you are coping. No one must know that you are not coping because everyone else seems to be fine. No one must know that you are weak and afraid. Think of the lion in *The Wizard of Oz* [7]. Do not hurt anyone.

I was still an alien. My cohorts were disappointing. They did not think like me – they liked partying, night-clubbing, drinking, gossiping and doing things that normal young people enjoyed. They did not speak my language and I felt my dream of finding my safe place in a literary world dissolving around me. I did try to fake it. I met a wonderfully vivacious and outwardly confident girl during my first year who befriended me. She was a good friend. She attempted to make me behave like a normal adolescent and was supportive of my relationship with John. When I had needed an escape from home I was able to crash in her university college apartment. I was forced to manifest huge levels of social energy that I was unaware that I had. Sometimes this charismatic energy seemed boundless: as though I was not quite inside myself – a different more likeable person. I was able to party all night and clean up the apartment whilst my fellow revellers slept and then attend the early morning lectures (which most of my fellow revellers skipped) as though I had just woken up from a good night's sleep. No sleep meant no nightmares.

These periods of high energy, and sociability were rare and in the beginning were free from elements of depression and anxiety. My first recollection of such a delightful feeling was when I was 16. I recall telling my mother that I felt extremely fertile. Probably not something that one should tell one's mother whilst walking down Queen Street, Brisbane – or at any time for that matter. It was spring; I could smell Christmas and jasmine. The world's colours were luminescent and glorious. I felt ethereal, effectual, beautiful and divine. No drugs; it was beyond being in love or being *fey*. This positive mood was coupled with high creativity – ideas for stories and paintings. It did not last long (perhaps four weeks) but I remember the mood fondly because it was in stark contrast to the prolonged, deepest, darkest depression that I experienced for the remainder of the year. Poor Mum. She must have been terrified. I certainly did not mean that I was feeling rampantly turned on – I was just turned on by life. Yep: I was mad. Exquisitely mad.

Fortunately for me, my appreciation for life and beauty prevented me from doing anything that could jeopardise my safety and enduring physical and psychological health. My loneliness did not lead to binge drinking, smoking, illicit drug use, or promiscuity. I did not consider an escape route other than death because there did not seem to be an escape route. Except one and that was not a choice I wanted to make so I didn't. Not consciously.

I met Julian at his 21st birthday party which had been held by his mother who had recently become a parishioner in my father's parish. I had been invited because everyone had been, and I attended because I habitually attended social occasions that my parents attended and I had nothing better to do. I was rather surprised when Julian approached me and began chatting. I was also very surprised when he later described me as the prettiest girl at the party. It did not occur to me that he was possibly chatting me up: however, it never ceased to amaze me and, to some extent, frustrate me that I seemed to attract unwanted masculine attention wherever I went. He was English, intelligent, handsome and charming. He had a sense of humour, had lovely manners and was easy to chat with. He was a civil engineer, worked locally and seemed to tick all the boxes that might appeal to my parents. It was too easy.

I did not fall in love with Julian but life became easier at home because I appeared to have ended my relationship with John. I did not want to end our relationship and struggled to write a letter to him that sounded convincing: that sounded like I had convinced myself. He drove 1500 kilometres overnight to try to change my mind but I was resolute. Although I had a wonderful relationship with Julian's mother my brief interlude with Julian was just that. He was consumed with the belief that relationships never last because his parents had divorced and I was still in love with John.

No matter how many times I told myself that John and I could not be together I could not stop thinking about him, dreaming about him, loving him, wanting him, and needing him. When Julian ended our dating period and I had absolutely no viable reason left to keep me from allowing myself to slip into the abyss I realised what I had done. I had pushed away the one person who loved me unconditionally and I believed that I would never be loved like that again. It seemed so final, so black.

One night, despite my attempts to refuse my friend's invitation to another university party which I desperately did not want to attend I found myself reluctantly driving there. I genuinely did not enjoy Dionysian type parties, did not want company, and I most definitely did not have the energy necessary to act my way through one. My familiar mantra was playing loudly on its background loop and I was finding it impossible to ignore its heavier, darker notes of unlovability and worthlessness. As I was driving through the rain, I had a strange feeling and thought that seemed to come from nowhere. It was as though part of me warned myself, *I am going to have an accident whether I continue to drive to the party or whether I turn around and go home now but I will be alright.* I was not frightened, just resigned.

I did ensure that I appropriately reduced my speed for the wet conditions and left a good distance between myself and the car in front. The back road to the university was not lit and there was no inside lane to drive in when the driver in front of me decided to turn right with little warning. I hit the brakes, rammed through the gears, swerved to the left to avoid the car, and said, "Oh!" I do recall feeling my face to ascertain whether I was alive. It was fortuitous that I had a solid car that protected me from its impact with the ditch and embankment. I was fortunate to be alive and I was grateful that I had been able to avoid hurting anyone. The driver behind me who was now directing traffic with his torch was an off-duty ambulance man. My car was a mess; I had whiplash and an injured knee from impact with the steering wheel and the state of my car meant that I had provided my parents with a new set of problems: somehow, I had to get to work and university.

I do not know how John's family heard about my accident but they sent me a card. I felt deeply moved by their gesture and I could not help but feel hope that he would love me again. With the help of a couple of friends who believed in our relationship, we were reunited and I still feel amazed at the way he accepted me and loved me completely without question. He asked me again to marry him and I said yes again because I wanted to be his wife. I wanted it to be possible. His family welcomed me again having openly accepted that they would have to support our inevitable marriage because they knew that my family wouldn't.

I know that his mother was angry at me for hurting him and expressed her concern that I had reconnected with John on "the rebound." She had every right to be angry with me for hurting him. I haven't forgiven myself for hurting him. However, there was no rebound: my love for John never changed. My friendship with Julian provided me with a brief period of time in which I was accepted by my parents: a buffer from that particular source of pain. It was a little like coming up for a lungful of air before being dumped by the next crashing wave.

John had withdrawn from his university course which I blame myself for, although he never did. He studied hard and joined the police force. It was a difficult time as a university student to maintain a relationship with a policeman during the Bjelke-Petersen era. He was constantly bullied in the academy because he had been a university student, was not a footballer, not a drinker, and was not a thug. He became careful about his choice of words, was unhappy about keeping a gun in his house, frequently told me to stay away from drugs (which he never needed to do), and continued to support my studies whilst I suspect he worried about my changing.

He transferred money into my savings account to help support me through university and encouraged me to study when I stayed overnight. I know that he would have supported me through university if I had left my parents but the thought had never occurred to me because it didn't seem possible. He would have been strong enough – I wasn't. My mother had told me that if I married John she would not be there. I could not discuss my life with my parents and my brother was still refusing to speak to me. I was the elephant in the room and I was skating on *very* thin ice.

I was not capable of thinking very clearly. I was extremely stressed by end of year exams (which I actually passed, and even scored an HD for sociology) and I was juggling two jobs. I had to lead a secret life with John and maintain a sociable façade within my father's parish. I attempted to seek counsel from a very charismatic, intellectual priest whom I had an affinity with. He had a passionate personality and did not seem to judge me. Occasionally his affectionate behaviour towards me bordered on the inappropriate but I always excused it.

He was entirely the wrong person to seek guidance from and John did not like him but never told me why. Many years later that particular priest was forced to leave the Anglican Church after allegations of sexual assault. I could not find the solutions to my problems and could not find a way to ease my anxiety. I lost my drivers' license because I obtained two speeding fines whilst on my provisional license. I had to sit a supplementary exam because I was too naïve to challenge my final results after I was failed for the entire academic year for not having submitted one assignment when, in actual fact, I had a stamped receipt evidence that I had.

It had not occurred to me that I could have shown the administrative staff all of my assignments as proof that they were wrong. I should have challenged the appropriate academic authorities but I didn't. I had been conditioned to believe that I was powerless in the face of authority. I did not have the strength. I was overwhelmed by anxiety and my mother's angry humiliation. I overheard her telling people I did not know that I had to sit the supplementary exam to pass the year. My life was never private. Tarring and feathering would have been a preferable punishment compared with parental disappointment and shame. I had lost face with my parents, my brother, some members of the parish who my parents had confided in and it was apparent that I had begun the year six feet under and I was still digging deeper. The trouble was I had the wrong digging technique and no light to guide me to the way out.

I began 1987 quietly. My one close university girlfriend had transferred to another university and I did not feel inclined to liaise with anyone. After studying media studies during my foundation year, I decided that I did not like the writing conventions associated with modern journalism. However, I knew that I loved literature, philosophy and psychology. I loved the way philosophy worked its way through art, music, literature, psychology, science, and political movements. I felt quite alive during lectures in which attending lecturers would debate with the delivering lecturer.

It was intellectually stimulating and provided me with some relief from my background loop. Whilst I was reading novels and revolutionary literature from the nineteenth and early twentieth centuries I could escape into worlds where I had understanding allies. I had my private backup troop comprising the likes of Freud, Nietzsche, Darwin, Hardy, E.M. Forster, Bronte, Jung, Edvard Munch, D. H. Lawrence, and Camus to reassure me that I was not marching to the beat of a so very different drum.

If truth be known, I was very lonely. My love for John had not altered but the way in which I was allowed to love him had changed. Not because he had changed, nor had he changed any of the conditions. My parents had. I could not love him with all of me because I did not love myself. My parents had robbed me of the ability to experience sacred love: that purest, most intimate and uninhibited sharing of spiritual, emotional and physical love. Their accusations, labels and punishments scarred the way I view myself and whilst I have learnt to respect myself, I have not been able to retrieve my beautiful self: the self John had shown me. I had lost hope. I had no expectations of experiencing real happiness again or of ever meeting someone – anyone who spoke my language.

I do not mean someone to replace John. I did not want that; I just wanted to meet another human being who did not want anything from me other than to be my friend – to share ideas, dreams, laughter, and to understand me. I was faced with a complex problem. I had a couple of friends who were girls and I had a *serious* problem with girls. They trusted me, some of them admired me and loved me, some of them were jealous of me and one of them in particular loved me too much. I cared about them, worried about them, listened to their problems but I felt on high alert when I was near them. I hated their affectionate touch, I was uncomfortable sharing their rooms at night, I felt physically repulsed when they casually undressed in front of me, and I could not understand why they depended on me so much. High alert, flash backs, smells, touches: that's what I got from girls. I could not trust them and I could not feel clean around them.

Now men were another matter. I like men. I feel comfortable around them and I enjoy their company. I tend to trust them. I have never had a shortage of male friends of all ages. How many men do you know who just want to be friends? I had a good male friend from youth group, (yes, I attended youth group as an atheist simply because I craved the company of male youths when I was still at school); who I continued to knock around with whilst I was at university. We had wonderful conversations, cooked together and shared a love of history.

We were priests' kids and although I was an atheist and he felt the vocation to be a priest we felt the pressures associated with our status. I loved Michael – his rebellious streak, his ear stud, the way he drove his little sport's car, his powerful masculinity, his confidence, his quick wit, his thirst for knowledge, and his sense of fun. I loved the way I could stay overnight in his house and know that I could trust him. I felt safe with him and I loved him as a friend and brother. I ignored the heat coming off his body when we stood really close. I palmed off his jealous questioning about John.

I felt sad when my mother told me that Michael had told his mother that I was his ideal woman. I did not expect him to ask me to marry him three times and each time I said no. I had never given him false hope or mixed messages. I had never been his girlfriend but I believe that we had shared the best of friendships and I always think of him when I listen to the Cure sing *Catch* [8].

1987 began quietly by choice. I had given up. I was not going to talk to anyone because it simply was not worth it; it just led to heartache and disillusionment. By a combination of circumstance and choice I had become a particle floating around in a seemingly expansive universe without a sense of purpose or direction. I was restricted by everything and nothing: blinded by a lack of light and unwittingly drawn along a terrifying, invisible path. A path that seemed impossible to resist - to gain a sense of time, location, or control. He was blacker than black the closer I moved towards his centre yet I was compelled to move towards him as soon as I was drawn into his path. It was not possible for me to escape.

Having privately assumed a vow of silence, I had poured myself a cup of coffee and settled in a corner of the Humanities' tea room to force myself to read Sir Walter Scott's *Waverley* [9]. It is still my opinion that one would have to be forced to read the novel because no one in their right mind, aged 18, would voluntarily read it for pleasure. I loved the Humanities block. In the true style of the university that was set in a nature reserve it was built around a tall, native tree. One had to walk through forest to the student carpark and the walk afforded one time to meditate whilst crossing winding, wooden bridges built around trees. It gave me time to mentally talk myself out of extreme anxiety and to create space from my problems: to escape.

I suppose it allowed me to temporarily ignore my problems and to assume an image of self-confidence. Unlike the other members of my regular student cohort who favoured whatever the latest fashion trends dictated (and I honestly had no real idea what they were) I was dressed in a navy straight skirt, a red, white and navy-blue striped top, a navy blazer, red court shoes and red lipstick; hardly the image of an 18-year-old humanities student. Furthermore, I was sitting alone, reading. In my mind I had disappeared but I definitely needed better camouflage if I had hoped to truly disappear.

I was ripped out of the nineteenth century into the present by his first question and was forced to break my secret vow of silence because I was polite. He asked me what I was reading, a rather simple question but I suppose it was a relief that it was about something I actually enjoyed talking about. I remember that his face was friendly, and that unlike other mature-aged students he wore shorts with an untucked business shirt rolled up at the sleeves; kind of business-like but quirky. Maybe that is why he gravitated towards someone who looked like she was wearing a "British Airways hostess uniform" as he later described my outfit.

We discovered that we were studying the same course and discussed *Waverley* in depth. I remember feeling stimulated by our conversation and astounded that I had irrevocably broken my vow of silence when our coffee room encounter ended seven hours after his initial question. He had unwittingly breathed on an oxygen-starved, barely smoking spark. He had spoken in a language that I recognised as my own and he gave me a glimpse of an alternative life that I had dreamed of but did not think was possible for me.

I had unconsciously moved onto his path and it was as though my own space-time continuum altered. No matter how many times I attempted to move away from him, and no matter how many ways in which I tried to find a way to keep a hold of who I was and who I wanted to be I was inevitably drawn into his path, compelled by his certainty, his ability to challenge my intellect and feed my imagination, and by his dark smouldering, mercurial love. I was frightened of him. I was frightened by the fact that I needed his friendship, his influence, his guidance but I did not want to need him. I was frightened by feeling even more out of control than I usually was. If John was my horizon, my sense of freedom, then Adrian was my maelstrom. And I loved both of them.

I cannot tell you when I fell in love with Adrian. I know I changed in his company. I was drawn into his circle of admirers – the young students, the mature-aged students and even the occasional lecturer who would gather around him in the tea room, enlivened by the literary, philosophical or cultural debates that he seemed to lead. How could I resist such a magic? He enchanted me with stories of his many years of travel, his musicianship; infiltrated my imagination, simultaneously expanding and splintering my worldview and sense of self. We became study partners and I learnt much from his professional, organised approach to research and study. I admired him, revered him, loved him. At times I feared him. Women who had been or were in love with him showed me open hostility or expressed resentment that I continued to be engaged to John and would not fall at Adrian's feet. I could not. I did not trust him.

Adrian did not move slowly. He knew what he wanted and he wanted me. I know hell and I know that there are depths of hell that some people never fall to. At 18 I discovered new depths of pain, despair, self-loathing, disorientation, abandonment of self: self-dissipation. Adrian's prodigious influence on my life surreptitiously seeped into my core sense of being, my worldview, my social life, my behaviour. He was 13 years older than me and 14 years younger than my parents and his ability to communicate easily and with confidence seemed to please them. I did not experience resistance from my parents if I spent time with Adrian because he was not John.

I could talk about Adrian; share with them our thoughts and experiences, and hence my life because he was not John. I did not experience resistance from my parents but I was terrifyingly aware that I was losing my tenuous grip on my core sense of values and identity. The more time I spent with Adrian the more I found an unfamiliar self and moved further away from my safe, solid sense of who I was when I was with John. I knew I needed and craved Adrian's friendship; his intellectual and creative stimulation. He made me feel alive but dangerously close to the edge of an invisible horizon: one that I was blindly feeling my way towards. A black hole.

Why was I scared of Adrian? He had the ability to draw out and encourage my potential yet he was deliberately and consciously obliterating my connection with John. He knew that I loved John yet he did not respect that part of me. He knew that I did not want to have a sexual relationship with him but he made it very clear that if I wanted to maintain our friendship then it had to be everything or nothing. I could not bear my life without his friendship and to me it seemed those moments of reluctant physical and psychological vulnerability followed by intense guilt, shame, and self-loathing was a necessary sacrifice. I loved Adrian and I was attracted to him: I just did not want to love him in that way. I was torn between the dark and the light: between the intoxicating unknown and the purity of something I could not hold on to. Adrian was leading me into a desert where I had to decide which self had to die and which self would be created and endure.

I wandered in that desert for nigh on eight months and I wanted to die. Mirages briefly enticed me with the impossible vision of a life in which I could love both John and Adrian. It is truly amazing how many different ideas of oneself can exist in one's mind: how some can be so incompatible yet the mind can rearrange them to justify certain behaviours that one knows are wrong. How one can justify certain uncharacteristic choices and behaviours as though one is a character in a Tolstoy novel. I experienced the effects of Festinger's cognitive-dissonance theory[10] 19 years before I studied it.

It is indeed a fine line between pleasure and pain and for much of those eight months the line was definitely blurred. I spent eight torturous months knowing that I loved two men with every fibre of my being; that they loved me, that I was hurting three people, that I would inevitably have to hurt two people, and that one of them did not deserve to be hurt and I did not know how to avoid it. I cannot write this without crying, without feeling a deep sense of grief and acute physical pain in my chest. I do not know if I ever would be able to.

John tried in so many ways to save us. He cooked vegetarian meals for me because Adrian had changed the way I ate. He encouraged me to study hard and always expressed his belief in my ability to succeed. He read books on saving marriages. He never gave up and when I expressed my distress at "losing my best friend" after I stopped seeing Adrian, he was dumbfounded that he was not my best friend. So was I.

Yet again, I returned to Adrian. Somewhere in my head I thought I could maintain a balance. As I left his home, he bent down to my open car window and said, "You can't keep sweeping this under the carpet." His words crashed into my conscious with the force of a meteor: I drove home totally and utterly out of my head. Something simply snapped in my brain. My emotions, my cognitions, my senses were overloaded and dangerously fused. I heard myself screaming, felt my face smash against the windscreen, my teeth shattered and my mouth filled with hot, salty blood. Yet I continued to drive home with an undamaged car and an undamaged face. Hallucinations are terrifyingly real. I could not verbalise the reason for my uncontrollable distress to my parents when I arrived home. I could not stop my sobbing and screaming other than to repeatedly gasp, "He's taken my soul!" I recall my mother putting me into her bed and telling my father to call the doctor. I don't remember what happened next.

I was in grave danger I knew that much. The cobalt sky was vast and all around me. I could not see the earth beneath me but I knew that it was a long way down and that I had no desire to meet it with the force that my current altitude would dictate. I had loved climbing the Poinciana as a child. Its friendly, generous limbs had offered a safe place to think, imagine and read. I loved its green canopy with glimpses of blue sky, and bright red splashes of joy in summer. I had no fear of climbing trees; I knew how to choose the safe and strong branches but I could hardly breathe now. The immense Poinciana's ancient, tired branches spanned the gaping canyon and provided my only means of progress. I was at the point of no return. I was responsible for which branch I chose to trust in to continue my journey – to survive. At this height they were confusing. There were too many and they appeared to be similarly fragile and potentially precarious.

Once again, my dreams were penetrated by my daily troubles. I encountered Dali-like landscapes filled with submerged dangers that could only be sensed rather than seen. I was forced to cross immense, caliginous swamps fearing the submerged hands that would attempt to grab my ankles and drag me under as I desperately attempted to wade across. I had no choice. Fear of the unknown. My wolf had many guises.

My grandparents were my solace – a safe place. I had often spent nights with them when I needed a break from home and no questions about visiting two men. I did not talk to them about my private life because it was a source of shame for my mother and I wanted to be loved by them and for them to be proud of me no matter what my mother told my grandmother. I loved spending time with both of them, sharing meals, watching television, cooking, chatting, discussing politics and science, or silently reading together in their patio's warm sunlight. They were aware that John was my boyfriend yet Adrian had met them and had met me at their home. They liked Adrian. They said nothing about my alternating boyfriends and I just pretended I was in control.

My grandfather was the catalyst in my decision to spend the rest of my life with Adrian and I love him for that. He asked me to accompany him to Manly to purchase lunch at the local fish and chip shop. It was not a regular activity and of course I agreed. It was a lovely day and after we ordered our sweet lip we decided to stroll along the beach whilst our lunch cooked. We began our conversation with naming which bird we would like to be if we had a choice. I had chosen a sea eagle and my grandfather chose a seagull and if you knew both of us you would probably say, "typical".

I would love to have been a sea eagle at that moment, looking down upon the two of us walking so companionably along the beach: Pa in his tweed trilby, my fair hair, and both of us walking with our hands in our pockets. The scene makes me smile because it was such a special, private moment to share with him. I cannot remember how my grandfather and I began to talk about his relationship with Nanny or knowing how he had made the right decision to marry her but I do know that he offered me some timely guidance that fitted neatly and subtly into our discussion and my life. *When you are married, sometimes you are lovers and sometimes you are friends. You should marry your best friend.* That message was an oasis in my desert and the air-conditioned bus ride out. No matter how painful the ramifications of my decision would be it felt like I was making a rational, logical decision to solve my problem and that there would be no running away from it. I was going to choose my best friend and my family would be at my wedding.

My second year of university was marked by the creation of new and enduring relationships and by the growth of my love for academia and cultural interests. It was vitiated by my increased sense of difference heightened by my disturbing dreams, my occasional compulsion to make socially-inappropriate verbal outbursts intended for shock value and my own amusement, a horrific visual hallucination and several serious "emotional meltdowns". 1987 also signified endings.

Adrian buried the remnants of my innocence and my experience of sacred love. Perhaps because he did not truly understand it or because he feared he would lose it before he could share it with me had I been granted the freedom to grow to want him in that way in my own time. He demanded that I demonstrate that my connection with John was over by my burning John's letters and cards and photographs. By destroying his ring. Every fibre of my being was silently screaming *NO* but I fulfilled his request because he needed me to - because I loved him. The ending of John marked the ending of the cold war at home and the return of the prodigal daughter to the fold.

1987 found me behaving in ways that I felt were opposed to my moral code – entirely wrong. I have often asked myself why I allowed myself to feel so vulnerable, so compromised. It is as though I was staring into huge beams of light that immobilised me and devolved me to a pre-pubescent child in a dark bedroom. Why did I allow myself to be vulnerable and abused as that child? I have only one honest answer. Because what I most wanted was more powerful than what I feared. My safety, my sense of self-respect, and at times my happiness, were worth sacrificing to belong, to obtain parental approval, to feel loved by my mother, and to prove to Adrian that I had crossed the desert to dance the ever-dynamic, endless dance of a woman in love with him.

Chapter 8

Deterioration, Disbelief and Diagnosis

There are only two mistakes one can make along the road to truth; not going all the way, and not starting.

Buddha

Much madness is divinest sense
To a discerning eye;
Much sense the starkest madness.

Emily Dickinson[1], *Much Madness is Divinest Sense.*

Suffering is permanent, obscure and dark,
And shares the nature of infinity.

William Wordsworth[2], *The Borderers.*

On the mountains of truth you can never climb in vain: either you will reach a point higher up today, or you will be training your powers so that you will be able to climb higher tomorrow.

Friedrich Nietzsche[3],
Human, all too human: A book for free spirits.

1988 was an exciting year. Brisbane matured into a vibrant, cosmopolitan city that welcomed the world's people, cultures, knowledge, and contributions. People seemed to be more friendly, open, curious and less suspicious of individual difference. World

Expo offered Queensland a safe window through which to see the wider world of difference and opportunities, and it was wonderful. Adrian and I spent many happy hours strolling through the Queen Street Mall, sipping coffee at Jimmy's on the Mall and *people watching*. *People watching* was one of our favourite things to do: observing behaviour and surmising about people's attitudes to life, or stages of relationships by the manner in which they walked or communicated with each other. We enjoyed the entertainment from buskers in the city mall and spent three tremendous days visiting the spectacular countries exhibited at World Expo along the Brisbane River.

In 1988 I saw world expo; was romanced by Adrian; successfully completed my Bachelor of Arts; enrolled in a Graduate Diploma of Education with the intention of studying post graduate literature so that I could lecture in the field I most loved; turned 20; and married Adrian. I had made the decision to spend the rest of my life with Adrian. He was my guiding light and I needed a sense of direction: someone to lead me out of the abyss. Without Adrian I doubt that I would have been able to cope with the speed at which my transition from adolescence to adulthood, and all that term implies, had suddenly accelerated. I was not ready for marriage, for leaving home and being an adult. To the outside world I had successfully waitressed at the same restaurant for three years and completed a degree. I looked like a responsible, quite mature, university student. Possibly even a *normal* human being.

It was not true. I knew I was masquerading as a normal person. I had learnt how to behave in certain situations because I had observed how people behave and I had taught myself how to cope with anxiety and depression: how to hide it from others. 1988 was one of my best performances. In fact, it was hard to follow it up. When I think of 1989, I do not automatically equate it with an image of freedom: of the tearing down of the wall. I think of black. 1989 felt like a cell. The cell had chinks of light, moments of shared happiness with Adrian but mostly 1989 was black. In some ways, 1988 was the colourful, enthralling, heady, skyrocket ride before my inevitable crash. As an adult, there was absolutely nowhere for me to go for help. How could I tell anyone that I did not feel like an adult, that I did not magically and automatically have all of the answers to my problems?

I did not feel in control of my situation, my emotions, my future, or my ability to gain control: to get a grip. I know the moment when I began to lose my grip in 1988. It was the moment when she physically re-entered my life and left a permanent physical stamp on my life. My parents' neighbours were known to be keen wedding photographers. How could I refuse their kind offer to photograph and video my wedding? What possible reason could I give my parents for refusing to speak with her in my home just days before my wedding?

She was in my bedroom on my wedding day. She was at my wedding. *I can see her face in front of mine whilst I am writing. If I close my eyes to block out her face, she is closer. I find it hard to breathe evenly. Over the years I have learnt to breathe shallowly rather than deeply: an anxiety response. I wish you weren't here. Ah – I meant to write she but I am leaving you there because for this moment it is more honest to leave you there. Your presence is strong. You pervade every moment of my wedding, every image. You were there for the last day that I was my parents' child before her transition to an adult. You were there at the moment when I joined Adrian as his wife. And you have remained with us. You bitch. I hate you now because you've made me cry. You stole something from me when I was six and you have continued to steal from me even in your physical absence. I am pressing and smoothing the muscles in my face. I do this to soothe myself. It is automatic. If I press my external self perhaps, I can contain my inner self. My sorrow, my hurt, my child.*

This moment will pass. I tell myself this. I will gain control again. There, I have wiped my eyes, blown my nose, regulated my breathing, taken two mental steps away from the feeling and her face. I am an adult again: I can cope. I spent much of my wedding night with my university friends being as bubbly and vivacious as possible – trying to feel busy and safe and maintaining the act to the end. I would like to do it again with just the people I love and truly enjoy the occasion but Pa and Nanny are dead and so is my childhood.

This is not a love story about Adrian and me. It is the story of how an individual experiences mental illness: how mental illness can develop, how it can be overlooked, underestimated, and most importantly; how it must be individually and for once – understood outside of a book. My experience of my specific mental illness does not fit neatly into eight pages of a text book dedicated to abnormal psychology nor can it be effectively described in the DSM. It most definitely should not be treated according to the psychiatric and medical guidelines prescribed by either medical source which unfortunately guide the majority of general practitioners and psychologists. It is not that the texts are essentially wrong. It is that it is dangerous to not listen and think beyond those sources of information: to fail to see the patient outside of the recognised medical box. Beyond confirmation bias.

I had moved from a family home with views of my beloved Moreton Bay to a tiny, two-bedroomed unit in a block of flats in Lutwyche, Brisbane City. I could not see the sea, and did not hear the birds. There were bars on the windows which obscured my vision of the night sky, the stars and the friendly moon. I had a good knowledge of South Brisbane but had never driven in the city or the north side and was terrified of driving in unfamiliar city traffic. My anxiety was exacerbated by feeling trapped. I did not know how to drive home and because I was anxious my ability to learn was impaired: I could not absorb and retain new information. It was an all too familiar problem.

The college that Adrian and I were attending was situated in Kelvin Grove and fortunately Adrian was familiar with the area so all I had to do was stick with him. We were inseparable and a formidable academic force. We worked well together and found the academic work a breeze compared with the demands of our previous study. The difficult part of the course was stomaching the "back-to-school" college environment. It was literally nauseating. We discovered that we felt sick whilst we were at the college yet when we returned to our flat, we recovered quickly.

There was no forest to walk through at the college. The refectory did not attract kookaburras to protect us from the dangers of potato chips. There was no tea room filled with the rejuvenating chorus of exuberant students and lecturers. University had been an endless kaleidoscope of new perspectives, possibilities, colours, and experiences. It had encouraged me to embrace E. M. Forster's mantra of *life, love, and beauty*. It had reinforced my pursuit of the eternal question – *Why?* Teachers' college was a grey, restrictive, dehumanising world.

Adrian and I were good teachers. We encouraged students to think for themselves, to be creative, to strive to fulfil their potential, to think outside of the box. The students loved us and it was clear to see that we were professional, efficient, effective, and worked hard for the benefit of our students. The majority of our students responded well to our teaching styles regardless of the various schools' socio-economic and cultural populations. Unfortunately, the bureaucratic, political, institutional nature of state education did not suit our individualistic approaches to education. We worked well together, and we worked well in teams at separate schools. We worked hard and we supported each other's efforts to remain in a profession that felt so wrong.

Adrian and I were misfits. We told ourselves that we only needed two years' teaching experience to meet lecturing requirements and then we would continue our academic studies but we were transferred to regions that prevented us from studying courses that were part-time and our dreams became more remote than our schools. Time, fate, chance – Hardy's ingredients for a modernist classic merged in our lives to influence and modify our relationship, our self-perceptions, and our aspirations for the next 13 years. They threatened our futures, and gave us new opportunities: setting new co-ordinates and a chance to grow.

Perhaps I could have continued teaching had I not been so ill. I had not had a happy school life and had no desire to teach. Yet teaching came naturally to me and I genuinely loved my students. I found ways to interest and motivate them. Music was often a conduit to their deeper understanding of poetry, or a novel, or history. Once one had captured their imagination, encouraged their empathy or compassion it was much easier to share knowledge and understanding, and sometimes even passion for a subject. It was not difficult for me to teach. It was difficult for me to remain untouched by the bitterness, pettiness, and small-mindedness of staff members who did not relate to their colleagues and did not like adolescents.

It was difficult for me to remain unaffected by colleagues who felt threatened by my drive to help students, my willingness to work hard, and my pursuit of personal excellence without the need to climb the power ladder. They bullied me because they could not step outside of their own insecurities to see that I posed no threat to them. They criticised me if I spent "too much" of my time helping students at lunch. They picked on me if I dressed well. They picked on me when I made efforts to make my classroom more like a friendly learning environment.

It hurt me because they misinterpreted my motivations. My students and the cleaners appreciated my efforts. The occasional, rare, ego-less head of department encouraged me but that only exacerbated uncomfortable peer relations. Did they fear what they did not understand and did not want to understand? Conflict, whether obscure or overt so often boils down to a fear of difference.

I became very depressed and very anxious. The most obvious symptoms were physical: asthma, eczema, and eye ulcerations. I was immobilised for brief periods of time because of complications associated with mild spina bifida. Painful muscular spasms in my back, and a lack of feeling in my legs simply disabled me. Once I discovered the magic of acupuncture for this specific problem, I could manage it. It was not "all in my head" but I am sure it was attributable to tension.

I was able to channel all of my energy into the hours I spent at work and to maintain a professional appearance. I did not have much time to sleep because of the hours of work required by our initial probation. Adrian and I spent most week nights up to 2 or 3am preparing work, knowing that we would start our day at 6am. We had little time for our relationship but at least we prepared work together and shared ideas. I was burning the candle at both ends and my state of mental health was in an untenable situation.

The beginning (1991).
Acrylic on board, 90 x 60 cm

Fecundity (1991/2021).
Acrylic on board, 90 x 60 cm

Hypervigilance, anxiety that cannot be turned off, endless depression, and disturbed sleep combined to dangerously spiral. I kept pushing myself to do what was expected of me but I lost control of my energy levels: my ability to regulate myself. I could not stop myself from needing to clean the house at 11 or 12 o'clock at night. I would feel compelled to paint at similar hours, claiming that I knew what David Bowie's *Starman* looked like, or that I could see his waves of sound and light.[4] I insisted that Adrian sit with me one weekend to rewrite a national curriculum for junior high school because I believed there was a better way to educate our students. Whilst I still hold similar views regarding education, I am painfully aware that my eccentric behaviour at home was not normal.

I would burn up that creative energy and then crash. I would be unable to hold the pain in and I would curl up and cry until I could not cry anymore. I would dig my nails into my arms or thighs just to redirect my internal pain. There was nothing more I wanted than to end the pain. I constantly thought about killing myself but I did not want to do that. I just did not want to live with me. I wanted help but I just did not know what help I wanted, or who to ask. Adrian's new professional commitments also created distance from me and I interpreted his distance as a sign of my own unlovability and worthlessness.

Starman (1990/2016). Mixed media on board. 74 x 48 cm

No doubt my behaviour at home seemed unusual and difficult to penetrate. So much more of it was concealed. My mother sent me a letter in which she told me that I had to finish my probation and become a fully qualified teacher; that I was behaving like an adolescent. I felt like I was screaming into the wind and that no one could hear my anguish. Of course, I did the "adult thing" and qualified with excellent results.

Each year that I left a school my students expressed their sorrow, their gratitude, and many their love. I attempted to leave schools, or teach different subjects just to maintain a semblance of sanity.

It was just too hard to pretend that I was functioning as a normal human being who was not trying to ignore the ceaseless white noise in her head; the fact that when she looked in the mirror the face that looked back at her was not symmetrical – the lower part of the face was twisted and distorted; that her left leg experienced electric shocks when she could not avoid stepping on cracks in the pavement; that sometimes the skin on the outside of her left leg felt painfully sunburnt – yet it wasn't.

When I was 23, we decided to have a baby. Adrian and I had been transferred to Central Queensland to a coal mining town. It was not a good cultural or social fit for us but we supported each other as much as we could. We were happy together and at least we had more time to share because we no longer had to meet the demands of the two-year qualification probation period.

We had decided that we could teach overseas and that it would be a wonderful experience for our children to grow up with an international education. It made the thought of teaching bearable and worthwhile. We had been considering teaching in Yemen just prior to the onset of the Gulf War. We were so happy when my pregnancy was confirmed and we believed that having our children was a natural extension of our love. My body was definitely not designed for pregnancy or birth. There was no such thing as morning sickness but there was such a thing as 24 hour a day nausea for 39 weeks.

I waited until Mother's Day to tell my mother the news: I wanted her to be the first person we would share our news with. *Don't expect me to be happy for you.* That is what she said and the memory of those words still has power. I had disappointed her again. I did not anticipate her rejection. I understand that she was disappointed because she believed that I would not have a chance to travel; that she feared that my actions had limited my future. She had not been thinking the way I had. She had not considered that Adrian is 13 years older than me; that I had to consider his life as well, and that we could still travel with children. I just was not the person she wanted me to be.

The coal dust simply was not good for asthmatics. Eventually I became very ill. My doctor told me that I could not have antibiotics because I was pregnant and advised me to cut back on my Ventolin. He refuted my concern that my baby would not have sufficient oxygen if I could not breathe. Fortunately, we chose to visit my parents in Brisbane for the winter holidays. I was blue by the time I had an appointment with a thoracic physician who immediately admitted me to hospital. I had not been confused about the advice I had been given by that GP. When I returned to Central Queensland I found a new doctor – a doctor who treated me with respect, who listened, and believed me.

My health did not improve in that environment. I was relying on my nebuliser, experiencing migraines accompanied with nose bleeds, and lonely at home on maternity leave. I was isolated from my family in Brisbane, suicidal and having to hide it from the friends we had made in the very small and visible community. I drew my pain on paper. I was losing my identity, my sense of self. I was drowning in a sea of black. I recall a desperate moment when I had gathered all of my medication in the belief that I could not tolerate the pain anymore. I was staring at my drawing – a depiction of suffering, loss of identity and the death of my inner child. I had decided to die.

I rang my mother just to hear her voice. Why her? Perhaps because I just wanted to give her one more chance to demonstrate that she loved me; that she could hear me. I told her that I was depressed. She told me that I was not *clinically depressed*. She said that someone who is clinically depressed cannot laugh and that when she had phoned me during a dinner party that I was sharing with friends, she heard me laughing. What could I say to convince her? That I had 17 years of acting experience? No volume, foreign language, no impact. Failed.

Victims (1992/1995). Watercolour pencil and ink 27 x 19.5 cm

I told my doctor and he believed me. He could see me and he could hear me. He was concerned that I was suffering from maternal depression and said that it was a very serious, real condition. He did not treat my situation lightly because a pregnant woman had recently committed suicide. I did not stay much longer in Central Queensland but I am grateful that his belief in me kept me alive. I spent the remainder of my pregnancy with my parents because my obstetrician advised that I stay close to my thoracic physician in Brisbane.

It was difficult living away from Adrian and having to hide my depression at all times. It was particularly hard for me to see her physically demonstrating maternal love towards my brother's girlfriend. She hugged her like I desperately wanted to be hugged. She hugged her at just the same times as I would have liked to be hugged. My brother's girlfriend was so lovable. She is still so lovable. Everyone loves my brother's wife, including me. I despise myself for feeling envious, for having felt so conflicted – so jealous. Jealous of the way my mother so effortlessly loved her and loved my brother. I understand the context of these feelings and the reasons why she behaved the way she did. I understand that it is all in the past but I do regret that it was the way it was.

I do not know what triggered the powerful flashback. I know that Adrian was returning to Central Queensland, leaving me with my parents and that I was feeling terribly vulnerable: that my remaining vestiges of armour were dissolving. I remember Charlie in the shower, talking me through my shower routine and that Charlie seemed to be talking out loud. The chatter in my head had become uncontainable. I was violently shaking and sobbing and absolutely exposed. Adrian had tried to comfort me but I was inconsolable, and probably making no sense. I do remember standing in my towel, dripping and shaking, and crying and my mother asking me in a serious, counsellor's voice, "Has someone touched you?" Her words reached into my little girl's reality and pulled out a far away, long ago and ever present *Yes*.

My mother was not there the day I told her. Perhaps she had to hide herself to protect herself. Perhaps she thought she had to hold herself back to help me. She sounded reserved, rational: distant. She had set boundaries like a professional counsellor. She believed me. "We can't tell Dad'. I accepted that she did not want me to tell my father. I understood that we needed to protect him. 'Would you like to see a counsellor?'

"No". I did not want to talk to a stranger. I did not want a counsellor right now – I wanted my mother. She seemed almost relieved. I recall her arriving at the conclusion that the event explained a lot: I am not sure what it explained to her. She also wondered aloud whether my abuser had been touched too. *Did she matter?* It was as though she was rationalising the event away. We did not talk about it again.

Perhaps I understand what triggered this flashback now that I have described the event. Adrian was about to leave me with my parents for several months. I had not lived at home since I had married Adrian. I had not had to see my neighbours' house every day for almost four years and this had helped create an unconscious barrier. I had seen her house, Adrian was leaving, and Charlie's firm reassurances were muffled and ineffectual in his efforts to repress my anxiety and terror. The irrepressible memories and emotions that I had attempted to contain from my parents erupted when I was most vulnerable, naked and exposed. I could not hide from myself and I could not escape me. They ran out of my eyes, flowed over my body, and flooded around my feet but they did not clean me. They did not evaporate when exposed to air: they formed a gas that pervaded my parents' house and no doubt my mother's life but they did not touch my father.

I did what was expected of me. I masqueraded as an adult, found a house for us to rent and prepared for the birth of our son. I coped as I always had: by putting one foot in front of the other because I believed I had no choice. I was relieved when my obstetrician decided that it was necessary to induce the labour and told me that I would have my first baby by that evening. Adrian was so excited and I was stoic in my effort to remain calm in appearance. I will not provide all the sensational details other than the birth of our first son was traumatic. My labour endured for 24 ½ hours after my waters were manually broken. An emergency caesarean was performed because our baby was distressed and dilation measured one centimetre. I glimpsed our son as he was whisked away in a humidifier.

We named him after a character in one of my favourite novels: a character who was brave and developed a strong sense of self. He was perfect. He looked like a baby doll with large eyes that were capable of meeting and holding one's gaze. He fascinated his paediatrician. I was overwhelmed with love when I was finally able to hold him. I literally felt like I had fallen in love and I believe that I have felt bonded to him ever since.

The obstetrician warned us that it would be dangerous for me to have another child and Adrian had been horrified by my experience. We decided that it would be sensible for Adrian to have a vasectomy and we accepted that our plans to have another child would have to be altered. It was definitely not pleasant to have to defend our decision when frequently criticised by individuals who believed that our son would be "lonely … an only child" and that we were "selfish". It is amazing how words have such power and how strong one has to be in one's own convictions to withstand their force.

I took a year's maternity leave to care for David. It was difficult to defend returning to work so soon but it was also a struggle to survive on one wage, pay rent and pay off our car loan so we did the best we could. For one very special year we had close support from my parents. We lived 15 minutes away from them and we enjoyed sharing David's development and family connectedness. I spent many hours talking to David, reading out aloud to him (sometimes I felt the necessity to censor words when Salman Rushdie's choice of words were inappropriate for a young baby to hear) and showing David pretty flowers and leaves in the garden. I held him on my lap whilst I painted and showed him how to blend colours. He stayed awake all day unless I lay down in the hammock or on the bed and then he slept spread-eagled on my chest. By 10 months of age, he knew how to hold a paint brush correctly. He was also able to use a combination of commands, verbs and nouns with clarity. His mind was very active and he needed little sleep. He was a very sociable baby, very alert. He still is.

Joy (1995). Watercolour pencil. 25.2 x 45 cm

I assumed that I was suffering from "the baby blues". I appreciated and loved being a mother and could not understand why I felt so down. I assumed all new mothers suffered from lethargy, exhaustion, nausea and acute sadness. I knew that my mother was concerned about the way I felt. She had also suffered illness through pregnancy and difficult childbirths. In fact, we had agreed that "there is nothing natural about pregnancy". She provided me great moral support and empathy having experienced the same difficulties. It was so good to have her support. In hindsight, my conjectured baby blues had masked a much deeper depression: a serious mental illness. I assumed that I would eventually pick up. I didn't.

At the end of 1993 we were transferred to a regional city six hours away from home because the education department assumed that my lungs were no longer in danger. Fairly ironic that they transferred me to a location recognised as the most dangerous area in the world for asthmatics but also typical. Once again, I put one foot in front of the other. I had to move to a new city, a new school, a new social setting. I was isolated from family support; I was ill and I was suffering from many stressors. Too many stressors. I was headed right into the danger zone and there were no signs saying *Wrong direction, Turn Back.*

Our new location was not a good cultural fit for us but it became our home for 21 years. The distance from our family and friends affected us greatly but we attempted to make the most of our situation. I have discovered that there are so many events that I am incapable of remembering from 1993 to 2010. It is not because I experienced trauma during those years. Rather, it is because the inkiest black depression erased memories.

I waded through a mire of debilitating depression for 17 years. It is so exhausting to appear to function; to work, to be a mother, a wife, a friend, a daughter, a student when one just wants to step off the Earth because the sadness is too great and the energy required to function *normally* is impossible to manifest at times. Social expectations, my own expectations combined with the symptoms of my undiagnosed illness formed an invisible, ever-restricting, compression suit: a vice that simultaneously diminished my sense of self and forced me to be bigger than I was. It blurred opportunities to be happy. At times it erased my belief that people needed me and loved me.

1994 was a tsunami that had built steadily. It was foreseeable but it had formed under the radar. It hit me in the dark; pummelled me, disoriented me, held me under until I could not breathe – until I did not want to breathe, and threw me onto a very distant shore. I gave all of my energy to teaching. It required everything I had to give and I often offered extra. Students absorbed so much and my passionate work ethic seemed to justify my need to operate on an extremely high stress level. It was a normal state for me.

Miraculously I had a couple of classes that had been allocated a teacher's aide for extra student support. I use the description miraculously because Jill was my lighthouse and my lifeguard in that tsunami. Her energy, her shared valuing of people, her appreciation of beauty, and her communication of absolute faith in me raised my head above the water. We naturally became a great egalitarian teaching team and firm friends. I loved Jill with all of my heart and she was the first woman I trusted. We shared a love of music and gardens and we both adored the same woman who would later become my best friend.

I knew there was something seriously wrong with me and that I needed help. I was appearing energetic in the classroom yet I felt like I was struggling to coordinate my movement to walk there. I was concerned that I was slurring my speech and confided in Jill. She loyally walked beside me to classrooms and observed me closely. She agreed that my eyes did not look "right" but did not notice any slurring. I had fallen over twice in the playground without warning and had large bruises on my legs and hips that I could not explain.

My doctor was concerned and ran a series of tests. He was a very kind doctor, a beautiful man and he never made me feel like I was stupid or a hypochondriac. He was not aware of all my symptoms because I had not described all of them. I had not known they were symptoms until I read about them. He had not been able to suggest a diagnosis because he was not aware of all of my symptoms. We had both been working on the same jigsaw puzzle with missing pieces and no illustration to guide us until I found a description in a book.

I liked the school guidance officer. He seemed different from the usual detached guidance officers: approachable, friendly, relaxed and human. He was observant and non-judgemental about students and he seemed to observe most human interactions. I believe he had observed me in the classroom and the general school environment. He appeared unsurprised and professionally helpful when I asked him for information on depression. He gave me copies of information about various types of depression including the then current Diagnostic and Statistical Manual of Mental Disorders' description of bipolar disorder[5]. The description of bipolar disorder 1 was a light bulb moment and a relief.

It did not describe how it *feels* to have the illness nor did it describe all of the symptoms because the illness has been somewhat difficult to research but it did describe enough of my symptoms to provide an answer for why I had been struggling to cope for so long. I objectively listed my symptoms on a sheet of A4 paper and I included the series of illnesses that I had been currently treated for (e.g., asthma, eye ulcers, eczema, etc.) and gave the list to my doctor. I told him that I thought I had bipolar disorder 1 and asked him what he thought. He supported my conclusion and made an appointment for me to see a psychiatrist who would interview me and provide his expert diagnosis. I felt safe because my doctor had trusted me, believed my suffering was real, and that I knew myself well enough to know that I was not imagining things.

Going to a psychiatrist is frightening and one has to be on one's best behaviour. I was worried that he would not think I had a mental illness but I was also afraid that he would think I was crazy. I was worried he would not ask me the right questions. Not that I knew what he was supposed to be asking. I was not the psychiatrist. I was just used to having to ask the big questions: used to nobody else asking them.

I recall Adrian driving me down to Brisbane, the fastest method for seeing a specialist when one lives in regional Queensland. How does one dress to see a psychiatrist? Funny little thoughts. We sat in a waiting room and waited. Over the years I have noticed that psychiatrists' rooms are never very optimistic or relaxing. They are often austere, dingy, clinical or eccentric. Most people in the waiting room avoid each other's gaze: they certainly avoid speaking to each other.

The waiting room mood tends to linger in the psychiatrist's consultation room. How does one sit? It is a little like sitting in the principal's office and trying not to anticipate whether one has passed or failed the final report, except that one does not expect a medal. In my case, I received a lifelong label. I needed the label to receive help but it is a double-edged blade. How does one answer the greeting, "How are you?" Automatically, politely: feel immediately dishonest, inaccurate.

Where does one look whilst he writes his lengthy notes? The room has high plaster ceilings decorated with classical, renaissance-type art deco moulds of curvaceous, naked women. It is incongruous with the Indian man sitting opposite me in a suit and bow tie. It felt surreal and anachronistic but I was not there to observe. I was there to be observed. I only remember one question, "Are you paranoid?" I answered with my typical quick wit, "I work for the education department, why wouldn't I be?" It was meant to be a tongue-in cheek comment but it was not met with a wry smile or any sign of a sense of humour. Possibly ill-timed, inappropriate. Heaven knows if my psychological report contains the word paranoia. I do know that my report contained the diagnosis of bipolar disorder 1 and obsessive-compulsive disorder. My family doctor told me the news on the 9th of August, 1994: my 26th birthday.

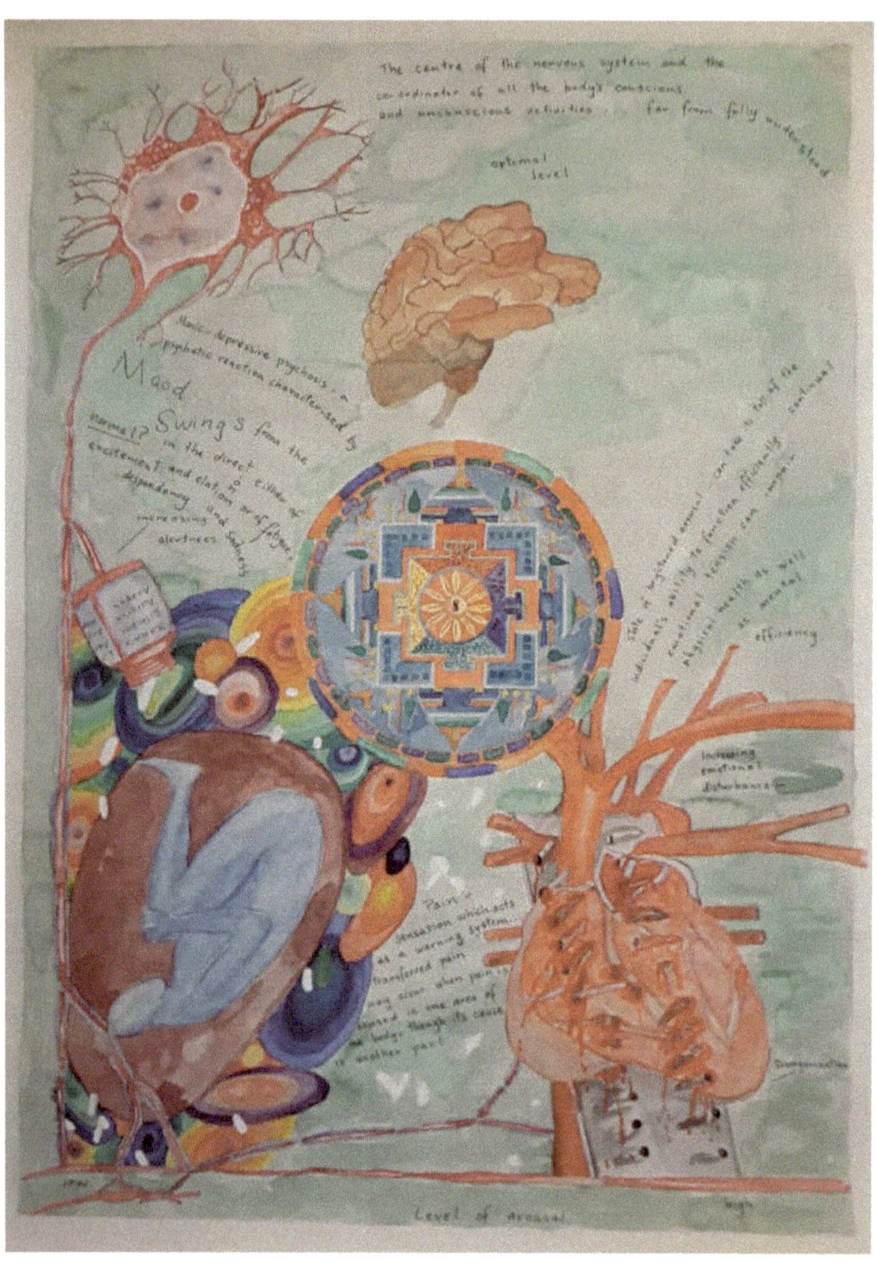

Lab rats, labels and loss. The unbearable darkness of being (2006).
Watercolour and ink 75 x 56 cm

Chapter 9

The Lion's Den

Virtual Alice I (1998) Water colour and ink.

Of a truth, Knowledge is power, but it is a power reined by scruple, having a conscience of what must be and what may be; whereas Ignorance is a blind giant who, let him but wax unbound, would make it a sport to seize the pillars that hold up the long-wrought fabric of human good, and turn all the places of joy as dark as a buried Babylon.

George Eliot[1], *Daniel Deronda.*

"The fault, dear Brutus, is not in our stars, but in ourselves."
William Shakespeare[2], *Julius Caesar.*

When you're down and they're counting
When your secrets all found out
When your troubles take to mounting
When the map you have leads you to doubt
When there's no information
And the compass turns to nowhere that you know well

When the doctors failed to heal you
When no medicine chest can make you well
When no counsel leads to comfort
When there are no more lies they can tell
No more useless information
And the compass spins
The compass spins between heaven and hell
Sting[3], Let your soul be your pilot, *Mercury Falling.*

I was not devastated by the diagnosis because I still had faith that my doctor could help me to feel better now that we had identified an illness. I suppose I thought that if I knew what the problem was, I could solve it. He prescribed me the new wonder drug, Prozac and told me that it would take four to six weeks before I would really notice any clinical benefits. I had never been treated with anti-depressants before but I had heard of *the happy pill* that the American pharmaceutical companies were claiming to be miraculous. I accepted that I had a mental illness: to me that was obvious. I wanted to feel truly happy again and I wanted to feel well so I was willing to follow medical advice. I also wanted to understand why I was ill.

Why me? Not in a, "Life's not fair, why does it have to be me?" way but in a, "If I can understand it, I can cope with it" way. If I know what I have to deal with, no matter how afraid I may be, I can face it. It was not easy for me to find helpful information. There was no whiz bang Wikipedia to provide me with some limited, evidence-based information, nor was I a student who had access to medical journals. My doctor treated me respectfully and assured me that I was "the

sanest person" he knew and that my "problem is you think too much".
Possibly so. He may have known a lot of insane people and people
who thought very little. It is all comparative. However, I wanted to
understand so I persevered in the best way I knew how.

I read about bipolar disorder, sometimes still referred to as
manic-depression in a psychology text book and learnt about
neuro-transmitters and serotonin. I read other shorter texts on
speculated theories for the development of the mood disorder,
including Andreasen's [4] *The broken brain: The biological revolution
in psychiatry,* and was left feeling under-informed, disconsolate and
literally broken. Simply defective and under-developed: not whole.

Stillborn (1994). Watercolour and ink, 27 x 19.5 cm

The puzzle pieces were incompatible and the then current descriptions of bipolar disorder did not adequately describe all of my symptoms. Quite often my symptoms were not described at all, or appeared to be described in convenient isolated boxes that did not blur. I discussed these matters with Jill because I trusted her, because she was highly intelligent and because she did not diminish my experiences in an effort to comfort me. Her acceptance and careful consideration of all the facts simultaneously communicated faith in my ability to manage my illness, and supported my effort to take one giant step away from myself to objectively assess my situation. She selflessly offered her energy, her honesty, and her insightful perceptions. Jill had the ability to identify an obscure, faintly glowing ember and the fortitude to encourage the ember to glow more brightly.

Fluoxetine (Prozac) is one of Eli Lilly's best-selling anti-depressants, is endorsed by the World Health Organisation as an essential medicine for primary health, and is commonly used in the medical treatment of a wide range of psychological disorders, including: depression, major depressive disorder (MDD) and obsessive compulsive disorder (OCD) in children and adults, trichotillomania, premenstrual dysphoric disorder, panic disorder, bulimia nervosa, post-traumatic stress disorder (PTSD), autism spectrum disorder, and alcohol dependence.

It is in the selective serotonin reuptake inhibitors (SSRIs) class of medications which function by increasing the number of serotonin, the monoamine neurotransmitters (chemical messengers), believed to be necessary for a sense of wellbeing. Serotonin helps to regulate appetite, mood and sleep, and contributes to cognitive functioning in learning and memory[5]. According to the helpful pharmaceutical pamphlet provided with the medication, fluoxetine helps to *maintain mental balance.* It did not help me.

Help (1995). Ink doodle on printer paper, 29 x 21 cm

My depression worsened. I dragged myself through my days at work, summoning up a cheerful countenance and energy for my students only to crumple in a heap when I returned home. There were nights when I could not feed myself because I found it impossible to hold my head up and my hand did not have the energy to raise my fork to my mouth. If Adrian had not fed me, I would not have bothered eating. I felt like living required manoeuvring my way through thick, black oil whilst pushing against an enormous, invisible, personal menhir. I wanted to die. I could not stop thinking about death. I constantly visualised my own death to the point of being terrified by my own compulsion. I felt drawn to sharp knives. I forced myself to give up driving because I felt compelled to take off my seatbelt, hit top speed and slam myself into a power pole.

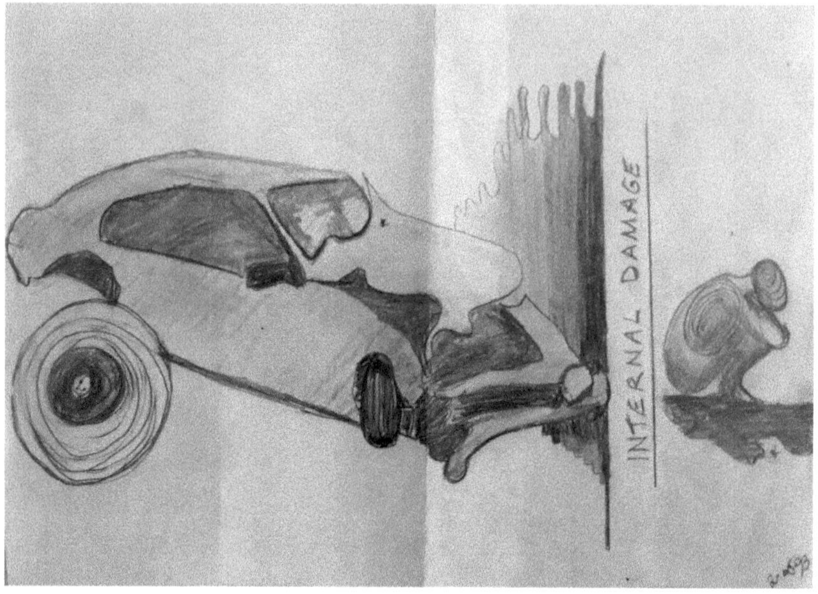

Internal Damage (1993) Pencil on A4 printer paper.

I was convinced that Adrian and David would lead better and happier lives without me. I recall watching David playing happily in his sandpit in our garden. I could feel nothing. I was aware that I told myself that he was so young that he would not remember me therefore it would not damage him if I died. I felt so messed up that one particular day I felt so ill that I spent the day in bed. I recall that my old school friend was visiting and that she was playing with David. Suddenly, I was convinced that I was dying, that I was crazy because I could see threatening geometric patterns around my head and I was aware that it was impossible despite the fact that they were clearly real. The only way I could make them disappear was by shouting at them to *GO AWAY!* They disappeared but my fear that I was crazy and that I would die did not leave me until I had made my friend promise me that she would look after Adrian and David.

No one told me that people with bipolar disorder can suffer from hallucinations.

I do not remember if I told anyone who loved me that I wanted to kill myself. I suppose I had tried in the past and my mother had not believed me. I also knew that it would hurt Adrian and Jill to hear such thoughts so I told my doctor. He believed me and prescribed a new medication for me which he assured me would help and rang me every night to check on my mental state. Lithium.

Wow: I had truly entered the stereotypical world that is reserved for *manic depressives*. Kassin's [6] glossary definition for bipolar disorder describes it as,

> "A rare mood disorder characterized by wild fluctuations from mania (i.e., euphoric, over-active state) to depression (a state of hopelessness and apathy)." (p. 753)

Descriptions of the manic phases sound attractive, appealing: even desirable. There is no doubt that some of my highs have been filled with uninhibited creativity, marvellous ideas, gregarious and entertaining behaviour, and boundless energy. I gave plenty of people the impression that I was a party girl, capable of being fun and possibly even wild. Those types of beautiful, euphoric highs when everything is magical, possible, probable, ethereal, scintillating and alive were exceedingly rare and short-lived. I doubt that if one were to sum the months of my life's worth of manic moments that they would amount to a year. However, the years of darkness, torment, hopelessness, shame, loss of sense of self and pain that is associated with my chronic, deep, dangerous depression would amount to decades.

Kassin paints a picture of gifted individuals, in particular famous writers, musicians, artists and poets who had bipolar disorder; warning students that whilst the manic state can promote creativity it can also be uncontrollable, disabling, and dangerous, leading to an inevitable emotional and physical crash, and sometimes suicide. His description of extreme, either/or mood states, highlighted with the well-known and much-loved stars of Loony Land (e.g., Vincent Van Gogh, Sylvia Plath, Handel, Virginia Woolf, and Schumann) is not inaccurate or misleading. It is incomplete. If he had added

Stephen Fry to the list, I would probably have slashed my wrists in a gesture of inferiority. How does one possibly live up to the social expectation attached to this psychiatric label: being brilliant, unbearably depressed, outrageously and notoriously mad, and successful? Furthermore, according to the research at that time, my illness should have had a strong genetic link.

Nevertheless, I had entered a world in which I could not escape stereotyping and stigma: much of it emanating from the medical world's limited research and understanding of the disorder and to some extent, the media's romanticised and sensationalised representation of mental illness. My efforts to learn more about my illness were limited to my original photocopy of the DSM's description of bipolar disorder[8], Andreasen's book, and a psychology text book. The psychology text confused me in the sense that I also identified with many of the symptoms associated with schizophrenia, both positive and negative symptoms. My lab rat/lab researcher mind was somewhat concerned about the hallucinations I was secretly aware of. Had I known in 1994 what I learnt in 2004 (i.e., hallucinations are not limited to visual or aural experiences but may also involve smelling, feeling or tasting something that does not exist) I would have been even more concerned.

What did I know about my illness? It is difficult to separate my understanding of the then current medical knowledge that I had access to and my own experience of my illness. I struggled to absorb and accept the fact that I had a life long illness that was difficult to treat. I had to accept that fact so I read about it, I attempted to talk about it, and I drew and painted it. My art works continued to provide solace and self-understanding through emotional expression but they also concerned me because my use of symbolism and style appeared to be in a similar vein to creative expressions by artists who suffer from schizophrenia.

I formed the impression that the term *mental illness,* when applied to an individual, was the Western World's term for *harijan*: an untouchable. Australian politicians call us *leaners*. It amazes me that so many educated people, privileged people, ordinary privileged people blessed with good health that allows them to grasp opportunities that facilitate their potential fulfilment assume that they righteously deserve what they have and that those who do not have the same living standards deserve their place in society because they did not try. The same people often assume that mental illness is different from having asthma or fibromyalgia: that individuals with mental illness cannot learn to manage their illness and that they have nothing useful to offer society. Those same people often assume that mental illness will not happen to them.

When my doctor informed me of my diagnosis, he also informed me that I was eligible for the disability pension. It had not occurred to me that I was disabled. Why would I be considered disabled when I was working professionally and full-time? In fact, I was meeting all of my deadlines ahead of time, returning marked work to my students within one week of receipt, helping to write work programs, working within departments that I had not originally trained in, and I was involved in extra-curricular activities.

I was actually contributing more than many of my colleagues, working harder and proving to be at least as competent. Properly medicated, I could reach my professional potential without having to regularly burn up all my energy reserves and not suffer from anxiety. Theoretically, a diagnosis should have made it easier for me to be a professional. I should have been able to stop hiding my diagnosis: it is such wasted energy. It was not the right time to *come out*. It still isn't.

I knew that people did not want to know about my mental illness. They were afraid of it. Were they scared of catching it: being touched by it? People are scared of the dark, of death, of what they cannot see, and of the unknown. They are embarrassed by it. Perhaps they feel shamed by it. My mother tried to tell me that bipolar disorder was on a continuum and that I was on the lower end of the continuum. She may have told herself that to help her cope with the label, just like she told me that I was not chronically depressed. Banging my head against an impenetrable brick wall. Screaming into the wind. How much did I have to continue to hide? How much did I have to reveal to convince her? It is a very fine line one has to walk. Falling either side of the line is damaging.

Virtual Alice II (1998).
Pastels on water colour paper, 35 x 25.2 cm

I knew bipolar disorder affects only 1% of the population: it still does[7]. I knew lithium was the recommended mood-stabilizing drug for the treatment of bipolar disorder and has been since the mid-1970s because research often suggests that lithium treatment is associated with lower incidents of suicide by preventing manic episodes.[8,9,10,11,12,13] Scientists have many theories regarding why some patients with bipolar disorder demonstrate a positive prophylactic response. According to research, it works for approximately 50% of patients[14,12] and even that researched percentage is dubious when one closely scrutinizes the experimental designs and the pharmaceutical companies that fund the research[8,15,16,17].

My extensive study of lithium's efficacy and side effects found that lithium research since Cade's 1949 published report[18] is contaminated by methodologically unreliable research trials (involving inconsistent dosage and combination treatments, and small populations of unrepresentative participants) conducted by pharmaceutical advisory panellists; misreported results of lithium treatment; and emotively argued with spurious "scientific evidence".

Malhi, Tanious, Das and Berk[19], and Pyle and Mitchell[20] describe lithium as the "gold standard" mood stabilising treatment for bipolar disorders. Indeed, Malhi, et al. describe lithium as a "magical element", particularly with respect to its claimed "unique anti-suicidal action … which remain an enigma" and simultaneously argue that lithium therapy practice must be founded on an established "… understanding of its clinical science" (p. 205). Their arguments for the continued use of lithium treatment are liberally supported with potential beneficial treatment effects preceded with words like "may, perhaps", and "suggest".

Bourgeois[21] lists its many beneficial effects including its neurodegeneration prophylactic capacity "… with a demonstrated positive action on neurogenesis in animals" (p. S93). Similarly, Shelton (MD, Chief, Adult Psychiatry Division, Vanderbilt University School of Medicine) described lithium as "a wonderful treatment"[22]. Such use of overtly subjective and persuasive language always directs me to reading the funding and declaration of interest sections of reports. No surprises: researchers that espouse the "unique" and "unequalled" benefits of lithium and warn of the "danger of [lithium] becoming obsolete" despite lithium's "60 years of clinical experience"[19] have received research support from Eli Lilly, AstraZeneca, Pfizer, Servier, and Wyeth, to name just a few of the pharmaceutical benefactors. The researchers also speak for, deliver lectures for, or serve on advisory boards for these pharmaceutical companies.

When one starts to cross-reference the "extensive studies of lithium" one soon discovers that the studies frequently rely on literary reviews stretching over the past 60 years, offering the same data from poorly designed, misreported trials and still fail to demonstrate an understanding, or provide a scientifically valid explanation of its action mechanism[23,21]. In summary, they have not shown how it works because they have not shown that it works.

Baldessarini, Tondo, Davis, Pompili, Goodwin and Hennen's (2006) meta-analytic review of long-term lithium treatment and suicide rates was evidently designed to find lithium effective in decreasing the risk of suicide. Despite the researchers outlining the extensive limitations to their studies' findings (i.e., inaccurate definitions of exposure times and participant numbers continuing to be at risk for extended time periods, inaccurate incidental suicide attempts reporting, inaccurate reporting of non-lithium treatments, over-representation of lithium-tolerant and lithium-responsive patients, exaggeration of lithium benefits that are not reflected in complex bipolar patients who are typically at high risk of suicide, and inadequate clinical information to provide analysis of the trial's data) Baldessarini, et al. reported positive results in the randomised control studies, the open studies, and the comparative lithium and non-lithium treated patient studies.

They concluded that their research "… findings provided strong support" for long-term lithium treatment to reduce suicide risk and the reduction of suicidal lethality in patients with bipolar disorder and major affective disorders (p. 636). Given the deficient and unethical research methodology and reporting, and the obvious bias I would posit that one could compare people who consume chocolate and find similar outcomes with possibly less dangerous consequences.

Mahli, et al. (2012) refer to Baldessarini, et al's (2006) research in their discussion of lithium's additional characteristics: namely "… the major benefit of long-term therapy is its demonstrated ability to reduce the risk of suicide/suicidal behaviour "(p. 199). Mahli, et al. make no reference to Baldessarini, et al's inadequate and unethical research practices. Whilst Malhi, et al. emphasise the importance of understanding lithium's science and the scientific practice of lithium therapy, Malhi, et al. clearly do not understand the purpose and importance of ethical and scientific research. They are more concerned with the plight of lithium's future - "… it is in danger of becoming obsolete" (p. 192) and its reputation that has been apparently tarnished with "… exaggerated fears surrounding lithium toxicity, acute and long-term tolerability and the encumbrance of life-long plasma monitoring" (p. 192) than they are with the patients who need safe and effective treatment for a life-long illness.

Malhi et al.'s claim that non-lithium treated patients are at a six times greater risk of suicide, based on Baldessarini, et al.'s rigged research findings is contemptible for a number of reasons. Firstly, the statement is founded on flawed data. For example, therapy efficacy trials for acute mania therapy have usually been concluded in 21 – 28 day randomised, placebo-controlled, parallel group, monotherapy trials in hospital-admitted patients who are not diagnosed with psychiatric or medical comorbidity, and are able to consent to the trial [24]. Secondly, non-lithium treated patients are generally not treated with lithium because lithium does not effectively treat their illness. Exclusion of comorbid and acutely ill patients, and non-responders to lithium, in addition to excessive drop-out rates unequivocally renders such study results ungeneralisable [14,16,24,17].

Yet published researchers frequently refer to lithium as the "first-line treatment" and "gold standard treatment" for acute mania, citing its 60 plus years of clinical research with the implication that lithium's veteran smoke and mirrors performance on the pharmaceutical stage (*now you see the participants – now you don't*) is the same as demonstrated evidence-based practice and clinical efficacy[25,26]. It's not.

Chou[8] aptly argued that lithium and anti-convulsant therapy have been preferred treatments for acute mania founded on the long historical use of the medications in lieu of comparative efficacy trials. Chou outlines the particularly complex difficulties associated with attempting to treat treatment-resistant bipolar disorder: an extremely common phenomenon. Treatment requires identification of the treatment phase, followed by best evidence-based therapy for mania, depression, or mixed episodes. Any one phase usually requires a combination of treatments – reflecting treatment resistance in the majority of patients, and is further complicated by a lack of standardised combination doses attributed to no evidence-based rationale for the combination of treatments that share no common action mechanism[8]. Furthermore, choice of treatment is complicated by patient comorbidity, history of episodes and history of treatment. [8,14,16,19,28,12]

According to Cookson,[14] lithium's delayed effectiveness (two to eight weeks to become fully effective) in treating mania limits its usefulness in the treatment of acute mania, and poses a risk for monotherapy excepting mildest cases. Lithium treatment has been demonstrated to be largely ineffective for patients with schizoaffective or mixed forms, destructive-paranoid mania, dysphoric mania, and rapid cycling. Patients who have previously suffered in excess of two mood episodes generally experience less benefit from lithium treatment than other patients; whilst patients who have experienced more than 10 episodes have been associated with a minimal probability of lithium response.[8,14,16,27,19,28,22,12]

Bourgeois [21] maintains that polypharmaceutical treatment courses before lithium treatment, particularly antidepressants, leads to lithium resistance. Furthermore, researchers have reported that lithium treatment provided for a shorter duration than two years may be harmful, if not unbeneficial to patients; therefore, some researchers[21] recommend long-term lithium therapy. It is reported that predictors of a positive response to lithium treatment include: patients with early onset; a familial history of the illness, a classical presentation of the disorder characterised by episodes of acute mania or mixed episodes, and major depression, lithium treatment early in the disorder's course, and an advantageous previous response to lithium treatment. [14,16,19,12]

Consider these facts: (a) treatment resistant bipolar disorder is extremely common, (b) any one treatment phase necessitates combination treatments, (c) diagnosis of bipolar disorder takes, on average, eight years from a patient's first remembered mood episode, (d) 25% of the aforementioned patients are originally misdiagnosed and ineffectively treated, (e) comorbidity is common in bipolar disorder patients, (f) on average, patients with bipolar disorder suffer from depression 33% of the time and more than 60% of patients experience at least four mood episodes annually, (g) treatment resistant depression and commonly experienced sub-syndromal depressive symptoms are extremely difficult to treat, and, (h) suicide risk is heightened during depressive phases.[29,8,14,30,31,32,33,34,35]

One wonders why lithium would be recommended as the safest, most effective, first-line treatment for a typically complex, difficult to diagnose psychological illness given that the capacity for lithium to effectively treat bipolar disorder is limited to a very narrow sector of its target population and inappropriate treatment with lithium is potentially dangerous.[8,14,16,27,19,28,32,12,35] Having critically studied these reports, amongst many, two pertinent questions repeatedly formed: (a) how many general practitioners, nurses, psychologists, psychiatrists, specialists and patients read these reports, and (b) how well do they understand them?

Furthermore, if they are specialists and they do critically read the reports independent from pharmaceutical funding influence why does the *Diagnostic and statistical manual of mental disorders: DSM-IV-TR* [7] recommend lithium as the "best choice as it is the only one which has been shown to be effective for all three phases of treatment for both manic and depressive episodes" (p. 6)? Given that Severus and Bauer[37] acknowledge lithium-induced nephropathy (kidney disease) as one of the dangerous side effects associated with long-term lithium treatment; why would they introduce their report with "For the last few decades lithium has been the most effective psychopharmacological drug in the long-term treatment of patients with recurrent unipolar and bipolar affective illness"? Similarly, who could challenge the DSM's[7] recommendation that lithium be the first-choice mood stabiliser with its compelling argument that "it has the longest track record"?

All phases of treatment? Despite Grunze's[16] recommendation that lithium be considered an "essential ... cornerstone of differentiated treatment" of bipolar disorder, he does warn that there is no methodologically acceptable study that demonstrates lithium's efficacy in the treatment of bipolar depression. Whilst individuals with bipolar disorder experience depression more frequently than mania there are very few studies of bipolar depression treatment and limited efficacy of the treatments that are currently recommended.[37,38,10,32,33]

Current research has found that the depressive phase of bipolar disorder is associated with the most impairment.[38,39,32,33,20] According to Judd, et al.'s natural history study of bipolar 1 disorder, the weekly symptomatic structure of the disorder is predominantly depressive instead of manic.[39]

Curran and Ravindran's [41] literary review of lithium purported to offer more current research findings on the efficacy of lithium in the treatment of all three phases. However, their effort to defend the usefulness of lithium was based on the same old experiments; there were no new designs focused on uncombined pharmacotherapy trials, resulting in limited literature and trials to base "new findings" on lithium treatment of bipolar depression.

Despite not finding any further evidence to recommend lithium as a monotherapy for bipolar depression, and outlining the problems associated with lithium's delayed anti-depressant effect (six to eight weeks) and potential overdose lethality, Curran and Ravindran reported, "Nevertheless, lithium remains a first-line agent for bipolar depression in several guidelines" (p. 1083).[41] Why? Quetiapine and a combination of fluoxetine and olanzapine are the only treatments for bipolar depression approved by the Food and Drug Administration. [8,10]

Marangell et al.'s [42] study of pharmacological impact on suicide attempts and completed suicides in patients with bipolar disorder found no relationship between lithium use, carbamazepine, lamotrigine, valproate (anticonvulsant), and atypical antipsychotic therapy and suicide attempts or suicide completions. Furthermore, the study's data did not demonstrate a suicide prophylactic effect of lithium.[37] Young and Hammond [43] purport that lithium's prophylactic efficacy could be attributed to the reduction of patients' manic relapses. Possibly a dubious hypothesis given that suicide risk is markedly raised throughout depressive episodes and that most suicides and suicide attempts occur during depressive episodes. [7,35] It pays to question Mahli's [19] unsupported claim that lithium possesses a "unique anti-suicidal action … (which) remains an enigma."

Whilst lithium has the reputation of being the first-line treatment for acute mania it is also interesting to note the way in which it is trialled and reported. For example, Storosum, et al. [26]

studied lithium's efficacy in short-term treatment of moderate to severe manic episodes. They acknowledged that the trial had many limitations, including over-estimation of the short-term effect of lithium (21 days), the exclusion of comorbid patients and those patients experiencing hypomanic episodes, and a generally high total drop-out rate (14-63% of the lithium-treated groups). They did not mention in the limitations that concomitant psychiatric medication was used throughout the trial (e.g., the administration of sleeping medication) and that 30% of the lithium-treated group was still using it at the end of the 3-week trial.[26]

How can these results be generalised to the greater population of patients suffering from bipolar disorder related mania? With the simple word *"Nevertheless ..."* (p. 797). "The results indicate that lithium is an effective drug in the treatment of moderate to severe manic episode." [26] Surely this conclusion, based on a minority of clients with bipolar disorder, which medical professionals accept and which other researchers use in their meta-analyses to apply to an entire population of patients with bipolar disorder should require more accuracy.

Recent and possibly more stringent research indicated that lithium should not be considered a first-line treatment for acute mania. Cipriani et al's [44] multiple-treatments meta-analytical study of comparative efficacy and tolerability of antimanic medications in acute mania demonstrated that antipsychotic drugs, such as risperidone, olanzapine and quetiapine, are considerably more effective than lithium in the treatment of acute mania. Risperidone and Olanzapine demonstrated superior efficacy and tolerability to lithium and valproate. Similarly, Yildiz, Vieta, Leucht, and Baldessarini's[45] meta-analysis of randomised, controlled trials examining the efficacy of antimanic drugs found antipsychotic medications like risperidone and haloperidol to have faster action, better efficacy and superior tolerability than lithium, valproate, and carbamazepine.

Yildiz, et al.[45] and Poolsup, Li Wan Po, and de Oliveira[46] highlighted the difficulty and limitations associated with selecting meta-analytic studies of efficacy therapies for mania that weren't affected by partiality toward recording positive trials, and failure or delays of reporting lack of separation of trialled treatment drug and placebo. Furthermore, if lithium is a highly effective antimanic treatment, why do so many studies report and recommend supplementary applications of high-level doses of benzodiazepines for sedation? [17,26,13]

One could be forgiven for arriving at the conclusion that the *real reasons* for failure to respond positively to the *magical* effectiveness of lithium lies with the patient. *Non-compliance* and *non-compliant patients*: they're a problem. Although some research reports have shown lithium efficacy in the prevention of manic relapse research has not demonstrated lithium's efficacy in preventing depressive relapse. [16,17,20]

Many patients receiving lithium treatment experience frequent and protracted depressive episodes. It is estimated that 20 – 50% of patients do not adhere to their lithium treatment.[20] That is, they are *non-compliant*. Rihmer and Gonda [12] emphasised criticism of the STEP-BD study's methodology because its data demonstrated that lithium has no suicide prophylactic effect. Rihmer and Gonda argue that the study lacked control over non-compliance in the later weeks prior to the suicide event and that non-compliance could explain patient relapse and suicide in comparison with those patients who remained compliant and non-suicidal. This argument begs the question: why did the patients cease lithium treatment if it was so effective?

Non-compliance is frequently discussed in journal articles dedicated to the study of bipolar disorder. Understandably so: it is a problem. Lithium-advocating researchers often attribute non-compliance to unhealthy lifestyles (e.g., substance abuse), interpersonal conflict, stigma, ignorance regarding the disorder, weight gain in women, and patient denial that they have the illness[19,12]. Poor adherence has also been attributed to "popular views of its alleged toxicity or lack of efficacy"[13]. Commonly reported reasons for ceasing lithium treatment include: weight gain, exacerbated psoriasis, severe acne, alopecia (hair loss), tremor, involuntary twitching, subjective cognitive impairment(dysphoria), impaired handwriting, general fatigue, mental confusion, headache, nausea, vomiting, fever, mild delirium, thirst, polyuria (excessive urine production), and diarrhoea.[16,27,19,17,13] Cogwheel rigidity is experienced by some patients on mono-lithium treatment.[14]

The combination of lithium with antipsychotic drugs, which is recommended for a more rapid response in patients suffering from acute mania, can increase extrapyramidal (Parkinsonian) side-effects.[14,24] Combined high level doses of lithium and antipsychotic drugs have been connected with severe neurological manifestations including diminished consciousness and irreversible brain impairment.[14] Current research points to a direct relationship between lithium treated patients experiencing serious adverse side effects, severe adverse side effects and treatment discontinuation.[47]

"… alleged toxicity or lack of efficacy" requires examination.[13] Recent research[36] demonstrates that long-term lithium therapy is correlated with lithium-induced kidney disease, an elevated risk for mortality and end stage kidney disease. Diabetes insipidus is the commonest kidney complication associated with lithium treatment, and whilst reversible through lithium withdrawal during early treatment can become irreversible because of structural damage.[19,48,43]

It is impossible to ensure prevention of lithium-induced diabetes so Young and Hammond[43] recommend using the lowest therapeutic application of lithium. Lithium alters thyroid and parathyroid gland operating: 8-19% of lithium-treated patients have clinically significant hypothyroidism compared with 0.5-1% of the general population.[19,10] Hypothyroidism increases the probability of developing rapid cycling and depression.[19] The optimum therapeutic level of lithium has not been established and it appears that there is significant disparity between published trial findings and clinical practice.[14,43]

The prevention of lithium toxicity is vital because it causes encephalopathy (brain function degeneration) and neurological impairment but lithium toxicity strength is not related to lithium serum levels: lithium toxicity can result from serum levels within the normal therapeutic range.[14,17,43] Therefore, lithium toxicity is based on clinical observation of symptoms rather than blood levels.[14] Uncertainty remains regarding whether lithium treatment is neuroprotective or neurotic yet it is certain that lithium has an extremely limited therapeutic indication and safety margin.[23,49,17,25] Severe lithium overdoses can be lethal and may be intentionally used for suicide.[23,41]

Salgado, et al.[25] report that parathyroid, thyroid and renal toxicity associated with long-term lithium therapy frequently contribute to discontinuation of lithium treatment. Oswald, et al.[50] refer to lithium therapy to illustrate the danger of the medical profession's employment of a consensus system that is conservative and reluctant to depreciate treatments when current efficacy evidence demonstrates that the treatments are less powerful or negative. They warn that current evidence base guidelines such as the APA guidelines[51] are not reflecting current research and are undoubtedly inaccurate.

Despite well-documented reports of lithium's numerous harmful effects, historical and social determinants have established lithium as a first-choice treatment founded on fallacious evidence.[8,42,16,17,20] Whilst some researchers may regard common side effects like weight gain, fatigue, brain fog, and tremor to be medically less severe than other side effects, they potentially significantly impair normal functioning and quality of life for many patients who are limited in choice of treatments and suffer from an inadequately and often poorly treated illness.[17,25,52,43]

According to research my lithium treatment was doomed from the start yet according to some of the research it should have been successful. Two complications with the current research are: (a) it is inconsistent, and (b) health professionals do not access all of the necessary information pertaining to the client and the treatment.

Lithium as a monotherapy is considered risky because of its slow action except for treating mildest cases: my depression was severe.[14] I was suffering from serious suicidal ideation and debilitating depression to the extent that I had taken stress leave from work. In contrast, lithium treatment should have been appropriate for me because I did not have schizoaffective or mixed forms, destructive-paranoid mania, dysphoric mania, and rapid cycling.

Similar to the majority of individuals who suffer from bipolar disorder, my diagnosis had been delayed more than the average eight years from my first remembered mood episode: I would estimate at least 11 and more likely 16 years.[53,54] Considering that patients who have experienced more than 10 episodes have been associated with a minimal probability of lithium response and that I had experienced at least 10 episodes it was less than likely that I would be responsive to lithium therapy.[8,14,16,27,19,28,22,12] It has been established that polypharmaceutical treatment courses before lithium treatment, particularly antidepressants, leads to lithium resistance.[21] I had been treated with numerous antidepressants before being treated with lithium.

Lithium may have been ideal for me given that I had early onset, and a classical presentation of the disorder characterised by episodes of acute mania or mixed episodes, and major depression. In fact, my first mixed episode was not experienced until I was 42 years of age. However, I did not have a familial history of the illness, I did not receive lithium treatment early in the disorder's course, I had comorbidity (OCD), and I did not demonstrate a favourable previous response to lithium treatment.[14,16,19,12]

I gained enough weight to change from a small size 12 to 14 within a couple of weeks. Throughout the two years that I endured lithium treatment I felt nauseous, fatigued, constantly depressed and unable to enjoy activities that I could ordinarily find some pleasure in. My general affect was flattened, preventing me from self-manifesting any energy that up until treatment allowed me to function. My world was dark grey. I constantly suffered from headaches and I found that I suffered from confusion and an inability to learn and recall new things quickly. My OCD was affecting much of my daily life; probably because I was not able to use my cognitive skills to regulate my mood as well as I had before treatment. Consequently, my self-esteem plummeted as I gathered more evidence for why I was broken and stupid. In short, I found lithium treatment toxic and destructive. It did not stabilise my mood unless one is aiming for chronic depression. I wanted to feel better. Bipolar disorder is a burden.

Alone (1998) Water colour.

A woman diagnosed with bipolar disorder at 25 years of age is estimated to lose 12 years of regular health, 14 years of productive functioning and nine years of her life.[35] I wanted to have faith in the medical profession and I wanted to be part of society. Therefore, I remained compliant.

Current research demonstrates that treatment resistant depression and commonly experienced sub-syndromal depressive symptoms are extremely difficult to treat, and, suicide risk is heightened during depressive phases.[8,14,31,55,32] My subjective experience of bipolar disorder has involved a constant struggle: I am a naturally optimistic person who has to consciously fight extremely oppressive sub-syndromal depressive symptoms most days of my life. I have not discovered a medication that has been able to cure that. I have to rely on my own superpowers – that is, my will to survive and be happy. Lithium suffocated those superpowers.

Depression is all pervasive and when it is severe it is inescapable. Internal pain becomes external and very difficult to mask. I know that I had set very high standards for myself to prepare an ideal 1996 Christmas for my family. I always look forward to Christmas because it's a magnificent celebration of family and love. I can actually smell Christmas well before it arrives: most often around October or November. I love putting up the Christmas tree, finding presents that I know will demonstrate my love and provide pleasure to the recipients. I also spend a lot of time preparing meals, cleaning, and becoming stressed because of over-stimulation and high expectations which are often not quite met.

I have learnt to control the stress in recent years but during my 20s, 30s and very early 40s Christmas was a very risky time for me. The sudden loneliness and lack of stimulation that followed Christmas (mostly due to isolation from family and friends who lived far away) was equivalent to a crash after a high. I did not experience mania during Christmas but I did experience a combination of joy and stress followed by loss that I often found unbearable.

1996 Christmas was different for a number of reasons. I was suffering from chronic stress which could be attributed to teaching full-time, building a house, moving, being the mother of a three-year-old, and feeling isolated from family members. I was feeling acute difference which had been exacerbated by disclosing my illness to work colleagues under the illusion that knowledge and respect should nullify stigma. I was feeling chronically ill because of treatment, and feeling severely depressed because of ineffective treatment. I had no reserves in my resilience bank to protect me from the straw that would break my back. Unkind words were enough to push me over the edge.

A much-loved individual's challenging of my perception of reality and understanding of emotions because of my illness was perceived as an insurmountable obstacle and my inner mantra of worthlessness and unlovability became deafening. If that person could not see me for who I was then there was no point living. I swallowed a near-full bottle of lithium. It was not a cry for help or an act of spite. I simply wanted to stop fighting and I wanted to stop feeling pain.

I do not want to describe all of the details surrounding my attempt to commit suicide. It is deeply personal and unnecessary. It is difficult for me to accurately recall details and large chunks of my life that have been affected by acute depression. The slow, floating feeling as I began to lose a sense of my surrounding was not particularly disturbing. I didn't care. My husband's efforts to persuade me to vomit appeared serious and I had no desire to distress him so I cooperated. It tasted disgusting and I felt significantly ill, as though I had been poisoned, for weeks. I do remember ringing my doctor and telling him that I had done "a stupid thing." I stopped taking lithium. It was the only time that I attempted to commit suicide. My experience is not consistent with research that espouses the magical anti-suicidal properties of lithium.

Paint it black (1996). Water colour pencil, 36 x 25 cm

Chapter **10**

Paint it Black

Hell is empty and all the devils are here.

Shakespeare[1] *The Tempest*

Ooh, a storm is threatenin' my very life today
If I don't get some shelter ooh yeah,
I'm gonna fade away.
  The Rolling Stones[2] Gimme Shelter, *Hot Rocks 1964 - 1971*

I see a red door and I want it painted black
No colours anymore, I want them to turn black …
I look inside myself and see my heart is black
I see my red door and I must have it painted black
Maybe then I'll fade away and not have to face the facts
It's not easy facing up when your whole world is black.
  The Rolling Stones[3] Paint it Black, *Hot Rocks 1964 - 1971*

And I'm not gonna take this all lying down
"Cause once I get started I go to town
"Cause I'm not like everybody else.
  The Kinks[4] I'm not like everybody else, *Kinks Greatest Hits.*

Current research indicates that the lifetime suicide risk in individuals with bipolar disorder ranges from 8 – 20%, almost 10 - 20 fold more than that of the general population.[5,6,7,8] Pompili, et al.[9], have reported a suicide risk for people with bipolar disorder at 20-30 times that of

134

the general population. It is estimated that between 25% and 56% of individuals with bipolar disorder attempt suicide: those who survive often suffer from consequential medical complications and typically shorter life spans.[5,7] More than half of patients with bipolar disorder who commit suicide have been found to have been untreated prior to their deaths.[9]

The World Health Organization's study of the global burden of disease found mental and behavioural disorders accounted for 12%, and that bipolar disorder ranked as the 7th most burdensome of all investigated medical disorders in terms of mortality or disability. Murray, et al.'s[11] global burden of disease study measured total years of life lost in addition to years existed with disability (DALYs) and found a significant increase in global burden of mental illness since 1990 (5.7% to 7.4%). Both studies emphasised the fact that mental health is essential to the general well-being of countries, societies, and individuals, and that the disproportionately high burden associated with human suffering, disability and economic burden needs to be addressed with government mental health policy that focuses on community-based care.

Bipolar disorder is difficult to diagnose and consequently is frequently under-diagnosed and misdiagnosed with serious deleterious clinical and economic results.[12,13,14] It has been reported that approximately 69% of individuals diagnosed with bipolar disorder were originally misdiagnosed. [15] Misdiagnosis can lead to higher treatment costs, loss of employment or work days, and reduced productivity of individuals with bipolar disorder.[13] Misdiagnosis, particularly when the illness generally manifests during adolescence and remains inappropriately treated for eight to 10 years, results in the disruption of lives that potentially negatively impacts interpersonal skills development, relationships, education, and career/earning potential.[16,12,13,14]

Bipolar disorder is the sixth principal cause of global medical disability in people aged 15 to 44 years, and is rated more disabling than serious chronic conditions, such as diabetes, asthma, osteoarthritis and human immunodeficiency virus infection.[17,12] People with bipolar disorder have reported greater difficulty attaining and keeping employment: unemployment rates of approximately 60% exist even within tertiary-educated patients.[12,14] They further reported great difficulty maintaining relationships, particularly with family members and friends.[16,18,12] Inadequate and incorrect pharmacological treatment can lead to individuals experiencing more and longer recurrences of mood episodes resulting in serious negative effects on functioning, medical costs, and may lead to iatrogenic harm and increased risk of suicide.[16,18,14]

Current research has shown that antidepressant (in particular, tricyclic) treatment, of bipolar disorder is associated with the experience of *switch*: the cause of mania or mixed mood episodes (simultaneous depression and mania), and rapid cycling.[19,20,21,18,22] This fact is sobering given that mixed episodes are difficult to treat and are associated with a greater suicide risk.[23,24,25]

Medical as well as psychiatric comorbidity is common in patients with bipolar illness and the associated functional disability is commensurate with that of numerous chronic medical illnesses.[12] Individuals with bipolar disorder are eight times more likely to suffer from obsessive-compulsive disorder and 26 times more likely to be diagnosed with panic disorder than people without a mood disorder in the general populace.[12] Bipolar disorder has also been associated with migraine and fibromyalgia.[12,26,27] Some research has also indicated that an increased number of bipolar disorder episodes is associated with the elevated risk of dementia development.[12] The approximated annual societal disease burden of bipolar disorder varies between $10 billion and $45 billion.[28,12]

Mental disorders represent 22% of Australia's DALYs: a demonstration that a significant proportion of the population affected by early onset mental illness are disabled by illnesses that require early intervention and support, and that a greater effort needs to be made to develop preventative measures and effective treatment.[29,30]

Pompili, et al.[9] list suicide, cancer, and cardiovascular disease as the three most common causes of death in people with bipolar disorder. This list is not surprising when one considers that the illness is under-treated; treated with medications containing properties that have the capacity to develop cancer and cardiovascular disease; and that the majority of individuals with bipolar disorder receive very limited and inadequate community/social support.[31,6,10]

The observation that rates of comorbidity involving anxiety disorders such as PTSD and substance abuse are high in patients with bipolar disorder is frequently reported.[23,33,34,15,7,35,30,10] Further studies should examine how well anxiety and PTSD is screened and treated in patients with bipolar disorder, and to what extent substance abuse can be explained by patient self-medicating because of ineffective medication, inadequate access to psycho-education/psychotherapy, and lack of social support.

Disappointingly, current research[7] continues to focus on impulsivity associated with mania in an attempt to understand and treat the neurobiological characteristics of suicide attempts and suicide in bipolar disorder. Predictably, such researchers[5,36] refer to lithium's unique suicide prophylactic effect because of its "strong anti-aggressive properties in humans and anti-impulsivity properties".[7] Their focus seems to be misdirected when there is sufficient evidence to suggest that most suicides are attempted and completed during depressive phases.[23,25]

Current research has established the predominant suicide risk factors are hopelessness and prior suicide attempt. The major risk determinants for non-lethal suicidal behaviour included early onset of the disorder, physical and sexual abuse especially during childhood, family history of suicide, severity of depressive symptoms, intensifying severity of mood episodes, rapid cycling, the existence of mixed mood states, comorbid Axis I disorders, alcohol and substance abuse.[24,25]

Hopelessness is the key word. Research consensus is that hopelessness is a significant suicide predictor.[37,38,39,40,41] Beck, et al., (1990) propose that the magnitude of hopelessness demonstrated during one episode of depression is predictive of the level that presents in future depressive episodes. Furthermore, indicators of acute suicide risk include hopelessness and sleep disturbances, particularly nightmares.[40]

Whilst many journal articles are dedicated to the pharmacological treatment of suicidal behaviours and bipolar disorder, few seem to be concerned with the cause of acute suicidal risk in people with bipolar disorder (other than attributions that conveniently and offensively seem to point to flaws/weaknesses of character), and fewer provide useful, comprehensive treatment and prevention guides that do not focus on pharmacological solutions. However, Van Orden's *interpersonal theory of suicide*[40] is a glorious oasis in the literary desert of theories for suicide and provides sound advice for clinical care that prioritises psychotherapy, pharmacotherapy, and public campaigns that promote social connectedness.

The interpersonal theory of suicide holds that the most perilous type of suicidal desire is produced by hopelessness regarding the simultaneous existence of a sense of "thwarted belongingness and perceived burdensomeness" (Van Orden, et al., 2010, p. 575). That is, a sense of feeling no hope: that life never can and never will get better because you are a burden on every one you care about and a burden to society. They are better off without you. You feel unloved, unlovable and disconnected from everyone. No one can or will be able to help you.

I have read many partial theories for suicide (such as, the diathesis-stress model, the cognitive behavioural model, an escape from negative self-awareness, and attachment theory) but none of them reflected the complexity and chronicity involved in a life impacted by bipolar disorder that leads to suicide desire.[42,43,7,41] Attempting to conveniently attribute serious suicide behaviours and lethal suicide to *impulsivity* or *feeling trapped* must be considered naïve, lazy, ignorant, and seriously irresponsible. Research has shown that individuals who commit suicide demonstrate multiple risk factors, instead of an isolated, single risk factor.[40]

Eroglu et al.'s study of suicide in bipolar disorder revealed that suicide risk increases with increased illness duration and mood episodes: especially with increased occurrences of depressive episodes[5]. The disorder's chronic course and its potential damaging effects, functional impairment, and anhedonia and hopelessness associated with depressive episodes are significant factors regarding suicidal behaviours. Gitlin et al.'s study of bipolar disorder relapse and impairment showed that many patients with bipolar disorder experience poor results from commonly recommended aggressive maintenance pharmacotherapy[44]. The study group's relapse rate was high; most participants who relapsed suffered multiple episodes; the study group endured prolonged periods of time with affective symptoms; and participants who did not relapse often suffered from serious mood pathology.

Significantly, Gitlin, et al. found that poor psychosocial (e.g., family or social dysfunction, and occupational disruption) results reflected inferior syndromal course. Impaired psychosocial functioning, particularly occupational disruption, signified a shorter duration to relapse.[44] Eighty-two percent of Gitlin, et al.'s participants were either divorced or single, reflecting the relationship difficulties commonly reported by individuals with bipolar disorder. Depressive episodes were most powerfully associated with family and social dysfunction: the predictors of relapse; yet the study showed that more aggressive medical treatment is not associated with better outcome. Gitlin, et al.'s study was published 11 years ago but little has changed in understanding and treatment of the illness, or the damaging impact on the quality of lives led by individuals who have bipolar disorder. *NB: written 2016

The Bipolar Disorder (STEP-BD) Study[19] indicated that earlier onset bipolar illness is associated with higher rates of substance abuse and comorbid anxiety, increased recurrences, shorter euthymic (i.e., relatively symptom-free) periods, and increased probability of violence and suicide attempts. The findings signify a more severe illness course regarding comorbidity and chronicity, and that bipolar disorder characterised by depressive-onset is markedly associated with increased lifetime episodes of depression and experience more time with anxiety and depression throughout the year. The STEP-BD Study also found that recurrence is associated with the existence of enduring mood symptoms on recovery, indicating the importance of targeting residual mood symptoms during maintenance therapy to reduce mood episode recurrence.

Suicidal behaviour research findings clearly indicate that suicidal behaviour prevention in individuals with bipolar disorder should involve consideration of established risk determinants in assessment and intervention, particularly during decision-making regarding treatment designed to reduce suicide risk.[24,6,25,] Gitlin et al.'s study[44] suggested that poor family, social and work functioning are stressors that potentially contribute to mood episodes. Occupational disruption appeared to be the most significant psychosocial factor in signifying a shorter interval to relapse.[44] It is vital that research investigating possible pharmacological treatments and psychosocial interventions designed to increase individuals' quality of life, and reduce stress, depression, suicide risk and suicide behaviour in individuals with bipolar disorder continues.[5,24,6,25]

Many researchers have argued that it is vital to formulate an effective suicide risk assessment.[38,5,6,] Data from the bipolar disorder (STEP-BD) Study patient sample revealed that the first 1000 participants had above average education, above average unemployment, and below average income.[19] Only 59% of the patients surveyed reported that their pharmacotherapy treatment (such as, lithium, valproate, selective serotonin reuptake inhibitors, and lamotrigine) met "minimally adequate" mood stabilisation irrespective of bipolar I or II condition, rapid cycling, or comorbidity.[19] Furthermore, participants reported that common comorbid disorders (e.g., anxiety disorders, attention-deficit/hyperactivity disorder, and substance abuse disorders) tend to be inadequately treated.[19]

Bertolote, et al.'s study of psychiatric diagnoses and suicide indicates that suicide prevention strategies should extend the focus of identification and treatment of psychiatric illnesses like depression to include the identification and treatment of mental illnesses as a whole: this necessitates considering comorbidity[38]. Effective risk assessment and treatment effectiveness of mental illnesses demands increased specialist and community knowledge regarding risk situations and factors of psychosocial risk.[38]

Early diagnosis, early intervention and effective treatment, effective risk assessment and holistic management that involves an informed, integrated team approach (i.e., patient, family, health workers, community) are essential in the reduction of stress, stigma, depression and suicide behaviours, and to the enhancement of quality of life for people with bipolar disorder. [29,38,44,30,10]

Early and accurate diagnosis of bipolar disorder is notoriously difficult and can be explained by: the complex nature and presentation of the illness; its manifestation and course; a dearth of comprehensive, information regarding the prevention and treatment of the disorder provided by experts who are unfettered by the vested interests of pharmaceutical companies; and media representations of *manic depressives* and *bipolars* that direct and reinforce social ignorance and stigma.

The greatest difficulty concerning accurate diagnosis of bipolar disorder involves distinguishing bipolar from unipolar depression.[16,18,12,13] Other difficulties include: (a) patients may provide their doctors with insufficient or irregular history, especially when they are experiencing acute mood episodes, (b) patients may not disclose information pertaining to manic symptoms because of a lack of insight associated with mania, (c) patients may not report milder symptoms (e.g., decreased need for sleep or racing thoughts) because they do not regard these symptoms as unhealthy, (d) patients may tend to report depression and not mania because one feels unwell when one is depressed but may not necessarily feel unwell when manic, (e) patients may under-report symptoms of depression or mania because of stigma, (f) psychiatric comorbidity features can overlap and blur symptoms – especially anxiety, (g) substance abuse and addiction may be prominent on patient presentation and mask bipolar disorder, (h) some misdiagnosis may result from long time intervals between patient reports of mood episodes, preventing identification of a recurrent mood pattern, and (i) many patients experience recurrent episodes of depression for numerous years prior to their experiencing hypomania or mania, thereby delaying identification of bipolar disorder.[18,13,14]

From a patient's perspective, I would also argue that when one has experienced the illness from a very early age, before one has developed words to describe and identify such pathological moods and symptoms, that state of being becomes normal: part of who you are. When one sees other normal people coping with normal life one may assume that one should be able to cope but even if one were to ask for help, who would one ask and what would one report? In my experience, very few general practitioners have the specialist knowledge, time, or motivation to ask their patients the right questions.

Very few take the time to ask for further information about my family, my work, my studies, my life; nor do they ask my family members about me. A failure to do so, equates to a failure to collect information about how I function, or fail to function. A failure to encourage me to make appointments with them when I am well equates to a lack of healthy/unhealthy comparisons. A failure to ask me, "Do you have thoughts about killing yourself? Do you ever imagine killing yourself?" is a failure to provide best practice for someone who has bipolar disorder.

Furthermore, I have certainly experienced stigma from medical professionals. My frequent reports of ill health were too often regarded as hypochondria rather than valid reports which negatively impacted the course of chronic conditions (e.g., migraine, and fibromyalgia), and endangered my life (e.g., two years to diagnose an invasive thymic tumour). I was particularly sensitive about being perceived a hypochondriac and reluctant to report feeling unwell: I also learned not to trust health professionals until they earned my trust.

Chapter **11**

Senses Working Overtime

Dispute not with her: she is lunatic.

Shakespeare[1] Richard III

Roll on, deep and dark blue ocean, roll!
Ten thousand fleets sweep over thee in vain.
Man marks the earth with ruin;
His control stops with the shore.

Lord Byron[2] Childe Harold's Pilgrimage

For man, as for flower and beast and bird, the supreme triumph is to be most vividly, most perfectly alive.

D. H. Lawrence[3] Apocalypse

Man has no Body distinct from his Soul; for that called Body is a portion of Soul discerned by the five Senses, the chief inlets of Soul in this age.

William Blake[4] The Marriage of Heaven and Hell

And all the world is foot-ball shaped
It's just for me to kick in space
And I can see, hear, smell, touch, taste
And I've got one, two, three, four, five
    Senses working overtime
    Trying to take this all in
    I've got one, two, three, four, five
    Senses working overtime

143

Trying to taste the difference 'tween a lemon and a lime
Pain and pleasure, and the church bells softly chime
Hey, hey, night fights day
There's food for the thinkers
And the innocents can all live slowly
All live slowly …
XTC[5], Senses working overtime, *English Settlement.*

Between 1997 and 2004 I was treated with a multitude of combinations of Epilim (anti-convulsant treatment for mania), selective serotonin reuptake inhibitors (SSRIs antidepressants) used to increase levels of serotonin believed to affect impulsivity and mood swings, and intermittent use of benzodiazepines (anti-anxiety medications), such as Valium, when my anxiety levels felt unbearable and I could not sleep.[6] I cannot recall all of the different names of the anti-depressants I attempted to use (other than Aropax, Zoloft and Effexor) however, I do recall that 1997 to 2004 was a period characterised by chronic depression, high anxiety, prolonged sleeplessness interspersed with unusual daytime sleeping, high energy, impulsivity and risky behaviour exacerbated by stress and an overwhelming feeling of disconnectedness and the perception that I was a burden.

My hours were preoccupied by full-time teaching in a high-stress, special needs school, parenting and family relationships, attempting to solve why I had bipolar disorder, and trying to heal the constant psychological pain. I became addicted to shopping.

God, I loved shopping! It began with small items: biros, coloured pencils, good lead pencils. Then it became lipsticks. They heralded the slippery slope. I have examined this phase of my life very closely and in hindsight it is relatively easy to understand how it developed. There was a cycle of feelings, thoughts, actions, and feelings. I felt depressed, alone, disconnected and black. I wanted to feel better. I wanted to feel happy, special and alive.

Several happy childhood memories involved one-on-one moments with my mother and with my grandmother. Moments that involved their listening to my thoughts about anything, whilst shopping with them and feeling special. Outstanding moments involved my mother purchasing a small talcum powder just for me when it wasn't my birthday, and my grandmother purchasing some beautiful shoes that I had chosen for my fifteenth birthday. Those memories have photo-like clarity in my mind and magically conjure warm, safe, happy, special and *lovable* feelings. Feelings I associate with connectedness. Being alive for me necessitates a multitude of colours, textures, smells, sounds, and flavours: preferably all at once. One has to make a conscious effort to fight a black world and I found my antidote in painting, music and, when the opportunity presented itself or compelled me: shopping.

I was primarily attempting to regulate and soothe myself by physically altering myself and my environment. Preceding the moment, and within the moment I believed that changing my hair colour or style, or purchasing the perfect dress or shoes that ultimately expressed the *real me* would stop my pain. If I couldn't buy the object I had my heart set on, I would feel intense physical pain and my mind was utterly obsessed with needing the object and how I would have to convince my husband of how necessary it was.

The planned shopping experience was the highlight of the day, if not the week. It took preparation, a build-up of excitement involving heightened energy and optimism, an increased appreciation of light and colour, and an anticipation of happiness and completion. I favoured clothing shops and book shops that were aesthetically pleasing and where I had already formed friendly relationships with the shop workers. I would be guaranteed sensory stimulation, conversation, positive attention, and an escape from feeling isolated, and trapped in a bleak, black, and highly stressful existence. I could elongate the pleasure by leaving the unopened special shopping bags on a chair where I could see them.

The shopping cycle nearly always ended with self-loathing guilt for having spent money that we could ill afford. It was like a self-fulfilling prophecy that inevitably proved to me that I was selfish and a burden. True, I didn't purchase diamonds, or expensive cars and pianos but we simply didn't have extra money for personal luxuries and leisure. A mortgage, high interest, unsupported child care fees, extra-curricular activities for children, private health insurance, and relatively modest wages did not stretch to regular self-medicating through shopping. When I eventually needed expensive hospitalisation, medical treatments and surgery, the expenses were added on to my burdensome existence: more money spent on me, and whether I was worth it was dubious.

Changing from teaching secondary school to special needs education in 1999 gave me a brief opportunity to work in a less environmentally stimulating environment and to focus on more creative ways of providing education. I was able to work in small teams, with small classes and introduced drama, play and relaxation therapy to the students. This new environment, combined with initial positive responses to a new antidepressant therapy that was not accompanied with health warnings against pregnancy offered me the chance to fulfil my desire to have the second child I had been previously told I could never have. Conditions appeared to be ideal. Nothing is simple.

I was never emotionally stable on anti-depressant medications and never felt physically well when I was treated with them but I accepted my doctors' advice because they were the medical experts. Research has shown that an indicator of bipolar disorder is a patient's rapid response to antidepressant treatment followed by an abrupt weakened response.[7]

This bipolar disorder indicator revealed itself in a monotonous pattern of regularity within my medical history but was not adequately addressed until 2011. However, I did attempt to investigate my familial history regarding bipolar disorder because I did not want to knowingly risk the chance of genetically passing on the risk of bipolar disorder to my child. There was no familial history of bipolar disorder.

Adrian consented to a vasectomy reversal. Having carefully read the fine print on my medication leaflet I decided that there was not enough researched evidence to suggest that it was safe to conceive a child, be pregnant or breast feed whilst medicated. Research is lacking because it is unethical to conduct such research trials on mothers and unborn foetuses. Furthermore, I was a special needs teacher and well aware of the enduring deleterious neurological, biological and social impacts of chemical substances on developing foetuses and their families. I therefore made the decision to cease medication three months prior to attempting conception, with the view to taking medication immediately after the birth because I was aware of the severe post-natal depression I had suffered after having David. It was a calculated risk I was willing to take.

Surprisingly, I was quite psychologically stable throughout the pregnancy. I felt supported by my general practitioner and female friends. My mother was particularly empathic regarding my 24/7 morning sickness that valiantly maintained its existence throughout the entire pregnancy, and concurred that, "there is nothing natural about pregnancy or childbirth". My gynaecologist had scheduled a caesarean operation founded on my previous birthing experience. Jude's birth should have been safe because I had been so careful. Yet there were factors beyond my control which contributed to his premature birth, and hospitalisation in intensive care for one month, and inevitably added to my biographical list of significant traumas and chronic stress.

Given that I was pregnant and that my baby was due in May, I requested that my principal did not allocate a physically violent student to my class group. I had been warned by the student's mother who was concerned about my safety. The principal did allocate the violent student to my class group. I did not fail to make a weekly request to my principal and deputy principal to reallocate that student to a more appropriate class. He was never moved. I was frequently punched in my stomach and had a desk thrown into my stomach by another class's student. I do not blame the students for the premature birth of our second child but the power and control games perpetrated by the school's principal were reprehensible.

It is difficult to satisfactorily outline and describe the many facets of Jude's birth that so poignantly illustrate the inadequacies of the medical profession to humanely meet the holistic needs of its patients, and the subsequent impact of its deficiencies. I am positive that the fact that my gynaecologist/obstetrician told me that I couldn't be experiencing contractions (which began immediately after I had been repeatedly punched in the stomach) when I reported feeling them throughout the week prior to my waters breaking did not help. In retrospect my fervent efforts to clean everything in sight at home (including the leather lounge) despite feeling exhausted and sick does suggest that I was *nesting*.

I do not understand why my gynaecologist/obstetrician made the decision for me to attempt a natural birth for four hours after my waters broke. There had been so much bleeding on my way to the hospital that the paramedic was visibly distressed. I had not dilated beyond a centimetre and we had contracted for a caesarean based on the previous emergency caesarean, provided after 24 and half hours of labour at one centimetre, and clinical data readings from a distressed baby. The fact that he changed his mind when he could see for himself that it was a complicated birth suggests that perhaps my personal experiences and needs were valid and worth investigating if not respecting.

At 36 weeks' gestation Jude's lungs were not developed and he could not breathe for himself. Once again, I was not able to hold my baby after he was born. The paediatrician at the base hospital strongly recommended to Adrian that we choose a name for our baby and that we should consider christening him immediately: they did not tell me this. Four hours after he was born, I was told that Jude would have to be flown to a metropolitan hospital that could provide intensive care. The nurses informed me that I would not be able to fly with my baby because I would not be able to walk after the operation: I would have to make the six-and-half hour drive with my husband.

No comfort was offered. I cannot describe how disempowered I felt by that experience nor the inner outrage and despair I felt. I stated quite firmly that I could walk and that I would be flying to Brisbane with Jude. I rose from my bed and I walked the perimeters of the ward to prove that I could. When the Royal Flying Doctor's plane arrived at the hospital I walked onto the plane.

When I arrived at the public hospital in Brisbane, I was transported to the maternity ward and left alone in a birthing suite until my mother arrived. Jude was taken to the intensive care in the paediatric ward. I have no words to describe how I felt when I could hear the women giving birth to their babies. My mother maintained a very brave and calm exterior: it took her five months to tell me that when she had arrived at the hospital and enquired how Jude was and where she could locate me, that the nurse had asked whether Jude was a boy or a girl, and had then said that because he was a premature boy he probably hadn't survived. The dehumanising power of statistics. I have no idea how she maintained her calm demeanour.

The nurses provided me with Panadol and every day for the week that I was a patient in the maternity ward (seemingly a million miles away from my baby) they asked me when I planned to leave the hospital. I insisted that I resume my antidepressant medication and endured and resisted the militant nurses who attempted to coerce me to provide breast milk for Jude; referring to the evils of *artificial feeding* in their efforts to shame me into expressing milk.

They had no idea that I had made every effort to safeguard Jude's development; that I had risked my own life by ceasing protective medication; and that I had made a conscious decision to protect my psychological health and Jude's cognitive development by resuming my medication and bottle-feeding Jude. Their ignorance regarding mental health, medication and cognitive development, and their blatant disrespect for their patient was abusive and dangerous. Their interactions with me reinforced the social stigma that so many nurses in my experience are so effective in maintaining.

Adrian and I visited Jude every day. We rode an emotional rollercoaster, experiencing fear, helplessness and grief in our own, very separate ways. Some days we were advised to rush to the hospital to say goodbye to Jude, other days we were told that he was progressing. There was no sense of safety. I requested the paediatrician not resuscitate Jude if he was brain damaged: I knew that I could not bear to see him suffer and I did not believe in medicine playing God with little human lives that nature did not intend to survive.

Perhaps it was easier for me to make this request because I had to stay strong. Perhaps it was because I had not held Jude and felt that I had never really had him. Perhaps it was because we were not allowed to hold him for the first three weeks of his life. Trauma typically involves dissociation and avoidance – grief isn't far removed.[8,9] At no point was Adrian, David or I offered any form of family support or counselling.

After three weeks we were given the joyful news that Jude would be flown back to our regional town's private hospital where he would be admitted into the special care unit until he learnt to suck and feed, and gain enough weight to thrive. The midwives were warm, supportive and nurturing. They demonstrated to me that Jude was so cognitively alert that they had to frequently provide him with new mobiles to encourage his stimulation. They provided opportunities for us to bond with our son, and for David with his brother. They were the antithesis of all we had previously experienced because they were non-judgemental and promoted relationship building.

I did struggle with depression after Jude's birth. Everything seemed so much harder and the antidepressants were not effective. We had little social support because our closest relatives lived seven hours away. We were exhausted from our ordeals and Adrian had returned to full-time teaching after having taken extended, unpaid leave: the joys of living in regional Australia.

I did not seek counselling or other psychological support: it had not been effective in the past. I had attended a number of counselling sessions in late 1996 with a general practitioner who practised counselling. I had believed that if I talked about my childhood sexual abuse and attempted to understand how it impacted my illness I could in some way understand why I was faulty and thereby diminish some of my pain. She did not recognise my sudden shift in mood from deep depression and hopelessness to an upbeat, *I've got a solution for everything* mood. Nor did she know that I had decided that my final solution to commit suicide was the best, most hopeful solution when she told me at the end of our counselling session that she enjoyed talking with me but she couldn't help me.

So how did I keep going? I put one foot in front of the other and existed. I spent money and whittled away the relationship I shared with Adrian. I worked too hard and attempted to be the perfect mother, teacher and daughter. I tried to be the best wife but I knew I was failing. I emotionally dissolved very easily if Adrian and

I disagreed about anything I highly valued, or if I perceived some criticism.

Adrian's own health impacted his behaviour and his ongoing medical treatment in Brisbane further drained our financial and emotional resources. Similar to when I was aged 15, my body screamed help out loud. My general practitioner began giving me Depo Provera (birth control treatment injections) in an effort to cease dysmenorrhea (painful menstruation and flooding), and premenstrual dysphoric disorder (PMDD) which were significantly affecting my private and professional life. There's no fun in raiding the students' spare clothes cupboard and doing a load of washing whilst you're at work.

I was not offered any information regarding the side effects of Depo Provera and was quite relieved that I didn't have to endure feeling like I was going crazy every couple of weeks. According to helpful women's health websites that are currently available (unlike in the early 2000s) common side effects of Depo-Provera comprise the ceasing of menstruation, nausea, stomach cramping/bloating, weight gain or loss, fatigue, dizziness, breast tenderness, diminished breast size, headache, irritability, diminished sex drive, hot flushes, joint pain, acne, and possible hair loss. This is useful information that I would have truly appreciated at 33 years of age.

Instead, I struggled with exhaustion from disturbed sleep caused by flu symptoms and hot flushes that I imagined could possibly be HIV. My having HIV was virtually impossible but thanks to successful media health campaigns I was familiar with such symptoms being associated with HIV, had an anxious and vivid imagination, and was ignorant of the side effects of the medication I was taking.

Was it because I had a mental illness that my general practitioner did not advise me of the side effects of Depo-Provera? Did he equate mental illness with cognitive impairment? I do not think so. He was kind and he was young, and he treated me with respect and warmth. Was his lack of information provision based on some arrogant white, middle class, male privileged assumption that I did not need to know because I was female and marginalised by madness? Given my awareness of his personal background, I do not think so.

It would be easy for me to feel a sense of justified anger and argue from a critical social, post-structuralist perspective that his failure to provide me with information was because of a patriarchal, neo-liberal, western prejudice aimed at reinforcing his power formed through institutionalised bio-medical discourse. Female doctors have also failed to provide me with vital information about medication, and nurses have positively delighted in sharing their "off-the record" diagnoses of my symptoms whilst espousing their political views of powerful doctors who don't know nearly as much as they do about medicine.

Perhaps these women had simply internalised and were demonstrating the patriarchal ideologies and behaviours embodied in the discourses they were a part of. However, this would excuse their behaviour and paint them as unconscious victims of an invisible power game and nullify the dominant reason and principles that people choose to work in human and health professions.

One only has to read the Hippocratic Oath and look to Médecins Sans Frontières to recognise that most medical professionals are motivated by compassion and a keen sense of human rights and social justice. It is simply not helpful to generalise individuals' characteristic flaws of ego, greed or ignorance, or indeed cultural differences, to entire institutions or sets of knowledge, thereby rendering potentially beautiful, useful and powerful knowledges impotent because of limited critical analysis masking political agendas.

It is entirely possible that medical professionals have to maintain such a broad awareness and understanding of an ever-growing and ever-changing knowledge base that it is humanly impossible for any general practitioner to have specialised knowledge of all aspects of health. A general practitioner may have a general knowledge of what has been deemed as generally effective for the general population, and has little time to pursue investigative research into anomalies unless they are visible and his or her patients are aware that they are experiencing anomalies.

It is certainly easier for doctors to now Google helpful medical information during consultancy and they appear to be more open to patients' participating in their own health management which sometimes involves questioning established practices. However, this requires the intentional development of a trusting, collaborative therapeutic relationship that encourages the sharing and validation of knowledge. It also requires time, an appreciation of holistic health (i.e., the interconnection of individuals, society, and the environment) and a cultural shift in which Australia's government recognises that no economy can operate effectively without well people, a healthy community, and a real valuing of a sustainable environment that enables global health.

However, at 35 years of age, with no medical expertise, multitudinous stressors, and flat-lined emotional and physiological strength a certain type of magic happened that changed everything for me. *There is only so much that any one woman can tolerate when she feels powerless to be self-determining within social structures that simply don't listen to her, attempt to understand her, and deny her repeated requested forms of help that she has clearly identified.*

Fuck Education Queensland, fuck medicine and fuck being a woman. Sometimes you need to be a real man to feel strong, independent and happy. It couldn't be more simple and quite honestly, when you have that kind of power who can touch you? Sometimes I'm a fucking genius and God, do I feel good! I even look good with the stubble. It's amazing how powerful you can feel wearing Doc Martens and a black leather jacket. It's also incredible how the whole outfit teams with long red and black tartan pyjama pants.

Who else would have thought of it? I'm getting a kick out of knowing that no-one else knows I'm wearing my pyjamas in real life outside of my house. Fuck fashion – I've invented my own and it's like a force shield. Now all I need to do is get my hands on a motorbike. Dad has one and I'm pretty sure I can talk him in to letting me borrow it. I've got a friend who'll teach me to ride it and I can get a blue heeler dog called Angus to balance on the back of my motor bike and we'll ride down to Victoria and eat cheese and bread, and drink wine and sleep in the vineyards.

Life's good. It looks good: beautiful in fact. I can actually feel the power of the universe and the way everything buzzes, connects, shines, throbs and sings. Smell it! Taste it! Who the hell needs to sleep when you can talk about music, drink red wine and ride other people's motorbikes as fast as you can? So what if you're not meant to combine alcohol and medication, and you're meant to be at home at 4am in the morning instead of in your friend's lounge room talking about every brilliant idea in your rapidly expanding, limitless brain? Why is it that normal people are so limited in the view of how things could be? Who makes the rules? Fuck the rules.

Resistance is so frustrating. Well-meaning, caring people simply refused to provide me with the key to personal freedom. There was no way anyone was going to provide me with a motor bike or teach me to ride. My default mechanism for flat-lining is self-manifestation of energy. It had worked for me for at least 18 years but something had gone wrong. It was out of control. I was experiencing my own Chernobyl disaster and the fallout associated with prolonged personnel mismanagement prior to, and following the disaster had globally impacted my life. I have likened my dangerously manic episode to driving a very red sports car at fantastically-exciting, super-human speeds. It's exhilarating, beyond responsibility, beyond consequences, beyond fighting to exist, beyond pain: beyond reality. Until one glimpses the sudden, impending, unavoidable wall that inevitably results in a near-fatal crash of depression. Survivor sustained internal damage.

I had sufficient internal dialogue and insight to know that I needed help and that I did not enjoy feeling out of control. I don't enjoy feeling inebriated and have never been truly tempted to use drugs because I hate not being able to control my thoughts and feelings. Perhaps this has saved me from becoming yet another statistic: that of the high population of people with bipolar disorder who also suffer from substance abuse disorder. [9,10,11,12,13,14,15,16] I can understand how this comorbidity exists. It is society's failure to address the underlying contributing factors that contribute to the development and experience of both disorders. I rang my doctor and begged that I be admitted to hospital. I wanted to be looked after.

I felt safe in the local private hospital where my family members and friends could visit me. My room was aesthetically pleasing and my ensuite ensured privacy. These are important points that I can't emphasise enough. The environmental and social conditions that promoted human dignity and respect were in stark contrast with my hospitalisation eight years later. My general practitioners, psychologist and psychiatrist visited me in hospital and were always kind. Most of the nurses were warm and nurturing. Warmth and kindness were precisely what I needed because I had been feeling so worthless and disconnected for so long.

Pharmaceutical treatment of my illness phase was a conundrum. Clearly, the antidepressants had not been effective in preventing mania. They had not prevented deep depression and anxiety (which in my view led to mania) but that was not the most pressing medical concern. I was prescribed the gold standard mood stabilising treatment: lithium. Of course I was. The effect was almost immediate.

I felt extremely nauseous and weak, and I felt as though my heart beat was, for want of a better word, erratic. I found my physical sensations distressing. True, the physical sensations eclipsed any euphoric mood I might otherwise have experienced but I honestly felt poisoned. I reported my concerns to a nurse whose condescending response, "You're not dying", effectively conveyed the message that *you are mad, you are not to be believed, and I resent having to care for people like you and I have no intention of reporting your concerns to your doctor.* I'm not suggesting for a moment that I wasn't mentally ill but I am arguing that I was capable of communicating my physical responses to the medication and that my experiences were valid, important and that I had a right to be heard and helped.

I am not sure of how many days I was treated with lithium but it was ceased when I told my psychologist that I felt so bad that I wanted to make myself vomit. He was horrified and implored me not to punish myself. I immediately assured him that it wouldn't be an act of self-punishment and that I felt like I was being poisoned. He was brilliant. He recalled that I had previously over-dosed on lithium and that my physical sensations were indicating an intolerance to the drug and that it was harmful. He had heard me and he believed me.

My psychiatrist was notified, lithium treatment ceased and I began treatment with the mood stabiliser, Epilim EC EC (500mg) and the anti-depressant Effexor –XR (150 mg). A systematic review, funded by Sanofi-Aventis, to decide valproate's effectiveness and tolerability in the pharmaceutical treatment of severe bipolar depression found some sign of an antidepressant response in patients with bipolar disorder.[18] I believe I was in hospital for a couple of weeks and during that time I gained a dress size and could not go home in my size 12 jeans. I certainly did not return home feeling well or less depressed.

Valproate (Epilim) is an antiepileptic medication commonly used to treat seizures. Its apparent mood-stabilising properties were observed during the mid-1960s in France. A number of open and controlled studies have found the drug to be well-tolerated and effective in the treatment of acute mania and the prevention of manic episodes, whether used as monotherapy or combined with other antimanic and mood-stabilising drugs.[18,19,20,21,22,23] Research trials indicated that patients suffering from concurrent significant depressive symptoms and mania, and patients who had experienced numerous previous mood episodes had increased likelihood of responding to acute therapy with valproate compared with lithium.[9]

Valproate has also been shown to be more effective than lithium in the treatment of manic patients experiencing mixed symptoms.[9,21,24] According to the American Psychiatric Association, unintentional and intentional overdosing of valproate is rare, and when compared with lithium, has less likelihood of being lethal.[9]

Manic episodes associated with bipolar disorder have been hypothesised as occurring as a result of disproportionate distribution and interaction between excitatory neurotransmitters (i.e., those chemicals that enable nerve cell communication), and neurotransmitters that calm nerve cells; thereby causing eruptions of electrical activity resulting in mood instability.[25] Sodium valproate is believed to function as an antipsychotic through augmenting inhibitory neurotransmitter (i.e. gamma amino-butyric acid, or GABA) activity which calms the excitatory neurotransmitters, stabilises the brain's electrical activity, and diminishes the impulses that produce manic episodes.[25,26]

Bowden, et al.'s study[19] of the maintenance treatment of euphoric and dysphoric (mixed) manic symptoms found patients who experience dysphoric mania are especially sensitive to negative effects resulting from valproate and lithium. They hypothesised that mixed mania symptomatology may be neurobiologically predisposed to increased negative effect burden associated with specific therapy dosage, or that mixed mania symptomatology may involve elevated subjective sensitivity to negative drug effects. Bowden, et al.[19] also conclude that whilst valproate may be more effective than lithium in treating dysphoric mania, and lithium's efficacy in treating euphoric mania may be more effective than valproate, the effective treatment of acute mania is not an accurate predictor of treatment efficacy, or prevention of developing depressive symptoms.

Commonly noted adverse effects of valproate include headache, gastrointestinal distress (e.g., nausea, anorexia, changes in appetite, vomiting, abdominal cramps, diarrhoea), sedation, light-headedness or dizziness, ataxia (muscular co-ordination loss, especially when walking), tremor, weight gain, and depression.[9,21,25,26] Given that I had demonstrated an intolerance to lithium and valproate had been shown to have some effectiveness in the treatment of mania in patients with bipolar disorder 1, Epilim seems to have been an obvious antipsychotic and mood stabilising therapy.

However, the National Institute for Health and Clinical Excellence[27] warns of the possible heightened risk of serotonergic effects associated with combined Epilim and Effexor therapy. Whilst consumers of Epilim may receive medication information that highlights possible side effects and interactions (which includes a frighteningly long list of risks and advice to discuss your concerns with your doctor) one needs to have several tertiary qualifications to recognise and understand the language, and the statistical probabilities of experiencing side effects.

One also requires an appreciation of self-fulfilling prophecy balanced with an ability to not overthink, a level of personal insight regarding mood and physical health, and an excellent collaborative relationship with one's doctor when navigating the effects of new medications regimes. Refreshingly, the American Psychiatric Association[9] acknowledges life-threatening side effects sometimes associated with valproate and recommends that "patients must be relied upon to report the often-subtle symptoms of these reactions promptly".

My continued support from my psychologist was invaluable. I began to recognise the adverse effect of chronic stress on my mental and physical health and the importance of acknowledging that there are simply some battles one cannot win when there is an imbalance of power. I ill-health retired from teaching, as did Adrian who was continuing to battle his own chronic illness. It was a pivotal life point: one that involved the disintegration of professional social identities equated with success to a plunging to the depths of the social barrel: the disability pension equated with failure, impending poverty, and shame.

I endured Epilim treatment for 11 months. My life felt fogged. I felt fatigued, nauseous, slow, and depressed. I began to develop an itchy rash on my face and was not convinced that I was benefitting in any way from the treatment. I was unaware of the aforementioned research on valproate and my complaints of adverse side effects had fallen on sympathetic but generally unresponsive ears.

Doctors sometimes have a way of kindly fobbing off patients with a message that implies, "*Mm, I know. It's not fun but I'm sure it's bearable because according to the fine print on the medication pamphlet it's to be expected and it may ease with time. Contact me if you're certain you're dying*". When it became obvious that I truly felt ill and that the rash was not going to disappear my Epilim treatment ceased and the Effexor dosage continued. The rash disappeared: the fog lifted slightly. The internal pain and darkness remained my constant companions; dulling my senses and seemingly casting a slow-motion spell on all that I experienced.

Chapter 12

Parthenogenesis

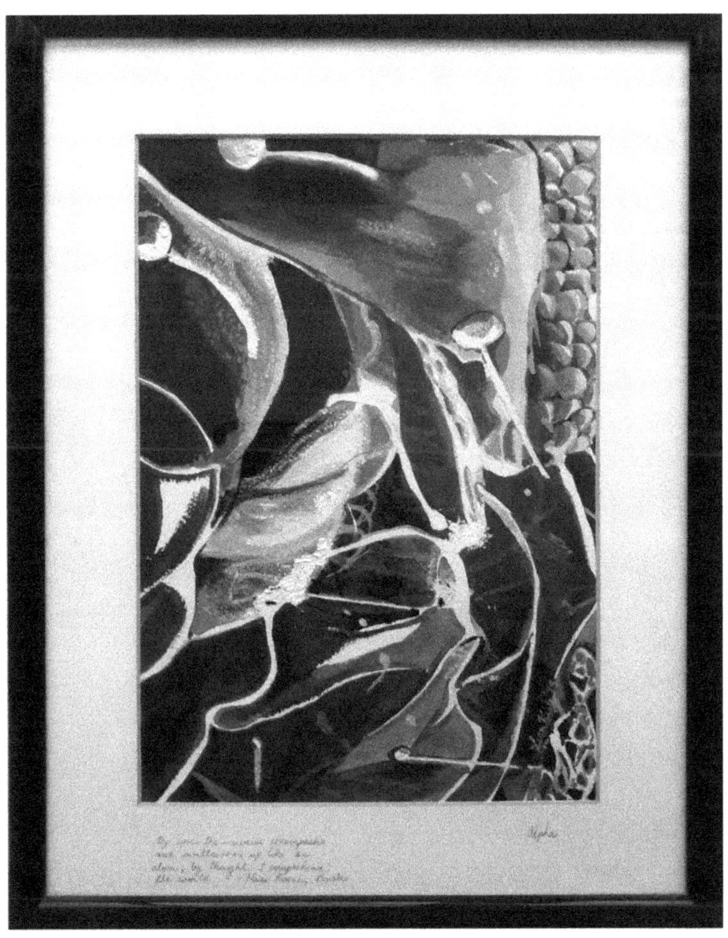

Alpha (1994). Watercolour 26.5 x 19 cm

By space the universe encompasses and swallows me up like an atom, by thought I comprehend the world.

Blaise Pascal[1] *Pénsées*

In every phenomenon the beginning remains always the most notable moment.

Thomas Carlyle[2], *Fraser's Magazine for Town and Country.*

I assess the power of a will by how much resistance, pain, torture it endures and knows how to turn to its advantage.

Friedrich Nietzsche[3] *The Will to Power*

Every man is a creative cause of what happens, a primum mobile with an original movement.

Friedrich Nietzsche[3] *The Will to Power*

This is my brain
And I live in it …
It's tucked away behind my eyes
Where all my screwed-up thoughts can hide
'Cause God forbid I hurt somebody
And the weird thing about a mind
Is that every answer that I find
Is the basis of a brand-new cliché

This is my brain
And it's fine
It's where I spend a vast majority of my time
It's not perfect, but it's mine
It's not perfect, but it's mine
It's not perfect
I'm not quite sure I've worked out how to work it
It's not perfect, but it's mine

Tim Minchin [4] *Not Perfect, So f#©king rock.*

Ill-health retiring from Education Department Queensland was a process that could be described as humiliating, dehumanising and shameful. The process involved proving that I was not fit to teach, and that in all probability, I never would be because I am mentally ill. One has to prove one is defective (thereby nullifying all that is not broken and effective) to receive help. One has to provide evidence to psychiatrists, psychologists, general practitioners and bureaucrats that one is a liability, and possibly a danger to the education department. That potential danger is recorded and prevents the retiree from reapplication for 10 years.

The Education Department's processes for reapplication after the 10-year freeze are complex, well-camouflaged in fine print, protected by human resources administrators who are largely inaccessible, over-worked, under-employed and act as obstacles to re-entry through the provision of paperwork without adequate information or support. In short, the possible danger associated with mental illness (which in my case was only ever a danger to me) is effectively transformed into a definite outcome that Education Department Queensland must ward against using complex, dehumanising and financially inhibitive means. Even if I had known that I would be well enough to teach after 10 years and that I would want to work as a school counsellor; and had I been aware that my ill-health retirement would create further obstacles for employment, I had no real choice but to ill-health retire. We had our superannuation and an opportunity to start again.

2004 simultaneously symbolised a break for freedom and a battle lost. I did not fit a social system; the system did not support me and I could not change it. 2004 is blurred. I know that we focused on our health, renovated our house, and took our children on a holiday to North Queensland during the winter school break. I cannot recall much of the holiday. I know I was so depressed that I cried when I heard Neil Diamond sing *September Morning* on the radio. I was an emotional sponge and was not physically responding well to a new atypical antipsychotic treatment: Risperidone. Risperidone is generally used to treat schizophrenia, irritability and behavioural problems experienced by children and adolescents with autism, and mania and mixed episodes in children, adolescents and adults diagnosed with bipolar disorder.[5,6,7,8,9]

From one distant perspective it is interesting that I was prescribed Risperidone. What was the reasoning that supported the decision to trial the medication on me? My mood patterns clearly demonstrated that I suffered from untreatable depression most of the time. I rarely experienced mania and was not manic when the drug was prescribed. I had no knowledge of ever experiencing a mixed mood episode and I was severely depressed. A vision is conjured of my body covered in Velcro, my eyes blindfolded, attached to a wildly spinning wheel of fortune whilst doctors and psychiatrists are desperately throwing drugs at my body in a desperate attempt to peg a serendipitously effective treatment at me. Perhaps one white-coated experimenter fervently called out "What she doesn't throw up or die from might just work. Fingers crossed lads!" It was literally the first medication that made me vomit.

Side effects commonly experienced by users of Risperidone are sleepiness, vision impairment, constipation, extrapyramidal symptoms (such as rigidity, muscle spasms, and restlessness), and weight gain.[5,7] I was not warned of the potential risk of the permanent motor disorder, tardive dyskinesia; nor of hyperglycemia, elevated suicide risk, and life-threatening neuroleptic malignant syndrome which is somewhat like an allergic response to an antipsychotic that can be confused for heat stroke or encephalitis.[5,7] Needless to say, it would have been advisable, respectful and pertinently nice to have been informed of the real side effects and risks that accompanied this drug and the argument for my use of it before I predictably consented to using it.

No doubt the side effects were listed on the pamphlet a patient receives when they have already bought the drug but how many patients have sufficient research skills, statistical awareness, and medical knowledge to understand what they are reading to make an informed judgement? Let's face it: how do you accurately assess what might be adverse side effects and what feels like normal when you feel like death warmed up for months on end?

I sincerely hope that it will not surprise you, Dear Reader, to learn that scientists don't have a substantial knowledge or understanding of Risperidone's mechanism of action, that is, how it works but they *believe* this 'first-line, second-generation antipsychotic' might act as a dopamine antagonist.[5] Yep, just what I needed: more magic. Treatment-resistant bipolar depression is an enduring problem for the medical profession. Double-blind, placebo-controlled data indicates that antidepressant monotherapy, or adjunctive tricyclic antidepressants can worsen the development of bipolar disorder.[10]

Some research suggests that electroconvulsive therapy or monoamine oxidase inhibitors may be switched to when a mood stabiliser combined with an antidepressant fails to aid patients with bipolar depression.[10] Risperidone has been approved as a monotherapy and adjunctive treatment for acute mania however, there seems to be little to no evidence that risperidone has potential in treatment-resistant bipolar depression.[5,10]

Research has shown unconvincing results for the efficacy of Risperidone in the treatment of bipolar depression.[5,11] In fact, Risperidone is considered to be effective as a maintenance therapy for the prophylaxis of manic episodes but there is no substantial evidence for the prevention of depressive episodes and there is a possibility that the long-acting, better-tolerated injectable Risperidone therapy may heighten the chance of depression.[11,12,6] Pae, et al.'s retrospective study of adjunctive risperidone, olanzapine and quetiapine treatment of hospitalised patients with bipolar 1 disorder[13] found the drugs combined with mood stabilisers for one month to have comparable effectiveness. However, the risperidone-treated group experienced a higher frequency of extrapyramidal symptom-related side effects than patients in the quetiapine and olanzapine groups.[13]

Cipriani, et al.'s multiple-treatments meta-analytical review[14] found that anti-psychotic medications, such as risperidone, olanzapine and quetiapine, were considerably more effective in the treatment of manic episodes without psychotic features than mood stabilisers like lithium and lamotrigine. Their study suggests that risperidone and olanzapine are significantly superior for acceptability and efficacy yet they note that the drugs' efficacy estimates were marginally higher in drug manufacturer trials.

Cipriani et al.'s multiple-treatments meta-analytical study reviewed trials that were perpetually short-term and patients with severe illness were excluded. Furthermore, the research did not investigate toxic effects, side effects, social or personal functioning, or quality of life which makes one wonder how researchers can claim to accurately measure acceptability and efficacy of a treatment.

It is indeed a sobering thought to consider that systematic reviews such as these, based on dodgy randomised control trials, are regarded as current 'gold standard' best evidence that informs public health policy promoted by the National Institute for Health and Care Excellence.[15,16] The researchers do emphasise the need for pharmaceutical treatments that offer better tolerability and efficacy than existing treatments often associated with extra-pyramidal, weight gain and metabolic effects.[14]

Gitlin, et al. stress the importance of prescribers being aware of the tolerability of various medications, the impact of tolerability and adverse side effects on user adherence, and the vital role that the patient-doctor relationship has on medication adherence.[11] Despite the fact that I was not adequately warned of the adverse effects of Risperidone, I believed that I maintained a strong therapeutic relationship with my general practitioner that was founded on communication and trust.

The relationship that I had with her was one of the most important relationships that I had during that period of my life and I believe that if it weren't for regular appointments that allowed her to monitor my moods, I would not be alive today. She made me feel that I mattered to somebody and that I was believed. She was aware that I was dangerously depressed and maintained phone communication whilst I was travelling. When I informed her that my depression had worsened and that I could not tolerate the medication she advised that I cease the medication.

I continued to take Effexor until October 2006, punctuated by 1 mg Kalma (i.e., alprazolam; an anti-anxiety medication derived from benzodiazepine) when my anxiety was unbearable. According to my medical records, I used Kalma from November to January. I characteristically used to find the Christmas season to be the most stressful time of year: a combination of great expectations, high excitement and a desire to feel happy and normal. An impossible mix.

I began studying psychology in 2005. I did not study it with the intention of making myself a personal case study: I was simply interested in human behaviour and had been attracted to the discipline since I had studied Freud and Jung as part of my comparative history and literature arts degree. I absolutely thrived on my studies and constantly surprised myself with my successes. I had been terrified of failure having experienced the anxiety-induced memory blocks whilst I was sitting exams at school. Therefore, I over-studied in preparation for my exams. My first exam involved neuroscience and the foundations of psychology: 100 random questions taken from any of the 759 pages the lecturer might choose to examine. I had to pass it to prove to myself that I wasn't stupid.

I was so terrified thinking about exams that I thought I was going to be sick. Being sick was excusable but an inability to think and recall was unforgivable. Prior to the exam period I met with the university's student welfare officer and was granted an extension of 10 minutes to be used for relaxation/anxiety management purposes during exams based on my "special needs" as a student with a mental illness. It is the only time I have asked for any kind of extra support at university based on my diagnosis. I believe that simply knowing that I had that support mechanism in place helped me to keep a level head when I entered the exam room for the first time.

I had mentally answered 96 of the 100 questions with absolute certainty within the 10-minute perusal period. I answered and proofread the exam paper within the first 15 minutes and made a mental note to check up the four questions I was uncertain of when I returned home. The exam supervisor noticed my inactivity after the first 30 minutes and apprehensively asked me if I had proofread my work and completed all the answers. He was very kind and let me slip out of the exam room well before it was deemed institutionally acceptable.

A High Distinction confirmed my estimated calculations and served to almost convince me that I wasn't stupid. I never needed to use that special 10-minute extension because I had taught myself to study, to overlearn, and to use silent positive self-talk to cope during times that I knew triggered disabling responses.

Studying psychology certainly helped to broaden my view of the world and of myself. I had always viewed myself as an arts girl: someone who was comfortable in the world of paint, music, books and philosophy. I certainly didn't see myself as someone who was just as interested in science beyond adoring David Attenborough and being a passionate Whovian (Dr Who fan). I felt excited that so much of what I had privately observed and experienced in life, the modifications I had made to my own behaviours in order to fit in, were substantiated by so many theories and that some of those theories also helped me to understand or explain some of my differences that I had previously criticised myself for.

I found the challenge of studying and learning a new discipline, a new way of writing thoroughly fulfilling and absorbing. I could focus for hours on end, studying on-line, independently and entirely self-motivated. Being totally focused on a problem or being absorbed in the flow of creativity helps me to block depression and physical pain. My arch enemy is stress and this is more often than not caused by factors beyond my control, such as poor health and economic disadvantage.

Despite my successes at university, I continued to struggle with serious depression and anxiety. Seroquel (25 mg) was added to my medication regime for five months during the first half of 2006. Epilim (200 mg) was re-introduced in October of the same year when I experienced my first mixed mood episode just prior to my major second year exams. I had not known that mixed mood episodes were possible. Mind you, I didn't know that one could experience sensory and olfactory hallucinations: I just suffered those sensations on my own and wondered why no one else could smell human faeces or why no one could give me a plausible reason for why my skin on my left thigh felt so painfully burnt despite not being exposed to the sun.

Studying abnormal psychology certainly helped illuminate a number of dark corners in my maze. However, I did find myself feeling frustrated with the paucity and superficiality of information provided on bipolar disorder. I found myself wondering why my experience of bipolar disorder: its aetiology, its symptoms, its complexity, and its treatment were barely, if at all, discussed. In fact, I felt like arguing with its inadequate description, and dare I say, its inaccuracy.

I attribute the dearth of knowledge and understanding of bipolar disorder to the underfunding of research. Research focus and funding are directly related to the relationship between those who have the power to know and to create the discourse of knowledge to be disseminated, and what they value as worth knowing. Hence, it seems apparent that the experience of those who suffer from bipolar disorder is insignificant and worth little value. My bio-psychiatric and psychological-angled gaze at myself was confronting, confusing, and effectively disempowering. I felt smaller, less human, and less inclined to disclose my illness to others.

It is not difficult to see how this social construction of current power relations involving those who are pathologised and politically disempowered, and those who are *normal* and possess power is self-internalised as mental illness stigma.[17,18] The discourse of discipline involves techniques and procedures which may be identified within various public institutions, including media, education and medical institutions, that involve surveillance, judgement, objectification of self and internalisation of rules to enforce a 'society of normalization'.[19,20,21,22,23]

Whilst mental illness affects most Australian people, personally or indirectly, public understanding of mental illness continues to be obfuscated by fear, misinformation, and incapacitating social stigma.[24] Mental illness stigma is demonstrated in various ways, including the social isolation and degrading labelling of individuals regarded as having a mental illness.[25,26,24] Stigma involves the identification and labelling of human differences; connecting labelled individuals to negative stereotypes; separating those individuals from the rest of society; and consequential loss of status and discrimination.[27,24]

Stigma is a social construction largely cultivated and perpetuated by the mass media's capacity to develop health attitudes, beliefs, and behaviours through news media and entertainment.[24] In my experience, and according to research,[26,28] doctors, psychiatrists, psychologists, nurses, mental health workers, and social workers are not immune to the effects of media constructed mental illness meanings. The deleterious effects of stigma on individuals experiencing mental illness include internalisation of stigma, diminished self-esteem, diminished quality of life, unwillingness to ask for help/treatment, poorer quality of health care, fewer employment opportunities, and fewer chances for acquiring housing.[26]

The National Depressive and Manic-Depressive Association (National DMDA) conducted a survey[29] to ascertain consumers' level of satisfaction with treatment, and reasons for ceasing medication. The survey's results were disturbing: both in levels of treatment satisfaction and in consumers' perceptions of their health practitioners' treatment of their illness. One third of respondents reported feeling very or somewhat satisfied with the treatment of their illness, and 28% expressed dissatisfaction with the treatment received from their health practitioner for their depression.

Fifty-six percent of the *dissatisfied* respondents reported that they felt their health practitioners did not understand depression.[29] Greater than a third of respondents felt that their depression was not taken seriously; that their practitioners lacked current knowledge regarding available treatments, and felt that their health practitioner did not care, and or did not respect them.

Reasons given for lack of treatment compliance included: (a) believing that medication is ineffective, (b) the usual three-to-four week wait for medication effectiveness, (c) financial restrictions, (d) inconvenience, and (e) side effects. Eighty percent of respondents reported experiencing side effects. One of the most significant findings of the survey was the underlying stigma associated with depression treatments. Twenty-three percent of self-reported non-compliant respondents indicated that they contemplated medication non-compliance because they believed medication would alter their personalities; and 18% of non-compliant respondents incorrectly believed taking medication may be habit-forming.[29]

It seems evident to me that ethical research signifies four glaring needs for the improvement of life opportunities and quality of lives of those who live with bipolar disorder: (a) the availability of medical treatments that do not force the consumer to choose between symptom alleviation and quality of life; (b) speedier diagnosis and effective treatment through improved and accurate symptom identification; (c) pharmaceutical treatments need to be effective faster, have fewer adverse side effects, be accessible and affordable, and need to be simpler to take; and (d) focused community education that effectively teaches *all citizens* that mood disorders are health problems - not character flaws.

The psychosocial factor of stigma significantly negatively impacts poor quality of life (QOL) and disability for those who live with bipolar disorder.[30,31] Internalised stigma (i.e., self-stereotyping, withdrawal, rejection, exclusion, and discrimination) is fundamental to understanding the psychological harm associated with self-esteem and QOL that is a direct consequence of stigma, and leads some people to avoid or cease treatment.[31]

The National DMDA[29] argues that medical practitioners should develop more empathy for individuals with mood disorders and that doctors should approach their mentally ill patients with the same levels of concern that they hold for their patients who suffer from other chronic diseases. Lewis laments that doctors have greater power and influence than consumers. She argues that pharmaceutical companies' markets rely on the existence of their consumers, and that the same consumers provide careers for clinicians and researchers.[29] Why is it that the consumers too often feel manipulated and invisible?

It is amazing how sensitivity to words, the power of words, the order of words and the messages overtly or insidiously inferred can affect the way one reads and understands journal articles. The more articles I read as a psychology student with a mental illness the more critical I became. I also internalised the stigma. It became increasingly hard to not define myself by my illness. So many researchers refer to people who live with bipolar disorder as *bipolars*. It is not rare to read sentences that refer to outcomes from pharmaceutical experiments involving human participants and rats as though they are interchangeable. For example,[32]

Lithium has many beneficial effects, beyond mood stabilization: it reduces mortality and morbidity, suicidal behaviour, viral infection and even protects against neurodegeneration with a demonstrated positive action in neurogenesis in animals (Bourgeois, 2002, p. s93).

It is rare for researchers to focus on the strengths and capabilities of those living with bipolar disorder. However, it is common for researchers to emphasise the *burden* of bipolar disorder: particularly the *economic burden*. I wasn't just a burden to my family and my family's budget: I was a burden to Australia's economy, a drain on the health system, the social welfare system, and the workplace. Oswald, et al.'s paper on *Current issues in bipolar disorder: A critical review* is simply one typical example of my observation of the clinical and financial gaze directed at such a small population.[33]

"… recurrence rate is high resulting in damaging interference with social and occupational activity for the individual and serious adverse effects for society at large. The burden and cost associated with bipolar disorder are considerable with even more bed days, absenteeism, poor social functioning and role limitation than that observed in depressive or anxiety disorders. Patients with bipolar disorders have a very low employment rate, most have a pension or disability benefits, a large proportion never marry and about 10% have forensic problems" (p. 688).

I suppose they could have emphasised our low self-esteem at the same time as squeezing lemon juice on our visible and invisible wounds just to make their points a little clearer. Carer burden is also severely impacted by bipolar disorder illness course and episode types.[34] Carers experience significant burden (e.g., increased time and financial expenditure, distress, stress and sorrow) when caring for individuals with bipolar disorder, whether experiencing mixed moods, mania, depression, euthymic state or subsyndromal manic symptoms.[34] *Spotlight shines brightly on guilty, impaired individual.* Rascati, et al.[35] offer a breakdown of the actual economic individual direct and indirect costs of people with bipolar disorder 1 and argue that,

In addition to the cost of work-place productivity losses, partial adherence and nonadherence to medications have been found to be associated with an increased risk of mood episode relapse, suicide attempts, and hospitalization, resulting in an increased cost to society (p. 1032).

Kleine-Budde, et al.[36] attempt to provide an international perspective of the direct, indirect and intangible costs of bipolar disorder illness because up until their own 'systematic review of the economic burden' of bipolar disorder research lacked vital information on 'the high cost-of-illness worldwide for bipolar disorder'. They point out that 'despite the low frequency, BD incurs high costs for both the healthcare system and society …. greater severity of disability, a longer duration of illness, greater losses of productivity' (p. 337).

Carlborg, et al.[37] and Stimmel[38] warn that the World Health Organisation has determined bipolar disorder as the 12th prominent cause of global disability and that the economic ramifications of the illness may have been previously underestimated. Unlike other researchers who tend to choose vocabulary and expression that resonate with conspiracy tones, Carlborg, et al.[37] and Stimmel [38] do recommend that such studies lead to earlier and accurate diagnosis, individualised therapy alternatives, and reducing the individual's and society's socioeconomic burden.

Do researchers really think that the primary argument for increased research into more effective medication is economic? Certainly, it appears that it is in the interest of their funders, namely AstraZeneca, Eli Lilly, and Pfizer, to make that argument. Mohiuddin [39] posits that

> People with BD have been found to use almost four times more healthcare resources and incur more than four times greater healthcare costs compared with those not with BD …. the health economist argues that choices between alternative healthcare interventions should be made on the ground of which intervention generates the highest health benefit from the finite resources available (p. 360).

This researcher certainly makes economic sense but there is far more involved in the health and well-being of an individual living with bipolar disorder than pharmacotherapy. There is far more to an individual living with bipolar disorder than bipolar disorder. When I came to this powerful realisation, I began to live with bipolar disorder rather than being defined by it. Bipolar disorder has been a burden for me but when I manipulate the lens rather than allowing others to control the gaze it has also been an enhancement.

Chapter 13

You Learn Something New Every Day

Knowledge is the most democratic source of power.
Alvin Toffler[1], *Powershift: Knowledge, wealth and violence at the end of the 21st century.*

I am in that temper that if I were under water I would scarcely kick to come to the top.
John Keats[2], *Letter to Benjamin Bailey.*

'Tis not enough to help the feeble up, but to support them after.
William Shakespeare[3], *Timon of Athens.*

The strongest principle of growth lies in the human choice.
George Eliot[4], *Daniel Deronda.*

Either life entails courage, or it ceases to be life.
E. M. Forster[5], *Pharos and Pharillon.*

I made several significant discoveries between 2004 and 2008: managing stress is the key to better health and that I had the ability to regulate my moods when all the necessary conditions were present. I discovered the diathesis stress model answered my question, *why me?* I learnt that mixed mood episodes occur and that all descriptions of Hell sound preferable to experiencing a mixed mood episode. I also realised that the more I know, the more I don't know.

I learnt to manage my illness to the best of my ability. I focused on my studies and rewarded myself with each high achievement. I maintained a balanced social life and discovered that regular walking and talking for an hour five times a week with my best friend was the best future-focused therapy. The shared time, laughter, support, and exercise was energising and emphasised a sense of connectedness and optimism. Prior to the Great Financial Crisis, Adrian and I could focus on developing new careers untainted by social welfare, and on encouraging each other. There was no blame when health concerns required money. It was a different matter post GFC. Economic burden and carer burden were certainly not key terms hurled around our domestic dialogue but they certainly impacted our relationship for at least six years.

Having an increased knowledge about the function of stress, the ramifications of chronic stress, and how to help minimise stress independent of medication was mind-blowing. Stress may be useful or adaptive in the sense that its symptomatic stages (i.e., alarm, resistance and exhaustion) function as a warning and defence mechanism.[6] However, stress presents itself more often than the occasional natural disaster and one cannot always remove oneself from stressful situations when surrounded by micro-stressors frequently underpinned by adverse life events and chronic illness.

Theoretically, I was informed regarding stress, micro-stress, acute stress, chronic stress and to some extent, PTSD. I knew that cortisol, the stress hormone, is associated with cancer: that stress jeopardises the immune system. And that it kills angry and stressed baboons. A quite interesting fact. I also thought I knew that I was coping with life rather well and could keep up an appearance of normalcy.

When my psychologist asked me how stressed I felt on a scale of one to 10 following my disclosure of a dream I had, I answered that

I felt 'okay, possibly around a six'. He asked me to complete a lengthy questionnaire and then provided feedback. He told me that I was operating at a level of stress equivalent to that of a person diagnosed with post-traumatic stress disorder. I was so used to living on high-alert: hypervigilant and prepared to run that a state of high stress was my sense of normal. It is still difficult for me to just sit and do nothing but his perceptive analysis made me mindful of the need to manage and alleviate stress. There's nothing attractive about an angry, stressed baboon.

I had naturally developed coping strategies to deal with stress that I had been living with for the past 35 years. I relied on problem-solving for thwarting problems that I could fix; emotion-focused coping when I could rationally talk myself through anxiety or fear; social interaction for support and distraction; and keeping busy on self-directed projects for my kind of relaxation and focused self-distraction. The more informed I became about my illness and what I was capable of, the greater sense of control I felt I had to protect myself from stress. I learned that despite suffering from a depressive illness I am essentially an optimist. Depression and optimism make strange bedfellows.

I regard 2008 as one of the best years of my life. I graduated with a Graduate Diploma of Psychology in 2007 and was accepted into the Honours programme. I deferred my studies to travel. Adrian and I took our children on a road trip to Sydney and Melbourne to provide our eldest son with an opportunity to attend lessons with the Australian Ballet. We travelled to Singapore to celebrate our youngest son's seventh birthday and have breakfast with an orangutan: a tradition we developed with our eldest son for his fifth birthday.

My parents invited me to travel with them in the UK for a month. Despite being Australian, it was like returning home. I felt immersed in a rich culture and history that I was very familiar with. I also benefitted from being 'the only child' [aged 40] for a month. I've got to say that being an only child for a limited time is brilliant.

Devon Geese (2020). Watercolour and pencil, 21x 16 cm

The first half of the year when we were living the high life was wonderful. Everything seemed a pleasure. I felt competent and successful but I still struggled with depression. My psychiatrist had given me a choice in 2007: either electroconvulsive therapy (ECT) or a new antipsychotic called Olanzapine. Progressive cognitive symptoms, particularly of memory, is a major concern associated with repetitive ECT treatments. Every ECT session has connate risks associated with short-term anaesthesia.[7] Yet, Australian health professionals continue to minimise patients' reports of long-term impairments caused by their treatment.

I knew all too well that there was no way that I would risk short-term or long-term memory impairment so I opted for the new drug. My psychiatrist did mention that Olanzapine could cause a little weight gain and that my eyes might flip back in my head and stay there *but* that was *rare*. I had worked so hard to lose the weight I had gained on other medications and felt good about being able to wear a two-piece bathing costume again. I thought I could manage the risk of 'a little weight gain' if I remained mindful. I simply blocked the eye flipping risk out of my consciousness.

I continued to lose weight on the lowest dose which surprised my psychiatrist. As the dose increased, without improvement in mood, my weight increased. Over time, my taste changed. I never described myself as a sweet tooth prior to taking Olanzapine, nor have I craved sugar since ceasing taking the medication but I was almost addicted to sugar whilst taking it. I could not understand why I felt like I was constantly hungry to the point that I experienced hunger pains and stomach rumbling. I also suffered from severe constipation and found myself relying on copious quantities of prunes and laxatives, despite having a diet high in fibre.

I maintained my exercise and joined Weight Watchers: adhering to a strict diet that involved more food than I had been eating previously. I remember asking the nurse who assessed me for Weight Watchers if she had knowledge about pharmaceutical side effects on weight and that she said yes. She was the same nurse who, after weighing me one week later, asked me if I understood the purpose of a restricted diet. I continued to gain weight, critical social comment, and became dangerously depressed. I was exhausted from attempting to explain to my doctors and some of my family members that I exercised and that I wasn't a glutton: I was just so hungry. I gained 26 kilos in 18 months.

When I returned from the UK, I enrolled in a Lifeline Telephone Counselling course because I believed that my psychology degree did not provide adequate development of therapeutic skills and experience. I enjoyed the course and my experience volunteering in crisis counselling. Following this experience, I began working fulltime in 2009 as an adults' and children's counsellor and studied psychology online part-time.

It wasn't easy. I maintained as balanced a life as possible, with two young children, a chronically ill husband who was frequently receiving chemotherapy, and we were living below the poverty line.

We had to sell our second car to afford the trips to Brisbane for his treatment. I was also struggling with diminishing eye sight. I relied on Adrian to read out digital object identifiers from journal articles so that I could type them in my assignments. It became impossible for me to judge distance. I seemed to have no peripheral vision and frequently dinged the side of my car against the garage walls. I began experiencing hypertension that needed medicating. I felt utterly stupid and a huge burden in every sense of the word.

Sheer commitment focused me enough to achieve grades that would walk me into a Masters course after I completed my thesis. Naivety created the greatest obstacle. I had not thought to advise my research supervisor that I had deferred my studies and he was not available to supervise my research one year later, in 2010. No other lecturer was willing to supervise the topic I had diligently researched for a year in preparation for the thesis. I began researching a whole new area of psychology and was forced to join a group research project.

I recall hearing part of a health report on ABC radio discussing Olanzapine and feeling so furious, whilst driving to work. I cannot recall if it was before or after I begged my GP to prescribe me Ziprasidone because I had been informed by another GP that Ziprasidone was known for helping weight loss. However, I do know that I first discovered Olanzapine caused excessive weight gain and diabetes in patients by listening to *All in the Mind* on the ABC National radio. I also recall that my weight gain was on par with the average weight gain of Americans who were waging legal battles against Eli Lilly, the pharmaceutical company producing and marketing Olanzapine as a wonder drug for depression.

Olanzapine and Ziprasidone are atypical antipsychotics, that are often combined with selective serotonin reuptake inhibitor antidepressants like Citalopram, to treat refractory or unresponsive depression.[8] Olanzapine is often used to treat psychiatric disorders, most commonly bipolar disorder, schizophrenia, autism and depression.[9] Atypical antipsychotics are proclaimed to provide a three-in-one treatment for mood stabilisation, antipsychotic effects and antidepressant effects.[8] Olanzapine is a favoured treatment for bipolar disorder because it is thought to be less likely than other antipsychotics like clozapine, to induce tardive dyskinesia: involuntary repetitive movements.[10]

Whilst lithium has been shown to be clinically ineffective in the treatment of mania in bipolar disorder, there appeared to be some evidence that Olanzapine has antimanic, and mood stabilising efficacy. Greater response rates have been reported when Olanzapine is administered as a combination therapy, using other mood stabilisers. However, some studies have shown that Olanzapine and Risperidone have precipitated or worsened mania in patients who are predisposed to experiencing mania.[10]

According to Lord et al.[9] Olanzapine frequently causes excessive weight increase and type 2 diabetes. People living with schizophrenia have a shorter life span: the main cause of death attributed to obesity-related metabolic syndrome. The prevalence of diabetes in atypical antipsychotic treated populations is four times greater than in sex-, race-, and age-matched controls. Unlike the general population, type 2 diabetes and morbid obesity develop in atypical antipsychotic treated patients within months, rather than years.[10]

Lord et al.'s experiment[9], targeting serotonin receptor 2c in female mice showed an 'acutely increased food intake, impaired glucose tolerance, and altered physical activity and energy expenditure' suggesting that Olanzapine operates some of its adverse metabolic side effects via antagonism of HTR2C (p. 3403). Despite being the most frequently prescribed atypical antipsychotic, Lord et al. assert that it 'causes the most weight gain and metabolic impairments in humans' (p. 3404). Furthermore, whilst Olanzapine may be effective for the treatment of mania in some patients with bipolar disorder, there is little evidence that it is efficacious in treatment of bipolar depression.[11]

Josefson[12] and Lenzer[13] reported that US drug companies were criticised by numerous journalists, doctors, lawyers and activists for their aggressive marketing Zyprexa (Olanzapine) to patients and the general population: including, offering students living with schizophrenia university scholarships to swap their existing medications with the new antipsychotic. Eli Lilly's marketing reaped extraordinary success: Zyprexa grossed US$550 m within its first year, 1996.[12] In 2006, the New York Times reported that Eli Lilly made US$4.26 b thanks to two million global consumers and Eli Lilly's decade-long concerted effort to minimise Zyprexa's health risks.[14,13]

It seemed that chief scientists of the Zyprexa programme were more concerned about the protection of their money-making molecule than they were of the health of their consumers.[15] I may be cynical but it isn't a giant leap of financial logic for pharmaceutical companies to calculate:

Vulnerable population + Zyprexa side effects
– *QoL* ÷ (morbid obesity+diabetes2)
= >medication
=>$

I recall parts of discussions that I had with my GP about my constant hunger, my change in taste, my inability to lose weight and my loss of vision. She told me that Zyprexa changes my metabolism and taste. She surmised that the changes in my brain, the swelling of my parietal lobe could be impacting my occipital lobe, hence causing loss of peripheral sight. I was devastated. It seemed that my life could not become more difficult.

I am still outraged that in 2021, the medical advice provided by Eli Lilly to medical practitioners is so vastly different to 'consumer information'.[16] Eli Lilly continues to minimise the very evident and probable long-term risks to patients and embellishes the wonders of their drug. The pharmaceutical company appears to load the responsibility on the medical practitioner, subtly removing choice from the patient by assuming that the patient lacks the prerequisite knowledge to make an informed decision.

I would argue that all health professionals have an ethical responsibility to promote and develop health literacy in their patients. Furthermore, they should spend adequate time researching the medications they choose to prescribe, including reading the fine print listing the generous 'research' funders.

I have worked hard to heal my traumas and to a great extent, I have succeeded. However, I continue to experience background emotional pain regarding how I perceive my body. I tell myself that I'm grateful that my limbs work and that my brain functions. However, I loathe my body. I am constantly frustrated that no matter how hard I try, I cannot convince my body that it is not wired to return to the weight that I gained on that insidious drug. I often feel deep mortification when I am standing near people who look the normal, comfortable size that I was. I regret that I didn't see what other people saw in me when I must have been beautiful.

Too many medications used to treat symptoms of bipolar disorder are linked with dangerous weight gain. Obesity increases the incidence of heart disease, hypertension, diabetes, hyperlipidaemia (high levels of fat in blood), various forms of cancer, respiratory diseases, gallstones, and global mortality. Therefore, the pharmacologic treatment of bipolar disorder may contribute to obesity and obesity likely exacerbates the development of bipolar disorder.[17]

At the time, I considered it serendipitous that my regular GP was on holidays when I consulted another GP about a heath concern that I can't recall: possibly my constant headache or pain in my sternum. The GP recommended that I switch from Zyprexa to a new antipsychotic called Zeldox (ziprasidone) because Zeldox was reported to help people lose weight. I was so excited! I made an appointment with my regular GP to request that she prescribe me this wondrous medication that would solve all my problems.

My GP was angry. She was indignant that another GP would suggest changing my medication. In retrospect, her indignation may have been motivated by a sense of protection of her patient. The other GP knew little about me. It may also have been a power struggle. Who knows? Regardless of her indignation, I began titrating off Zyprexa in December 2010 and began taking Zeldox in January 2011. I continued to combine my antidepressant treatment with the SSRI Cymbalta. My dreams of completing my Honours program and returning to my ideal weight were reignited. I could be good enough.

I felt unwell during December and received treatment for a chest infection. My blood pressure treatment had also been increased.

I thought that I was unusually anxious because my body simply felt wired: unable to be still. I could not understand it because I had every reason to feel better about myself. I had employment that I loved and allowed me to feel like I was a worthy citizen. I was studying Honours, which meant that I must be intelligent and my parents could be proud of me. Most importantly, I was losing weight.

By May, I had lost 10 kilos but at what expense? I could not sit still: I had to keep moving. I was trying to teach myself post graduate level, advanced statistics because I was studying online whilst working, yet I found it impossible to concentrate and to learn new things. Admittedly, the majority of my cohort was struggling to teach themselves too: some becoming suicidal because of the lack of support and high expectations of our absent lecturer who advised us to practise cognitive behavioural therapy (CBT) on ourselves.

However, my struggles were not familiar to me. My body seemed to be communicating something I could not comprehend. I continued to feel depression which normally made my body feel like it was having to operate under seven feet of wet cement but my body was screaming run, albeit it in an uncoordinated, involuntary way.

I recall feeling utterly stupid when I attended an appointment with my thesis supervisor. He was a kind and patient man who was rather breathtakingly good looking. In fact, he reminded me of the perfect combination of Clark Kent and Superman without the glasses. His attributes made my situation even worse when I discovered to my horror that my hand had forgotten how to write. I kept dropping my pencil and scribbled his answers on my tightly gripped notebook. I felt utterly embarrassed, infantile and terrified.

I was driving Adrian crazy because I could not sit still. I had to keep walking. I couldn't sleep because my legs wanted to keep walking. I was exhausted but compelled to move. I could not sit in the patients' waiting area of the medical clinic I attended. I completed numerous laps of the block until I could see my GP. My GP explained to me that I had an adverse response to Zeldox that presented as

Parkinsonian effects. It would have been more accurate to have said, *Lisa, you have taken your first step of your descent into Hell.*

Drug-induced movement disorders like Parkinsonism are most commonly caused by dopamine receptor blocking pharmaceuticals such as antipsychotics. Symptoms can occur after starting treatment, dose increase, or when changing to a different medication.[18] Movement disorder symptoms generally abate over a period of weeks to months from ceasing the antagonising medication.[19]

Yet again, I had not been warned about the side effect risks of a medication that I was prescribed. Research showed in 2008 that the primary disadvantage of Olanzapine is excessive weight gain and its propensity to cause long-term increased glucose and lipid levels in consumers' blood.[20] Furthermore, research trials in the use of Ziprasidone for mixed episodes and mania showed extrapyramidal symptoms, somnolence (drowsiness), and activation: a type of akathisia oft misinterpreted as anxiety and restlessness. The strong risk of the patient's switch to depression remains linked to antipsychotic treatment. [20] Vieta and Sanchez-Moreno[20] observed that more effective, tolerable treatments are desperately required for most people who are diagnosed with bipolar disorder.

There remains a dearth of evidence regarding safe, efficacious pharmacotherapy for people diagnosed with bipolar disorder who live with depression, mania and mixed states.[7, 22] The ISBD task force report on the use of antidepressants in the treatment of bipolar disorder[22] observed the glaring paradox between widespread prescription and unsubstantial evidence for the safety and efficacy of antidepressant medication in the treatment of bipolar disorder. The report found a scarcity of adequately-designed, long-term trials of preventative benefits having been administered, and insufficient evidence for treatment advantages with mood stabilisers combined with antidepressants.[22]

From my perspective, researchers don't find the answers because they aren't asking the right questions. They are blinded by their medical discourse, maintained by their affiliations with their benevolent funders. They focus on the warning signs (like cardiovascular disease, obesity and non-compliance) and attribute the cause to an innate fault in the person sending the distress signal.[23,21,24] Furthermore, they continue to conduct meta studies, citing previous studies and drawing the same conclusions from flawed and limited trials.[7,25]

My GP wanted me to go to hospital to receive adequate care whilst I began entirely different treatment so she made the call. I wanted that too. It would be safe there. Despite my having private health insurance and having been a patient of the private hospital in the regional centre, the hospital refused to admit me because I was 'mentally ill'. My GP argued that I had previously been their patient and that she was referring me for care for side effects of a medication, not because I was struggling with my mental health. Their answer remained the same: no. I felt like I had received the Coward's Punch of Discrimination to the back of my head. It didn't matter how compliant or rational I was, there was no way I was going to have the personal power to challenge and change the private medical system.

My GP called the psychiatrist who had previously provided psychotherapy and prescribed me Olanzapine. She smiled and said to me, 'He remembers you. He said you were very interesting'. Small comfort. She followed his recommendations and prescribed me a combined therapy of Diazepam, Epilim and Zoloft. Within three days of taking the Zoloft my 24/7 treatment resistant migraine developed and continued for at least two years. I withdrew from my Honours program. It was impossible for me to sit the stats exam. My research proposal was effectively null and void because it was a group experiment that would continue without me. I wasn't good enough: I was a failure. I would never be a psychologist.

My life was shrouded in ink black darkness and physical pain. I frequently reported the pain in my sternum and heart to my GP who repeatedly said, 'Your blood tests show inflammation. It's probably a virus. We'll look at it closely if it still shows inflammation next time', which I guess signalled to me *You're a hypochondriac without a clear vision of reality. Please go away.*

My body ached, my head ached and my chest hurt. Worst of all my heart was broken and I had a no hope-filled sense of my future. I had previously resigned from counselling to study fulltime to ensure that I could produce the best thesis possible. I also had my second bout of pneumonia. I was incapable of putting on a happy face for anyone. I lost all interest and joy. I spent most of my day lying in front of ABC 24 watching horrible news stories.

We had experienced devastating floods caused by global warming that the Australian government refused to acknowledge. Murdoch's media had prevented Kevin Rudd retaining the position of Prime Minister and effectively established at least a decade of ecological vandalism, social division, racism, and systemic marginalisation and discrimination of people who never thrive and profit from neo liberalism and its 'trickle-down economy'. What was there to be happy about? The rest of my time was spent sleeping. I became dangerously depressed.

Chapter 14

Death is Preferable

A first sign of the beginning of understanding is the wish to die.

Franz Kafka[1] *The Zürau Aphorisms*

You have your way. I have my way. As for the right way, the correct way, and the only way, it does not exist.

Friedrich Nietzsche[2] *Thus spoke Zarathustra*

Nobody realizes that some people expend tremendous energy merely to be normal.

Albert Camus[3] *Notebooks*

Judging whether life is or is not worth living amounts to answering the fundamental question of philosophy.

Albert Camus[4] *The myth of Sisyphus*

Where choice begins, Paradise ends, innocence ends, for what is Paradise but the absence of any need to choose this action?

Arthur Miller[5] *After the Fall*

When you have to make a choice and don't make it, that is in itself a choice.

William James[6], *The Will to Believe and Other Essays in Popular Philosophy.*

The difficulty in life is the choice.

George A. Moore[7] *The Bending of the Bough*

The strongest principle of growth lies in the human choice.

George Eliot[8] *Daniel Deronda*

That time in my life is hard to recall with words. Impenetrable black, and pain come to mind. Existential pain. I needed someone to rescue me and make me feel valued but I felt utterly alone, not understood, unheard and worthless. I wanted the pain to end. At that time, I believed that I would have been overjoyed to receive a diagnosis of an inoperable brain tumour: an end point would equate to the light at the end of the tunnel. Suicidal ideation was morphing from a Plan B (i.e., a means of flexibility and choice: a lifeline) to terrifying, intrusive images, thoughts and compulsions.

I had verbally contracted with my GP to go to the hospital if I didn't feel safe. It took all of my emotional and mental strength, and perhaps my remaining will to survive, to drive myself to the base hospital emergency department to stop myself from suiciding. I had to override the constant urge and intrusive images of my unfastening my seatbelt, and accelerating directly into telephone poles the entire way. I knew what I needed. I needed to access my former psychiatrist who made me feel heard; I needed to not be prescribed another SSRI because they were making me feel terrible; and I needed to be treated with kindness.

I was triaged and taken into a small consultation room. The emergency doctor asked me if I would provide permission for a medical student to observe the consultation – in front of that medical student. I didn't want to give permission. I felt vulnerable and overwhelmed but I gave consent because I felt outnumbered.

I was advised that I could not access my psychiatrist because he was working in the public system with children. I stressed that I did not want to be prescribed a new SSRI and explained that they did not help: they just made life more unbearable. I recall being asked if I intended to kill myself and my answer was that I didn't want to – that I was spiralling down and that was why I was at hospital.

The attending doctor left the room, leaving the door ajar, to discuss me in the hallway. Apparently, *bipolars* are deaf. The doctor returned with a new script for another SSRI. Knowing that I was a counsellor, they advised me to 'get some counselling' and sent me home.

I don't experience pain anymore when I think about that moment but it was traumatising. It was as though I had been trapped at the bottom of a well with my last lit match guiding my rescue party, only to have my rescuers snuff out the match and abandon me. I feel outrage when I consider the layers of disrespect, ignorance and malpractice that was later explained away as the problem being that 'she is high functioning'.

No one asked if I had someone to take me home safely. No one asked me about the nature of my suicidal thoughts or whether they were more frequent or intense. No one asked me how I felt after imagining my suicide. No one offered me comfort, or safety planned: they just sent me home with no hope and my imagined method.

Mental imagery manifests when perceptual knowledge is retrieved from memory. Mental imagery is different from verbal cognition because it has sensory characteristics that can be consciously described and its image can be shown on a neural level.[9] Imagination uses memory to allow us to relive previously experienced events. It also permits us to create new blends of never-experienced images and the capacity to 'time travel' to the future to what could possibly happen. Autobiographical (past) memory processes and processes that enable our ability to imagine our future require shared neural processes.[9]

People use guided visualisations to alter their emotional states. People create visual story boards and goal setting images as inspiration to strengthen their likelihood of success by elevating the importance of their thoughts. Therefore, it is far more probable for us to carry out actions we have practised in our imaginations than those we have merely talked about.[10,9,11] Imagery in nightmares and flashbacks is the indication of post-traumatic stress disorder: imagery can elicit powerful emotions linked to the stored memory of the original trauma.[12,11] Such mental images can simultaneously cause emotional and psychological distress, and reinforce the maintenance of numerous psychological disorders, such as PTSD, anxiety, phobias and depression.[11]

The individual's adopted perspective of mental imagery bears affective and behavioural ramifications: first-person perspective usually eliciting emotional influence.[11] Such facts need to inform current suicide prevention policy when one considers the combined power of repeated mental imagery reinforced by amplified, distressing emotions to distort perception and increase the likelihood of practised behaviours. The 'how do I feel about the outcome of my imagined scenario' heuristic is involved in increasing the likelihood of the imaginer's subjective probability estimation and the imagined suicidal behaviour.[11] In other words, practice makes perfect.

Hales, et al.'s[10] study of cognitions in bipolar depression and unipolar depression revealed individuals living with bipolar depression were substantially more absorbed with *flashforward* imagery, considered the imagery to be more compelling, and were 'more than twice as likely to report that the images made them and to take action to complete suicide'. Furthermore, participants diagnosed with bipolar disorder reported a higher trait disposition to use mental imagery ordinarily. Of all mental illnesses, bipolar disorder carries the greatest risk of completed suicide.[13.10]

Most of Hales et al.'s[10] participants reported, without being prompted, that they never talked about their suicidal images with their clinicians. Exploration of mental imagery and rehearsal does not feature in suicide prevention training for clinicians in 2021. Little has changed in 11 years. Holmes et al.[9] argued the necessity of considering the non-traumatic, anxiety-related-imagery people diagnosed with bipolar disorder experience because of the high rates of OCD and social phobia comorbidity.

Now consider the impact of insight on suicidal ideation. Greater awareness or insight is associated with improved adherence to treatment and therapy, and to more effective outcomes. Cognitive impairments, such as memory and executive functions, and severe psychotic symptoms are associated with impaired insight.[14] Health literacy, including illness and wellness awareness and the individual's capacity to recognise and identify abnormal mental events (i.e., hallucinations and delusions) is essential to recovery and relapse prevention.[14]

Psychoeducation is a vital component of therapy in the development of insight. At no point throughout my diagnosis or experience of illness, was I ever provided psychoeducation about my diagnosis, the aetiology of the disorder, or the treatments. That was my puzzle to solve. The more questions I had, the more complex the problem became. It was an intersectional problem of gigantic proportions that tended to eclipse hope.

Látalová[14] argued that increased suicidality in people diagnosed with schizophrenia and bipolar disorder may be associated with better awareness. Impairment of insight is greater in the course of an illness episode than during remission, in mixed than in manic episodes, in patients diagnosed with bipolar 2 than in bipolar 1 disorder, in pure mania than in unipolar or bipolar depression. Látalová recommended the use of concordance therapy (brief cognitive therapy) to help patients develop insight regarding their illness, its management, and results.

Such therapy necessitates all of the factors missing from my experience of the public health system, and later, the private health system, unless I demanded it. That is, a collaborative approach taken by the patient and the doctor, empowerment of the patient through the provision of sufficient information, respect for the patient's articulated perspectives and desires, and offering the patient a significant part in treatment determinations.

Mental illness insight is not a black and white measure: existent or non-existent. Nor is it as simple as well or unwell. It involves awareness of: illness, individual and social health, the aetiology of the symptoms, the need for care, treatment and recovery, and the social consequences of the patient's illness. I maintain that the understanding of mental illness and the development and maintenance of mental health requires a bidirectional growth of insight between the health practitioner and the patient. In other words, try listening to your patients and you might learn something.

The order of events is muddled in my head now. I refused to begin taking a new SSRI and I think I asked my GP to contact my original psychiatrist for help. He is a lovely man: non-judgemental, generous and kind. In fact, he is the only psychiatrist who I am aware of who provides talk therapy and bulk billing. He prescribed me a new medication which I had not used before and I cannot remember what it was.

The pharmacist asked me if I had taken it before and explained to me that it was an antipsychotic. I recall my feelings of horror and shame. I felt betrayed that my trusted psychiatrist had not advised me that I needed antipsychotics (having no knowledge that antipsychotics are often used to 'treat' depression) and ashamed that my nice pharmacist would think that I was insane. What I clearly remember is that I was seriously depressed and that the medication immediately caused insomnia. I calculated that I had fewer than eight hours sleep during the best part of three weeks.

My GP convinced me that I needed to be admitted to a private mental health hospital on the southside of Brisbane. I had told her that Adrian did not want me to go to hospital but I just wanted to be looked after. She assured me that it was a nice hospital with lovely gardens. I rate my five and a half weeks' treatment at that private hospital as being in the top five of my most traumatising life experiences.

Erving Goffman's[15] description of the *total institution* of asylums had stuck in my head since I read about his theory when I was 18 years old. I doubt that he would need to add many more notes now to his original observations documented in 1961. From my perspective, patients are still treated as inmates, rewarded for conforming and their illnesses remain a mystery that may only be *understood* by those in power of the medical model.

Adrian drove me to the hospital which was approximately seven hours away from home. I had packed a bag with toiletries and sleepwear, having become an expert at the hospital environment. I was simultaneously terrified of being so far away from the regional centre, and relieved that I was going to be looked after. I was expecting a pleasant room, similar to other private hospital rooms and the *lovely gardens* had sounded like the promise of healing.

On my arrival, I was presented with a welcome pack at reception that was a small clear sealed plastic bag consisting of ear plugs and a mini-Mars bar. The hospital was being renovated. I was shepherded to my room and sternly told that I would require more clothing and that I was not allowed to wear my pyjamas all day. The nurse seemed horrified that I had expected otherwise and I felt like a stupid child when I explained that it was normal to wear pyjamas in hospital in the regional centre.

There were no paintings on the walls of my room and the windows would not open even though it was a single storey building. My shower had no curtains or screens (presumably to prevent suicide attempts) so the water went all over the floor and the room steamed up. I vaguely recall being told to not trigger an alarm in the bathroom by having hot showers. It was winter. I had to pay extra to have a TV in my room and spent a good week chasing down an antenna. I think we also paid extra for a phone to be in my room so that I could make a daily call home. My environment was depressing, alien and lonely. It was also terrifying.

I felt guilty for having extremely high blood pressure that frustrated a nurse because he tried three monitors when he didn't believe the reading. No one seemed to link my fear with the reading, even though I had been followed by a very disturbed patient who was clearly experiencing psychosis and paranoia and had expressed angry suspicions of me. I felt exhausted and was accused of not knowing my own mind when I didn't sleep during my first night, having been assured that I would because I had been provided Seroquel, Valium and Rohypnol.

I would defy anyone to sleep in a noisy hospital when they regularly have a torch shone on their face during the night, whilst being terrified, alone and simply not able to sleep. I may have been experiencing symptoms of a mental illness but I was not a liar. The next night they gave me two Rohypnol. I didn't sleep. I guess I must have begun sleeping on the following night.

A nurse dumped clean bed linen on the end of the bed and told me to remake my bed on the morning after my arrival. All meals were shared by patients in a large buffet-style dining room. Trapped. I absolutely hate food courts in shopping centres to this day because they trigger my sense of being observed whilst I eat and they have no sense of space, much like cattle being herded before they're slaughtered. We had to line up for our medication. The nurse had her favourites and they seemed to be the patients who didn't ask questions and were very compliant or sedated. I secretly called her Ruby 40.

She started off as Ruby, then became Ruby 20 and progressed to Ruby 40 according to the average time she took to address my needs.

Ruby 40 definitely had an attitude towards patients and doctors. She tested my urine and advised me that I had blood in it. She asked me if I had my period. I replied no. She asked me if I was certain. I said I was sure and that I had often been told that I have blood in my urine but nothing has ever been made of it. Ruby 40's theory was that my kidneys were shot 'but don't tell the doctors because they don't like being told anything by nurses'. It seemed Ruby 40 wasn't a fan of the medical model either.

I also unwittingly made an enemy of a locum GP sometime during my first week. I had dressed respectfully to travel to Brisbane. I wore a black dress with a black lace overskirt, sheer black stockings, black Italian leather, medium-heeled shoes and a striking red, black, and ochre yellow Kisi stone bead necklace that my best friend had given me. My mother had taught me to dress well when one goes to the city, attending appointments, or when one is working as a professional.

My attire seemed appropriate for driving to hospital and then changing into sleepwear. I felt horribly out of place as a patient. I also had to wash my one outfit regularly until Adrian could freight down a carton with clothes and books to last the duration of my stay. I apologised to the female locum GP for being overdressed. She immediately became hostile and asked me if I thought she wasn't dressed well enough. Nothing I could say would convince her that I wasn't being a bitch.

I told her about the pain in my chest, my constant headache and my experiencing breathing difficulties. Every time she took my blood pressure over the next five and a half weeks, it was elevated. It was never elevated when the kind, older male locum GP took it. She asked me if I studied maths at school. I replied that I had. She then asked me, 'Do you remember the circle?' I refrained from asking her if that was the one with four sides. I nodded. She then described to me how one measures the area of a circle to explain to me that I was getting enough oxygen. Never in my life have I encountered her equal in being such a condescending bitch. It took me another six months to have my breathing difficulties and chest pain addressed. It certainly didn't involve someone testing my geometry skills to save my life.

The general Australian public most commonly connects with mental illness via the movies or media.[16,17] Research of media depictions of mental illness has found that both news media and entertainment most frequently provide negative and inaccurate images of mental illness. The most common depiction involves mentally ill people as childlike and helpless, or unpredictable, aggressive, violent, and a potential danger to others and themselves.[16,18,17,19] The way in which I was treated by that particular GP and many nurses in that private mental health hospital was merely evidence to me that mental health workers are not immune to the effects of media constructed mental illness meanings.

We were expected to attend group sessions, typically CBT and art therapy. I stated emphatically that I would not be attending CBT sessions because I knew there was absolutely no point my being there. I was afraid of going to the art therapy group because I was worried that I had forgotten how to draw.

I'm glad that I went because it was the most effective therapy I received: I led my own recovery through colour and symbolism. It was pure mindfulness. My mandalas kept me occupied in my room and away from other depressed or dangerous patients who had no semblance of boundaries and personal insight.

Psychedelic Peace (2011)
Pencil on black paper Circ. 18 cm

Tsunami (2011)
Pencil on black paper Circ. 18 cm

There is a pecking order amongst patients. The highest level of awe is reserved for those who are in the secure wing: the patients who *really* tried to die. Then there are the frequent flyers: those who are regularly admitted for treatment. Some of the frequent flyers can be identified by their vague sense of place and poor memories. I discovered that they had also received ECT and claimed that it didn't affect them … every time we had the same conversation. Next, the patients with decent diagnoses like schizophrenia or bipolar disorder. I have no idea who is on the bottom rung but I certainly didn't aspire to rising through the ranks. I wanted to get out.

I spent as much time as I could out of the hospital on day leave at the enormous shopping centre directly opposite the hospital. It was disastrous on almost all fronts. I was suffering from serious anxiety being in the hospital: a sense of loss of control and entrapment. At that time, shopping was my default mechanism for such feelings. Clothes, jewellery, shoes and expensive colouring pencils. Brilliant. Poor Adrian. We needed me to spend money like we needed holes in our heads.

However, I did eventually calm my anxiety and curb my shopping with my drawing, and shopping was far better than the initial urge to step in front of the oncoming traffic when I was crossing the road to the shopping complex. It still amazes me that I was allowed out when I was feeling so dangerous to myself. In hindsight, I suppose I only had therapy with a psychiatrist once each week so who would have known I was feeling so bad?

I recall posing the question of the impact of childhood sexual abuse on my mental health and diagnosis with one of the psychiatrists. I don't recall his response other than he didn't think it was good to leave 'the elephant in the room' with my father. I still haven't told him and I don't think I ever will even though I wish he really knew me. Perhaps, that is my choice.

I am not certain of when I was prescribed Valdoxan 25mg (Agomelatine) but I think it was towards the end of my hospital stay. Being prescribed this medication made my five and a half weeks' sentence worthwhile. My request to be treated with a medication that was not an SSRI was finally met. Seroquel was dropped. It would have been wonderful to have had a mental health practitioner explain to me that atypical antipsychotics are often prescribed to patients as mood stabilisers to remove some of the shame I felt at the time that I associated with the medication.

Best of all, the head psychiatric nurse treated me with respect when I asked for information about my new medication. He was surprised and commented on the fact that my inquiry was unusual for a patient but good. He provided me with printed information about Valdoxan and I recall feeling like an equal when we conversed.

I have reflected on my equal surprise that I was an unusual patient. This has been a common theme throughout my experience of the medical system and it greatly concerns me. Health literacy is not promoted in Australia. The paucity of health awareness, both physical and psychological, is an indictment of the neo-liberal political system whose main interest appears to be the maintenance of power via the jealous guarding of knowledge and the sustained elevation of corporate greed. This perspective needs to change.

My psychiatrist informed me that Valdoxan was a very new drug that worked differently from SSRIs and had few side effects. He stated that 25 mg was as effective as the initially recommended 50 mg and I remained on that dose for 10 years. Valdoxan has unique pharmacological processes (i.e., it simultaneously acts as melatonin agonist and a selective serotonin antagonist) that can restore disrupted circadian rhythms in people suffering from depression.[20,21]

It has been reported to be an effective antidepressant for both response and remission rates, and is superior in tolerability, having less side effects.[20] Circadian rhythmicity is essential for humans to physiologically and behaviourally function, and to manage significant variations happening in the extrinsic environment. Mood disorders such as seasonal affective disorder, unipolar and bipolar depression and major depressive disorder have been connected to circadian rhythm irregularities.[21]

Interventions such as light therapy and medications targeted at resynchronising patients' circadian systems have shown antidepressant effects. Sleep problems are a predominant characteristic of depression. At least 80% of patients diagnosed with depression report impaired quality of sleep, whether it be difficulty falling asleep, maintaining sleep, or waking early in the morning.[21,22] Studies have identified polymorphisms in specific circadian genes that link with mood disorders, particularly bipolar disorder. The circadian clock genotype has been linked with more severe insomnia during antidepressant therapy, more frequent recurrences of bipolar episodes, and a decreased sleep requirement for patients with bipolar disorder.[21]

It wasn't my imagination. Research shows[20,21,22] that most patients diagnosed with depression are medicated with manufactured drugs such as SSRIs that affect the monoaminergic system; norepinephrine and dopamine reuptake blockers; serotonin norepinephrine reuptake inhibitors (SNRIs); monoamine oxidase inhibitors; and tricyclic antidepressants which demonstrate limited or no amelioration of depression and cause side effects like sexual dysfunction, fatigue, cognitive disorders, and sleep disorders. In fact, SSRIs reduce restorative sleep (REM), thereby exacerbating insomnia symptoms.[22] It doesn't take Stephen Hawking to tell you that any individual who lives with depression, experiencing those side effects for a lengthy period of time, would feel depressed. Sleep deprivation is known to be an effective torture technique designed to break the strongest of individuals.

The comorbid disorders caused by antidepressants are often treated with benzodiazepines, despite the high-risk side effects associated with them.[22] Agomelatine has been shown to be effective in the treatment of people diagnosed with depression by its successful reduction of sleep complaints, increased duration of slow wave sleep and normalised sleep structure. Agomelatine has demonstrated to be a fast performing, dual action medication that can simultaneously improve the quality of sleep and diminish depressive symptoms.[22] Furthermore, no author of any peer-reviewed journal article discussing agomelatine I have studied, has declared benefits, or affiliations with any pharmaceutical company.

In my experience, Agomelatine (Valdoxan) is an ideal antidepressant medication that offered me quality sleep, increased daytime alertness and appeared to improve my mood: helping me to be a much happier bunny during my day and night.

Chapter 15

Emerging

Raison d'être (2017). Watercolour, 24 x 24 cm

Let your pain, be my sorrow
Let your tears, be my tears too
Let your courage, be my model
That the north you'll find, will be true
When there's no information
And the compass turns to nowhere
To nowhere, that you know well
        Sting[1] Let Your Soul Be Your Pilot, *Mercury Falling.*

Now the darkness only stays at night time
In the morning it will fade away
Daylight is good
At arriving at the right time
It's not always going to be this grey
All things must pass

George Harrison[2] All things must pass.

So, if you meet me
Have some courtesy
Have some sympathy, and some taste
Use all your well-learned politeness
Or I'll lay your soul to waste,
Pleased to meet you
Hope you guessed my name,
But what's puzzling you
Is the nature of my game

Jagger-Richards[3] Sympathy for the Devil, Beggars Banquet.

Valdoxan isn't a wonder drug: it doesn't cure trauma. My life didn't suddenly flood with technicoloured brilliance like Dorothy's transition from Kansas to Oz. I returned home to the regional centre, deeply depressed. I received one follow-up call from the hospital during which I was advised that my continued experience of depression was 'normal', that many people feel depressed when they leave hospital because hospital 'feels safe'. The nurse's explanation could not have been further from the truth. However, my environmental stressors had not altered: we were still experiencing financial hardship and I was not going to become a psychologist. I continued to have a constant migraine, a pain in my sternum, difficulty breathing and poor eyesight.

I felt pretty miserable and had to get a handle on my situation. I had my eyes tested. I consulted my GP to obtain a referral to a psychologist. She also gave me a referral to an allergist located in Brisbane. I knew the type of therapeutic approach I needed a psychologist to demonstrate and knew who I wanted to see but felt too ashamed to ask to be referred to him. I was scared that my supervisor (a clinical psychologist) would question my capacity to be a therapist if I had experienced mental illness.

I agreed to see another clinical psychologist who my GP recommended because 'he practises EMDR'. I knew very little about Eye Movement Desensitisation and Reprocessing Therapy at that stage and like all good psychology students of the time, was very sceptical about the practice. I arrived at the therapy room feeling like I was at rock-bottom despair and ready to break: the very last thing I felt I needed to do was complete several evaluation forms to measure my level of depression.

My pain was very visible. I did not want to talk out loud to a stranger about my experiences in the hospital. In 2011, I thought, 'if someone waves their finger in front of me in the name of therapy, I am likely to stick two fingers up at them'. My attitude was a reflection of the lack of respect I had felt from the medical system and was utterly misplaced with that psychologist but I did not make further appointments beyond my initial assessment.

I summoned the courage to make a therapy appointment with the clinical psychologist who had previously been my supervisor. It was the best action I could have taken: I felt safe. Spencer consistently communicated a genuine valuing of me as an individual and he demonstrated respect. He heard me and didn't attempt to retraumatise me by opening old wounds. Spencer didn't need to be convinced that I had experienced five and a half weeks of hell. When you're doing time, you don't forget the *and a half.*

He spoke to me on my level: drawing on my love of music, psychology, philosophy and culture to connect with me, inspire me and dispel any possible power differential. Spencer was attuned. I felt he could see me. He played a YouTube video of a guitarist playing an exquisite acoustic rendition of *While my guitar gently weeps* and said, 'This is you'. I felt visible. He challenged me when I said that I wasn't intelligent enough to finish my honours degree in psychology because I couldn't make myself face statistics again. He made direct eye contact with me and said, 'bullshit.'

I enrolled in a Masters of Guidance and Counselling for 2012 having decided that I wanted to work with grief after listening to an interview with David Kuhl, and reading his book, *What dying people want*[4] and Irvin Yalom's *Staring at the sun*[5]. The course coordinator assured me that I would be qualified to work in palliative care.

The allergist informed me that I would need desensitisation treatment for allergies to dust and cats. The treatment cost an absolute fortune and would be imported from France. I had hope that the treatment would help ease the constant pain in my face and my painful breathing. The optometrist informed me that I would need new glasses, that my eyesight had deteriorated six times faster in one year than the normal person and that I was legally blind.

I could recognise familiar faces when they were close to me. I could see dark blobs where eyes and mouths were when I watched the TV. I had been interpreting text according to the shape of words for quite some time and I had been extremely cautious in judging distance when I drove. I was terrified because I knew, even though we had private health insurance, we couldn't really afford new glasses that wouldn't be unbearably heavy on my sore nose and face. I was an economic burden on Australia and my health was an endless economic burden for my immediate family. The financial strain caused painful ruptures in my relationship with Adrian, and deep-seated guilt in me. The miserable darkness of 2011 merged seamlessly into 2012, blotting out the silver glints of hope that I had held for a new, purposeful career.

I cannot recall the date in January 2012 when it was impossible for me to lie flat in bed to sleep. I was scared. I told Adrian that the pain in my sternum and heart was referring to my back and that I was finding it too painful to breathe lying down. I can't remember if we waited until morning to drive to the base hospital, or if we drove there that night.

As per usual, I had the impression that the hospital staff thought I was a hypochondriac. The staff in emergency are busy and pressured, hence they really don't have time to reassure concerned patients to make them feel safe. It just infuriates me when I am fobbed off with the standard phrase, 'it will probably be a blood clot' because I interpret it as 'you're overweight and have probably brought it on yourself because of your lifestyle'. I know that I told them that the pain had existed for approximately 18 months and that it had become more painful, closer to my heart, in my back and that it was harder to breathe. Blood tests and chest x-rays were conducted.

I recall a doctor telling me, 'The good news is you don't have a blood clot. The bad news is that you have a mass where you shouldn't have'. Apparently, I had a thymic tumour that wasn't possible to be operated on in the regional centre, and I would need an MRI before driving to Brisbane for immediate surgery. The doctor informed me that I shouldn't really need a thymus at my age. I now assume he meant I didn't have a developmental need for a thymus beyond puberty but it made me feel more of an unfortunate freak than comforted me. The MRI was terrifying. I wouldn't normally describe myself as claustrophobic but I certainly cried the entire time I was being scanned: my whole world was uncontrollably shrinking and I felt trapped and powerless.

I didn't ask what the operation would involve: I was in a state of shock. We drove to a private hospital in Brisbane for my surgery, understanding that I would need to convalesce for a month with my parents before I could return to the regional centre, to fully recover. I am glad that I wasn't aware of the surgical procedure prior to my surgery: I doubt that the staff would have been able to focus on my speed-of-light form disappearing over the horizon. I know that when I briefly experienced consciousness after the surgery that I said, 'I want to die' before falling unconscious again. I thought the anaesthetist said, 'No, you don't. My poor baby' but I recently discovered it had been Adrian.

I was in intensive care for a couple of days before moving to a private room. There were three very significant moments that occurred whilst I was in hospital. My brother briefly visited me and insisted on reading my patient file. It's amazing how doctors can make demands of nurses whether they work in the same hospital or not. I believe he reported reassuring information to my parents and told them that it would be a rough recovery. I knew he cared. He had visited me in the mental health hospital too and took me to an Indian restaurant for lunch. He wasn't warm and overtly affectionate but he was real: he was my brother and he cared about me.

My parents very briefly visited me shortly after my surgery. I remember preparing for their visit: showering and struggling to change my hospital gown for a nightie so that I would look less unwell. It was extremely painful for me but I wanted to look OK for them. I was shocked and disappointed at how soon they left but I will never forget the look of horror on my mother's face when she saw me. Edvard Munch's *Geschrei* is the most accurate depiction of internal pain made visible: no doubt we were embodying that anguished figure.

The third visit was devastating and reminiscent of when I was ambushed by my parents and the deputy principal during my final year at school. I had indicated on my hospital forms that I am an atheist and did not want hospital chaplain visits. I was very polite but firm when the Anglican hospital chaplain discounted my instructions and visited my room to offer pastoral care. I was 42 years old and within my rights to assert my boundaries.

My father visited not long after the pastoral visit and disclosed to me that the chaplain informed him that I didn't want pastoral visits. Dad was visibly upset. I tried to explain to him as gently as possible that I am an atheist and he cried, lamenting that he had failed me. I was angry at the hospital administration's and chaplain's breaches of confidentiality but I was more concerned about causing my father pain. I immediately told him that he had not failed me, that he had taught me the values of love and compassion and those are the greatest gifts. I feel acute pain when I recall the third visit because I know that my father still prays for my soul – that I will see the light, and he fears my damnation in Hell for all eternity. The truth is, I've spent many years in Hell. I no longer fear it because I've learnt to manage it. Some would argue that I will be in good company.

The month I spent with my parents after Adrian returned to the regional centre, to look after our sons was painful and transformative. I slept seated in a recliner in the sunroom because I couldn't lie down. At first, my father cut my food up so that I could feed myself. I avoided laughing, sneezing and coughing because any sudden movement or pressure on my chest and ribs was unbearable. I sat to shower and my mother washed and dried my long hair.

I treasure the moments when she combed my wet hair because she was so gentle: so very different from when I was little and she felt stressed and seemed to resent the presence of knots. I felt loved and safe. Dad insisted on taking advantage of a captive audience by playing recorded André Rieu concerts for me until I thought my ears would bleed or I would give up the will to live. Mum and I binge-watched *Poldark*, read novels and discussed politics which was far more my scene. The days were bearable because I was generally occupied and was medicated with Targin (oxycodone). At night I was utterly vulnerable.

In retrospect, I was in a similar situation to the one when I was pregnant with David and living with my parents. I was living in close proximity to the source of my trauma and I felt as though I had as much personal power to protect myself as I had when I was six. Before Adrian left, he told me that he had to wake me from my nightmares. Adrian had been sleeping in the spare bedroom downstairs and had heard me howling in my sleep. My howls were so loud that they had woken him.

After Adrian left, my father woke me from my nightmares. I don't recall the dreams I had then other than they involved being hunted and that I felt terrified. I was not capable of lucid dreaming and dream reconstruction during that time: perhaps the medication prevented me. Each moment I spent at my parents simultaneously brought me closer to my mother and closer to my need to resolve my trauma.

It took approximately eight months to fully recover from surgery. My GP told me that my surgeon didn't explain the surgical procedure to me because it was better for me to not know that he would saw my sternum in half and break every rib to remove the tumour. The tumour had placed pressure on my aorta but was benign: I was extremely lucky. I deferred my studies until 2013 and focused on my recovery.

I jumped through hoops to register as a provisional teacher and worked as a supply teacher. I had to complete two years fulltime to be considered a fully-registered teacher because 13 years of teaching and several degrees can fall out of your head if you haven't been paying registration fees. I was offered a fulltime contract by the school principal and deputy principal who wanted to employ me and offered to write a letter to the department but the department wasn't flexible.

It was impossible for me to successfully re-enter the education system as a guidance counsellor because I wasn't a fully-registered teacher. It wasn't until I embarked on a placement that I discovered that the course coordinator had misled me regarding being able to work as an allied health professional with a Masters of Guidance and Counselling. What is a degree between friends, other than time and further debt?

Over the following two years, my immune system refused to benefit from desensitisation treatment and my symptoms worsened. My neurologist diagnosed me with tension migraines and fibromyalgia. I guess my overall pain and breathlessness wasn't hypochondria after all. My father paid for me to have eye surgery that involved grinding down my corneas, laser surgery and replacing my lenses. I discovered that I could read without glasses, catch things left and right-handed and that I wasn't especially stupid and uncoordinated. It was like discovering a superpower.

Two conversations led me to consider writing and two conversations provided the passion to follow through. I genuinely enjoyed the company of my regional manager of Lifeline in the regional centre. He is a gentle, compassionate, perceptive, humorous man with an inquiring intellect and twinkly eyes. We met for green tea and stimulating conversation on numerous occasions after we had both left the service. It was during one of those occasions that he suggested that I should write.

It wasn't an outlandish thought but it surprised me because I had no idea why he would think that I could. I pondered the question out loud with my best friend, Noelene, as we walked along the beach. I told her, 'My favourite writers are Salman Rushdie, E.M. Forster, Robin Hobb and J.K. Rowling. I could never write as well as them so what's the point of writing? I have to write well and all the best books have been written'. I suspect Noelene invented a potion for personal agency: she certainly emanates unwavering belief in my ability to climb mountains that seem insurmountable, 'Why do you have to write like them?' Noelene immediately began providing me with newspaper and magazine clippings about publishing. My main obstacle was that I had nothing to write about.

During another walk, I was furious. I had been bottling up my sense of social injustice and hurt at the maltreatment and discrimination I had received from the health system. As far as it is possible to stomp on sand, I stomped for a good kilometre, verbally fuming about the many occasions on which I had to search for answers, beg for help and fight to receive equal care. When was somebody going to help me? Noelene's reply wasn't what I expected. It was something like, 'It's up to you'. My emotional response was a sense of betrayal and my unspoken thought was 'It's always up to me' but it provided the fuel for my unlit fire.

I had a secret fear that I needed to articulate. I never provided details of my first traumatic event with Esther to Spencer. It was too painful and too shameful. I remained riddled with shame, disgust, self-loathing and confusion. I was worried that the development of my mental illness was evidence that I was not as strong as others who had experienced far worse adversities: that I was weak and abnormal. Furthermore, I was still aware of the chatter in my head and the internal *we* that provided reassurance and courage.

'Am I normal?' Spencer was thoughtful. He summarised the typical emotions survivors of childhood sexual abuse feel, like shame and grief. He then said, 'You're exceptional'. I spent most of my sessions analysing, avoiding feeling too much and sobbing, wishing that I would not cry. Spencer smiled, 'You won't cry on the day that you don't need to be here'. It was during my darkest moment of despair when I felt like I had lost all hope and would rather die that Spencer breathed hope. He described my hope as being a fire that had died down, leaving dimly glowing embers that just needed me to gently blow on them to bring them to life. His powerful metaphor inspired me to find my invisible sun. I began researching, writing and supporting Adrian through another round of chemo.

Life wasn't meant to be easy but I felt certain that life was particularly difficult until we sold our house and moved to the Sunshine Coast in late 2014. We had no choice but to sell our house because we could not afford the small loan we'd taken before the

Global Financial Crisis had hit Adrian's business. The floods had inflated insurance fees and made it very difficult to sell houses in the regional centre, despite our house being a pole house especially designed and built to withstand cyclones and floods. Two floods that never impacted our house devalued its selling price by $180 000. The sale did not cover the loan but we could move closer to better health services and the Sunshine Coast offered more opportunities for our sons' tertiary education and employment.

I drove to Townsville single-handed (because I had carpal tunnel in my right hand) with Adrian slumped against the passenger door to deliver my master's research presentation. I typed a 44 400-word assignment left-handed because I was advised not to use my right hand or I would lose my fine motor skills. The surgeon told me that I needed surgery immediately and he wasn't aware of any reason why I would need to postpone it. He hadn't factored in Adrian's chemo and my need to go to Brisbane for surgery. I had the surgery prior to moving to the Sunshine Coast. New eyes, new hand, a Master's qualification and a house on the Sunshine Coast – things were moving on a more positive trajectory.

Despite my qualifications, I discovered that it was almost impossible to find employment as a woman in her forties. I was frequently told that I was over-qualified. I didn't have barista training so I couldn't rely on my old waitressing skills. I reached the desperate point of consulting with our local MP to report the difficulties of employment when one has been out of work for various reasons and when one is considered 'too old or too qualified' to be employed. Peter Wellington was very kind and known for his honesty. He was very aware that underemployment and unemployment rates were high and that it was common for 'overqualified' people to struggle to find meaningful work, especially experienced workers. I was one of many of his constituents struggling with the same range of difficulties, so he took my concerns to parliament.

In 2015 I returned to counselling as a domestic and family violence prevention practitioner. Whilst my experience working for a large non-government organisation ended traumatically after about eight months (and is another story regarding the church's abuse of power and exploitation of employees) it was the catalyst for my recovery from trauma. I formed many enduring friendships with good women, I developed a sense of community, a reputation for being a highly-skilled therapist, wrote my own social theory and completed a Master of Social Work.

I was employed by a community organisation and appointed the role of clinical practice manager of its domestic and family violence prevention service. It was a service with a difference because my team of therapists helped women and children recover from trauma using evidence-based, trauma-informed and attachment-focused interventions. Our practice framework employed the Power Threat Meaning Framework: a non-pathologising conceptualisation of an individual's psychological distress caused by threatened personal power[6]. Best of all, my dear friend Fiona banished my perpetual threatening night sky to a distant realm outside of my sun's orbit.

Moonage Daydream (2020). Acrylic on canvas, 45 x 60 cm

Chapter 16

Finding My Invisible Sun

The Sound of Silence (2021). Acrylic on canvas, 34.5 x 44 cm.

Inky black night. We are running from the familiar terror that is never visible: never identified. We are running from death, or worse: endless suffering and execration. An abomination. Its breath is on our neck, coursing through our airways, filling our lungs and we throw our head back and howl our epiphanous agony to the empty heavens. We are one and the same, and there is no escape. How can one escape one's self?

I had been running for 40 years yet my night terror had never been so illuminating in its obscurity. I had been running from shame, self-hatred: a metaphorical self-perception of evil. I feared the wolf and the wolf was me. I loathed who I was and I feared who I might become.

My colleagues, clients and friends were shocked and appalled by the actions of the church organisation I had worked for. The details surrounding what happened are not relevant to this narrative but the impact on my mental health is. My shock was palpable. My friends later described my expression as 'traumatised'. It was as though I had lost my sense of reality, purpose, and self. Yet again, the betrayal, disempowerment and accumulated harm was inflicted by women. Upon reflection, they were women who upheld and represented the patriarchal system they served. It was the only way they had any semblance of power, whether it was moral and just or not.

The community organisation that I had closely liaised with, contacted me and asked that I establish a private practice because they wanted me to continue providing therapy for the women seeking shelter from domestic abuse. They saved my life and restored a little of my self-worth. Another wonderful friend encouraged me to study a Master of Social Work, arguing that I would be able to practice as an allied health worker and fulfil my dreams of working in palliative care. I am ever so grateful that Siobhan was impressively persuasive because my profession as an accredited mental health social worker allows me to practise from an informed stance, using my combined tertiary education and practice wisdoms.

Between 2016 and 2018 I studied fulltime, and ran my private counselling practice. The community organisation's CEO had asked me to write an early intervention program for women and children to obtain a funding grant. She said, 'If we get it, the job's yours'. I had never made an application for a funding proposal and was busy studying fulltime but I was grateful for the support the staff of the women's shelter had offered me so I agreed to help. To my great shock, we obtained the grant. The one-year pilot project was a success.

There was only one factor that was holding me back from working safely in the same community that I had grown to love when working for the church organisation. I was terrified that I would encounter the two women who had so effectively annihilated my fragile, incipient sense of self-worth. Fiona was furious when I voiced my fears to her. 'I'm not going to let them take your power'. The next afternoon, I drove to her house to receive eye movement desensitisation and reprocessing (EMDR) therapy. I had no idea what to expect but I trusted Fiona implicitly.

It was a deeply ontological experience, involving a painfully exquisite connectedness with nature, beings, emotions, the past, the present and the future. Fiona's house was just like Fiona: it appeared to have grown out of its natural landscape, at ease with the soil, the forest and sky. I felt as safe as I could possibly feel with the unknown that I was approaching with Fiona's assistance. I won't lie: I was still scared. Fiona provided me the option of receiving therapy on her verandah which I gratefully accepted.

Fiona is a brilliant, highly perceptive, and creative woman: a people whisperer. I'm fairly certain that Fiona could tame any wild brumby with her novel ukulele compositions and tea. She certainly intuitively knew what I needed that day. Only fools would be duped by her quirkiness: her wombat earrings (sometimes hastily mismatched), and oft dramatic and eccentric stories. I see her brilliance: her capacity to gently and lovingly approach the vulnerable with humility. Fiona is so at ease with herself that she can laugh at herself and say to all around her: *keep your power. Your power is yours, and mine is mine. I don't need anymore. In fact, I'll help you find yours, if you want to.*

We sat opposite each other and Fiona provided me with an A4 list of negative and positive beliefs. I was directed to choose the negative beliefs that resonated with me most: the ones I believed. I don't recall my beliefs but I may have chosen *I am powerless* and possibly *I am permanently damaged.* I know that I definitely believed that. Fiona provided me with water and a large box of tissues (she frequently needed to remind me of the latter for the following 90 minutes). Fiona didn't ask me about my target memories: we were there to process my latest memory, and Fiona had no knowledge of my diagnosis or trauma history. I was careful not to share my diagnosis with Fiona because I was aware that the diagnosis carried stigma and I didn't want her to think less of me. It didn't occur to me that none of my colleagues ever suspected it of me because I didn't demonstrate any 'bipolar behaviours'.

Fiona measured my level of belief in my negative belief and the positive belief that we were to replace the negative belief with. She measured my SUDS (subjective units of distress scale) and explained to me that I would need to 'just look' at my memory like I were travelling on a train and observing the scenery. I would just be noticing. Whilst I was looking at the scenery, she would tap my hands. Every now and then she would tell me to take a deep breath in and then, in my own time, let it go. She would ask me to report to her what I noticed. I wasn't to try to understand it, or analyse it, just notice it. Sometimes she would check my negative belief or SUDS and we would be aiming for a zero. Fiona asked me to place a cushion on my lap and then asked me where I felt comfortable for her tap. I chose the back of my hands. I liked the fact that I didn't have to tell her what happened: I didn't have to relive it.

My problem began when I was asked to imagine a flower. Fiona began the process with a visualisation to calm me and introduce me to a safe place. Any ordinary person would have loved it. If you hadn't noticed, I am a highly visual person. I use symbols and images to communicate my thoughts and feelings. I used visualisations to help teach relaxation skills to my students in special education and regularly made my teacher aide fall asleep.

I couldn't follow Fiona's visualisation to save my life. What type of flower would I choose? What colour? OK. That's impossible! I can't allow a flower to breathe for me! I was the worst client. I chose to tune in to the smells and sounds around me. I could smell the native vegetation and earth. I could hear the birds, the snuffling and movement of her dogs, and I could hear Fiona. I was safe. When I think of Fiona's home, I think of wood, forest, and the sounds of the forest. There is an image of growth.

I couldn't imagine the train ride. The images were too vivid and forcing me to look closely. I refused to pass them by and wanted to deal with the two women. I kept seeing them sat opposite me. The one on the left sat, speechless and expressionless. The other was talking but said nothing that made sense and most of it seemed incongruent with the messages she had given me two weeks prior. Why was I so scared of them? Have you ever listened to Dire Straits[1], Les boys (Making Movies, 1980)?

Les boys got leather straps
Les boys got SS caps
But they got no gun now
Get dressed up get a little risqué

That's precisely how I rewrote the narrative. I provided their costumes, enjoyed their performance, got up and left the room. My SUDS and negative belief dropped a little. We needed to go further back. Could I think of another target memory? In my head, I knew where I needed to go but I wouldn't. I knew that no one could change what happened to me and I would be ill forever. Nothing could change that because no one could undo it and my life would always be affected by her.

I travelled back to 2011, to the hospital. I was angry. I didn't stay on the train. I walked into reception, and informed them of their ignorance and discrimination. I gave them the British victory sign or the Australian 'ups'. Interpret the gesture how you like: I'm sure you will arrive at the most accurate interpretation. I strode out to the carpark, climbed into a Mini Cooper and drove away. It was the best feeling! I had wanted to drive a Mini since I was enthralled by the original and best film, *The Italian Job*[2], starring Michael

Caine. Again, my SUDS and negative belief dropped. Fiona asked me if I was at a solid zero. 'That's impossible', I replied. 'How can something be solid if it's not there?' Fiona laughed, and described me as something that amounted to being incorrigible. We needed to go further back.

I couldn't. There was no point. It was impossible and too painful. I was sobbing and using so many tissues that I had to stop apologising because it was too hard to multitask. Fiona was gentle. Perhaps she had intuited the source of my problem but I didn't tell her until 2020 when she introduced me to Family Constellations (another interesting form of therapy used for transgenerational trauma). She invited me to rescue little me. I don't remember how she invited me but I knew where to go and what to do. I would save me.

I walked into their house via the workshop space where her father was always busy working on his carpentry. It was dark and filled with the smell of sawdust. We always entered from the side entrance closest to the paddock that separated my home from theirs, not the front door. I stepped up into the timber, low-set house, straight into the hall that led to the kitchen. I smelt fear. My body felt tense, my heart was pounding and every fibre of my body told me to run but I wasn't leaving without me.

I could hear Fiona asking me if I could see her. I nodded. She is so small and she is standing alone in a very dark room. She's so vulnerable and powerless. 'How old is she?' *She's six.* 'Tell her she's safe. Tell her you will protect her and keep her safe now'. I'm sobbing and nodding. I don't look around to see if Esther's there. I don't care. I pick her up because I'm the adult, and I feel her cling to me. My mind tells her, *I have you now. I can protect you. I will keep you safe.* Fiona must be watching me. I don't know because I have had my eyes closed for most of the process. Her steady tapping keeps me in the present. I hear Fiona say, 'Have you got her?' I nod. 'Take her with you. Is she in your car?' I nod. 'Does she have her seatbelt on?' I nod again. I'm lying to Fiona. This job required so much more than an ordinary car. I was flying her home on a double-decker bus and I was holding her all the way. She has never left me.

Fiona measured my SUDS and my levels of belief in my negative and positive belief. It was nothing short of a miracle. I didn't quite believe it. I felt wrung out. Fiona advised me that I would feel exhausted and that my brain would continue to process the memories. She warned me that other memories may surface, that we could process those if they did and gave me a post-EMDR therapy record sheet to document any memories that surfaced. She checked in on me the next day to make sure that I was OK.

Dear Readers, I have never shared all those details with anyone. You are the first to read of what happened in that house and my thought processes during EMDR. I have offered glimpses of the processes when they have been useful for clients to transcend trauma but I have always guarded them as deeply personal. I believe it's necessary for me to share the power of this process because it was so life-changing.

The next morning, I drove to work but there was something that I had forgotten. I scanned my brain for what I may have forgotten, whilst driving. I knew my briefcase was packed because I always prepared the evening before work. I had remembered my lunch and handbag because they were on the passenger seat beside me. I suddenly had a moment of panic when I thought to myself, *Have I forgotten to put on my underwear?* I quickly felt for seams through my dress. I laughed with relief: I was fully dressed.

Enlightenment hit me with such force that Newton's famous apple assault and Buddha's fig were simply healthy snacks compared with my 16-hour mental feast. I felt miraculously lighter. The internal burden I had carried for 42 years had been magicked away. I didn't need to run anymore: I could see my sun.

Ontology (2020). Acrylic on canvas, 50 x 60 cm

Chapter 17

The Missing Piece

Enlightenment (1991/2016). Acrylic on board, 90 x 70 cm

I'm fixing a hole where the rain gets in
And stops my mind from wandering
Where it will go

I'm filling the cracks that ran through the door
And kept my mind from wandering
Where it will go

And it really doesn't matter if I'm wrong, I'm right
Where I belong, I'm right
Where I belong
The Beatles[1] Fixing a hole, *Sgt Pepper's Lonely Hearts Club Band.*

That was it. In his befuddled, sleepy state, he leant out of their bed, picked up their furry, little white dog and plonked her onto what he believed to be the space beside him. In fact, it was her leg. She was simultaneously shocked, angry, disappointed and very much awake. She would never know what the handsome, young blond man, who always ordered the aubergine meal from the pretty, dark-haired young waitress serving in the vegetarian restaurant would order.

My recurring nightmares ended. I am not afraid of the wolf and I am not afraid of me. I have a normal range of emotions; I have healed my trauma and I am whole. I had not stopped asking why: what I needed was someone to give me permission to protect myself and to say no. I had been gathering the pieces of my puzzle for two decades, attempting to know and understand why I was the way I was. Fiona had helped me find the missing piece that integrated the image: personal power was the answer I needed.

It always comes down to power: those who have it, those who don't and those who abuse it. I am angry with the Australian government's persistent commodification of knowledge and the bastardisation of the tertiary system, resulting in a neo-liberal business that promotes mediocrity, short-sightedness and passive minds. I was furious when the then course coordinator refused to give me credit for prior learning for more than two subjects for the master's course in social work.

She told me that it made her physically ill to provide me credit for advanced research and reflective thinking, discrediting the notion anyone could learn and develop the skills of critical reflective thinking within any other discipline. She said, 'You've wasted your time studying anything else'. I still shake my head when I remember her saying that. Wow, if only I had known that I wouldn't need those four degrees: that someone who originally said 'knowledge is no burden' could be so wrong. What was I thinking?

I sat through an introductory lecture and refrained from automatically leaving the room when we were told that humanists, modernists, educators, psychologists, and counsellors were all ineffective because change only happens at a social level. Boo to those who would think otherwise. I wryly thought to myself, 'I wonder which part of me I should hate the most.' This new and pervasive message was promptly followed by the next message, the biomedical model is evil. What can I say? Two legs bad, four legs good? The most common comments I received from the lecturers and tutors during the two-year degree were: *You should be lecturing, When you do your PhD …*, and *You don't think like a social worker*. I set a goal to achieve a GPA 7 without ever telling them what they wanted me to think. Nobody tells me what to think or how to think. Nobody will ever define me.

I attended sociology, despite having completed a minor in sociology in my arts degree. I observed that John Howard's push to make history studies a thing of the past was very effective. Recent efforts of the federal coalition government, beginning with Tony Abbott, to obliterate the study of humanities, thereby cauterising critical thinking has also been terrifyingly effective. It was evidenced throughout most levels of the university system, from the top down. The lecturers' insistence that any type of thinking before post-modernism was to be disregarded, and that no cultural knowledge gleaned from any source that was not collectivist was in some way misguided reminded me of the Dark Ages masquerading as the Reformation.

I believe that there has never been a greater sociologist than Foucault and no one who has really contributed anything further to his observations but I became so surfeited by labels, boxes and stigma that I drafted my own social theory in 2016 whilst watching *Rage* (a popular Australian music show like MTV).

Points of Resistance: An Epistemological Theory

Points of Resistance Theory (PORT) employs post-modernist, contextual, inclusive, deconstructive and reconstructive analysis of knowledge and discourse to access portals to knowledge and emancipation through means of curiosity and subversion.

PORT recognises that no one discourse provides truth, knowledge or reality. It acknowledges that all knowledges are useful and that it is only after the examination and deconstruction of many knowledges that a reconstruction involving a synthesis of components of knowledges can offer a new, incomplete but useful reflection of truth, knowledge and reality regarding the posed question at that point in time, for that person. In relation to any one discourse the point of resistance is also the point of access.

It is the central interdisciplinary paradox of this theory that where there is resistance to oppression there is the opportunity to learn. By approaching knowledge and discourse with a stance of curiosity one may perceive the point at which discourse renders one simultaneously vulnerable and powerful: the point of resistance. The point of resistance is the starting point for questions, exploration and dialogue that provides the direction and means for new direction and change.

PORT intentionally assumes a political, subjective standpoint. It holds that the personal is political and that it is only through the eternal questioning of reality (that is, our own personal experiences) that we recognise the need for subversion. By interfacing personal experience and discourses of knowledge and power, one can merge and share knowledge and power. The sharing of knowledge and power results in agency and liberation. Hence, PORT pays tribute to the French Resistance. It draws on Nietzsche's modernist, deconstructive theory, the humanist philosophies of E.M. Forster and Carl Jung, and Foucault's post-structuralist theory to devise a theory that provides the means to ontologically question: the way things are, why they are the way they are, should they be the way they are, and could they be another way? PORT therefore, promotes and provides the theory and method for questioning and affirming what it means to be human.

The fundamental principles of PORT follow:

1. There is oppression and this causes suffering
2. The Will to Power causes oppression 'Where I found the living, there I found will to power; and even in the will of those who serve I found the will to be master'.[2]
3. To eliminate oppression, one must relinquish the Will to Power
4. The means of relinquishing the Will to Power is to walk the spectral tightrope intersecting disciplines of knowledge

By *spectral* I mean the breadth of knowledge encompassing all disciplines: the sum total of human knowledge. This spectral path allows for a widening of perspective to reveal opportunities and develop solutions for change. The tightrope represents three characteristics of subversive action: a) the danger of challenging accepted truths (discourses), b) the balance required to negotiate and transcend dichotomies, and c) the courageous maintenance of focus on the path to solution.

PORT contends that it is impossible to understand and achieve full human agency and potential by adhering to one discourse. A singular discourse fails to recognise the complexity of human experience and only serves to limit human potential and agency. PORT aims to transcend dichotomous traps: to free people from social constructs that limit self and social understanding, and possibilities for growth and change. It provides an accessible language for multitudinous perspectives to be explored and explained without imposing universal, fixed prescriptions for social change. In other words, what works for me will not necessarily work for you but it is worth considering.

This theory developed as a reflexive response to academic constraints of what a 'valid research theory' should look like. That is, if my knowledge and understanding of my experience is not presented within academically recognised and approved theoretical discourse, and if my argument is not evaluated by recognised quantitative and qualitative research models embedded in recognised social theory, it is not valuable or valid. My life experiences have led me to questions that do not benefit from an analysis employing one or two discourses that inevitably further reinforce the oppressive structures that have led to my questions. I am multifaceted. My experiences are multifaceted. I propose that solutions to my perceived problems require a complex explanation derived from synthesised knowledges.

This way of thinking may help others like me, and I believe it would prove helpful when applied in broader social contexts. However, if you are expecting an anti-positivist approach, or a Marxist analysis, or feminist standpoint theory you will be sorely disappointed. My subversive curiosity refuses to be limited by that game.

I apply my social theory combined with my long-standing raison d'être to all that I do. The combined perspectives provide my moral compass, courage and strength. I had little time to work on *Finding my invisible sun* between 2016 and 2022 but I continued researching whilst I had free access to peer reviewed articles, and world-class professional development from renowned trauma specialists, such as Dr Bessel van der Kolk, Janina Fisher, and Pat Ogden. I also trained to become an EMDR therapist and member of EMDRAA.

Towards the completion of my Master of Social Work degree at the end of 2017, I provided further assistance to the community organisation I was working part-time with when the CEO pursued funding for a wrap-around domestic violence service. The CEO was a brilliant policy writer and funding grant applicant and successfully won the government funding. I was offered a fulltime position as a D&FV practitioner in October 2017.

I fulfilled my personal goal to obtain a GPA 7 (achieving High Distinctions/7s across institutions evidenced that there was no subjective bias or fluke). I didn't attend the graduation ceremony, nor did my family witness my award for academic excellence because we couldn't afford the $100 attendee invitation. I didn't accept the invitation to join the Golden Key Society because I had a greater need for underwear without holes (except the necessary ones) and petrol.

Nevertheless, during those two academic years I honed my argument for an interdisciplinarian approach to mental health and formulated the perspective that one can fully recover from trauma and shake off the shackles of labels if one has access to knowledge and power. The political struggle for dominant discourse and institutionalised power amongst health professions, including social workers, psychologists, nurses, and doctors, in tertiary institutions, health and helping environments is a maleficent distraction at the expense of mental health consumers.[3]

For consumers of the Australian mental health system, the political is personal – and the personal is political. Stigma silences: consumers of the mental health system hold a realistic perception that the dominant discourse has not changed and it is not safe to educate those in power if consumers desire to work in parity with them in the health system.[4,5]

Australia's *Fifth National Mental Health Plan*'s[6] vision for more people with improved health outcomes, and fewer people experiencing stigma and discrimination begs the question, 'How many, and how will we be able to know?' The policy provides no evaluation guidelines or goal. Accountability and transparency are rhetorical illusions in this policy. As Rosenberg[7], senior lecturer in mental health policy at the Brain and Mind Institute, Sydney, indicates, the FNMHP lacks funded commitments for independent data collection and analysis, thereby perpetuating the previous four national mental health plans' failures to establish legitimate accountability.

Similar to flawed research trials and data collection pertaining to the pharmacological treatment of mental illness that sustains profit for pharmaceutical companies, the federal government has established reporting (or lack thereof) methods to ensure that it can claim to have spent more on mental health than any previous government and to have provided better services with more positive outcomes than ever before. Its deliberate disconnection of Australia's primary and local health networks from the state and federal funding bodies conjures the smoke and mirrors necessary for it to shift the blame for systemic failure to mental health workers and mental health consumers.[7] It doesn't require the observational skills of Sherlock Holmes to discern the obvious discrepancy between the positive rhetoric of the FNMHP and the reported negative experiences of those working for, or those who have accessed the mental health services.[7]

Many stakeholders are involved at social policy and practice levels. Some of those stakeholders' interests are powerfully represented and articulated in policy but not all of the stakeholders enjoy equal representation, equal opportunity to access health and social resources that are deemed basic human rights necessary for health and wellbeing.[8] Those stakeholders who are supposed to be at the centre of a 'whole-of-person, whole-of-life' policy[6] aiming to reduce discrimination and stigma have the least voice; are systemically, adversely affected by devaluing dominant discourses that formulate social policy and deliberately under-resource mental health consumer needs

Helping professionals, whether they be mental health clinicians, allied health workers or medical practitioners, study various theories and models of health and are sometimes encouraged to think critically about how discourses develop, who developed them, and how they are used but not often enough. We are often presented these discourses in ways that have underlying assumptions about power, who wields it, and how we need to redress power imbalances.

I do not find it difficult to sit back quietly and listen to conversations involving members of interdisciplinary teams articulating power struggles founded on historical and tertiary-educated assumptions about dominant knowledges and ensuing power relations. How often do you critique the biopsychosocial and biomedical models, or the attachment-focused or trauma-focused approach, or the Power Threat Meaning Framework instead of the DSM with limited knowledge of any? How often do you assume that yours is the only profession that promotes critical thinking and the gold standard treatment for mental health with limited formal education or experience in other disciplines?

Ignorance, discrimination, stigma, lack of trust, lack of respect for difference leads to fear, anger and suffering. In our case, when health and helping professionals are struggling for recognition, or struggling to maintain power relations, it is to the detriment of the mental health consumer.

Let's critically think about how we can work together using socially-just, human-rights practice frameworks to emancipate society from divisive and marginalising discourses. Almost two decades have passed since Ian Hickey cautioned, '*What we do not need* is continued blaming of those who use the services, those professionals who provide the services or those independent bodies who report on them. Continuation of this culture of blame will only worsen the workforce crisis in public sector mental health services'.

As a mental health practitioner, I have lost count of the number of times I have heard my colleagues blame their clients for irregular or non-attendance, or for sounding like a broken record. Where do individuals who require mental health support go if their needs are too complex for a basic mental health care plan comprising 10 (and if 'fortunate' enough to be ill during a pandemic, 20) psychotherapy sessions? What if their needs aren't sufficiently acute to be hospitalised? Where do they go to regularly access good mental health support (e.g., weekly trauma-informed clinical support) if they can't afford the gap fee? What should they do if they aren't one of the privileged deserving few who can afford lengthy private hospital care? What if their needs are not being met so they feel compelled to repeat their stories until someone hears them and provides them the information and clinical support that they know they need?

What if there is no such thing as a simple answer to a complex problem?

Consider the phrase *their needs are not being met so they feel compelled to repeat their stories until **someone hears** them*. I have deliberately presented *Finding my invisible sun* to you as a mystery. My future and experiences surrounding my mental illness were mysteries to me. I felt lost, unheard, invisible, unknown and alone for several decades. Unlike many people diagnosed with bipolar disorder and major depressive disorder, whether or not they have a diagnosis of comorbid PTSD, I maintained a core sense of self that I clung onto and desperately fought for.

Many clients I work with have experienced childhood trauma and adulthood trauma. The majority of them eventually ask me to help them 'find me again' or 'find the old me' or 'feel something'. They describe themselves as permanently damaged, unlovable and incapable of trusting others. They experience a sense of having forgotten or lost something very important. It takes great courage and strength for them to ask for help. I know what it's like to feel unheard and to be told that I am beyond help.

Unlike normal, daily life events unaffected by trauma, traumatic experiences are saved in memory in a disorganised process. Traumatic memories interrupt the natural narrative flow, disrupting people's sense of place in their personal history: disconnecting their sense of past, present and future. Hence, trauma fragments and scatters an individual's personal identity and self-integrity.[10]

Eye Movement Desensitisation and Reprocessing (EMDR) is an evidence-based, psychotherapeutic treatment created by psychologist Francine Shapiro in 1987 to treat clients suffering from trauma. Pagani et al.'s[11] EEG study of neuronal activation during EMDR sessions concluded that EMDR therapy processes effectively alter brain wave activity, making Shapiro's approach the first with evidenced neurobiological effect.

EMDR is recommended by the National Institute for Care Excellence to treat adults with PTSD.[12] The World Health Organisation recommends EMDR as the preferred treatment for children, adolescents and adults diagnosed with PTSD.[10,13,14]. Recent research[12,16,17,] has shown that EMDR is also an effective and safe therapy for the treatment of complex diagnoses such as attachment, dissociative and personality disorders, schizophrenia, psychosis, unipolar depression, bipolar disorder, major depressive disorder, anxiety disorders, phobias, substance use disorders, chronic back pain and eating disorders. [10,13,14]

Van der Kolk et al.'s[18] comparison of the treatment efficacy of fluoxetine, with EMDR therapy and a pill placebo in participants diagnosed with PTSD measured the effects and maintenance of treatment gains at a six-month post-trial follow-up. The study found that EMDR therapy was more successful than the pharmacotherapy intervention in effecting sustained decreases in PTSD and depression symptoms, chiefly for participants diagnosed with adult-onset trauma.

The six-month follow-up revealed that 75% of adult-onset compared with 33.3% of child-onset trauma participants receiving EMDR attained an asymptomatic functioning outcome in contrast to none in the fluoxetine group. Most significantly, an eight-month follow-up showed a 73% cure rate in adult-onset PTSD and 25% in child-onset trauma. Van der Kolk[19] and Fisher[15] similarly argue intentional trauma-specific therapies such as EMDR are more effective, less expensive in the long-term and safer. Furthermore, trauma-informed, psychotherapy treatment plans are context-focused and tailored to the needs of the client.

My trauma was cumulative and began in early childhood, so why did it work so dramatically for me? I believe it was a combination of factors involving inherent and environmental protective buffers and coping skills. In other words, I possessed factors of resilience, and self-efficacy.

Resilience is characterised by positive developmental consequences despite elevated-risk conditions, sustained coping with stress, and recovery from cataclysmic events or serious deprivation.[20] Masten and Coatsworth[21] describe resilience as evidenced competence within the context of critical threats to development or adaptation. Identification of resilience depends on two evaluations: (a) the individual has experienced a critical threat (e.g., born into a marginalised and disadvantaged community) or survived serious hardship or trauma (e.g., domestic and family abuse, death of a caregiver, sexual abuse), and (b) the individual demonstrates high-quality adaption or development.

Resilience research describes seven key protective factors in an individual's manifestation of resilience: (a) social skills, (b) intelligence, (c) a faith in a higher power superior to oneself, (d) loving caregivers who employ authoritative parenting approaches, (e)unconditional love, and (f) community connectedness[22,21,20].

Lazarus[23,24] defined coping as a dynamic process involving continuous attempts to cognitively and behaviourally regulate psychological stress. This process is influenced by the individual's appraisal of his or her context, resources, and self-perception.[24] Effective coping behaviours such as problem solving, information seeking and acting on problem solving are correlated with superior competence and efficacious functioning.[25] Coping involves a positive attitude, belief in one's ability to manage a situation, and a variety of adaptive coping strategies.[26]

Self-efficacy concerns one's convictions in one's abilities to execute a specific behaviour necessary to produce a specific result.[27] Self-efficacy expectations develop from, and may be increased by the use of four efficacy information determinants: (a) performance successes, (b) vicarious learning, (c) anxiety, and (d) verbal encouragement.[27] Perceived self-efficacy affects coping behaviour, stress response levels, helplessness, motivation, the amount of effort expended on a specific task, perseverance when confronted by impediments or failure, and career choices.[28]

According to resilience researchers, I had a lot going for me. I had many of the ingredients they consider necessary to be a resilient child and adolescent. I had good intellectual functioning (when not under threat) and an open, sociable, conscientious disposition. Whilst my self-esteem and self-confidence were seven feet below the Earth's surface, my early exposure or experiences of the principles of self-efficacy, combined with some talents and high creativity allowed me to tread water long enough to survive.

My sense of self and place in the universe more than made up for a need for faith in a superior power beyond me. My close relationship with my father provided the pillars necessary to develop a healthy attachment style that I later formed with my mother and others. The structure my family provided me and high expectations of success were simultaneously lifesaving and torturous. It gave me an insider's understanding of the high prevalence of prisoner recidivism.

My strong connections to prosocial adults, friends, honorary grandparents, aunts and uncles outside my family gave me a broader, safer, more optimistic perspective of the world than the hell that I endured during my primary and secondary education. The people I admired or chose to trust visually communicated to me, *we value you, respect you and have faith in your capacity to make it.*

The oft pathologised symptoms that medical and mental health specialists have attempted to treat, correct or explain the difference in achievement or behaviours (e.g., 'You think too much', 'you're so fey', 'you use a lot of images when you talk') that loved ones have questioned were and are simply evidence of my extraordinary effort to use ordinary or 'normal' human adaptive processes to survive and to be the best version of myself.

Chapter 18

A Road to Peace of Mind

Cornish Man (2019). Watercolour and ink, 30 x 21.5 cm

Sometimes I'm in the sunshine
And Lisa you're in the rain,
Enemies are charging down,
You battle with the pain.
I'm sorry if it hurts you baby,
I love you, lord above,
We keep the peace on the frontline,
In the revolution of love.
We won't fight another man's revolution,
As a road to peace of mind.
Won't take a substitute solution,
There's nothing there to find.

Adrian King[1] *Revolution of Love*

'Eating cardboard isn't good for you.'

Adrian King 2022

And the shame, was on the other side
Oh we can beat them, for ever and ever
Then we could be Heroes, just for one day

David Bowie[2], *Heroes, Heroes.*

Holmes et. al[3] reported feedback from patients diagnosed with bipolar disorder who reported that cognitive behavioural therapy (CBT) was unhelpful. Bessel van der Kolk[4] noted that trauma treatment recommendations for survivors of the 9/11 attacks on the World Trade Centre were limited to CBT and talk therapy. However, a survey of 225 survivors conducted by St Vincent's Hospital in 2002 revealed survivors found massage, yoga and EMDR to be most helpful.

For millennia, people have been saying, 'I have no words to describe what happened to me. I was speechless'. People struggle to identify and describe emotions that have not felt safe or bearable to feel. Some have the superpower to forget. Most protect themselves (or 'avoid' in psycho-medical language) to think about and deliberately retraumatise themselves by talking about or thinking about what they most dread or don't understand.

Trauma-informed therapists know that trauma is sensed through perception, experienced physiologically, and stored in our bodies, our limbic system and memory to protect us from being vulnerable again. People will recall images, words, sensations, emotions, sounds, and smells at lightning speed to throw up their defence walls, invisible force fields or launch attack for as long as they can to survive. It's instinct. Suicidal ideation and suicide are the last bastions of the system's survival response.

Yet, 'non-responsive' or 'avoidant patients', those individuals with strong survival responses that are prepared to fight to the death to protect their threatened selves, are blamed for not recovering from trauma.

People diagnosed with PTSD re-experience traumatic memories through *flashbacks* of sensory features of the memory (e.g., smells, physical sensations, sounds or images) coincided with a powerful distressing emotion, such as terror. Flashbacks feel very real, as though the person is re-living the event and that they are just as vulnerable as they were at the time of the trauma. EMDR is recommended for the treatment of PTSD to desensitise and reduce the traumatic memories, and reprocess the negative beliefs that have protected the patient from being vulnerable by replacing the negative belief with a more helpful, protective belief founded on a new understanding of the experience.[5,6,7]

EMDR processing targets the individual's thoughts, emotions, images and physical sensations comprising their traumatic memories. The purpose of EMDR therapy is to reprocess and restructure the fragmented and scattered traumatic memories as part of the individual's private narrative memory.[8,9,6]

I had done the preliminary work necessary to develop stabilisation: coping skills that allowed me to maintain emotional regulation. I had intentionally researched and studied human development, trauma responses and the causes of mental illness to solve the puzzling problem of *why me?* Intellectually, I understood why my group of *symptoms* were described as 'textbook bipolar' by my psychologist in 2003. I hadn't experienced psychotic symptoms since then, nor dangerously clinical levels of depression since 2011 yet I believed I was permanently damaged and that nothing could change the reason. No medication could fix that truth. So why was EMDR different?

It was safe. Fiona's tapping made me physically aware that I was in the present at all times and that it was impossible for my body to travel back to an unsafe place. Her verbal reassurances and regular check ins (i.e., 'what do you notice now?') meant that I was never alone and I was never back there. The EMDR therapy process was individually tailored to focus on my beliefs, images, feelings, physical sensations: essentially, my truth. I didn't have to speak my truth out loud because I didn't need to have the words. I could rewrite the images with my special power: creativity.

Mental imagery amplifies negative and positive emotions which undoubtedly intensifies experiences of anxiety, stress, depression and pleasure and mood states observed in people diagnosed with bipolar disorder.[3] This does not have to be a bad thing, nor should the use of imagery in language and storytelling be pathologised, regarded only as a symptom of an elevated state, or overlooked in individuals diagnosed with mental illness. Gold standard cognitive approaches like CBT and talk therapy have been found unhelpful for many patients diagnosed with bipolar disorder and for people diagnosed with PTSD and complex childhood trauma.[5,3]

Lewis[10] argued that if consumers' efforts to inform legislation had been successful when the National DMDA formed, then millions of people living with mood disorders could have been spared existences marked by suffering and underachievement. The answer to most people's problems seems to be a matter of communication. Communication takes more than one person screaming into the ether. Successful communication depends on someone being receptive to the message. Patients diagnosed with bipolar disorder who reported that they found CBT unhelpful stated that CBT's '*focus* felt wrong' (Holmes, et al.,2008, p. 1256).[3] From my perspective, listening to my clients' use of language, whether they can find words, describe images or sensations, provides me with the means to their recovery and recreation.

The answer to my mystery was deeply embedded in the one desirable trait that researchers and the media have attributed to people assumed to have bipolar disorder: creativity.[11,12,13,14,15] My imagery susceptibility, and hyperawareness of feelings, and physical sensations allowed me to perceive my problems, describe my experiences, and find my solutions. Being more informed about the aetiology of trauma responses helped me to tie up the loose ends of my mystery and provided me with greater clarity regarding what is mine to feel responsible for: replacing shame with self-compassion, and vulnerability with empowerment.

Creative success necessitates generation of new ideas, critical thinking and attention to detail across the arts and sciences.[15,16] Many creative traits mental health specialists and doctors associate with bipolar disorder may be considered strengths: openness to new experiences, positive emotion, high energy levels, and motivation to attain success. Creative traits don't simply apply to people living with bipolar disorder, or people living with psychosis. There is no one-size-fits-all clinical treatment or evidence-based therapeutic approach that is suited to any individual seeking therapy for a psychological disorder caused by trauma. However, creativity is required to solve complex problems and I used it to solve my complex problem.

Whether my diagnosis of bipolar disorder was accurate or not, I had experienced accumulative trauma that caused trauma responses and the development of autoimmune disorders. I attribute much of my survival and recreation to my personality traits and creativity. Creativity is defined as the capacity to create something simultaneously original and adaptive or beautiful.[11,17] Creativity is intimately associated with personality and interacts symbiotically with environmental, cognitive, intelligence and personality variables to generate creative success.[12]

Rutter[18] posited that resilience is identified by a type of action with a specific goal in mind and a considered strategy to achieve the goal. Essentially, to be resilient, one must be creative and that demands a certain set of personality traits. The Five Factor Model of personality describes individual differences in personality as existing within five broad traits: neuroticism or emotional stability, extraversion, openness, agreeableness, and conscientiousness.[19]

Having recently completed a Five Factor model of personality test [International Personality Item Pool] developed by Goldberg[20] I feel pleasantly reassured that my claims to be an optimistic problem-solver despite my experience of depression are indeed accurate.

My very high score (95) on the dimension of emotional stability reflects my tendency to be consistently secure and relaxed. My colleagues, clients and acquaintances often refer to me as 'calm' and 'gentle': descriptions that often surprise me because I see myself as rather passionate. My score (50) on the dimension of extroversion indicated that I am neither extroverted nor introverted. This possibly explains my ability to be naturally sociable, friendly, affectionate, playful and talkative balanced by my need for solitude to focus my energy and attention inwards.[17] I cannot tolerate a herd mentality, superficiality and mediocrity: it is as satisfying as sitting down to a meal of cardboard.

My very high score (96) on the dimension of openness or intellect and imagination indicates my tendency towards originality, imagination, broad interests and curiosity, and daring.[19] I would further describe my daring as courage and a sense of adventure, not impulsivity. My very high score (95) on the prosocial dimension of agreeableness is demonstrated in my strong selfless regard for others. The trait of agreeableness is characterised by affability, benevolence, courteousness, and receptiveness.

Finally, my very high score (97) on the dimension of conscientiousness is evidenced by the traits required to complete five degrees and research and write a manuscript in the face of complex adversity: perseverance, self-discipline, striving for excellence, purposefulness and hard work. I have often been described by my colleagues as hard-working, energetic and thorough. My friends and clients have often remarked on my 'solid sense of self'.

Eysenck's[12] claim that 'simple survival of the creative person may demand personality characteristics more like those of the street-fighter than those of the ivory-tower academic!' (p. 171) may be more accurate than he ever hypothesised. When one is under threat, one has to suppress pain and fear to focus on the threat, leaving oneself free to respond reflexively and automatically to the circumstance.

Survival requires adaptation and an assumption of personal power actualised with sufficient support, resources and knowledge.

My personal qualities and protective buffers, such as a safe home and parents with positive intentionality did not equate to an effective force field. Adding a label to explain my strange moods, physiological symptoms and seeming failure to achieve as much as what was expected of me did not help. It added to my personal burden by making me blame myself for my perceived inadequacies and corroded my physical health with ineffective medication. Rutter's[18] advice regarding 'Resilience in the face of adversity' is 'to focus on ensuring that interactions are as adaptive as possible, avoiding scapegoating and fostering positive elements in personal interchanges, rather than slipping into vicious cycles of coercive interaction' (p. 608).

Resilience and recovery are two very different things.

Understanding the processes required for an individual's recovery requires a knowledge and understanding of human development and the impact of uncontrollable stress and trauma on young children. Development involves learning to comprehend and control one's experiences and to move from being one's experiences or sensations to having responses, sensations, movements and reflexes.[21]

Children need continuity and predictability to develop a reliable sense of causality and become proficient at categorising their experiences. Children need to form categories to enable them to situate specific experiences in larger contexts. These developmental skills are necessary for children to have the capacity to appraise what is occurring and consider their available options when making decisions to achieve their desired outcomes. When children are able to imagine themselves having the power and ability to influence outcomes, they develop problem-focused coping skills.[21]

When children experience uncontrollable stress and their caregivers are unable to regulate their arousal [that is, to make them feel safe], children will be unable to make sense of their experiences.[21] Physical, emotional, cognitive and psychosocial development is a lifelong process. Hence, infants and young children are particularly vulnerable and depend on their caregivers to protect them. Children do not possess the equivalent levels of cognitive functioning or personal power that adults have; therefore, they depend on them for their survival.[22,21]

Children who experience trauma before they have the understanding and language to describe or make sense of what has happened to them, don't have the capacity or opportunity to disclose, remove themselves from their situation, or find some means to protect themselves. Their inability to articulate their experiences leads to their development of defence strategies, trauma responses or survival responses designed to maintain their incomprehensible, terrifying secret. They may cope with their helplessness via compliance or defiance, and adapt to unsafe environments as best they can.[21]

Bessel van der Kolk[21] warns that the impact of professional's combined lack of awareness of children's requirement to adapt to traumatising environments, and ill-informed expectations that children should conform to adult qualities of autonomy, self-determination, and rational choices, is the labelling, stigmatisation, mistreatment, and rejection of children's survival responses, erroneously perceived as maladaptive behaviours.

Such 'maladaptive behaviours' may be experienced by children who have experienced trauma as difficulty understanding, identifying, feeling, or controlling their experience of emotions. They may lose a sense of self, behave impulsively, appear aggressive towards themselves or others, find it difficult to trust themselves and their gut instinct. Children who have experienced trauma may feel extreme psychological distress and confusion associated with their inability to trust others and their tendency to either mistrust or over trust. They may experience serious loneliness and isolation because they disconnect from themselves, their bodies and struggle with intimacy. Traumatised children are often the most caring of peace keepers who live to serve and please others, and find it extremely difficult to say no. Essentially, they do not feel safe.

Children who have experienced chronic trauma (e.g., those who have lived with domestic and family abuse, or with caregivers who are chronically ill, or in war zones) often suffer from impaired memory (e.g., amnesia, hypermnesia), flashbacks and nightmares about specific events, disorientation in time and space, dissociation, derealisation and depersonalisation, impaired focus and concentration, and sensorimotor developmental disorders. Unsurprisingly, living with inexplicable, cognitive, emotional, and somatic symptoms impedes traumatised children's capacity to learn new things and to be open to change. Some children possess the superpower to fragment and compartmentalise parts of their personality to make the unbearable bearable.[23,24]

How could young children possibly describe such terrible, invisible, painful and inexplicable experiences? Traumatised children rarely articulate their traumatic memories and fears without prompting. This may be attributed to having no words to describe how terrible their trauma was, or because they fear being disbelieved, punished or rejected. Furthermore, young children have very limited insight regarding the association between their behaviours, their emotions, and what has happened to them.[21] To understand and communicate their traumatic past, children tend to re-enact their experiences during play and in their imaginations.[21]

Similar to many children who have experienced sexual abuse[21], I have developed immunological disorders: fibromyalgia, Hashimoto's disease and Mast Cell Syndrome. I am intimately familiar with internalised terror and its many expressions. The most painful of trauma responses I experienced were my feelings of shame, self-loathing and assumption of guilt for something that was done to me.

It is vital that health professionals not neglect the thorough assessment of children's trauma history when they present with symptoms associated with the common psychiatric disorders they are given, such as PTSD, separation anxiety disorder, attachment disorder, generalised anxiety disorder, phobic disorders, oppositional defiance disorder, conduct disorder, ADHD, bipolar disorder, major depression, psychosis, eating disorders, non-suicidal self-injury, and substance use disorders.[25] Failure of patients diagnosed with comorbid diagnoses to benefit from evidence-based treatment may be partially explained by untreated symptoms of traumatic stress which simultaneously erodes their health, reduces their quality of life, and increases the national economic and public health burden.[26]

Although many people seeking mental health support and treatment present with both serious mental illness and trauma, their trauma is rarely assessed or treated. Serious mental illness symptoms, such as psychosis and anxiety, remain the medical model's focus of treatment, whilst the very real influence of trauma is excluded from the essential case conceptualisation and treatment plan.[21]

People's real experience of disorders like PTSD or bipolar disorder, is far more complex, widespread and enduring than a neat group of symptoms conveniently organised into a label bestowed by the DSM. The devaluation and treatment of trauma according to one handy diagnosis. The deleterious outcome of at best, frugal and at worst, negligent health care is too many patients living with the legacy of their trauma perpetuating rather than healed.[21]

Van der Kolk[27] explained that traumatic events leave impressions on the mind, influencing the traumatised person's emotions and biological and immune systems. Therefore, health and helping professionals must conceptualise and treat each person's experiences of trauma through a holistic lens.[27] Most health and mental health professionals maintain that they use evidence-based practice: a combination of (a) patients' illness self-management, management of medication, health promotion, and psychological interventions, (b) social interventions, and (c) service-level interventions. Evidence-based practice is often guided and measured by research.[21,27]

I have discussed at length the flawed designs and limited nature of *gold standard* randomised control trials (RCTs). Trials often exclude comorbidities and patients with severe mental illness. They rarely include trauma. Hence, the research designs tell us very little about how severe mental illness develops and progresses.[21] Unlike RCTs that depend on probability decisions based on homogenous samples, therapists often make subjective decisions regarding treatment plans for individuals with severe mental illness and comorbid issues.

A common comorbid condition typically overlooked is trauma exposure with or without PTSD.[21, 27] Lutton and Swank attribute the disregarding of trauma to (a) the overlapping symptoms of severe mental illness and trauma, (b) many people's experiences of trauma are not explored when they are diagnosed prior to entering the mental health system, and (c) limited coverage of trauma criteria in the DSM.[27]

However, I have observed throughout my studies and career a serious lack of intentional training in psychological trauma and assessment across medicine, psychology, social work and counselling. In fact, trauma-informed therapy appears to be considered either a niche interest favoured by therapists who are prepared to dedicate their own time and money to the study of trauma and trauma interventions, or 'the dark side' comprising 'alternative', 'non-mainstream', unprofessional hippy types. Yet again, the traditional medical model appears to favour othering difference, and hoarding knowledge and power to the detriment of those they purport to protect: the people seeking their help.

Trauma specialists emphasise the gravity of identifying and treating trauma holistically to enable connection with the mind, body, emotions and spirit.[23,28,29,27] Trauma therapists adopt a holistic approach rather than depending on one limited evidence-based therapy like CBT because they know that a lack of a sense of emotional and physical safety does not solely reside in faulty thinking.

CBT is either inappropriate or simply fails to completely treat trauma for many people who experience severe mental illness because it does not recognise the profound associations of trauma. Rather than healing trauma in people diagnosed with PTSD, CBT and prolonged exposure therapy fails to address their negative beliefs and emotions, retraumatises them, and leaves the trauma stuck in them, resulting in perpetuated problems across physical, interpersonal and emotional domains.[23,19,21,29,27]

It is apparent to me that traumatised individuals, individuals who live with severe mental illness, have suffered and continue to suffer from symptoms directly caused by threats to their personal power. Their complex problems require creative, individually-tailored solutions formed from the examination, deconstruction, synthesis and reconstruction of many knowledges accessed from the point of resistance: the point in time and place where their questions are first posed. Who am I? Why do I feel so terrible and can you help me to feel better?

A creative, critical, flexible, reflexive and responsive interdisciplinary framework recognises that where there is resistance to oppression there is the opportunity to learn. A critical psychology approach to mental health therapy demands the therapist to adopt an ethic of care: to pay attention to and learn from the particular language and narrative of their client. The therapist must consider the application of therapeutic interventions to their client's language, cultural, social, spiritual, and interpersonal context.[31] The critical psychology model is open to varying ways of knowing the world, supporting theoretical diversity instead of dominance of one model over another, thus enriching the potential for effective psychological and therapy practices.[30]

By supporting clients to approach their narrative with a stance of curiosity the therapist and the client may collaboratively perceive the point at which discourse renders the client simultaneously vulnerable and powerful: the point of resistance. The point of resistance is the starting point for questions, exploration and dialogue that provides the direction and means for new direction and change.

Trauma specialists posit that trauma-focused treatment is not exclusively beneficial for people who have a diagnosis of PTSD but may also benefit people whose history of subjection to traumatic stressors does not meet the PTSD diagnostic criteria but they experience emotional or behavioural responses that may be associated with or aggravated by their trauma histories. [23,5,26,31] Trauma treatment focuses on three fundamental domains: (a) safety and stabilisation, (b) development of acceptance of trauma memory, and (c) integration and meaning making.[5,21]

There are many, multidimensional trauma-informed approaches to recovery: 'to feeling free to know what you know and feel what you feel without becoming overwhelmed, enraged, ashamed or collapsed' (van der Volk, 2014, p. 203). Personal experience, peer-reviewed literature, and my practice-based evidence working with clients with complex diagnoses including PTSD and trauma, schizophrenia and trauma, and attachment, personality and dissociative disorders indicate that the chief goals are to restore or instil hope, self-worth, safety, empowerment and connection.

This is possible whether you use EMDR therapy, resourcing, desensitisation, processing, mindfulness, meditation, yoga, forming earned secure attachment with traumatised child parts, or reconstruction of the client's personal narrative through the use of the Power Threat Meaning Framework. I have found that respect, curiosity and the capacity to attune to my client guides me to respond reflexively to my client's needs and an effective approach.

My path to recovery and the work I do has led me to the conclusion that there is absolutely no substitute for peace of mind.

Afterword

There has to be an invisible sun
It gives its heat to everyone
There has to be an invisible sun
That gives us hope when the whole day's done
Police[1] Invisible Sun, Ghost in the Machine.

Little darling, I feel that ice is slowly melting
Little darling, it seems like years since it's been clear
Here comes the sun do, do, do
Here comes the sun
And I say it's all right
The Beatles[2] Here comes the sun, Abbey Road.

'From so simple a beginning endless forms most beautiful
and most wonderful have been, and are being evolved'.
Charles Darwin[3] The Origin of Species
by Means of Natural Selection.

Every day I wake up and marvel at my freedom to know what I know
and to feel what I feel without the need to justify or to defend. I rejoice
in my sense of empowerment and clarity of thought. I feel purposeful
and generally calm. I am able to identify, experience and express a
full range of emotions without questioning whether I am normal. I
remain an optimist without a tinge of melancholy. I have replaced the
loop, *I'm not crazy, I'm not stupid, I'm not a hypochondriac* with my

own soundtrack and recreated me in my own image. My triumphant transformation involved paying attention to my trauma responses, self-sourced psychoeducation, talk therapy, EMDR therapy and a hell of a lot of determination.

I love what I do. I love being me. The last phrase is a phrase that I couldn't even imagine being able to say eight years ago. I have not needed psychiatric help since 2011. I have not needed the support of a therapist since early 2014. I no longer use Valdoxan. I suspect that I hadn't needed it for many years but I was worried that perhaps I couldn't trust my judgement regarding recovery. I know I'm not wrong.

My personal transformation hasn't been powerful enough to thwart the liability of being a woman in a world designed specifically to maintain male privilege and power. Nor can it provide a refund for years of lost income, health and opportunities to afford to travel or complete a PhD. Essentially, it can't obliterate mental illness discrimination or reverse the legacy of systemic abuse.

A small part of me remains hopeful that one day Adrian and I will be able to make a reality of our shared dreams to make use of our much-loved Lonely Planet copies of *Travelling on a shoestring* and witness the sun rise and set on new horizons. A bigger part of me hopes that my experiences and observations challenge the current dominant discourse pervading Australian academic institutions, mental health systems and public health policy.

I have not attempted to create a self-help book or a therapist's guide to trauma counselling. There are plenty of these texts available and I simply don't know as much as Bessel van der Kolk or Janina Fisher but they are ideal starting points for therapists and doctors who aspire to best practice.

Remaining questions exist for me. Was my initial diagnosis correct? If so, does my experience provide some evidence that bipolar disorder should not be assumed a lifelong illness?

I believe that I no longer experience the legacy of my traumas and have not merely recovered from accumulated trauma: I have transformed from it. Does this mean that I will be free from discrimination when my story is read? If not, why not?

There is one very significant message that I want to impress upon you Dear Readers: *where there is trauma, there is space for recovery* and *where there is hope, there is potential for recreation and transformation.*

Finding My Invisible Sun presents a longitudinal study of my emergent development within much larger systems than my immediate family and school communities. It is a longitudinal case study that has developed around my need to understand and recover from trauma. It is a critical discourse analysis of my life and experiences of threats to my power that led me to develop my *Points of Resistance Theory. Finding My Invisible Sun* illuminates and elucidates an individual's capacity for, and path to, recovery and transformation from cumulative, systemic trauma.

Self-knowing (1998/2015). Acrylic on canvas, 7' x 5'.

References

Prologue

1. Harrison, G. (1967). Within you, without you. *Sgt.Pepper's lonely hearts club band* [Album]. EMI Studios, London: ParlophoneSee comment in PubMed Commons below.

Sentient

1. Shakespeare, W. (1603/1973). Alexander, N. (Ed.). *Hamlet.* London: Macmillan Education.
2. Atwood, M, (1977). *Dancing girls.* Toronto: McClelland & Stewart.
3. Kundera, M. (2000). Kussi, P. (Trans.). *Immortality.* London, UK: Faber & Faber.
4. Orff, C. (1936). O Fortuna. *Carmina Burana* [CD]. Sydney, Australia: The Rainbow Music Group.
5. Bandura, A. (2001). Social cognitive theory: An agentic perspective. *Annual Review of Psychology, 52,* 1 – 26. Retrieved from http://*www.annualreviews.org/*
6. Freud, S. (1924/1975). Richards, A. (Ed.). *Volume 4: The interpretation of dreams.* Harmondsworth, Middlesex, England: Penguin Books.
7. Bandura, A. (1977). Self-efficacy: Toward a unifying theory of behavioral change. *Psychological Review, 84*(2), 191-215. Retrieved from http://www.apa.org
8. Carlyle, E. (1969). *The very hungry caterpillar.* NY: World Publishing Company.

White Bears and Lost Innocence

1. Jung, C. G. (1968). *Analytical psychology: Its theory & practice.* NY: Vintage Books.
2. Williams, K. (2012). How Salman Rushdie (finally) wrote a memoir: Born-digital materials are reshaping memory and the creative process. Retrieved from http://www.emory.edu/EMORY_MAGAZINE/issues/2012/spring/of_note/rushdie.html

3. Choir of the Monks of the Abbey of Santo Doming de Silos (1969) *Gregorian chants*. [Album]. Hamburg: Polydor International GmbH.

4. Etain, B., Henry, C., Bellivier, F., Mathieu, F., & Leboyer, M. (2008). Beyond genetics: Childhood affective trauma in bipolar disorder. *Bipolar Disorders, 10,* 867-876. Retrieved from https://www.onlinelibrary.wiley.com

5. Larsson, S., Aas, M., Kluungsøyr, Agartz, I., Mork, E., Steen, N. E., … Lorentzen, S. (2013). Patterns of childhood adverse events are associated with clinical characteristics of bipolar disorder. *BMC Psychiatry, 13,* 97-106. doi:10.1186/1471-244X-13-97 *bmcpsychiatry.biomedcentral.com*

6. Leverich, G. S. & Post, R. M. (2006). Course of bipolar illness after history of childhood trauma. *Lancet, 367,* 1040-1042. Retrieved from https://www.thelancet.com

7. Subica, A. M. (2013). Psychiatric and physical sequelae of childhood physical and sexual abuse and forced sexual trauma among individuals with serious mental illness. *Journal of Traumatic Stress, 26,* 588–596. doi:10.1002/jts.21845

8. Wright, J. H., Basco, M. R., & Thase, M. E. (2006). *Learning cognitive-behavior* therapy: An illustrated guide. Washington, DC: American Psychiatric Publishing, Inc.

9. Wegner, D.M. (1989). *White bears and other unwanted thoughts: Suppression, obsession, and the psychology of mental control.* NY: Viking.

10. Wegner, D.M. (1994). Ironic processes of mental control. *Psychological Review,* 10(1), 34-52. doi:10.1037/0033-295X.101.1.34

11. Wegner, D.M., Schneider, D. J., Carter, S.R., & White, T. L. (1987). Paradoxical effects of thought suppression. *Journal of Personality and Social Psychology, 53,* 5-13. Retrieved from https://www.apa.org/pubs/journals/psp/

12. Milne, A. A. (1989). *The complete Winnie-the-Pooh: Containing Winnie-the-Pooh and The house at Pooh Corner.* London: Chancellor Press.

13. Williams, E. (1949). *The wooden horse.* London: Collins.

14. Minney, R. J. (2013). *Carve her name with pride.* South Yorkshire, UK. Pen and Sword Books.

15. Le Carré, J. (1963). *The spy who came in from the cold.* London: Victor Gollancz & Pan.

16. Brickhill, P. (1950). *The great escape.* London: Faber.

17. Orwell, G. (1945). *Animal farm: A fairy story.* London, England: Secker and Warburg.

18. Bronte, C. (1847/1996). *Jane Eyre.* London: Penguin Books.

Shattered

1. Shakespeare, W. (1605/1962). Walter, J. H. (Ed.). *Macbeth.* London: Heinemann Educational Books.

2. Kundera, M. (2000). Kussi, P. (Trans.). *Immortality.* London, UK: Faber & Faber.

3. Brandeis University. (2008). Illusion vs. reality: Age-related differences in expectations for Future happiness. Science Daily. Retrieved from www.sciencedaily.com/releases/2008/09/080911154216.htm

4. Carroll, L. (1865). *Alice's adventures in Wonderland.* London: Macmillan.

5. Mayle, P. (2000). *Where did I come from?* NY, US: Kensington Publishing.

6. Mayle, P. (2003). *What's happening to me?* NY, US: Kensington Publishing.

7. Cervantes Saavedra, M., de (1605/2008). *The life and adventures of Don Quixote de la Mancha, volume 1.* Charleston, US: Bibliolife.

8. Nietzsche, F. W. (1885/1978). Kaufmann, W. A. (Trans.). *This Spoke Zarathustra.* Harmondsworth, Middlesex, England: Penguin Books.

9. Turner, E. (1894/2010). *Seven little Australians.* Melbourne: Penguin Books.

Year of the Cat

1. Stewart, A. (1976). Year of the cat. *Year of the Cat* [CD]. UK: EMI.

2. Lennon, J., & McCartney, P. (1969). Because. *Abbey Road* [Album]. EMI Studios, London: Apple Records.

3. Saltzman, H., & Fisz, B. (Producers), & Hamilton, G. (Director). (1969). *Battle of Britain* [Motion picture]. United Kingdom: Ealing Studios.

4. Shakespeare, W. (1609/1993). *The Sonnets.* Twickenham: Tiger Books.

5. Abba. (1976). *Greatest hits.* NY: Atlantic.

6. The Beatles. (1969). *Abbey Road* [Album]. London: Apple Records.

Fugitive

1. Locke, J. (1726). *An essay concerning human understanding: Volume 1.* Retrieved from https://books.google.com.au/books

2. Wheelock , J. H. (1963). *What is poetry?* NYC, NY: Scribner.

3. Stewart, A. (1976). If it doesn't come naturally, leave it. *Year of the Cat* [CD]. UK: EMI.

4. Frydenberg, E., & Lewis, R. (2009). The relationship between problem-solving efficacy and coping amongst Australian adolescents. *British Journal of Guidance & Counselling, 37*(1), 51-64. doi:10.1080/03069880802534054

5. Zimmer-Gembeck, M. J., & Skinner, E. A. (2008). Adolescents coping with stress: Development and diversity. *The Prevention Researcher, 15*(4), 3-7. Retrieved from http://www.TPRonline

6. Spence, E. (1976). *October Child.* Oxford, UK: Oxford University Press.

7. Boss, P. (2004). Ambiguous loss research, theory, and practice: Reflections after 9/11. *Journal of Marriage and Family, 66*(3), 551-566. Retrieved from http://www.*onlinelibrary.wiley.com*

8. Holm, A. (1980). Kingsland, L. W. (Trans.). *I am David.* London: Magnet.

9. Bronte, C. (1847/1996). *Jane Eyre.* London: Penguin Books.

10. Sting. (1987). History will teach us nothing. *Nothing like the sun* [CD]. Los Angeles: A&M

11. *Lawrence, D. H. (1923/1950) Kangaroo. Harmondsworth, Middlesex, England: Penguin Books.*

Salvation and Sacrifice

1. Sting. (2010) When we dance. *Symphonicities* [CD]. London, UK: UMG Recordings.

2. Springsteen, B. (1984). Cover me. *Born in the U.S.A.* [CD]. NYC, NY: Columbia.

3. Stewart, A. (1976). Year of the cat. *Year of the Cat* [CD]. UK: EMI.

4. Schweitzer, A. (2010). The philosophy of civilization: *Part 1, the decay and the restoration of civilization; Part 2, civilization and ethics.* Whitefish, Montana: Kessinger Publishing.

5. Copernicus, N. (1543/2016). Edward Rosen (Trans.) *De revolutionibus (On the revolutions),1543 C.E.* Baltimore and London: The John Hopkins University Press.

6. Freud, S. (1924/1975). Richards, A. (Ed.). *Volume 4: The interpretation of dreams.* Harmondsworth, Middlesex, England: Penguin Books.

7. The Carpenters. (1972). Top of the world. *A song for you* [Album]. Los Angeles: A&M Records.

8. Nietzsche, F. W. (1973). Hollingdale, R. J. (Trans.). *Beyond good and evil.* Harmondsworth, Middlesex, England: Penguin Books.

9. Shakespeare, W. (1603/1973). Alexander, N. (Ed.). *Hamlet.* London: Macmillan Education.

Event Horizon

1. Shakespeare, W. (1603/1973). Alexander, N. (Ed.). *Hamlet.* London: Macmillan Education.

2. Blake, W. (1804-1820/2016). *Jerusalem the emanation of the giant Albion* [Poem]. Retrieved from http://www.blakearchive.org/exist/blake/archive/ transcription. xq?objectid=jerusalem.e.illbk.04

3. Boulton, J. T. (2002). Letter to Thomas Dunlop in, *The letters of D. H. Lawrence.* Cambridge, England. Cambridge University Press.

4. Boulton, J. T. (2002). *The letters of D. H. Lawrence.* Cambridge, England. Cambridge University Press.

5. Miller, A. (1980). *After the fall.* London, UK: Penguin Books Ltd.

6. U2. (1987). With or Without You. *Joshua Tree* [CD]. London, UK: Island.

7. Baum, L. F. (1900/1950). *Wizard of Oz.* New York City, NY: Random House.

8. The Cure. (1987). Catch. *Kiss me, kiss me, kiss me* [CD]. London: Fiction Records.

9. Scott, W. (1972). Hook, A. (Ed.). *Waverly.* Harmondsworth, Middlesex, England: Penguin Books.

10. Festinger, L. (1957). *A theory of cognitive dissonance.* Stanford, CA. Stanford University Press.

Deterioration, Disbelief and Diagnosis

1. Dickinson, E. (1830-1886). *Much madness is divinest sense.* [Poems: Packet XXVIII, Fascicle. 29]. Houghton Library, Harvard University, Cambridge, MA. Retrieved from http://www.edickinson.org/editions/1/image_sets/235910

2. Wordsworth. W. (1842). The Borderers. Retrieved from https://www. oxfordreference. com › q-oro-ed5-00011734

3. Nietzsche, F. W. (1878/1994). Fabian, M. (Trans.). *Human, all too human: A book for free Spirits.* Harmondsworth, Middlesex, England: Penguin Books.

4. Bowie, D. (1972). Starman. *The Rise and Fall of Ziggy Stardust and the Spiders from Mars* [Album]. NYC, NY: RCA Victor.

5. American Psychiatric Association. (2000). *Diagnostic and statistical manual of mental disorders: DSM-IV-TR.* Washington, DC: American Psychiatric Association.

Lion's Den

1. *Eliot, G. (1876/1996). Cave, T. (Ed.). Daniel Deronda. London, UK: Penguin Classics.*

2. Shakespeare, W. (1599/1985). *Julius Caesar.* London: Macmillan Education.

3. Sting. (1996). Let your soul be your pilot. *Mercury Falling* [CD]. Hollywood, CA: A&M Records.

4. Andreasen, N. C. (1984). *The broken brain: The biological revolution in psychiatry.* New York: Harper & Row.

5. Barlow, D. H., & Durand, V. M. (2009). *Abnormal psychology: An integrative approach* (5th ed.). Belmont, CA: Wadsworth Cengage Learning.

6. Kassin, S. (2004). *Psychology, 4th ed.* Upper saddle river, NJ: Pearson, Prentice Hall.

7. American Psychiatric Association. (2000). *Diagnostic and statistical manual of mental disorders: DSM-IV-TR.* Washington, DC: American Psychiatric Association.

8. Chou, J. C-Y. (2011, July 6). Treatment-resistant bipolar disorder. *Psychiatric Times, 58-63.* Retrieved from https://www.psychiatrictimes.com

9. Kim, E. Y., Miklowitz, D. J., Biuckians, A., & Mullen, K. (2007). Life stress and the course of early-onset bipolar disorder. *Journal of Affective Disorders, 99,* 37–44. doi:10.1016/j.jad.2006.08.022

10. Mitchell, P. (2013). Bipolar disorder. *Australian family Physician, 42*(9), 616-619. Retrieved from https://www.racgp.org.au/afp

11. Renk, K., White, R., Lauer, B., McSwiggan, M., Puff, J., & Lowell, A. (2014). Bipolar disorder in children. *Psychiatry Journal, 214,* 1-19. doi:10.1155/2014/928685

12. Rihmer, Z., & Gonda, X. (2012). The effect of pharmacotherapy on suicide rates in bipolar disorder. *CNS Neurosciences & Therapeutics, 18,* 238-242. doi:10.1111/j.1755-5949.2011.00261.x

13. Tondo, L., & Baldessarini, R. (2009). Bipolar disorder treatment: Lithium. In *The International encyclopedia of depression.* New York, NY: Springer Publishing Company. Retrieved fromHttp://search.credoreference.com/ content/entry/Spiedep/ bipolar_disorder_treatment_lithium/O

14. Cookson, J. (2001). Use of antipsychotic drugs and lithium in mania. *British Journal of Psychiatry, 178*(41), 148-156. Retrieved from https://*bjp.rcpsych.org*

15. Gitlin, M.J., Swendsen, J., Heller, T.L., & Hammen, C. (1995). Relapse and impairment in bipolar disorder. *The American Journal of Psychiatry, 152*(11), 1635-1640. doi:10.1176/ ajp.152.11.1635

16. Grunze, H. (2003). Lithium in the acute treatment of bipolar disorders – a stocktaking. *European Archives of Psychiatry and Clinical Neuroscience, 253,* 115-119. doi:10.1007/ s00406-003-0427-4

17. Moncrieff, J. (1997). Lithium: Evidence reconsidered. *The British Journal of Psychiatry, 171,* 113-119. doi:10.1192/bjp.171.2.113

18. Cade, J. F. J. (1949). Lithium salts in the treatment of psychotic excitement. *Medical Journal of Australia, 36,* 349-352. Retrieved from *https://www.mja. com.au*

19. Malhi, G. S., Tanious, M., Das, P., & Berk, M. (2012). The science and practice of lithium therapy. *Australian & New Zealand Journal of Psychiatry, 46*(3), 192-211. doi:10.1177/ 0004867412437346

20. Pyle, D. I., & Mitchell, P. B. (2007). Maintenance treatments for bipolar disorders. *Australian Prescriber, 30*(2), 70-73. Retrieved from https://*www. australianprescriber. com*

21. Bourgeois, M. (2002). Lithium and the treatment of mania. *European Neuropsychopharmacology, 12,* 93. doi:10.1016/S0924-977X(02)80023-2

22. Peck, R. L. (1999). Atypical antipsychotics for treating depression. *Behavioral Health Management, 19*(4), 44-45. Retrieved from https://*www. worldcat.org/title/behavioral-health-management*

23. Baldessarini, R.J., Tondo, L., Davis, P., Pompili, M., Goodwin, F.K., & Hennen, J. (2006). Decreased risk of suicides and attempts during long-term lithium treatment: a meta-analytic review. *Bipolar disorders, 8,* 625-639. Retrieved from https://www. onlinelibrary.wiley.com

24. Keck, P.E. Jr. (2003). The management of acute mania. *British Medical Journal, 23*(7422), 1002-1003. doi:10.1136/bmj.327.7422.1002

25. Salgado, M. E. F., Sutor, B., Albright, R. C., & Frye, M. (2014). Every reason to discontinue lithium. *International Journal of Bipolar Disorders, 2*, 12-14. doi:10.1186/s40345-014-0012-y

26. Storosum, J.G., Wohlfarth, T., Schene, A., Elferink, A., van Zweiten, B. J., & van den Brink, W. (2007). Magnitude of effect of lithium in short-term efficacy studies of moderate to severe manic episode. *Bipolar Disorders, 9*(8), 793-798. doi:10.1111/j.1399-5618.2007. 00445.x

27. Jefferson, J. W. (1998). Lithium: Still effective despite its detractors. *British Medical Journal, 316*(7141), 13330-1331. Retrieved from https://www.bmj.com

28. Monteleone, P., & Maj, M. (2008). The circadian basis of mood disorders: Recent developments and treatment implications. *European Neuropsychopharmacology, 18*, 701–711. doi:10.1016/j.euroneuro.2008.06.007

29. Angst, J., & Sellaro, R. (2000). Historical perspectives and natural history of bipolar disorder. *Biological Psychiatry, 48*, 445-457. doi:10:1016/S0006-3223(00)00909-4

30. Highet, N. J., McNair, B. G., Thompson, M., Davenport, T. A., & Hickie, I. B. (2004). Experience with treatment services for people with bipolar disorder. *Medical Journal of Australia, 181*(7), S47–S51. Retrieved from https://www.mja.com.au

31. Morselli, P.L., Elgie, R. & GAMIAN-Europe. (2003). GAMIAN-Europe/BEAM survey I: global analysis of a patient questionnaire circulated to 3450 members of 12 European advocacy groups operating in the field of mood disorders. *Bipolar Disorders, 5*, 265-278. Retrieved from http://onlinelibrary.wiley.com/journal/

32. National Collaborating Centre for Mental Health. (2006). *The management of bipolar disorder in adults, children and adolescents, in primary and secondary care. National Clinical Practice Guideline Number 38.* London: Gaskell & The British Psychological Society. Retrieved from https://www.bps.org.uk

33. Perlis, R. H., Ostacher, M. J., Patel, J. K., Marangell, L. B., Zhang, H., Wisniewski, S.R., … Otto, M. W. (2006). Predictors of recurrence in bipolar disorder: Primary outcomes from the systematic treatment enhancement program for bipolar disorder (STEP-BD). *The American Journal of Psychiatry, 163*(2), 217-24. Retrieved from http://ajp.psychiatryonline.org/

34. Post, R. M. (2012). Acquired lithium resistance revisited: Discontinuation-induced refractoriness versus tolerance. *Journal of Affective Disorders, 140*, 6-13. doi: j.jad.2011.09.021

35. Singh, T., & Rajput, M. (2006, October). Misdiagnosis of bipolar disorder. *Psychiatry*, 57-63. Retrieved from https://www.hindawi.com/journals/psychiatry

36. Severus, E., & Bauer, M. (2013). Managing the risk of lithium-induced nephropathy in the Long-term treatment of patients with recurrent affective disorder. *BMC Medicine, 11,* 34-36. doi:10.1186/1741-7015-11-34

37. Fawcett, J., M.D. (2008). What we have learned from the systematic treatment enhancement program for bipolar disorder (STEP-BD) study. *Psychiatric Annals, 38*(7), 450-456. Retrieved from http://search.proquest.com/docview/217046641?accountid=28745

38. Frye, M. A. (2011). Bipolar disorder – A focus on depression. *The New England Journal of Medicine, 364,* 51-59. Retrieved from http://www.nejm.org

39. Judd, L. L., Akiskal, H. S., Schettler, P. J., Endicott, J., Maser, J., Solomon, D. A., … Keller, M.B. (2002). The long-term natural history of the weekly symptomatic status of bipolar 1 disorder. *Archives of General Psychiatry, 59*(6), 530-537. Retrieved from http://archpsyc. jamanetwork.com

40. Kessler, R. C., Akiskal, H. S., Ames, M., Birnbaum, H., Greenberg, P., Hirschfeld, R. M. A., … Wang, P.S. (2006). Prevalence and effects of mood disorders on work performance in a nationally representative sample of U.S. workers. *The American Journal of Psychiatry, 163*(9), 1561-1568. Retrieved from http://*ajp.psychiatryonline.org/*

41. Curran, G., & Ravindran, A. (2014). Lithium for bipolar disorder: A review of the recent literature. *Expert Review of Neurotherapeutics, 14*(9), 1079-98. doi:http://dx.doi.org/10.1586/14737175.2014.947965

42. Young, A. H., & Hammond, J. M. (2007). Lithium in mood disorders: increasing evidence base, declining use? *British Journal of Psychiatry, 191,* 474-476. doi:10.11 92/bjp.bp.10.043133

43. Cipriani, A., Barbui, C., Salanti, G., Rendell, J., Brown, R., Stackton, S., … Geddes, J.R. (2011). Comparative efficacy and acceptability of antimanic drugs in acute mania: a multiple-treatments meta-analysis. *Lancet, 378,* 1306-1315. doi:10.1016/s0140-6736(11)60873-8

44. Yildiz, A., Vieta, E., Leucht, S., & Baldessarini, R.J. (2011). Efficacy of antimanic treatments: meta-analysis of randomized, controlled trials. *Neuropsychopharmacology, 36,* 375–389. doi:10.1038/npp.2010.192

45. Poolsup, N., Li Wan Po, A., & de Oliveira, I. R. (2000). Systematic overview of lithium treatment in acute mania. *Journal of Clinical Pharmacy and Therapeutics, 25*(2),139-156. Retrieved from https://www.onlinelibrary.wiley.com/journal

46. Rybakowski, J. (2006). Lithium in mania: from John Cade to New Deli Study. *European Neuropsychopharmacology, 16,* S587. Retrieved from http://www.journals.elsevier. com/european-*neuropsychopharmacology/*

47. Wellman, N. (2007). Bipolar disorder. *Primary Health Care, 17*(5), 31-34. Retrieved from http://journals.rcni.com/journal/phc

48. Keks, N. A., Hill, C., Sundram, S., Graham, A., Bellingham, K., Dean, B., ... Copolov, D. L. (2009). Evaluation of treatment in 35 cases of bipolar suicide. *Australian and New Zealand Journal of Psychiatry, 43,* 503-508. doi:10.1080/00048670902873680

49. Oswald, P., Souery, D., Kasper, S., Lecrubier, Y., Montgomery, S., Wyckaert, S., ... Mendlewicz, J. (2007). Current issues in bipolar disorder: A critical review. *European Neuropsychopharmacology, 17,* 687-695. doi:10.1016/j.euroneuro.2007.03.006

50. American Psychiatric Association. (2002). Practice guideline for the treatment of patients with bipolar disorder (revision). *American Journal of Psychiatry, 159*(4), 1-50. Retrieved from http://www.ncbi.nlm.nih.gov/pubmed/11958165

51. Sanches, M., Newberg, A. R., & Soares, J. C. (2010). Emerging drugs for bipolar disorder. *Expert Opinion, 15*(3), 453-466. doi:10.1517/14728214.20 10.492393

52. Mantere, O., Suominen, K., Leppämäki, S., Valtonen, H., Arvilommi, P., Isometsä, E. (2004). The clinical characteristics of DSM-IV bipolar I and II disorders: baseline findings from the Jorvi Bipolar Study (JoBS). *Bipolar Disorders, 6*(5), 395-405. Retrieved from https://www.onlinelibrary.wiley.com

53. Sajatovic, M. (2005). Bipolar disorder: Disease burden. *The American Journal of Managed Care, 11*(3), S80-S84. Retrieved from http://*www.ajmc.com*

54. Eroglou, M. Z., Karakus, G., Tamam, L. (2013). Bipolar disorder and suicide. *The Journal of Psychiatry and Neurological Sciences, 26, 139-147.* doi: 10.5350/ DAJPN2013260203

Paint it Black

1. Shakespeare, W. (1610/1994). Carabines, K. (Ed.). *The Tempest.* Ware, Hertfordshire, England: Wordsworth Classics.

2. The Rolling Stones. (1971). Gimme shelter. *Hot Rocks 1964-1971* [CD]. NYC, NY: ABKCO.

3. The Rolling Stones. (1971). Paint it black. *Hot Rocks 1964-1971* [CD]. NYC, NY: ABKCO.

4. The Kinks. (1993). I'm not like everybody else. *Kinks greatest hits* [CD]. Sydney, Australia: Castle Communications Australasia Ltd.

5. Eroglou, M. Z., Karakus, G., Tamam, L. (2013). Bipolar disorder and suicide. *The Journal of Psychiatry and Neurological Sciences, 26, 139-147.* doi: 10.5350/ DAJPN201326020

6. Keks, N. A., Hill, C., Sundram, S., Graham, A., Bellingham, K., Dean, B., ... Copolov, D. L. (2009). Evaluation of treatment in 35 cases of bipolar suicide. *Australian and New Zealand Journal of Psychiatry, 43,* 503-508. doi:10.1080/00048670902873680

7. Mathews, D. C., Richards, E. M., Niciu, M. J., Ionescu, D. F., Rasimas, J. J., & Zarate, C.A., Jr. (2013). Neurological aspects of suicide attempts in bipolar disorder. *Transitional Neuroscience,* 4(2), 203-216. doi:10.2478/s13380-013-0120-7

8. National Collaborating Centre for Mental Health. (2006). *The management of bipolar disorder in adults, children and adolescents, in primary and secondary care. National Clinical Practice Guideline Number 38.* London: Gaskell & The British Psychological Society. Retrieved from https://www.bps.org.uk

9. Pompili, M., Gonda, X., Innamorati, M., Sher, L., Amore, M., Rihmer, Z., ... Girardi, P. (2013). Epidemiology of suicide in bipolar disorders: A systematic review of the literature. *Bipolar Disorders, 15,* 457-490. doi:10.1080/00048670902873680

10. World Health Organization. (2001). *The world health report - Mental health: New understanding, new hope.* Retrieved from http://www.who.int/whr /2001/ en/whr01_en.pdf?ua=1

11. Murray, C. J. L., Vos, T., Lozano, R., Naghavi, M., Flaxman, A. D., Michaud, C., ... Alvarado, M. (2012). Disability-adjusted life years (DALYs) for 291 diseases and injuries in 21 regions, 1990–2010: A systematic analysis for the Global Burden of Disease Study 2010. *The Lancet, 380*(9859), 2197–2223. doi:10.1016/S0140-6736(12)61689-4

12. Sajatovic, M. (2005). Bipolar disorder: Disease burden. *The American Journal of Managed Care, 11*(3), S80-S84. Retrieved from http://*www.ajmc.com*

13. Singh, T., & Rajput, M. (2006, October). Misdiagnosis of bipolar disorder. *Psychiatry,* 57-63. Retrieved from https://www.hindawi.com/journals/ psychiatry

14. Wellman, N. (2007). Bipolar disorder. *Primary Health Care, 17*(5), 31-34. Retrieved from http://journals.rcni.com/journal/phc

15. Hirschfeld, R. M., Lewis, L. & Vornik, L. A. (2003) Perceptions and impact of bipolar disorder: how far have we really come? Results of the national depressive and manic-depressive association 2000 survey of individuals with bipolar disorder. *Journal of Clinical Psychiatry, 64,* 161–174. Retrieved from https://*www.psychiatrist.com*

16. Bongards, E. N., Zaman, R., & Agius, M. (2013). Can we prevent under-diagnosis and misdiagnosis of bipolar affective disorder? Repeat audits to assess the epidemiological change in the caseload of a community mental health team when bipolar disorder is accurately assessed and diagnosed. *Psychiatria Danubina, 25*(2), 129-134. Retrieved from http://www.hdbp. org/psychiatria_danubina

17. Murray, C. J.L., & Lopez, A. D. (1997). Global mortality, disability and the contribution of risk factors: Global Burden of Disease Study. *Lancet, 349*(9063), 1436-1442. doi:10.1016/ S0140-6736(96)07495-8

18. Perlis, R. H. (2005). Misdiagnosis of bipolar disorder. *The American Journal of Managed Care, 11(9)*, S271-S274. *Retrieved from* http://www.ajmc.com

19. Fawcett, J., M.D. (2008). What we have learned from the systematic treatment enhancement program for bipolar disorder (STEP-BD) study. *Psychiatric Annals, 38*(7), 450-456. Retrieved from http://search.proquest.com/docview/ 217046641?accountid=28745

20. Grunze, H. (2003). Lithium in the acute treatment of bipolar disorders – a stocktaking. *European Archives of Psychiatry and Clinical Neuroscience, 253*, 115-119. doi:10.1007/s00406-003-0427-4

21. Kyooseob, H., Perugi, G., Kasper, S., Amsterdam, J. D., Hirschfeld, R. M., & Kapczinski, F. (2013). ISBD task force report on antidepressant use in bipolar disorders. *American Journal of Psychiatry, 170*, 1249-1262. Retrieved from http://ajp. *psychiatryonline.org/*

22. Rihmer, Z., & Gonda, X. (2012). The effect of pharmacotherapy on suicide rates in bipolar disorder. *CNS Neurosciences & Therapeutics, 18*, 238-242. doi:10.1111/j.1755-5949.2011.00261.x

23. American Psychiatric Association. (2002). Practice guideline for the treatment of patients with bipolar disorder (revision). *American Journal of Psychiatry, 159*(4), 1-50. Retrieved from http://www.ncbi.nlm.nih.gov/pubmed/11958165

24. Hawton, K., Sutton, L., Haw, C., Sinclair, J., & Harriss, L. (2005). Suicide and attempted suicide in bipolar disorder: A systematic review of risk factors. *Journal of Clinical Psychiatry, 66*(6), 693-704. Retrieved from https://www.psychiatrist.com

25. Marangell, L.B., Dennehy, E.B., Wisniewski, S.R., Bauer, M.S., Sachiko Miyahara, M.S., Allen, M.H., … Thase, M.E. (2008). Case-control analyses of the impact of pharmacotherapy on prospectively observed suicide attempts and completed suicides in bipolar disorder: Findings from STEP-BD. *Journal of Clinical Psychiatry, 69*(6), 916-922. Retrieved from http://www.psychiatrist.com

26. Simmel, G. L. (2004). The economic burden of bipolar disorder. *Psychiatric Services, 55*(2), 117-118. Retrieved from http://ps.psychiatryonline.org

27. Wilke, W. S., Gota, C. E., & Muzina, D. J. (2010). Fibromyalgia and bipolar disorder: A potential problem? *Bipolar Disorders, 12*, 514-520. doi:10.1111/j.1399-5618.2010.00848.x

28. Kleine-Budde, K., Touil, E., Moock, J., Bramesfeld, A., Kawohl, W., & Rössler, W. (2014). Cost of illness for bipolar disorder: A systematic review of the economic burden. *Bipolar Disorders, 16*, 337-353. doi:10.1111/bdi.12165

29. Andrews, G., Hall, W., Teeson, M., & Henderson, S. (1999). *The mental health of Australians.* Canberra, ACT: Commonwealth Department of Health and Family Services.

30. Strober, M., Birmaher, B., Ryan, N., Axelson, D., Valeri, S., Leonard, H., … Keller, M. (2006). Pediatric bipolar disease: Current and future perspectives for study of its long-term course and treatment. *Bipolar Disorders, 8*, 311-321. Retrieved from https://www.onlinelibrary.wiley.com

31. Johnson, J.G., Cohen, P. & Brooks, J.S. (2000) Associations between bipolar disorder and other psychiatric disorders during adolescence and early adulthood: a community-based longitudinal investigation. *American Journal of Psychiatry, 157*, 1679–1681.

32. Lewis, L. (2000). A consumer perspective concerning the diagnosis and treatment of bipolar disorder. *Biological Psychiatry, 48*, 442–444. Retrieved from hhtp://www.biologicalpsychiatryjournal.com

33. Carlborg, A., Ferntoft, L., Thuresson, M., & Bodegard, J. (2015). Population study of disease burden, management, and treatment of bipolar disorder in Sweden: a retrospective observational registry study. *Bipolar Disorders, 17*, 76–85. doi:10.1111/ bdi.12234

34. Cassidy, F. (2011). Risk factors of attempted suicide in bipolar disorder. *Suicide and Life-Threatening Behavior, 41*(1), 6-11. Retrieved from http:// onlinelibrary.wiley.com/ journal

35. Oswald, P., Souery, D., Kasper, S., Lecrubier, Y., Montgomery, S., Wyckaert, S., … Mendlewicz, J. (2007). Current issues in bipolar disorder: A critical review. *European Neuropsychopharmacology, 17*, 687-695. doi:10.1016/j. euroneuro. 2007. 03.006

36. Malhi, G. S., Tanious, M., Das, P., & Berk, M. (2012). The science and practice of lithium therapy. *Australian & New Zealand Journal of Psychiatry, 46*(3), 192-211.doi:10.1177/ 0004867412437346

37. Beck, A. T., Brown, G., Berchick, R. J., Stewart, B. L., & Steer, R. A. (1990). Relationship between hopelessness and ultimate suicide: A replication with psychiatric outpatients. *The American Journal of Psychiatry, 147*(2), 190-195. Retrieved from http://ajp.psychiatryonline.org/

38. Bertolote, J. M., Fleischmann, A., De Leo, D., & Wasserman, D. (2004). Psychiatric diagnoses and suicide: Revisiting the evidence. *Crisis, 25*(4), 147-155. doi: 10.1027/0227-5910.25.4.147

39. Smyth, C. L., & Maclachlan, M. (2005). Confirmatory factor analysis of the Trinity Inventory of Precursors to Suicide (TIPS) and its relationship to hopelessness and depression. *Death Studies, 29*, 333-350. doi:10.1080/07481180590923724

40. van Orden, K. A., Witte, T. K., Cukrowicz, K. C., Braithwaite, S. R., Selby, E. A., & Joiner, T. E. Jr. (2010). The interpersonal theory of suicide. *Psychological Review, 117*(2), 575-600. doi:10.1037/a0018697

41. Wright, J. H., Basco, M. R., & Thase, M. E. (2006). *Learning cognitive-behavior* therapy: An illustrated guide. Washington, DC: American Psychiatric Publishing, Inc.

42. Baumeister, R. F. (1990). Suicide as escape from self. *Psychological Review, 97*(1), 90-113. Retrieved from http://www.apa.org

43. Baumeister, R. F., & Leary, M. R. (1995). The need to belong: desire for interpersonal attachments as a fundamental human motivation. *Psychological Bulletin, 117*(3), 497-529. Retrieved from http://*www.apa.org/ pubs/journals/bul*

Senses Working Overtime

1. Shakespeare, W. (1593/1960). Wright, L. B., & LaMar, V. A. (Eds.). *Richard III*. NY, NY: Washington Square Press.

2. Byron, G. G. (1812/2013). Bowler, L., & Widger, D. (Eds.). *Childe Harold's pilgrimage*. Retrieved from http://www.gutenberg.org/files/5131/5131-h/5131-h.htm#link2H_4_0006

3. *Lawrence, D. H.* (1930/1995). *Apocalypse*. London, England: Penguin Classics.

4. Blake, W. (1790). *The marriage of heaven and hell. Retrieved from,* http://www.bartleby. com/235/253.html

5. XTC. (1982). Senses working overtime. *English Settlement* [CD]. London, UK: Virgin Records.

6. Barlow, D. H., & Durand, V. M. (2009). *Abnormal psychology: An integrative approach* (5th ed.). Belmont, CA: Wadsworth Cengage Learning.

7. Singh, T., & Rajput, M. (2006, October). Misdiagnosis of bipolar disorder. *Psychiatry,* 57-63. Retrieved from https://www.hindawi.com/journals/psychiatry

8. Carlson, E. B. (1997). *Trauma assessments: A clinician's guide*. NY: The Guilford Press.

9. American Psychiatric Association. (2000). *Diagnostic and statistical manual of mental disorders: DSM-IV-TR*. Washington, DC: American Psychiatric Association.

10. Carlborg, A., Ferntoft, L., Thuresson, M., & Bodegard, J. (2015). Population study of disease burden, management, and treatment of bipolar disorder in Sweden: a retrospective observational registry study. *Bipolar Disorders, 17*, 76–85. doi: 10.1111/ bdi.12234

11. Cassidy, F. (2011). Risk factors of attempted suicide in bipolar disorder. *Suicide and Life-Threatening Behavior, 41*(1), 6-11. Retrieved from http://*onlinelibrary.wiley.com/ journal*

12. Hirschfeld, R. M. and Vornik, L. A. (2005). Bipolar disorder--costs and comorbidity. *American Journal of Managed Care, 11*(3), S85-90. Retrieved from http://*www.ajmc.com*

13. Mathews, D. C., Richards, E. M., Niciu, M. J., Ionescu, D. F., Rasimas, J. J., & Zarate, C.A., Jr. (2013). Neurological aspects of suicide attempts in bipolar disorder. *Transitional Neuroscience, 4*(2), 203-216. doi:10.2478/s13380-013-0120-7

14. Oswald, P., Souery, D., Kasper, S., Lecrubier, Y., Montgomery, S., Wyckaert, S., … Mendlewicz, J. (2007). Current issues in bipolar disorder: A critical review. *European Neuropsychopharmacology, 17,* 687-695. doi:10.1016/j. euroneuro. 2007.03.006

15. Strober, M., Birmaher, B., Ryan, N., Axelson, D., Valeri, S., Leonard, H., … Keller, M. (2006). Pediatric bipolar disease: Current and future perspectives for study of its long-term course and treatment. *Bipolar Disorders, 8,* 311-321. Retrieved from https://www.onlinelibrary.wiley.com

16. World Health Organization. (2001). *The world health report - Mental health: New understanding, new hope.* Retrieved from http://www.who.int/whr /2001/ en/whr01_en.pdf?ua=1

17. Smith, L.A., Cornelius, V.R., Azorin, J.M., Perugi, G., Vieta, E., Young, A.H., & Bowden, C.L. (2010). Valproate for the treatment of acute bipolar depression: Systematic review and meta-analysis. *Journal of Affective Disorders, 122,* 1-9. doi: 10.1016/j.jad.2009.10.033elsevier.com/european-neuropsychopharmacology/*

18. Bowden, C. (2006). Valproate in mania: From Pierre Lambert to New Deli Study. *European Neuropsychopharmacology, 16,* S587. Retrieved from http://www.journals.elsevier.com/european-*neuropsychopharmacology/*

19. Bowden, C. L. & Singh, V. (2005) Valproate in bipolar disorder: 2000 onwards. *Acta Psychiatrica Scandinavica, 111,* 13-20. doi:10.1111/j.1600-0447.2005.00522.x

20. Grunze, H. (2006). Comparison of lithium and valproate in the treatment of mania: predictive factors and tolerance issues. *European Neuropsychopharmacology, 16,* S588. Retrieved from http://www.journals. elsevier.com/european-*neuropsychopharmacology/*

21. Murray, C. J.L., & Lopez, A. D. (1997). Global mortality, disability and the contribution of risk factors: Global Burden of Disease Study. *Lancet, 349*(9063), 1436-1442. doi:10.1016/ S0140-6736(96)07495-8

22. McElroy, S. L., Keck, P. E. Jr. (2000). Pharmacologic agents for the treatment of acute bipolar mania. *Biological Psychiatry, 48*(6), 539–557. doi:10.1016/ S0006-3223(00)00961-6

23. Rybakowski, J. (2006). Lithium in mania: from John Cade to New Deli Study. *European Neuropsychopharmacology, 16,* S587. Retrieved from http://www.journals.elsevier. com/european-*neuropsychopharmacology/*

24. Nivoli, A. M.A., Murru, A., Goikolea, J. M., Crespo, J. M., Montes, J. M., González-Pinto, A.,García-Portilla, P., Bobes, P., Sáiz-Ruiz, J., Vieta, E. (2012). New treatment guidelines for acute bipolar mania: A critical review. *Journal of Affective Disorders, 140*, 125-141. doi:10.1016/j.jad.2011.10.015

25. www.medicines.org.uk

26. Zawab, A., Carmody, J. (2014). Safe use of sodium valproate. *Australian Prescriber, 37*, 124-7. Retrieved from http://www.australianprescriber.com

27. National Collaborating Centre for Mental Health (2010). *Depression in adults with a chronic physical health problem: Treatment and management.* Leicester, UK: British Psychological Society; 2010. (NICE Clinical Guidelines, No. 91.) Appendix 16, Table of drug interactions. Retrieved from http://www.ncbi.nlm.nih.gov/books/NBK82914/

Parthenogenesis

1. Pascal, B. (1670/2016). *Pensées.* New York, New York: Philosophical Library.

2. Carlyle, T. (1834). *Fraser's Magazine for town and country, 9*, 177. Retrieved from https://books.google.com.au/

3. Nietzsche, F. W. (1885/1968). Kaufmann, W. A. (Trans.). *The will to power:* In science, nature, society and art. NY: Random House.

4. Minchin, T. (2013). Not perfect. *So f#©king rock.* [CD]. Australia: Inertia Music.

5. Barreto, M., & Souery, D. (2006). Role of risperidone in the treatment of bipolar disorder. *Future Neurology, 1*(5), 535-543. doi:http://dx.doi.org. ezproxy.usc.edu.au: 2048/10.2217/14796708.1.5.535

6. Muralidharan, K., Ali, M., Silveira, L. E., Bond, D. J., Fountoulakis, K. N., Lam, R. W., & Yatham, L. N. (2013). Efficacy of second generation antipsychotics in treating acute mixed episodes in bipolar disorder: A meta-analysis of placebo-controlled trials. *Journal of Affective Disorders, 150*(2), 408-14. doi:10.1016/j.jad.2013.04.032

7. www.nim.nih.gov, 2016

8. Nivoli, A. M.A., Murru, A., Goikolea, J. M., Crespo, J. M., Montes, J. M., González-Pinto, A., García-Portilla, P., Bobes, P., Sáiz-Ruiz, J., Vieta, E. (2012). New treatment guidelines for acute bipolar mania: A critical review. *Journal of Affective Disorders, 140*, 125-141. doi:10.1016/j.jad.2011.10.015

9. www.nps.org.au, 2016

10. Nierenberg, A. A., Ostacher, M. J., Calabrese, J. R., Ketter, T. A., Marangell, L. B., Miklowitz, D. J., … Bauer, M. S. (2006). Treatment-resistant bipolar depression: A STEP-BD equipoise randomized effectiveness trial of antidepressant augmentation with lamotrigine, inositol, or risperidone. *The American Journal of Psychiatry, 163*(2), 210-6. Retrieved from http://search.proquest. com.ezproxy.usc.edu.au:2048/docview/ 220509499?accountid=28745

11. Gitlin, M.J., & Frye, M. A. (2012). Maintenance therapies in bipolar disorders. *Bipolar Disorders, 14*(2), 51–65. doi:10.1111/j.1399-5618.2012.00992.x.

12. Hegerl, U. (2012). Review: Risperidone, olanzapine and haloperidol are the most effective drugs for acute mania in adults with bipolar 1 disorder. *Evidence Based Mental Health, 15,* 45. doi:10.1136/ebmental-2011-100476

13. Pae, C-U., Ghaemi, S. N., Patkar, A., Chae, J-H., Bahk, W-M., Jun, T-Y., & Masand, P. (2006). Adjunctive risperidone, olanzapine and quetiapine for the treatment of hospitalized patients with bipolar 1 disorder: A retrospective study. *Progress in Neuro-Psychopharmacology & Biological Psychiatry 30,* 1322–1325. doi:10.1016/j.pnpbp.2006.03.020

14. Cipriani, A., Barbui, C., Salanti, G., Rendell, J., Brown, R., Stackton, S., … Geddes, J.R. (2011). Comparative efficacy and acceptability of antimanic drugs in acute mania: a multiple-treatments meta-analysis. *Lancet, 378,* 1306-1315. doi:10.1016/s0140-6736(11)60873-8

15. Bright, G. & Harrison, G. (2013). *Understanding research in counselling.* London: Learning Matters, Sage.

16. Parikh, S. V., LeBlanc, S. R., & Ovanessian, M. M. (2010). Advancing bipolar disorder: Key lessons from the Systematic Treatment Enhancement Program for Bipolar Disorder (STEP-BD). *Canadian Journal of Psychiatry, 55*(3), 136-143. Retrieved from https:// us.sagepub.com/en-us/nam/the-canadian-journal-of-psychiatry/ journal202498

17. Foucault, M. (1973). Howard, R. (Trans.). *Madness and civilization: a history of insanity in the age of reason.* NY: Vintage Books. Retrieved from, https://libcom.org/ files/Michel%20Foucault%20-%20Madness%20 and%20Civilization.pdf

18. Powers, P. (2013). Rawlinson's three axes of structural analysis: a useful framework for a Foucauldian discourse analysis. *Aporia: The Nursing Journal, 5*(1), 6-12. Retrieved from, http://www.oa.uottawa.ca/journals/ aporia/articles/2013_01/ powers.pdf

19. Foucault, M. (1976/1999). Power as knowledge. In C. Lemert. (Ed.) *Social theory: the multicultural and classical readings,* 2nd ed. Boulder, CO: Westview.

20. Foucault, M. (1980/1985). Power, sovereignty and discipline. In D. Held, et al. (Ed.). *States & societies,* Oxford, UK: Basil Blackwell Ltd.

21. Foucault, M. (1982). The subject and power, *Critical Inquiry, 8*(4), 777-795. Retrieved from, http://www.jstor.org/stable/1343197

22. Foucault, M. (2008). 'Panopticism' from discipline & punish: the birth of the prison. *Race/Ethnicity: Multidisciplinary Global Contexts, 2*(1), 1-12. Retrieved from, http:// www.jstor.org.ezproxy.usc.edu.au:2048/ stable/25594995

23. Seidman, S. (2013). *Contested knowledge: social theory today, 5th ed.* Oxford: Wiley-Blackwell Publishers.

24. Quintero Johnson, J.M., Riles, J. (2016). "He acted like a crazy person": exploring the influence of college students' recall of stereotypic media representations of mental illness. *Psychology of Popular Media Culture,* 1-18. doi:10.1037/ppm000012

25. Arboleda-Flórez, J. (2003). Considerations on the stigma of mental illness. *Canadian Journal of Psychiatry, 48*(10), 645-650. doi:10.1177/070674370304801001

26. Covarrubias, I. & Han, M. (2011). Mental health stigma about serious mental illness among MSW students: social contact and attitude. *Social Work, 56*(4), 317-325, doi:10.1093/sw/56.4.317

27. Holland, K. (2012). The unintended consequences of campaigns designed to challenge stigmatising representations of mental illness in the media. *Social Semiotics, 22*(3), 217-236. doi:10.1080/10350330.2011.648398

28. Klin, A., & Lemish, D. (2008). Mental disorders stigma in the media: Review of studies on production, content, and influences. *Journal of Health Communication, 13*(5), 434-449. doi:10.1080/10810730802198813

29. Lewis, L. (2000). A consumer perspective concerning the diagnosis and treatment of bipolar disorder. *Biological Psychiatry, 48,* 442–444. Retrieved from hhtp://www.biologicalpsychiatryjournal.com

30. *Geddes, J. R., & Miklowitz, D. J. (2013). Treatment of bipolar disorder. The Lancet, 381 (9891), 1672-1682.* doi:http://dx.doi.org/10.1016/S0140-6736(13)60857-0

31. Michalak, E., Livingston, J., Hole, R., Suto, M., & Hale, S. (2010). "It's something that I manage but it is in not who I am". Reflections on self-management strategies and stigma in bipolar disorder. *Journal of Affective Disorders, 122,* S47. doi:10.1016/j.jad.2010.02.041

32. Bourgeois, M. (2002). Lithium and the treatment of mania. *European Neuropsychopharmacology, 12,* 93. doi:10.1016/S0924-977X(02)80023-2

33. Oswald, P., Souery, D., Kasper, S., Lecrubier, Y., Montgomery, S., Wyckaert, S., ... Mendlewicz, J. (2007). Current issues in bipolar disorder: A critical review. *European Neuropsychopharmacology, 17,* 687-695. doi:10.1016/j.euroneuro.2007.03.006

34. *Erten, E., Alpman, N., Özdemir, A., & Fistikci, N. (2014). The impact of disease course and type of episodes in bipolar disorder on caregiver burden. Turkish Journal of Psychiatry, 25(2), 114-122. doi: 10.5080/u7446*

35. Rascati, K. L., Richards, K. M., Ott, C. A., Goddard, A. W., Stafkey-Mailey, D., Alvir, J., ... Mychaskiw, M. (2011). Adherence, persistence of use, and costs associated with second-generation antipsychotics for bipolar disorder.

Psychiatric Services, 62(9), 1032-40. Retrieved from http://search.proquest. com.ezproxy.usc.edu.au:2048/ docview/1095834915?accountid=28745

36. Kleine-Budde, K., Touil, E., Moock, J., Bramesfeld, A., Kawohl, W., & Rössler, W. (2014). Cost of illness for bipolar disorder: A systematic review of the economic burden. *Bipolar Disorders, 16,* 337-353. doi:10.1111/ bdi.12165

37. Carlborg, A., Ferntoft, L., Thuresson, M., & Bodegard, J. (2015). Population study of disease burden, management, and treatment of bipolar disorder in Sweden: a retrospective observational registry study. *Bipolar Disorders, 17,* 76–85. doi: 10.1111/bdi.12234

38. Stimmel, G. L. (2004). Economic grand rounds: The economic burden of bipolar disorder. *Psychiatric Services, 55*(2), 117-118. doi:http://dx.doi. org/10.1176/appi.ps.55.2.117

39. Mohuiddan, S. (2014). A systematic and critical review of model-based economic evaluations of pharmacotherapeutics in patients with patients with bipolar disorder. *Applied Health Economics and Health Policy, 12,* 359-372. doi:10.1007/s40258-014-0098-5

You Learn Something New Every Day

1. Toffler, A. (1990). *Powershift: Knowledge, wealth and violence at the edge of the 21st century.* New York: Bantam Books.

2. Keats, J. (1818). *Letter to Benjamin Bailey.* Retrieved from https://www. oxfordreference.com/view/10.1093/acref/9780191866692.001.0001/q-oro-ed6-00006160

3. Shakespeare, W. (1607/2015). *Timon of Athens.* London, UK: Penguin Classics.

4. Eliot, G. (1876/1996). Cave, T. (Ed.). *Daniel Deronda.* London, UK: Penguin Classics.

5. Forster, E. M. (1923). *Pharos and Pharillon.* London: Hogarth Press.

6. Selye, H. (1936). A syndrome produced by diverse nocuous agents. *Nature, 138*(3479), 32.doi:10.1038/138032a0

7. Grunze, H., Vieta, E., Goodwin, G. M., Bowden, C., Licht, R. W., Azorin, J., … Kasper, S. (2017). The World Federation of Societies of Biological Psychiatry (WFSBP) Guidelines for the Biological Treatment of Bipolar Disorders: Acute and longterm treatment of mixed states in bipolar disorder. *The World Journal of Biological Psychiatry, 19*(1), 2-58. doi:10.108 0/15622975.2017.1384850

8. Peck, R. L. (1999). Atypical antipsychotics for treating depression. *Behavioral Health Management, 19*(4), 44-45. Retrieved from https://*www. worldcat.org/title/behavioral-health-management*

9. Lord, C. C., Wyler, S. C., Wan, R., Castorena, C. M., Ahmed, N., Mathew, D., ... Elmquist, J. K. (2017). The atypical antipsychotic olanzapine causes weight gain by targeting serotonin receptor 2C. *Journal of Clinical Investigation, 127*(9), 3402-3406. Retrieved from https://doi.org/10.1172/JCI93362

10. Cookson, J. (2001). Use of antipsychotic drugs and lithium in mania. *British Journal of Psychiatry, 178*(41), 148-156. Retrieved from https://*bjp.rcpsych.org*

11. Oswald, P., Souery, D., Kasper, S., Lecrubier, Y., Montgomery, S., Wyckaert, S., ... Mendlewicz, J. (2007). Current issues in bipolar disorder: A critical review. *European Neuropsychopharmacology, 17,* 687-695. doi:10.1016/j.euroneuro.2007.03.006

12. Josefson, D. (1998). Marketing of antipsychotic drugs attacked. *British Medical Journal, 316*(7132), 648-648.

13. Lenzer, J. (2007). Drug company tries to suppress internal memos. *British Medical Journal, 334*(7584), 59-59. Retrieved from https://doi.org/10.1136/bmj. 39090. 484074.DB

14. Berenson. A. (2006). Eli Lilly said to play down risk of top pill. *NYTimes.com.* Retrieved from, https://www.nytimes.com/2006/12/17/business/17drug.html.

15. Anonymous. (2007). Side-effects secret. *The Ecologist, 37*(1), 13. Retrieved from https://theecologist.org/

16. *Eli Lilly. Canada Inc. (2020). Product monograph: Zyprexa® (olanzapine), [Product Monograph]. Retrieved from http://pi.lilly.com/ca/zyprexa-ca-pm.pdf*

17. Wang, P. W., Hill, S. J., Childers, M.E., Chandler, R. A., Rasgon, N. L., & Ketter, T. A. (2011). Open adjunctive ziprasidone associated with weight loss in obese and overweight bipolar disorder patients. *Journal of Psychiatric Research, 45*(8):1128-32. doi:10.1016/j.jpsychires.2011.01.019.

18. Duma, S. R., & Fung, V. S.C. (2019). Drug-induced movement disorders. *Australian Prescriber, 42,* 56-61. doi: 10.18773/austprescr.20

19. Shin, H., & Chung, S. J. (2012). Drug-induced Parkinsonism. *Journal of Clinical Neurology, 8,* 15-2. doi:10.3988/jcn.2012.8.1.15

20. Vieta, E., & Sanchez-Moreno, J. (2008). Acute and long-term treatment of mania. *Dialogues in Clinical Neuroscience, 10*(2). Retrieved from https://www.ncbi.nlm.nih.gov/ pmc/articles/ PMC3181868/pdf/DialoguesClinNeurosci-10-165.pdf

21. Mangge, H., Bengesser, S., Dalkner, N., Birner, A., Fellendorf, F., Platzer, M., ... Reininghaus, E. (2019). Weight gain during treatment of bipolar disorder (BD)—Facts and therapeutic options. *Frontiers in Nutrition, 6*(78), 1–8. doi:10.3389/fnut.2019.00076

22. Pacchiarotti, I., Bond, D. J., Baldessarini, R. J., Nolen, W. A., Grunze, H., Licht, R. W., . . . Vieta, E. (2013). The international society for bipolar disorders (ISBD) task force report on antidepressant use in bipolar disorders. *The American Journal of Psychiatry, 170*(11), 1249-1262. doi:10.1176/appi.ajp.2013.13020185

23. Kidnapillai, S., Bortolasci, C. C., Panizzutti, B., Spolding, B., Connor, T., Bonifacio, K., … Ken Walder, K. (2019) Drugs used in the treatment of bipolar disorder and their effects on cholesterol biosynthesis: A possible therapeutic mechanism, *The World Journal of Biological Psychiatry, 20*(10), 766-777. doi:10.1080/15622975.2019. 1669823

24. Prabhakar, M., Haynes, W. G., Coryell, W. H., Chrischilles, E. A., Miller, D. D., Arndt, S., … Fiedorowicz, J. G. (2011). Factors associated with the prescribing of Olanzapine, Quetiapine, and Risperidone in patients with bipolar and related affective disorders. *Pharmacotherapy, 31*(8), 806-812. Retrieved from http://onlinelibrary.wiley.com/journal/

25. Smith, L.A., Cornelius, V.R., Azorin, J.M., Perugi, G., Vieta, E., Young, A.H., & Bowden, C.L. (2010). Valproate for the treatment of acute bipolar depression: Systematic review and meta-analysis. *Journal of Affective Disorders, 122,* 1-9. doi: 10.1016/j.jad. 2009.10.033

Death is Preferable

1. Kafka, K. (1931/2014). *The Zürau Aphorisms.* UK: Random House.

2. Nietzsche, F. W. (1885/1978). Kaufmann, W. A. (Trans.). *Thus Spoke Zarathustra.* Harmondsworth, Middlesex, England: Penguin Books.

3. Camus, A. (1962/2010). *Notebooks 1942-1951.* Chicago, US: Ivan Dee, Inc.

4. Camus, A. (1955/2000). *The myth of Sisyphus.* UK: Penguin.

5. Miller, A. (1980). *After the fall.* London, UK: Penguin Books Ltd.

6. James, W. (1979 [1897]). *The Will to Believe and Other Essays in Popular Philosophy,* ed. Burckhardt, F., Bowers, F. and Skrupselis, I.K. In Burckhardt, F. (gen. ed.), *The Works of William James.* Volume 6. Cambridge, MA: Harvard University Press. Google Scholar

7. Moore, G. (1900/2019). *The Bending of the Bough.* Sydney, NSW, Australia: Wentworth Press.

8. Eliot, G. (1876/1996). Cave, T. (Ed.). *Daniel Deronda.* London, UK: Penguin Classics.

9. Holmes, E.A., Geddes, J.R., Colom, F., & Goodwin, G.M. (2008). Mental imagery as an emotional amplifier: Application to bipolar disorder. *Behaviour Research and Therapy, 46,* 1251-1258. doi:10.1016/j.brat.2008.09.005

10. Hales, S. A., Deeprose, C., Goodwin, G. M., & Holmes, E. A. (2011). Cognitions in bipolar affective disorder and unipolar depression: imagining suicide. *Bipolar Disorders, 13,* 651-661. doi: 10.1111/j.1399-5618.2011.00954.x

11. Holmes, E.A., & Mathews, A. (2010). Mental imagery in emotion and emotional disorders. *Clinical Psychology Review, 30,* 349-362. doi:10.1016/j.cpr.2010.01.001

12. American Psychiatric Association. (2000). *Diagnostic and statistical manual of mental disorders: DSM-IV-TR*. Washington, DC: American Psychiatric Association.

13. Gregory, J.D., Brewin, C.R., Mansell, W., & Donaldson, C. (2010). Intrusive memories and images in bipolar disorder. *Behaviour Research and Therapy, 48*, 698-701. doi:10.1016/ j.brat.2010.04.005

14. *Látalová, K. (2012). Insight in bipolar disorder. Psychiatric Quarterly, 83, 293-310.* doi:10.1007/s11126-011-9200-4

15. Goffman, E. (1961/1991). *Asylums: Essays on the social situation of mental patients and other inmates.* London, UK: Penguin Books Ltd.

16. Arboleda-Flórez, J. (2003). Considerations on the stigma of mental illness. *Canadian Journal of Psychiatry, 48*(10), 645-650. doi:10.1177/070674370304801001

17. Klin, A., & Lemish, D. (2008). Mental disorders stigma in the media: Review of studies on production, content, and influences. *Journal of Health Communication, 13*(5), 434-449. doi:10.1080/10810730802198813

18. Corrigan, P.W., Powell, J., Michaels, K., & Patrick, J. (2013). The effects of news stories on the stigma of mental illness. *The Journal of Nervous and Mental Disease, 201*(3), 179-182. doi: 10.1097/NMD.0b013e3182848c24

19. Quintero Johnson, J.M., Riles, J. (2016). "He acted like a crazy person": exploring the influence of college students' recall of stereotypic media representations of mental illness. *Psychology of Popular Media Culture*, 1-18. doi:10.1037/ppm000012

20. Chen, F., Chen, S., Liu, J., Amin, N., Jin, W., & Fang, M. (2021). Agomelatine softens depressive-like behavior through the regulation of autophagy and apoptosis. *Biomed Research International, 2021*, 1-10. doi:10.1155/2021/6664591

21. Monteleone, P., & Maj, M. (2008). The circadian basis of mood disorders: Recent developments and treatment implications. *European Neuropsychopharmacology, 18,* 701–711. doi:10.1016/j.euroneuro.2008.06.007

22. Pandi-Perumal, S. R., Moscovitch, A., Srinivasan, V., Spence, D. W., Cardinali, D. P. & Brown, G. M. (2009). Bidirectional communication between sleep and circadian rhythms and its implications for depression: Lessons from agomelatine. *Progress in Neurobiology, 88,* 264–271. doi:10.1016/j.pneurobio.2009.04.007

Emerging

1. Sting. (1996). Let your soul be your pilot. *Mercury Falling* [CD]. Hollywood, CA: A&M Records.

2. Harrison, G. (1970). All things must pass. *All things must pass* [Album]. EMI Studios, London: Apple.

3. The Rolling Stones. (1968). Sympathy for the devil. *Beggars Banquet* [Album]. Olympic, London: Decca.

4. Kuhl, D. (2002). *What dying people want: Practical wisdom for the end of life.* Sydney, NSW: ABC Books.

5. Yalom, I.D. (2008). *Staring at the sun: Overcoming the terror of death.* San Francisco, CA: Jossey-Bass.

6. Johnstone, L. & Boyle, M. with Cromby, J., Dillon, J., Harper, D., Kinderman, P., Longden, E., Pilgrim, D. & Read, J. (2018). The Power Threat Meaning Framework: Towards the identification of patterns in emotional distress, unusual experiences and troubled or troubling behaviour, as an alternative to functional psychiatric diagnosis. British Psychological Society: Leicester.

Finding My Invisible Sun

1. Dire Straits (1980). Les Boys. *Making Movies* [Album]. UK: Vertigo.

2. Deeley, M. (Producer) & Collinson, P. (Director). (1969). *The Italian Job* [Motion Picture]. UK: Paramount Pictures.

The Missing Piece

1. The Beatles. (1967). Fixing a hole. *Sgt. Pepper's Lonely Hearts Club Band* [Album]. London: EMI.

2. Nietzsche, F. W. (1885/1968). Kaufmann, W. A. (Trans.). *The will to power*: In science, nature, society and art. NY: Random House.

3. Boyce, R. (2006). Emerging from the shadow of medicine: allied health as a 'profession community' subculture'. *Health Sociology Review, 15*(5), 520-534, doi: 10.5172/hesr.2006.15.5.520

4. Corrigan, P.W., Watson, A.C., Byrne, P. & Davis, K.E. (2005). Mental illness stigma: problem of public health or social justice? *Social Work, 50*(4), 363-368, doi:10.1093/sw/ 50.4.363

5. Lewis, L. (2000). A consumer perspective concerning the diagnosis and treatment of bipolar disorder. *Biological Psychiatry, 48*, 442–444. Retrieved from hhtp://www.biologicalpsychiatryjournal.com

6. Department of Health (2016). *Fifth National Mental Health Plan - Draft for Consultation,* retrieved from http://www.health.gov.au/internet/main/ publishing.nsf/Content/ 8F54F3C4F313E0B1CA258052000ED5C5/$File/ Fifth%20National%20Mental%20Health%20Plan.pdf

7. Rosenberg, S. (2016). Magical realism and the Draft Fifth National Mental Health Plan, *Croakey.* Retrieved from https://croakey.org/magical-realism-and-the-draft-fifth-national-mental-health-plan/

8. *Universal Declaration of Human Rights* (UDHR) 1948, (resolution 217 A), adopted 10 December 1948. Retrieved from http://www.ohchr.org/EN/ UDHR/Documents/ UDHR_Translations/eng.pdf

9. *Not for service: experiences of injustice and despair in mental health care in Australia*, Mental Health Council of Australia, Canberra. (2005). Retrieved from https://www. humanrights.gov.au/sites/default/files/content/disability_rights/notforservice/documents/NFS_Finaldoc.pdf

10. Perlini, C., Donisi, V., Rossetti, M.G., Moltrasio, C., Bellani, M., & Brambilla, P. (2020). The potential role of EMDR on trauma in affective disorders: A narrative review. *Journal of Affective Disorders, 269*, 1-11. https://doi.org/10.1016/j.jad.2020.03.001

11. Pagani, M., Di Lorenzo, G., Verardo, A.R., Nicolais, G., Monaco, L., ... Siracusano, A. (2012). Neurobiological correlates of EMDR monitoring: An EEG study. *PLoS ONE, 7*(9), e45753. doi:10.1371/journal.pone.0045753

12. Calancie, O.G., Khalid-Khan, S., Booij, L., & Munoz, D. P. (2018). Eye movement Desensitization and reprocessing as a treatment for PTSD: current neurobiological theories and a new hypothesis. *Annals of the New York Academy of Sciences, 1426*, 127-145. doi: 10.1111/nyas.13882

13. Shapiro, F. (2014). The role of Eye Movement Desensitization and Reprocessing (EMDR) therapy in medicine: Addressing the psychological and physical symptoms from adverse life experiences. *The Permanente Journal, 18*(1), 71-77. Retrieved from https:// www.ncbi.nlm.nih.gov/pmc/articles/PMC3951033/pdf/permj18_1p0071.pdf

14. Valiente-Gómez, A., Moreno-Alcázar, A., Treen, D., Cedrón, C., Colom, F., Pérez. V., & Amann, B. L. (2017). EMDR beyond PTSD: A systematic literature review. *Frontiers In Psychology, 8*, 1668-16678. doi:10.3389/fpsyg.2017.01668

15. Fisher, J. (2017). *Healing the fragmented selves of trauma survivors: Overcoming internal self-alienation*. New York, NY: Routledge.

16. Forgash, C., & Knipe, J. (2012). Integrating EMDR and ego state treatment for clients with trauma disorders. *Journal of EMDR Practice and Research, 6*(3), 120-128. http://dx.doi.org/10.1891/1933-3196.6.3.120

17. Moreno-Alcázar, A., Radua, J., Landín-Romero, R., Blanco, L., Madre, M., Reinares, M., M Comes, J., Jiménez., E, Manuel Crespo., ... Amann., L. (2017). Eye movement desensitization and reprocessing therapy versus supportive therapy in affective relapse prevention in bipolar patients with a history of trauma: Study protocol for a randomised controlled trial. *Trials, 18*, 160-170. doi 10.1186/s13063-017-1910-y

18. van der Kolk, B.A., Spinazzola, J., Blaustein, M.E., Hopper, J.W., Hopper, E.K., Korn, D.L., & Simpson, W.B. (2007). A randomized clinical trial of eye movement desensitization and reprocessing (EMDR), fluoxetine, and pill placebo in the treatment of posttraumatic stress disorder: Treatment effects and long-term maintenance. *Journal of Clinal Psychiatry, 68*(1), 37-46. doi: 10.4088/jcp.v68n0105. PMID: 17284128.

19. van der Kolk, B. (2014). *The body keeps the score: Mind, brain and body in the transformation of trauma.* New York, NY: Penguin.

20. Resnick, M. D., & Taliaferro, L. A. (2011). Resilience. *Encyclopedia of Adolescence, 1*, 299-306. doi:10.1016/8978-0-12-373915-5.00035-8

21. Masten, A., & Coatsworth, J. D. (1998). The development of competence in favourable and unfavourable environments: Lessons from research on successful children. *American Psychologist, 53*(2), 205-220. Retrieved from http://www.apa.org

22. Blum, R. W., McNeely, C., & Nonnemaker, J. (2002). Vulnerability, risk, and protection. *Journal of Adolescent Health, 31S*, 28-39. Retrieved from http;//www.jahonline.org/

23. Lazarus, R. S. (1993). Coping theory and research: Past, present, and future. *Psychosomatic Medicine, 55*(3), 234-247. Retrieved from http://www.psychosomaticmedicine.org

24. Lazarus, R. S. (2000). Toward better research on stress and coping. *American Psychologist, 55*(6), 665-673. doi:10.1037//0003-066X.55.6.665

25. Zimmer-Gembeck, M. J., & Skinner, E. A. (2008). Adolescents coping with stress: Development and diversity. *The Prevention Researcher, 15*(4), 3-7. Retrieved from http://www.TPRonline

26. Rutter, M. (1993). Resilience: Some conceptual considerations. *Journal of Adolescent Health, 14*, 626-631. Retrieved from http://www.jahonline.org/

27. Bandura, A. (1977). Self-efficacy: Toward a unifying theory of behavioral change. *Psychological Review, 84*(2), 191-215. Retrieved from http://www.apa.org

28. Bandura, A. (2001). Social cognitive theory: An agentic perspective. *Annual Review of Psychology, 52*, 1 – 26. Retrieved from *http://www.annualreviews.org/*

A Road to Peace of Mind

1. King, A. (1993). *Revolution of Love.*© [Excerpt from song lyrics].

2. Bowie, D. (1972). Heroes. *Heroes* [Album]. NYC, NY: RCA Victor.

3. Holmes, E.A., Geddes, J.R., Colom, F., & Goodwin, G.M. (2008). Mental imagery as an emotional amplifier: Application to bipolar disorder. *Behaviour Research and Therapy, 46*, 1251-1258. doi:10.1016/j.brat.2008.09.005

4. van der Kolk, B. (2014). *The body keeps the score: Mind, brain and body in the transformation of trauma.* New York, NY: Penguin.

5. Forgash, C., & Knipe, J. (2012). Integrating EMDR and ego state treatment for clients with trauma disorders. *Journal of EMDR Practice and Research, 6*(3), 120-128. http://dx.doi.org/10.1891/1933-3196.6.3.120

6. Shapiro, F. (1989). Eye movement desensitization: A new treatment for post-traumatic stress disorder. *Journal of Behavior Therapy and Experimental Psychiatry, 20*(3), 211–217. https://doi.org/10.1016/0005-7916(89)90025-6

7. van der Kolk, B.A., Spinazzola, J., Blaustein, M.E., Hopper, J.W., Hopper, E.K., Korn, D.L., & Simpson, W.B. (2007). A randomized clinical trial of eye movement desensitization and reprocessing (EMDR), fluoxetine, and pill placebo in the treatment of posttraumatic stress disorder: Treatment effects and long-term maintenance. *Journal of Clinal Psychiatry, 68*(1), 37-46. doi: 10.4088/jcp.v68n0105. PMID: 17284128.

8. Harricharan, S., McKinnon, M.C., Tursich, M., Densmore, M., Frewen, P., Théberge, van der Kolk, B. & Lanius, R.A. (2019). Overlapping frontoparietal networks in response to oculomotion and traumatic autobiographical memory retrieval: implications for eye movement desensitization and reprocessing. *European Journal of psychotraumatology, 10*(1), 1586265. doi: 10.1080/20008198.2019.1586265

9. Shapiro, F. (2014). The role of Eye Movement Desensitization and Reprocessing (EMDR) therapy in medicine: Addressing the psychological and physical symptoms from adverse life experiences. *The Permanente Journal, 18*(1), 71-77. Retrieved from https://www.ncbi.nlm.nih.gov/pmc/articles/PMC3951033/pdf/permj18_1p0071.pdf

10. Lewis, L. (2000). A consumer perspective concerning the diagnosis and treatment of bipolar disorder. *Biological Psychiatry, 48*, 442–444. Retrieved from hhtp://www.biologicalpsychiatryjournal.com

11. Andreasen, N. C. (2008). The relationship between creativity and mood disorders. *Dialogues in Clinical Neuroscience, 10*(2), 251-255. doi:10.31887/DCNS.2008.10.2 /ncandreasen

12. Eysenck, H.J. (1993). Target Article: Creativity and personality: Suggestions for a theory. *Psychological Inquiry, 4*(3), 147-179. Retrieved from http://www.jstor.org/stable/ 1448958.

13. Johnson, S. L., Moezpoor, M., Murray, G., Hole, R., Barnes, S. J., CREST. BD., and Michalak, E. E. (2016). *Creativity and bipolar disorder: Igniting a dialogue. Qualitative Health Research, 26(1), 32-40.* doi:10.1177/1049732315578403

14. Murray, G., & Johnson, S. L. (2010). The clinical significance of creativity in bipolar disorder. *Clinical Psychology Review, 30*, 721–732. doi:10.1016/j.cpr.2010.05.006

15. Rothenberg, A. (2006). Creativity, self creation, and the treatment of mental illness. *Medical Humanities, 32*(1), 14-19. doi:10.1136/jmh.2004.000185

16. Schou, M. (1979). Artistic productivity and lithium prophylaxis in manic-depressive Illness. *The British Journal of Psychiatry, 135*, 97-103. doi:10.1192/bjp.135.2.97

17. Feist, G.J. (1998). A meta-analysis of personality in scientific and artistic creativity. *Personality and Social Psychology Review, 2*, 290-309. doi:10.1207/s15327957pspr0204_5

18. Rutter, M. (1995). Resilience in the face of adversity: Protective factors and resistance to psychiatric disorder. *The British Journal of Psychiatry, 147* (6), 598 – 611. doi:https://doi.org /10.1192/bjp.147.6.598

19. McCrae, R. R., & Costa, P. T. (1987). Validation of the five-factor model of personality across instruments and observers. *Journal of Personality and Social Psychology, 52*(1), 81-90. doi:10.1037/0022-3514.52.1.81

20. Goldberg, Lewis R. (1992). The development of markers for the Big-Five factor structure. *Psychological assessment, 4*(1), 26-42. doi:10.1037/1040-3590.4.1.26

21. Van der Kolk, B. A. (2005). Developmental Trauma Disorder: Toward a rational diagnosis for children with complex trauma histories. *Psychiatric annals, 35*(5), 401-408. doi: 10.3928/00485713-20050501-06

22. Papalia, D. E., Feldman, R. D., & Martorell. (2012). *Experience human development* (12th ed.). NY: McGraw-Hill.

23. Fisher, J. (2017). *Healing the fragmented selves of trauma survivors: Overcoming internal self-alienation.* New York, NY: Routledge.

24. Subramanyam, A.A., Somaiya, M., Shankar, S., Nasirabadi, M., Shah, H.R., Paul, I. & Ghildiyal, R. (2020). Psychological interventions for dissociative disorders. *Indian Journal of Psychiatry, 62,* S280-S289. doi:10.4103/psychiatry.IndianJPsychiatry_777_19

25. van der Kolk, B., Ford, J.D. & Spinazzola, J. (2019). Comorbidity of developmental trauma Disorder (DTD) and post-traumatic stress disorder: findings from the DTD field Trial. *European Journal of Psychotraumatology, 10*(1), 1562841. doi:10.1080/20008198.2018.1562841

26. van der Kolk, B., Ford, J.D. & Spinazzola, J. (2019). Comorbidity of developmental trauma Disorder (DTD) and post-traumatic stress disorder: findings from the DTD field Trial. *European Journal of Psychotraumatology, 10*(1), 1562841. doi:10.1080/20008198.2018.1562841

27. Lutton, S. S. & Swank, J. M. (2018). The importance of intentionally in untangling trauma from severe mental illness. *Journal of Mental Health Counseling, 40*(2), 113-128. doi:10.17744/mehc.40.2.02

28. van der Kolk, B. (2014). *The body keeps the score: Mind, brain and body in the transformation of trauma.* New York, NY: Penguin.

29. Levine, P. (2010). *In an unspoken voice: How the body releases trauma and goodness.* Berkeley, CA: North Atlantic Books.

30. Ogden, P., & Fisher, J. (2015). *Sensorimotor psychotherapy: Interventions for trauma and attachment.* New York: Norton.

31. Larner, G. (2001). The critical-practitioner model in therapy. *Australian Psychologist, 36*(1), 36-43. Retrieved from http://www.psychology.org.au/publications/journals/

32. Tounsi, H., Pacioselli, P., Riou, L., Gouret, C., Gross, L., Quaderi, A., & Palazzolo, J. (2017). Psychotherapies for complex trauma: A combination between EMDR and mindfulness. *25th European Congress of Psychiatry / European Psychiatry, 41S*, S710–S771. http://dx.doi.org/10.1016/j.eurpsy.2017.01.1320

Afterword

1. Police (1981). Invisible sun. *Ghost in the Machine* [Album]. Hollywood, CA: A&M Records.
2. The Beatles. (1969). Here comes the sun. *Abbey Road* [Album]. London: Apple Records.
3. Darwin, C (1979). *The origin of species by means of natural selection.* New York: Avenel Books (Original work published 1859).